Praise for **Farmer's Son**

This is an enlightening and uplifting story. Those of us with learning disabilities will find special meaning but everyone will enjoy the story of Bobby and his family. A thoroughly good read.

Thomas H. Kean
Dyslexic
Governor, New Jersey 1982 – 1990
President, Drew University 1990 – 2005
Chairman, 9/11 Commission

Words cannot begin to describe how important this novel is to me both personally and professionally. With my being a "Bobby" and also leading a specialized school for "Bobbys," **Farmer's Son** has made my short list of MUST READS! I read this brilliant book in two days. I couldn't put it down!

Janet George, M.S., M.ED., F/AOGPE
Dyslexic
Founder and Headmaster, Fortune Academy-Indianapolis, IN

As a dyslexic, I know the many challenges of learning to read and write. N.E. Lasater has written a first novel which I believe readers will find captivating. It is especially worth the struggle for a dyslexic, giving us characters and experiences to identify with. N.E. Lasater has a true understanding of the struggles and isolation many feel. I highly recommend **Farmer's Son**.

William Gaston Caperton, III
Dyslexic
Governor, West Virginia 1989 - 1997
President & CEO, the College Board 1999 – 2012

N.E. Lasater has created a fantastic novel that grabs the reader in the first chapter. This wonderful story describes what it is like to be dyslexic and the amazing ways dyslexics overcome their challenges. Thank you for this outstanding work.

Peter G. Ruppert
CEO, Fusion Education Group and Fusion Academies
California, New York, New Jersey and Texas

Wow. An adult book for dyslexics. Thank you. N.E. Lasater is an excellent writer and this is a wonderful book.

Victor Villaseñor
Dyslexic
5-Time Bestselling Author
3-Time Pulitzer Prize Nominee

Dyslexia is a debilitating disorder affecting too many of our friends and neighbors and people from all walks of life, yet it does not receive nearly the attention it deserves. I hope that this compelling novel will not only help lift the stigma that is sometimes associated with this lifelong reading disability, but also serve as a source of inspiration for those with dyslexia to assure them there are others like them who are triumphing over the struggles they face.

Representative Gerald E. Connolly (VA 11th)
United States Congress

Growing up with dyslexia made life difficult, forcing me to think and work in ways different from those around me. Yet despite, or perhaps because of this, it didn't prevent me from achieving my dream of becoming a scientist and working for the US space program. Everyone with dyslexia needs to read this book and realize like the protagonist Bobby they can ultimately reach for their own star.

Simon J. Clemett, PhD.
Dyslexic
Astromaterials and Exploration Science Directorate
NASA Johnson Space Center

Farmer's Son reminds us that dyslexia affects people and relationships, not just test scores and classrooms. Everyone who is considered "different" will appreciate the challenges faced by the McAllister family in this saga of generations so weighed down by perceived weaknesses they are unable to appreciate and celebrate their very real strengths.

Paul Orfalea
Dyslexic
Founder of Kinko's
Philanthropist

How wonderful that N.E. Lasater has the talent and the understanding to put into words what so many of us have experienced.

P. Buckley Moss
Dyslexic
Artist

A great read. . . If I could have changed but one thing growing up, it would have been to understand why reading and spelling were so hard.

Bill Samuels, Jr.
Dyslexic
President & CEO (1975-2011) Maker's Mark Bourbon

N.E. Lasater's candid view of a family impacted by dyslexia will hit home to anyone who has felt misunderstood, embarrassed or ashamed of themselves because of their struggles with the written word. **Farmer's Son** is a powerful example of the incredible, lasting impact families have on children with learning differences.

Ben Shifrin
Head, Jemicy School in Owings Mills, MD
Vice President, the International Dyslexia Association

Dyslexia made certain school subjects difficult for me (reading) and others nearly impossible (math). However, thanks to some great role models, I have learned it also offers many gifts. There are brilliant dyslexics in the world who use the fact that they see the world differently to their advantage. **Farmer's Son** may use dyslexia as a backdrop, but its real story is about the universal needs we all share to be free of shame and connected to our families. This is a read everyone will enjoy.

Jewel
Dyslexic
Singer/Songwriter

Farmer's Son deftly describes the multi-generational impact dyslexia has on children and families. Through rich, descriptive character development, N.E. Lasater accurately captures the emotional and self-esteem issues that have a profound effect on children and adults with learning disabilities. Too often incredibly talented individuals are shamed because their minds work in different but wonderful ways.

Casey Crnich, Ed.D.
Executive Director
Hyde Park Day School at the University of Chicago

farmer's son

N.E. LASATER

Farmer's Son / N.E. Lasater— 1st ed.
ISBN-10: 0990306909
ISBN-13: 978-0-9903069-0-0

To Dr. Frederick C. Rimmele, III

BOBBY
Spring
1971

1.

From underneath the planter where he lay flat on his back, Bobby Rowan McAllister heard the roar of the Chevy's engine as soon as his father's truck cleared the top of the hill. Even from that distance, the pickup's old motor gunned so loud the twitching finches on the power line above him stopped chattering. Even Will, the gray-haired hired man who knelt next to Bobby, handing him tools, shut up the moment he heard it and cocked his head like the birds to follow the sound.

The old red truck spun off clods of dirt and yellow dust as it charged toward the tiny brick farmhouse and the gravel yard on the uphill side of it where the teenager and the hired hand were working. Sweating and crammed in tight under a metal seed tube, Bobby could hear but he couldn't see beyond the mechanism that hung almost to the ground next to his cramping left shoulder.

Will was already standing by the time Bobby threw down his wrench and scuttled out crablike from the twelve inches of space he had between the metal parts and the rubber wheel. There were five tires in all, alternating with the six row units attached to the planter's long metal arm. Bobby had spent the morning inching himself between them, working on the steel mechanisms, and he was hungry.

He had barely straightened up when the Chevy careened, braking hard around the corner, and jerked his father to a cloudy stop, nose-in less than a foot from the side of the shoebox house. Bobby squared his shoulders and planted his feet apart as his fa-

ther had taught him, then gripped both his freckled hands behind his back. He took in his breath.

"Jesus Christ!" Garrett McAllister shouted as he climbed
down from the pickup and slammed the door, clunking metal
against metal. "What the hell are you doing up here?"

"You said it was too wet."

"The hell I did!"

"This morning, you—"

"I told you to come out and see what was going on!" Garrett
rolled his shoulders and strode toward him across the gravel.
Bobby saw the harm in his eyes.

"You told me to fix the seed tubes, Dad, and that's—"

"Don't you ever use your head?" Garrett kept coming but
pumped his arm out, pointing to his right but not looking as he
stepped onto the high spring grass that Will hadn't mown yet.
"You're eighteen goddamn years old. Don't you see it?"

Bobby followed the finger to his left, then swung his whole
body, searching.

"Over there!" Garrett stopped in front of Bobby. "Jesus!" A
spray of spittle wet Bobby's face.

Bobby scanned the hill on the other side of the machine shed.
"I'm sorry, Dad. I don't see—" He twisted around the other way
to find Will, but the hired man had slunk back into the shadow
of the open barn. Bobby caught a glimpse of thin bars of sunlight
streaking the sags of his face.

"Don't look at him, Bobby! He's just as ignorant as you are.
Bertram's running. Can't you see it?"

A few dark birds circled low beyond the machine shed that
blocked Bobby's view. Stretching even taller than his six feet, he
squinted above it to see the small specks reeling and turning in
the sky. "I swear, he wasn't running when I came in. And I went
all over the county like you said, to see what everybody else was

2

doing before I—"

Garrett's finger jabbed him in the chest. Bobby looked down at it. "Do I have to be here all the time? Bertram's the dumbest farmer in this state. He doesn't even get his beans in until after the Fourth of July. But there he is, while you two just sit here with your thumbs up your asses."

"But Dad—"

"You've already cost us half a day! I want you down there on the other side of that ditch. You hear me?"

"Yes, Dad."

Garrett leaned in so close tuna salad filled Bobby's nose. "What did you say?"

The boy blinked. "I said yes."

Garrett stepped the hard toes of his hard boots over top of Bobby's own. He stared up at Bobby towering above him. "What did you say?"

The air around them stopped moving. The trees and even the grass stopped waving. There was nothing but sun and the heat in his father's eyes.

"Yessir."

Garrett pressed down on Bobby's toes.

He said it like his father had taught him. "Sir. Yes. Sir."

Garrett raised his eyebrows. His feet didn't move.

"You're the boss. I'll do whatever you say."

Garrett grinned wide, blasting his small sharp teeth. "You're damn right you will." He spun around and headed for his truck again, his narrow shoulders rolling. "I'll be back in an hour. One hour. You hear me? Will!" he shouted. "You're a coward. You know that?"

Garrett opened the driver's door and turned. "And Bobby, don't you dare plant too shallow. That seed cost me a fortune. It's dry. You take it all the way down to proper depth."

A moment later, the truck backed up eating yellow dust again, then turned and charged up the gravel road. Bobby didn't move until the spinning swirl behind it had disappeared long after the bright red had crested the hill. The finches twitched once the sound was gone, as Will re-emerged blinking into the bright, hot sunlight.

He still held the tools he had been handing Bobby. "Your father's full of crap," he said. "It's not gonna be dry enough to plant for at least another day."

Bobby waited, but Will said nothing more. "So what do you want to do?"

"I told you. I'd leave it another day."

"But—"

"Your dad's a fool, Bobby. He doesn't know the first thing about farming."

"But you heard what Dad said."

Will shrugged. "Then I guess you've got a choice."

"Me? Why me?"

"Because he's talking to you, that's why. He's not talking to me anymore." Will paused to manage the sound of his voice. "I'm sorry, but it has to be you now. So you can either tell him no, or you can do what he wants. Only he didn't tell you what that was, did he?"

"What do you mean?"

"What the hell is "proper depth'? An inch makes all the difference in whether you kill the seed or not. You plant it two inches down if the ground's dry, and not just on the top here. It has to be dry all the way down to that little seed or it'll drown in all that moisture and never come up. If it's wet underground, like I know it is, you've got to plant shallow so the seed'll survive. No deeper than an inch."

Bobby looked at the ground by his feet.

"That's not going to tell you anything. It looks dry on top. And you can't dig down either. It might be dry in one place but wet as hell a few feet over. The only way to know is from experience, from looking at the whole field. And how much of that has your father got?"

"But he said—"

"Bobby, I'm telling you. If we do what he says and plant deep, you're gonna have a cocked-up planter gummed with mud you're gonna have to fix. Again. But it's up to you. Either way, we still have to get this last tube fixed." Will threw down the tools as he crouched and turned, putting himself on his back with his knees bent and the soles of his boots flat. He began to wriggle under the low-hanging machinery, inching to get back under the same row unit where Bobby had been working.

"But what if he's right?" Bobby said to Will's jiggling paunch.

Will snorted.

Bobby brought his right hand to his mouth to bite his ragged thumbnail as his eyes found the dark birds again, circling low above the unseen Bertram. There were more of them now.

Will's hand searched on the patchy grass for the pliers and found them.

"I'm gonna go see," Bobby said. "Maybe it is dry. Maybe it's drier there than it is here. Maybe Dad's right."

Will didn't answer.

Bobby headed to his dirty Rambler, which he had parked early that morning next to the picnic table by the back door of the house. A few steps away, along the same narrow plateau that paused the steep slope to the bottom land, aqua blue bath towels swayed on two clotheslines strung between a pair of rusted Y-poles that faced each other across the green. One small hand towel had slid loose and fallen. Bobby picked it up and gently smoothed it over his left arm before putting it on the line again in its assigned spot next to its brothers.

The gravel road bordered the western edge of his father's property. On the other side of it and up a hill, the neighboring farmer was planting corn as he sat high and proud on his shiny new red tractor. Bertram's planter was new too, a clean eight-row he was pulling like a giant rake behind him, cutting the ground as it made eight furrows where seed tubes shot the corn in, then buried each kernel under a carefully measured layer of dirt.

"Damn," Bobby said to himself as his stomach rumbled.

The black birds circled, screeching and diving for worms. From the car, Bobby watched Bertram get to the end of the long field, then turn the tractor and planter in a wide half-circle to head back in Bobby's direction. He even waved at the boy when he spotted him. Bobby had no choice but to smile and wave back.

Bobby took the gravel road downhill, passing Will again on his back in the farmyard. At the bottom, Bobby crossed a cement bridge that spanned a deep drainage ditch cutting a wide gorge in the broad, fertile valley that stretched ten miles north to a smudged gray line of distant hills. Garrett's land stopped at the dark trees half a mile away.

Bobby climbed out and started walking. As he entered his father's fields, he breathed deep, filling his lungs with the moist rich smell. It relaxed him, easing the stiffness he had already begun to feel in his shoulders. He rubbed the base of his neck, which felt better already now that he was in the fields alone.

He raised his legs high above the rows of dead, long, veined leaves and corn stubble that snapped under his boots. Chopped off a foot from the ground by the slicing combine during the last harvest, the old brown corn stalks stuck straight up like the broken teeth of a comb. When he was a child, Bobby had walked the marching rows, crushing them, jumping on each little pole with both laughing feet.

Now, when he got to the middle of the field, he kicked the ground, digging in the toe of his boot. Dry topsoil flew up to powder the air. He followed the wind current and watched the weight of the dirt.

He squatted and laid one thin forearm on his knee, then picked up a clod with his bare hand and crumbled it. He tilted his head and looked west to where the fronts came. The sky there was clear and sparkling blue.

He put both his palms down and rubbed the ground. He dropped to both knees as he touched the dry chunks and stroked the new weeds that blasted happily through the stubble. He closed his eyes as he laid his hands on the willing earth and tried to divine without seeing it the state of the underground beneath his fingers.

"Dad was right!" Bobby yelled to Will as he jumped out of his car back at the farm three minutes later. "Bertram's running and the ground down at the bottom's dry. If we don't get out there, he's gonna kill us."

2.

Will shook his head as he wiped the tools clean. "It only looks dry. I don't care what you saw."

"But the dirt's powdery. It's not chunky."

"I don't want to be fixing these seed tubes again. If they get snapped off, we won't be able to find replacements. You know how old this thing is."

Bobby flicked his wrist to check the Timex he wore under his left forearm. "He's gonna be here in fifty minutes. He's always on time."

Will snorted again. "That's the one thing he does do. He—"

"Will! I don't have a choice."

Will looked at him.

"I'm sorry," Bobby said. "I don't mean to be disrespectful."

Will held up one hand. "It's okay. What a man to have for a father."

Bobby turned away. "Mom says it's me. I'm too willful. I'll get the tractor." Bobby went over to the open barn and climbed on their one old Farmall and drove it out and swung it around so his back was to the planter's front. Will straddled the hitch of the old planter, rolling his right hand for Bobby to back up at a crawl. From five feet up on the tractor's hard seat above the big rear tires, Bobby had to make sure the two holes in the planter's u-shaped clevis stacked precisely around the single one in the tractor's drawbar. If they didn't, Will couldn't drop in the pin.

Bobby twisted his back so he could see better. He broke out in a wide smile when he got it done in one motion, without stopping. Will held both thumbs up. "I think that's a record," Will shouted above the noise of the motor. "Less than a minute."

Bobby hopped down and bounced as he walked back into the barn. Will drove his own truck, a dirty white one, to the sliding rear door where Bobby was already waiting by the tall, squared-off towers of fifty-pound bags that were piled in alternating rows to the roof on wooden pallets.

Bobby hauled six bags of seed corn over the tailgate while Will idled, then walked through the barn again and back outside, climbing once more on the tractor, which was now towing more than fifteen feet of perpendicular metal frame. The planter connected to the tractor with just the one hitch to create a "T" with the tractor in front dragging the wide planter behind it. As he rumbled onto the road, getting ready to make the right down the long hill from the gravel farmyard, Bobby had to watch carefully so he didn't sideswipe the mailbox or the electric pole.

On the other side of the narrow cement bridge, which he had to cross with both outside planter wheels dangling, he made a wide turn and brought the rig thundering onto the same shorn field where he had been, then snaked it left so it all pointed north. The tractor had its back to the farmhouse midway up the hill behind him. Will pulled up next to him in his dirty white pickup.

"So here's what you do," Will said after they had clamored up on the planter's long metal arm to pour seed corn into the six plastic bins that topped the six hanging row units. "Don't set it too deep. Only go down an inch or you'll pull up that mud once you get going and cock up the planter." Will coughed as he clutched the huge, heavy bag and brought his forearm up to rub across his forehead. Corn dust had floated up onto his eyebrows and eyelashes.

Bobby copied the older man, scraping his own thin arm across his nose. "But Will, look at that tan color." The compacted soil on the ground four feet below them, under the planter's long metal arm, shone smooth and flat like the top of a hamburger bun in the hot sunlight. "And it's not supposed to rain all week."

"Listen to me. I've been doing this a long time. One inch. The seed won't starve. It'll draw up the moisture."

"But if we do it your way—"

"My way?" Will was staring.

"He'll rage, Will. You know how he is. And we'll have to buy new seed. We can't afford it. Listen, if we're gonna screw up, I mean really screw up, why not do it his way?" Bobby was talking fast, hugging the bag of seed corn against his chest. "At least he can't get mad."

Will's face softened. "You really do believe your father."

Bobby scanned the sky, finding the dark birds again at Bertram's. He looked down again at the dry earth beneath the planter's small wheels.

"I need to do what he wants." He took a deep breath. "Assuming he's right, how deep do I go?"

Will nodded, finally. "On dry ground, you set it to two inches."

"Then that's what I have to do."

"Go slow. I'll be here. I'll honk if you need to stop, so listen for me. You'll be driving it. You won't be able to see when the mud starts coming because it'll be happening to the planter, behind you."

Bobby hopped off and walked to the first row unit at one far end to manually set two inches as the depth on the first pair of gauge wheels. As the boy sped down the line setting the other five the same way, Will filled the rest of the bins then stepped off the planter holding his paunch and drove his white pickup out of the way. He opened his door and leaned out, planting his left boot on the ground as he pressed his backside against the cushion.

Bobby got up on the tractor and sat, then started it and pulled a lever that sent the right marker out seven and a half feet from the planter's end. The metal disk hit the dirt like the top of a tin can and banged as it sent up a puff of dust. He squared his back as he set his sight on a distant county road sign to keep his rows straight, and put it into gear and started forward. The tractor roared, chewing the ground as it lumbered.

Everything was okay at first, but then he hit a little rise in the field and chugged down the other side into a low spot that started mud slinging off the rubber tires and onto the metal frame, then onto the six dangling row units. Another ten yards and the muck had oozed up to cover the sharp rim blades of the units' opening wheels as they cut deeper into the wet soil and lifted it glistening, curling and folding it like butter under a knife. Soft mud churned out of the ground and rose in heavy waves that stuck to everything, clumping and dripping off every part. The planter was crippled and choking.

Will saw it happening. He pounded the truck's horn, but Bobby couldn't hear it. The boy was listening to the tractor's engine, which had just dropped in sound as it started to lug, straining to pull the growing mountain. He had never heard that sound before, so it took him another instant.

Will had already jumped in the truck. He was flooring it, laying on the horn as he came bouncing over the old furrows.

Bobby stomped the clutch, then heard the engine whine as it revved out of gear. He stood up to grip the wheel and he locked his elbows and his legs to counter the brute force of his foot, which he'd shoved down like a piston. He grabbed the gearshift that was between his legs and jammed it into reverse, pulling back on the hydraulic lever at the same time to raise the planter.

But it took more seconds to do than he gave it, and the planter was still partway in the muck when he let out the clutch too fast and started backing up. He twisted his neck and his whole body around to watch where he was going. The engine roared as it shoved, pressing back against the wet earth.

He heard two sharp pops, loud enough to be heard above the thundering motor. He heard them even though he hadn't heard the blaring of Will's horn.

Bobby jumped on the clutch and the two brakes, slamming both brake pedals with his right foot. Will yelled as he ran up. "Bobby, it's sprung! The bolts popped when you backed up on it!"

The whole third row unit had bent, pleating out from the frame with buckled metal. Only one pair of bolts attached it now to the long arm of the planter, when there were supposed to be two, one each on either side of the heavy mechanism. Without the second pair, the entire assembly had twisted. Folded sideways, it looked like a dangling baby tooth that needed to be pulled.

"Oh shit." Will had one dusty hand to his face. "It's gonna have to be replaced and it's gonna be days before we find another one. You know how old this thing is? Jesus, Bobby. Your dad's gonna be pissed."

3.

Garrett barreled down the hill, crossed the bridge and bumped over the gully as he came onto the field squeaking the struts of his red pickup. He gunned straight toward them like he was going to hit them, but he veered at the last second to stop alongside Will. He cranked down his window. "You broke it! Look at that!"

Will kept his back turned to him, facing the front side of the planter, scooping wet mud out from around the twisted row unit. "It was gonna happen anyway."

"The hell it was!"

Bobby knelt in the hot sun beyond them, on the other side of the planter's arm, his legs and boots soaked with mud. In his hands, he cradled the metal tube he'd taken off to see how badly it was broken. He was wiping it with a cloth that was already filthy. His head was down and he kept it there as he rubbed.

"You planted too deep," Garrett shouted at Will. "Any fool can see that. How far down did you go?"

Will didn't answer right away. He straightened up and put one lumpy hand on the shovel handle, blocking Garrett's view of Bobby kneeling on the ground behind him. "Did it ever occur to you that this is bottom land?"

"Shut up! Move!"

"Your buddy Bertram up there. He's riding on top of a ridge."

"Bobby!"

"It's drier up there. Water runs downhill, you know."

"Bobby! How deep?"

Will didn't move. He answered for Bobby. "Two inches, just like you wanted."

"I never said two!"

Behind Will, Bobby struggled to his feet with his wet jeans sticking.

"You're trying to ruin me," Garrett said. "That pretty little wife of yours, did she put you up to this?"

"My wife?"

"Dad!" Bobby cried out.

"Bobby, shut it."

"But Dad!"

"You and her both," Garrett told Will. "You're gonna pay for this."

"Listen to me!" Bobby had stepped around so he stood next to Will, facing his father. "I screwed up. Not Will. I made the decision to put it down to two inches. And I put it in reverse."

"Reverse?"

"And then two of the bolts popped and I sprung the unit."

"Reverse in all that mud?"

"Only I didn't lift the planter all the way up."

"Jesus. How stupid are you?"

Will bent low to look through the driver's side window. "You know what he was doing? He was trying to please you. You came out here like a bat out of hell and you told him to get running, and that's what he did."

"I never said two inches!"

"Nah, you were careful about that, weren't you? You left the boy hanging and made him decide for himself."

"He's not capable of deciding. He can't even think! That was your job."

"You dumb son of a bitch," Will said. "Your son's a lot smarter than you are. You know what he's already done? He's already

14

been up there on the telephone and he's found another one. The row unit's a hundred years old, just like that planter, and it's all the way over in White County, but it's there and it's cheap. We've only got to get it and put it on. That's only two days lost. He's just saved your year."

But Garrett wasn't listening. "I never said to go down that far," he shouted to his son. "Did I?"

"Hey!" Will said. "Didn't you hear me?"

"Bobby! Answer me."

"Look!" Will thrust his muddy left fist in under Garrett's nose. "This is why it popped off. You see that?" Will had opened his palm.

"No, Dad," Bobby said quietly.

Will held a broken bolt cut in half, sheered off across the middle of the shank. But Garrett wasn't looking. He had started to smile, staring at Bobby. "Say that again."

"It's the bolt that popped." Will jiggled it against his wedding ring to make it jangle. "It was already cracked halfway through, and rust had gotten in. See that line there, making it look like a half circle? It was weak already because of that crack. The good half was all that was holding it. That unit was going to pop anyway at some point because of metal fatigue."

But Bobby had said, "No, Dad. You're right. You never said to go down two inches. Everything was my fault."

Garrett looked at Will, ignoring the bolt. "I've got a question for you, Mister Know-It-All. If Bobby's so good at farming, like you say, if he's a 'natural' like you say, then why didn't he see it? Where's that 'knack' he's got?"

"He couldn't have seen it," Will answered quickly. "Nobody could have seen it. It was inside the part, too far in."

"Some knack," Garrett said loud enough for Bobby to hear him. "All I see is a knack for fucking up."

4.

He had to go home. There was nowhere else to go when night finally came and they were done in the field. Bobby waited for as long as he could, but eventually he was just standing with Will outside the back door of the old farmhouse, talking.

Will's sweet wife opened the door to tell them dinner was ready. She asked Bobby if he wanted to eat too but he said no, thanks Anna, he had to get home. But he didn't move after Will went inside and closed the door. Through the window, Bobby watched him climb the stairs and smile and kiss his wife in the warm, welcoming light. Will had told him once she had wanted children, but it was too late now. Plus, he'd said, what kind of life would that be, moving all the time to go where the work was? Children needed a home and a place to be rooted.

Bobby dug out his keys. As he walked to his Rambler, he could hear crickets singing in the orchard grass across the gravel road. Down the steep hill, cicadas hummed, echoing. He waited, stopping at the car door until he heard it. A barn owl stuttered, hooting low far off to his right. Underneath it all, close by and quiet, the fat leaves of the catalpa trees danced with each other in front of the porch.

He looked up. The bright stars shimmered. Bobby stretched out his thin arm, still dirty from the mud, and traced the glimmer of the Milky Way in its thick band from one end of his father's land to the other, bowing over his head in the soft night.

He pulled out and drove slowly away with the high beams shining. He motored up the hill, then over top of it and away from the fertile valley. Bobby headed down the long decline into town, turning left finally at the "T" that dumped him onto the county road heading south. Ten dark miles later, he passed a cement plant and rumbled over sharp railroad tracks. He turned left into the first small lane alongside them. There were only two houses, and they both backed onto the tracks—his father's was the older white bungalow with a small yard around it.

Bobby pulled up next to the neighbor's hedge and cut the lights.

His father's voice came out to him, angry and loud as the freight trains that ran past every night. Even from across the street, he could hear the force of it if not the words. Bobby shifted in his seat to try to peer into the neighbors', but their new, tall squared-off hedge blocked his view. He could see the gold light of their shielded front room, though, speckling through the foliage.

He turned to look beyond his mother's homemade lace curtains into his own kitchen. His short father stormed back and forth in front of the closed window. Bobby got out and moved across the street with his head down, trying not to hear it.

"I don't care!" Garrett's voice pursued him on the asphalt.

Bobby walked around to the back yard where the basement steps were, underneath the picture window at the far end of the den upstairs, and he went down and took his boots off before opening the heavy door. His caked socks had dried so they were stiff as he shuffled them across the gritty concrete floor of the foundation, feeling his way in the dark past his father's golf clubs, the pool table, old bikes and laundry, toward the bathroom he'd helped construct in the far corner. The two outside walls had been framed up against the concrete. Bobby had cut through the dry wall in order to keep the window, a small high one three inches from the planks above his head. Even on the brightest day, the window shared only the dullest sunlight, diffused and glowing bluish from the street where his old car was parked now in the pitch black and ready to run again the next morning.

He closed the door and locked it, then pushed aside his mother's ruffled curtain to crank the shower faucet as hard and hot as he could. The pipes clanked with the new heat as Bobby yanked off his brittle clothes and checked the time on the wall clock, which had silver spikes with metal balls on the ends that made it look like a satellite. 10:30 p.m., and his father still hadn't turned on the television.

Naked, Bobby stood under the driving steam without moving for a full five minutes feeling the hammer of the water.

His father was still raging when he got out. Right above him, the floorboards creaked with new pacing closer to the kitchen sink. Bobby stared up and listened, his eyes fastening on the sharp points of the raw nails that came at him through the planks.

"No I can't trust him," his father was saying.

His mother answered, but Bobby couldn't hear her.

"He does so mean it!" his father said. "He's just as willful as Garrett J. was."

She spoke. Bobby strained but couldn't get it.

"They are too the same!"

Her murmuring again, soft and low, blocked by the floorboards.

"I'm sick of you taking his side. He thinks he can get to you just like Garrett J. did. Bobby's stupid, but when it comes to you he doesn't miss a trick."

Standing damp on the cold concrete, Bobby started to pull on the new clothes his mother had put out for him on the lid of the wicker hamper next to the toilet. He fit his clean socks over his wet feet and reached for his pressed jeans.

"No, he didn't 'misunderstand' me! I said an inch. I specifically said it. 'Whatever you do, don't go down more than an inch.'
Any five year-old knows you don't go any deeper on wet
ground."

Bobby stopped tugging, holding his trousers. "You never said
that," he told the floor. "But she believes you, and you know it."

"So then what?" his father said to her above him. "You think
he saw Bertram up there and figured it was dry. 'Hey it's a nice
day. Let's take it down to two inches?' You think he's so stupid
he doesn't know Bertram's on a ridge?"

Bobby looked up at the planks. He heard footsteps, then a
small smash of dishes going down on the Formica counter next
to the sink. She was over his head now. The two sets of faucets
shared the same pipes.

Garrett had followed her. "—plain and simple. And you en-
courage it because you molly-coddle him. Bobby's trying to run
my farm."

"You asshole," Bobby whispered.

He heard the hard heels of her shoes and followed the pivot.
Her soft voice came down because it had taken on the slightest
edge that had turned it and sliced it sideways through the floorboards. "No he's not. He's a good boy. And he's your son. He
may not get it all the time, but he's trying. He's just like you."

"No I'm not!" Bobby hissed.

"No he's not!" Garrett told her at the same time. "He's nothing like me. He takes after your mother."

The kitchen faucet came on. Bobby took a deep breath and
zipped his fly and found the slippers his mother had left him.

"Of course it's fair!" Garrett said. "He's not worth it. I'm not
paying Will sixty percent of my crop. You know how long it's
gonna take to fix it? We're screwed if it's not all in by the end of
the week."

She said something under the noise of the water.

"No, I'm not gonna wait. I'm gonna tell him. It's not like he's got a lot of leverage here." Bobby heard his father's stomp above him and the refrigerator door open. A moment later, Garrett walked off to the den and the television came on.

Bobby moved his few coins from his grimy jeans to his new pants pocket, then flipped open the hamper and flung the dirty clothes in. He unlocked the door and padded in the darkness toward the bare wooden basement stairs that rose from the center of the slab to his mother's pink kitchen. As he climbed, he carefully blanked his sunburned face.

She was still at the sink, facing away from him in front of a window that looked out to the separate garage in the backyard. Taller than his father and bird thin, Cora Rowan McAllister had corded legs she dressed in skirts and long, narrow, bony feet she housed in flat shoes with little buckles. Her stringed neck was bent and her shoulders hunched to allow her big hands to find the pots she had just added to the soapy water.

Bobby crept across the linoleum toward the dining room beyond the kitchen, through an arched doorway. He heard the television blaring from the back wall of the den beyond, but he couldn't see yet the black and white screen.

He moved as fast as he could, but she spoke to him without turning. "Did you get dinner? I don't have any meatloaf left, but I could make you some eggs."

"No," he said. "It's all right."

She turned then, her hands bumping in the water. Her glasses glinted from the little rhinestones on the curved tips. She smiled at him and he felt his shoulders relaxing. "Did Anna feed you again?"

His pause was so small. "Yeah," he said. "We had spaghetti."

"I'm glad. You're awfully skinny."

Bobby took a step more. "Well, good night."

"Wait." She cocked her head at him, motioning for him to come over. She grabbed a dishtowel.

"What happened out there today?" she asked once he was close enough to whisper. "He says you disobeyed him. He says he told you specifically to only go down an inch, but you ignored him."

"But that's not what happened!"

"Shh!" She swung a glance at the doorway.

He lowered his voice. "Mom, I'm telling you. He never told me any specific depth at all. He just yelled at me and took off."

"He says he told you." She clutched her dishtowel, peering eye-to-eye through the thick lenses of her glasses. "Didn't you hear him? You know sometimes you have trouble, uh, paying attention."

"No! He didn't."

She put her hand on his upper arm and rubbed. The dishwater had made her long fingers warm and soft against his skin. "Didn't you hear him? You know that's happened before. Where was Will? Was he there?"

Bobby brightened. "Yeah!"

"What did he say about how deep to plant?" Her glowing hand moved up and down.

Bobby looked at her. "He said to only go down an inch."

She nodded like she'd already known it. "Then why didn't you listen?"

"I did, but I—"

"Will should have stopped you. That's the problem. It's him. Not you. You can't help it if you didn't hear."

5.

Bobby crossed the dining room. As he did, he peered into the den, where the white top of his father's small head crested the broad flat back of the old blue armchair that faced the console television against the far wall. Garrett was alone in there with nothing but a newspaper that had slipped to the floor face down in a tent a foot below his suspended right hand. Bobby's father was asleep.

Bobby climbed the stairs. At the top of the landing, the whole second floor opened into one large room with three beds in a row along the wall. His two younger brothers were both wide-awake and staring.

"What happened?" John asked from behind the tall pile of history books open on a desk. Loose sheets of lined, three-holed paper were anchored by his right elbow.

Bobby crossed the big room and went past John toward his dresser.

"Man," John said to his back. "I thought he was gonna cut you a new one."

"He already did that out at the farm." Bobby fished the coins out of his pants and dumped them in a little ashtray.

"Did you really put it in reverse?"

"Bobby—" said his little brother Tommy.

"And you broke it?" John interrupted. "The whole unit?"

Bobby didn't turn around.

"—Daddy scared me," seven year-old Tommy said from his bed.

"You broke the whole unit?" John said. "Not just a piece of it?"

"Bobby," Tommy's high voice broke. "Daddy scared—"

"Is it really gonna take two days—"

"—me just now. He was yelling and—"

"—find another one? Don't we need to get it all planted this week? That's what Dad said. If we don't—"

"I screwed up, okay!"

Bobby had turned around so fast John's mouth was still open. "I screwed up."

"Shh!" John said. "Dad's gonna hear you."

"I made a big mistake. I know that," Bobby said more softly. "And I'm the one responsible to make it right."

"Daddy's been raging all night," Tommy said. He was sitting upright in flannel pajamas covered in red bucking broncos. "He scared me."

"You're okay," John said to him. "You've been up here with me."

Bobby forced a smile at the little boy whose feet twisted under his blanket. "I promise I'll make it okay, and the crop will get in and we'll be fine again."

Tommy blurted, "But Daddy says we're gonna lose the house."

"He did? Well, we're not."

John put his chin on the heel of his hand. Blue ink stained his fingers. "Are you really gonna have to pay half? That's what Dad says. And what about Will? What do you think he's gonna do when he finds out?"

"About what?"

"Dad's cutting his share, starting right now. He's taking it down to fifty-fifty and he's gonna apply it to this year's crop."

Bobby's eyes grew big. "Will won't stay another minute if he does that. Heck I don't even know if he'll stay now. It's sixty-forty. It's never fifty. The tenant farmer always gets sixty percent for doing all the work."

"But Dad gives him the house for free," John said.

"He couldn't get any rent for it if he wanted to, it's so run down."

Their father's voice came up to them then, loud and fast. He was standing in the dining room, at the foot of the stairs, yelling up to them in the top of the house. "John!" he shouted. "Bobby! I can hear you."

They all froze, their eyes darting,

John swallowed, then yelled back, "Yes, Dad?"

"I don't want you talking to Bobby. He's in enough trouble already."

Young Tommy reached to switch off the light on his bedside table.

"And John, I want those books open," Garret called out.

"Sir! Yessir!" John said.

"Is Tommy in bed with the light off?"

"Yes, Daddy!" the boy sang out as he burrowed under the covers with his flannel arms out.

"Don't make me come up there and check. Debbie! Your book open?"

They heard her shout through the closed door of her bedroom downstairs, next to the dining room. "Yes, Dad!"

"I don't want you slacking off. Just because you're going to Southern next year doesn't mean you can stop studying. Bobby!"

Bobby screwed up his face. "Yessir!" He called down.

"I don't care what you do up there, but don't bother John. He's got studying to do."

6.

The next afternoon Bobby sat in the last seat in the far left row of his Senior English class, hunched with pointed shoulder blades over the paperback book in his big hands. Next to him, the bottom of the old casement window was swung open. He listened to a lawn mower buzzing on the playing field at the side of the school.

Up front, five columns of battered desks away, a young woman teacher with long brown hair was saying, "Let's do something different today. Instead of starting up front like we always do, let's start in the back. With you ... Bobby." Standing against the blackboard, she tilted far to her right so she could see him. "Did you do the assignment?"

Her long straight hair swung out from her side, glossy in the slanted sunlight.

Bobby clenched the small book even tighter.

She waited. "Bobby?"

"Yes, ma'am." He cleared his throat for her. "I did."

"Okay, let's hear it. We're all waiting."

"We sure are," one of the other dumb boys next to him in the back of the room whispered. "What's it gonna be this time?"

Bobby spoke up so she could hear him. "It's not so much what's there, in the passage, as what's not."

"Excuse me?" She looked baffled, still leaning.

"What's missing. That's what I thought about. See, the book is about the call of the wild. What happens to the dog, Buck, when his master gets killed. He goes out and he goes wild. Well I was wondering. You know, what would have happened if his master hadn't died? How would the dog have turned out?"

"You mean," the pretty teacher said, "because somebody loved him?"

"And if he wasn't alone. You know, if he had somebody who believed in him, and thought he could change."

"But he did die," a smart boy in the front of the class said. "Jim died. He got killed by the Indians. That's the whole point."

"Quiet, Samuel," the teacher said. "Bobby, so you think that would have made it a better book?'

Bobby nodded. "At least there would have been a choice. Isn't that what it's about? Life, I mean. The choices we make, and who we want to be?"

The same smart boy butted in. "But that would have been stupid. Who needs a happy ending like that?" He turned around in his seat to say to Bobby at the far back of the room, "It's a dog-eat-dog world out there. I'm surprised you don't know that."

Bobby leaned forward. "You think I don't?"

"Boys! Samuel. Bobby, you go on." She waited, but Bobby didn't say anything. "Is that it? Is that all you want to tell us?"

Bobby shrugged. "I guess so."

"Don't you have a passage for us?"

"A passage?"

"From the book. You were supposed to find a passage. That was the assignment. You were supposed to pick one you liked in terms of the English. Did you do that?"

Bobby looked down at the thin book in his hands.

"You didn't? Bobby, I can't hear you."

"No."

"You want some time to find one?"

He started flipping.

"You think you can do that in the next few minutes?"

26

He didn't look up. He could hardly breathe. "It's a lot of pages, Miss Nunley."

"It's actually a pretty short book." She paused. "Michael," she said to the boy immediately in front of him. "Have you got one?"

"Yes, ma'am."

"Bobby, you keep looking, and if you don't find one you can do it tomorrow. I'll call on you first thing. Now, Michael, which is it?"

7.

Bobby met Sarah on the staircase after class. She was climbing up as he trudged down. He started to smile at her, but then he saw her eyes. "Hey. Are you all right?"

Kids surged past them, twisting to squeeze through on the narrow landing.

Her skin was pale as his mother's bone china and her eyes had the same turquoise rims. "It's my mom again. She just dropped me off here. She's mad at my dad and she says she's going to spend the night somewhere else."

"Where's she gonna go?"

A blonde angled by them. "Can you guys move?"

Sarah smiled a little as she looked up. "How about your place? Can we send her over to your house, so she can live with your dad?"

"Sure, but then where would I go?" He smiled back.

Teenagers shoved by, knocking them with their gawky arms and heavy notebooks. Bobby put his arm around Sarah to shield her and bring her close.

"Are you going tonight?" she asked. "Because if you are, I'd like to ride with you. My dad's too tired. He can't make it."

"Sure. I'll pick you up. Mom's got to feed Dad before she leaves, so she's gonna take the truck."

"Oooh," someone sang out. "Look at the two lovebirds. Sarah and Bobby, sittin' in a tree ..."

Sarah pulled away. She was blushing.

Bobby tugged her close again. So was he.

8.

Bobby and Sarah sat high up, on an aisle in the balcony, under the big faceted window of the old brick gymnasium that had been built in the 1920s. With his arm around her and Sarah nestled in, he watched as their high school principal marched to the front, under the stage that had been cut into the far front wall, and turned to face the noisy crowd.

"Students! Ladies and gentlemen." The man waited until the assembly quieted. "I'm so glad to see so many of you here tonight, to honor these fine young people. Moms and dads, I know how proud you are of your children. They've worked hard and they've accomplished a lot. When I call out their names, you can go ahead and clap."

With his left arm, he pointed toward the back of the gym, near the doors, where a long dessert table was set up under one of the basketball hoops. "We've got some wonderful cakes and pies for everyone at the end. Mrs. O'Bannon has organized a terrific spread, as always. Many thanks to all the mothers who brought things tonight. I just wish my waistline would let me try everything."

He patted his stomach hanging over his belt, then swept his arm toward the side of the gym, where a tight ring of tidy adults in metal chairs circled a long folding table. "Over here are the scholarship presenters. I'll introduce them as we go along, but why don't we go ahead and give them all a round of applause now?"

When the clapping stopped, he went on. "As we always do, we'll start with the awards to the seniors. Then we'll move on to the other classes. So let's begin with our honors students. These are the boys and girls who've kept up a grade point average of at least 3.0 since their freshman year. As I call your name, please come up front. When we've got everybody, Dennis here will take a group shot. Okay, Dennis?"

He called out twenty-two names, and each time a scrubbed, awkward teenager shuffled to the front.

"Now these next ones are the students who've averaged at least 3.5 all four years. I'm proud to say that every one of them is going on to college. Andy Biggerstaff," he read from a sheet. "MaryAnn Campbell. Come up here and get your awards. Susan Epperson. Teresa Harper. Deborah McAllister."

They all clapped as Debbie stood up from where she sat with the other student honorees in short rows of metal chairs on the gym floor. In the balcony, two rows below Bobby and Sarah, Cora sat proudly with spit-and-polished Tommy, who kept bouncing in his seat to some music in his head.

"Leslie Moore. Jeffrey Rohrer. And Elizabeth Sykes."

When the photographer took their picture, Debbie was standing in the middle. Like all the rest of the girls, her long legs fell out of her miniskirt and stretched miles to the floor.

When he had finished with the honors students, the principal began the scholarships. The third presenter was a heavy-set middle-aged woman who bustled forward in a tight fuchsia suit. "Thank you, Mr. Harris," she boomed into the microphone. "As you all know, every year I get to award the Martin J. Morris memorial scholarship, which is named after my late husband. He was a student here, just like I was, about a hundred years ago."

Mr. Harris was nodding, trying to get her to speed up.

"Every year I get to see all you fine young students," she said. "I'm so happy to be able to say that I've known this year's winner since before she was born. I went to school with her mother. She has high honors too, just like her mother, and she's the sweetest girl. And of course she's going to Southern this fall, just like her sister and her late brother before her."

Cora turned in her seat to smile up at Bobby.

"The five hundred dollar Martin J. Morris memorial scholarship goes to Deborah Claire McAllister!"

Bobby, Sarah and Tommy jumped up, pounding their hands together and yelling. Cora waved at them to sit down, but she didn't mean it. She was clapping hard too.

Beaming, Debbie looked up at her mother as she trotted to the front again, pulling on her skirt. The photographer's flash went off as Mrs. Morris bear-hugged her, the parchment scroll and red ribbon crushed flat against Debbie's chest.

When all the scholarships had been awarded, Mr. Harris began naming the honors students in the lower grades. When he called out the sophomores, Bobby and Sarah and Tommy stood up twice more, for John and for Sarah's pretty sister Gina.

Sarah's mother left with the McAllisters. A short woman with heavy breasts and dark eyebrows, she congratulated John and took the time to inspect Debbie's parchment, which the happy girl thrust at her. "You must be very proud," black-haired Esther said to Cora, who returned the compliment about Gina.

Cora asked whether she and Sarah cared to come over for ice cream to celebrate, but Mrs. Winston said no, she had to get home to her husband, who was ill again. She gave Sarah permission to come over, though, after which Bobby politely thanked her and walked the stolid woman to her car in the dark school parking lot.

"Shot gun!" John ran to Bobby's blue Rambler.

"No." Bobby said as he opened the door for Sarah. "Not this time."

# # #

They were all laughing as they tumbled in the back door of the house. Bobby had his arm around John's neck in a hammer-lock while Tommy giggled. Sarah came in quietly behind them, then leaned against a counter.

The television blared from the den as they talked in a big circle, clanking their spoons into six huge mountains of vanilla ice cream with canned chocolate syrup. After a few mouthfuls, Sarah stepped to look out the kitchen doorway into the dining room. She whispered to Debbie, "Aren't you going out there?"

"Why?" Debbie said.

"To show him your award."

Debbie turned to her mother, who was standing next to John. "She wants me to talk to Dad."

"Why?" John said in surprise to Sarah.

"She's right," Cora cut in, and all three of her children looked at her. She scooped Debbie's award off the kitchen table and held it out to her. "Here, honey. You go tell him. He'll be proud."

Debbie glanced at Bobby.

"I'll go with her," he told his mother.

"Why not take Sarah?" Cora said to Bobby. "You can introduce her."

Sarah smiled, then fell into line behind the two others.

"Dad!" Debbie had to raise her voice over the blaring variety show as she crossed the long room. "There's something I have to show you."

"I'm busy. I'm reading."

Debbie stopped in mid-stride but Bobby touched her back to keep her going. He stepped next to his sister as she bent at the waist, leaning in, making her face appear over top of the newspaper Garrett held open. "I won this, Dad. The Martin J. Morris scholarship." She held the parchment aloft so her father would take it.

Garrett didn't move. All Sarah saw was newspaper and two small hands. "How much is it?"

"What?" Debbie said, unsure.

"It's a scholarship. How much money do we get?"

"Five hundred dollars. See?" She wiggled the parchment to make the red ribbon flutter.

"When do we get it? Cora!"

The fluttering stopped. "I don't know. They didn't tell me."

"You've got to find out these things or people will screw you. Cora!"

"But Dad—"

"Yes?" Cora had leaned out.

"Where's that coconut cake?"

"I took it to school. You knew I was going to."

"Dammit woman. I had my mouth around that cake all afternoon."

"I can get you some ice cream."

"I don't want ice cream. I want your coconut cake."

"Dad?" It was Debbie. "Don't you want to read this?"

"I've already read it. I read Jeanne's, and I read Garrett J.'s."

"But it's mine."

"All I want to know is, did they spell my name right?"

"Your name?"

"They made it m-a-c one time."

She looked down. "McAllister. Yes, they did."

"Then I've seen all I need."

9.

Bobby drove Sarah home. She lived in the center of town so her mother could walk to work at the lawyer's office where she was a secretary. Just a block away, the redbrick county courthouse squatted in the precise middle of the town square, which was skirted by two main roads that converged then kinked around the corners before heading straight out again through the flat fields on their way to the next county and the next, in the asphalt grid that webbed the state. From Garrett's sloped white bungalow at the railroad tracks it took them only five minutes to pull up at the curb in front of Sarah's two-story clapboard house.

She turned to him. There were no streetlights. Her inquiring face was lit only along the edge of her nose, on the tip of her chin, and over the soft curve of one cheek by the dim glow of the porch light twenty feet away.

"Is your dad always like that?" she asked.

"Like what?" He didn't turn to her but kept his hands on the wheel. His knobby knuckles caught the same pale light.

"Maybe I shouldn't say anything, but he's mean. My dad's not like that. He's always glad to see me. But your dad, he cut off Debbie like she was nothing. Even back where I was standing, I could see her face."

"I could too."

"Why wasn't he at school tonight? Did he have some other place to go?"

Bobby snorted. "No. All he does is play golf with his buddies. Other than that, he's out at the farm or at home or running up and down the road like a maniac. At night he sits there, and he reads. He eats there, and then he goes to bed."

"He eats there too?"

"Didn't you see that TV tray? That thing's planted. It's got roots."

"He doesn't eat with you?"

Bobby shook his head. "Not unless we've got company and he wants to put on a show. It's just him and that newspaper, like it's his best friend. Plus that TV."

She shook her head. "How can you live there?"

"Where else am I supposed to go?" He was angry. "It's not like I have a choice. You want to take care of your dad when he comes home. All I want to do is avoid mine. That's all any of us want to do, except my mother."

Sarah had her hand on the door handle, but she didn't open it. "Is that what Jeanne did? Your sister. She never moved back here."

He nodded. "She left as fast as she could, before she was eighteen. She could have lived at home while she was at Southern, but she didn't, and it's only an hour away."

Just one car sat in the short dirt driveway next to Sarah's house, and it was the same Chrysler Mrs. Winston had driven to the awards assembly. It looked to Bobby like Sarah's father wasn't home.

"Garrett J." she said. "Was your dad the same way with him?'

Bobby thought. "Worse. The only one of us boys he likes is John. He and Garrett J. fought all the time until Garrett J. left. He never came back, not even when he had a wife and a baby."

"What happened to him?" she asked quietly.

The light in the front room flicked on behind the drapes.

"Shot down. His plane went down over the Sea of Japan."

"When?"

"Sixty-seven."

"Were you close?"

"You sure do ask a lot of questions." He smiled, though.

"I know, I'm sorry. Mom says that too."

"Yeah, we were close. He used to let me tag along all the time. I was little. Maybe four. He was in high school then. I don't know how he stood it."

"What did they fight about?"

Bobby shrugged. "Who's boss. No matter what they talked about, it always came down to that. Dad wanted him on the farm, but Garrett J., I guess he knew how that was gonna be. So he got his degree and left. He moved out to San Diego and joined the Navy."

Bobby looked out the windshield. "The whole town thought he was king of the hill. Valedictorian. President of the Senior Class. Even the leading scorer on the basketball team senior year. The old guys, they've got this picture of him in his uniform over at the VFW hall. They never did find his plane."

"That must've been hard on your mom."

"Yeah." Bobby's voice had gone hollow, remembering. "Some days I'd come home and she'd be sitting in the living room with that pink Bible she wouldn't let anybody touch, and her rosary. She'd say she was praying, but I could tell she'd been crying. The tissue would be all over the place. I asked her about it once, years after. She said she didn't want to worry us, so she did her crying by herself, when no one was home."

"How was your dad when he died?"

Bobby smirked. "My dad? One time Jeanne started crying. It was right after they called. Dad got mad and told her not to. He said there wasn't anything to cry about. There she was. Just lost her big brother. And he tells her there's no reason to cry."

"Is that why you're going all the way to Nashville? To get away from him?"

Bobby shook his head. "It really is the best school for what I want to do. But I tell you what. If I could, I'd do the same thing they did, my sister and my brother both. I'd get out of here and I'd never come back." But he looked over at her. "At least, not to see him."

She smiled. "Is your dad ever nice to anybody?"

"Sure. He'll tell my sisters they look pretty in a new dress. And he loves my mother. Sometimes it seems like they're in their own little world."

Bobby leaned forward to look up at the sky. "I remember this one time, Dad took me out to see the stars. We were in the back-yard by the railroad tracks. You know there's that big expanse of ground."

Sarah nodded.

"Well it was just him and me. He made a point of it. I think my brother John wanted to go, but for some reason he wouldn't let him. I think it was the only time we ever went out alone.

"And I remember him standing there, pointing up. It was a clear night. I remember the wind. It was warm. Probably summer. And he took maybe an hour, telling me all about the stars and the planets. He showed me everything that was up there. I remember it was the first time I ever saw the Belt of Orion, or the Pleiades. You know, that cluster of stars that's so hard to see. You're not supposed to look at stars with the naked eye. Did you know that? You're supposed to look at them on an angle. You'll see them. That's what he taught me. He said he learned it onboard ship."

"How old were you?'

"Maybe eight. He didn't yell that night, not once. He was quiet. He talked to me like I was a real person. It was the only normal conversation we ever had. I remember he even laughed once. Like I counted. Like I actually had a brain."

Bobby smiled to himself. "He even acted like he was glad I was there. After a while, he decided to go in. But I didn't want to. I remember. I wanted to stay out there all night."

10.

The three boys sat together upstairs later that night. Bobby was hunched over in the corner at his desk, staring down at The Call of the Wild, riffling pages of the paperback and reading out loud to himself. Every once in a while, he blinked and had to rub his tired eyes with the pads of his fingers.

Bobby's mumbling was the only sound anyone made. John and Tommy heard him as they were studying, but they never looked at him.

Bobby murmured, "Buck had accepted rope … the rope … with quiet … dignity … Sure was … No … To be sure … it was an … an …"

His voice died, and the pages started turning again.

He stopped. "It was enough … No … It was all well enough …"

John called out. "Debbie! You down there?"

"in the …"

"Yeah!" she shouted up. "What do you want?"

"… Southland …"

"This French! Can you come help me?"

"… under law … under the law … of … No."

Debbie's light feet came gently up the stairs.

"This French," John said to her. "It doesn't make any sense."

She stopped next to him at his desk. "Join the club," she laughed. "It doesn't make sense to anybody."

"How'd you do it? These verb tenses."

"I just crammed them into my head."

Bobby started again. "He was beaten … "

"Going, coming, seeing, all the verbs for what people do most," Debbie said. "They're all gonna be irregular, just like in English."

"… He knew that …"

"'If I'd known, I would have done something else,'" John read from his book. "What verb tense is that?"

"… But he was broken … No … not broken …"

Debbie turned to him, in his corner. "Bobby," she said.

He looked up. "Huh?"

"You're reading out loud again."

"Oh. Sorry."

"Why do you do that? You always do that."

Bobby shrugged. "I don't know."

11.

Bobby came down the stairs to the kitchen. His father was asleep again in front of the TV. Cora was alone with the radio on, flouring two cake pans, turning and knocking them with the palms of her hands so the flour skittered around the insides.

"Mom, can you read this for me?"

"Of course." She put the pans down and reached for a towel. "What is it?" She turned the radio off.

"The Call of the Wild."

"Oh, I didn't like that one," she said, making a face. "Dogs killing other dogs, while they all watched. And people being killed. You reading that for school?"

He nodded, handing her the little book. "I just want to see if I got this one part right. Page eight, the second paragraph."

She turned to it. "You want me to read it?"

"No. Can you follow along while I say it?

Bobby closed his eyes. He recited, flatly but without stopping, "'He was beaten (he knew that); but he was not broken. He saw, once and for all, that he stood no chance against a man with a club. He had learned the lesson, and in all his after life he never forgot it.'"

"That's right," she said.

He opened his eyes and smiled. "Thanks," he said and reached for the book.

"Is that all you want me to do?"

"Yeah. Goodnight."

"Goodnight," she said. "Sleep tight."

12.

"Bobby, it's your turn," Miss Nunley said with the paperback in her hands, standing up front with her pert backside once more against the distant chalkboard. "Do you have it?"

"Yes, ma'am. Page eight, second paragraph." He slid down low behind the tall boy in front of him.

"Go ahead." She leaned over but he had made sure she couldn't see him.

Bobby closed his eyes. "He was beaten (he knew that); but he was not broken," Bobby recited. "He saw, once for all, that he stood no chance against a man with a club. He had learned the lesson, and in all his life …"

"All his after life," she interrupted.

"Huh?" He opened his eyes.

"All his after life," she said from her far distance. "You missed a word."

"Oh."

"Go on."

"Um … All his … All his…" Bobby sputtered to a stop. "I need to start over."

"No, just go on."

"I … I need to say the whole thing right."

She sighed. Bobby could see it in her shoulders. He shrank low again and repeated, going slow. "He was beaten (he knew that); but he was not broken. He saw, once and for all, that he stood no chance against a man with a club. He had learned the lesson, and in all his after life he never forgot it."

He brought his head up, searching for her face, and he smiled.

"Okay. Now why'd you pick it?" she asked.

"It's the difference between losing and really losing, you know. He had to give in to the man in the red sweater, but he didn't have to sell his soul. It's all about not having to sell your soul."

"That's right," she nodded. "Now tell me about the English."

"It's clear. It makes sense, and the words are simple. He gets his point across without a lot of long words."

"Uh-huh," she said, then waited. "Is that it?"

Bobby shrugged. "I guess so."

"But there's a lot more to this passage, don't you think? For one thing, why's there a semicolon?"

"A what?" Bobby looked down at the page.

"He could have used a comma," she said. "Or a period. Why the semicolon?"

Frozen, he didn't answer.

"Bobby?"

"I don't know," he finally said dully, staring down.

"Well read the sentence again and tell us. Just read it out loud."

She waited, but he didn't speak.

"Don't you see it?" She had leaned all the way over now, her long hair falling straight from her center part. "The semicolon?"

Bobby closed his eyes.

"Right there in the first sentence?" she nudged.

She waited, but he didn't answer. Then, "Anybody else? Nancy?"

A girl spoke right up. "It's there to make a stop, but not a full stop. He was trying to put those two thoughts together, but to make two different points."

"That's right. Bobby, do you see it now?"

"Yes ma'am," he lied to his desk.

"Let me ask you," she said to him. "Why'd you pick that passage, and not the one at the end of the paragraph? I agree with what you said about not losing your soul, but doesn't the end of the paragraph say it better?"

His voice had gone far away. "I guess so."

"Read it for us, please."

But he didn't start.

"Bobby?"

The letters swirled. He couldn't see it.

"Start with 'a man with a club...'"

They spun and he couldn't hold them down. "I'm sorry. I don't ..."

"Good Lord!" She counted with her finger. "It's six lines up from the bottom."

Bobby counted, then held the words tight in his gripping fingers. "'A man with ... a club was law ...'"

"'A lawgiver.'"

"'A lawgiver ... A man with a club was a lawgiver ... A master to obey ...'"

"'To be obeyed,'" she said, starting to walk toward him.

"'To be obeyed ... Though not ... not ness ... not ness ... '"

"Not what?" She walked down the long line of desks. As she passed them, the other kids turned to stare at him, row by row.

"Not ness ... not ness." Bobby stopped.

"What's wrong?" She neared him, seeing him now.

He didn't answer.

She got to him, staring down, waiting, her eyes watching.

"I'm sorry." He could feel her, feel her body next to him, but he kept his head down. He could feel them all, watching.

"Are you okay?"

Utterly still now, the whole room heard the tremble in his voice. "I just can't get it. I'm sorry."

The black-rimmed clock over the classroom door did the only talking.

"You can't read it?" she asked.

He kept his eyes on his book. She crossed her arms, waiting.

"Bobby," she said. "I'm sorry too. Steven, can you read it?"

"I sure can!" The other boy jumped in and the others started moving again, shifting with relief in their hard seats as she returned to her station in the front. "'A man with a club was a lawgiver, a master to be obeyed, though not necessarily conciliated. Of this last Buck was never guilty, though he did see beaten dogs that fawned upon the man, and wagged their tails, and licked his hand.'"

13.

After school that day, Bobby drove Sarah to the local community college. It was a long way, and she shuffled her papers nervously the whole time. She talked non-stop about the classes she was going to be taking, telling him again how she wanted to become an x-ray technician at Memorial Hospital in their town.

Bobby listened and smiled along with her as they drove, but his eyes never left the fields. The days were more humid and they could feel it. Still, Bobby never liked to turn on the air conditioner. He preferred to sit with the window down on the driver's side and his left arm out, elbow to the wind.

"Since we're here," Bobby said. "Do you want to stop and see your dad at the rail yard?"

"No," she said quickly. "That's okay."

After she registered for the fall and they left again, they stopped for dinner on the road. Bobby insisted on paying, telling her with a broad smile that he'd never taken an almost-college-girl out before.

Later, as they got nearer to home, he asked quietly whether she had to get back right away. He didn't look at her as he said it, and he tried to sound as casual as he could. She looked at him, then turned to look out the windshield. Just as quietly, she said no. Not right away. At least not for a little while.

The night was clear and the stars shone above them. Bobby found the small red dot of Mars above the tree line.

He slowed, then turned off the hardtop and onto a dirt lane that ran away into a field. After a minute, it became rutted and they bounced along until it finally stopped, facing a plot of corn. Bobby cut the engine and the lights, and turned to Sarah. He took her in his arms and they began to kiss.

Across the bucket seats, she reached up to his hair and stroked it, taking possession of him. He brought his lips to her soft, willing neck. She smelled of lilacs.

He felt himself rise. Into her ear he whispered, "I want to show you something."

She had brought her breasts up, curving her back. He could feel them pressed against him. "Bobby, I ..."

"Sit up," he told her.

"Sit up?"

"Yeah, sit up. Move up a little."

She opened her eyes. Her black hair was everywhere and her pale, china skin was rose pink and glowing. He pulled away from her and brought one of his hands out from behind her.

"What are you doing?"

"Just watch." He reached between the two seat backs, by her left shoulder. Suddenly, her seat back dropped all the way down with a thump. Sarah was on her back with her head touching the rear bench seat, staring up at the ceiling. Bobby was already on his way over to her, trying to get his legs around the wheel.

"Bobby McAllister! You get me up this instant!"

"Sarah—"

"Get me up!"

He fumbled, trying to get himself back into the driver's seat. "Sit up. You've got to sit up. It won't come up if you're lying back."

She brought herself up as he reached for the lever. "Who do you think I am?" she said. "Mary Ellen Sandowsky?"

He got the seat up. She arranged herself on the seat and wrapped her arms around her chest.

"You've got the wrong girl. Take me home!"

"Sarah—"

She glared straight ahead in the dashboard light. "What kind of girl do you think I am?"

He tugged desperately at the knees of his jeans. "I didn't mean—"

"Take me home."

He started the car and got back to the road. It was another ten silent minutes before she said, "What'd you do to my seat?"

"I ... um ..."

"You never did that before."

He slid a look over to her, but she had her back turned to face out her window. "I switched them," he said.

"You what?"

"I switched the seats. I did it last week."

"How come?" Her voice was sharp.

At first he didn't answer, but then he said, "Remember I had all that pipe to get up to the farm? Well I figured if I switched them, the levers would be on the inside. I could just reach up and drop that passenger seat from my side. You know, without my having to get out of the car and walk all the way around to get that lever on the window side. I'm in here so much, hauling so much, I'm trying to use it as a pick-up. I just lay that pipe next to me here, with your seat down."

She twisted all the way around to stare at the space between the front bucket seats. "So if you pull this knob," she asked, looking at the silver lever, "my seat goes down? And this one here on yours puts your seat down?"

"Yep."

"And they used to both be on the other sides? By the doors?"

"Pretty clever, huh?" He smiled at her, but she wasn't looking.

"And to do that, you had to switch the seats? Literally take them out of the car and put them back in again, reversed? So mine's the seat from the driver's side. And yours used to be mine?"

He was grinning. "Yep, you're a smart girl."

Through the open windows warm air rushed in, bringing the cicadas' song and the high sound of crickets rubbing their hind legs together, advertising for love.

When she finally looked at him, her eyebrows had marched up her forehead. "And you thought you'd try this out on me?"

"Maybe. What do you think?"

"I think I'm never getting in this car again. Mom was right."

"About what?"

"About boys and Ramblers. Nothing but rolling beds. That's what she says. Did you really think you were gonna get something back there?"

"I don't—"

"Because you weren't. And you may not ever, now."

He didn't say a word.

After another few long minutes, they made the last turn at the county courthouse square on the way to Sarah's, and he sent his eyes over to her again. She caught him doing it, and she smiled, and then she started to laugh. "So how'd you know you could do that? Switch the seats."

"I just figured it out. It seemed logical."

He pulled up at her curb, which was shedding aggregate and crumbling into the old asphalt of the street. As she collected her college papers and her purse, he said, "I didn't mean to get you upset. I wouldn't disrespect you. I thought you wanted me … I mean us … I thought …"

Her mother had already come out onto the porch. Bobby saw the shelf of her bosom in the dim light above her. She clasped her arms at the elbows, pressing them down on her chest. "Sarah," Mrs. Winston called to them. It was a statement, not a question.

Sarah got out, but then she turned to lean in the passenger-side window, taking her time and showing her mother her rear-end. "Bobby, you're full of it," she said. "You didn't switch those seats to load pipe."

"I didn't?'

"If you wanted to load pipe, you'd want the lever on the out-side here, where my door is. Because you'd be starting on the outside with your arms full. Now that it's on the inside, you have to either come around to your side and lay down my seat by leaning in around the steering wheel or you have to lean all the way in from my side to grab the handle. You wouldn't do that."

"Well," he said slowly. "Maybe you're right."

"You didn't change those seats to load pipe. You did it so you could drop my seat when you were already inside the car. You wanted to take me out there like you did and do that, tonight. That's why. You planned it."

"Sarah! Time to come in now," Mrs. Winston called from the porch.

Sarah peered at Bobby, ignoring her mother. "You want to try another explanation?"

He smiled wide. "I don't have another one. But if you give me a minute, I'm sure I could think of something."

14.

It was even hotter the next day when Bobby stopped after school to pick up some new scraper blades he had ordered for the broken planter. The sun cooked, and it hadn't rained all week, leaving the young grass dry and browning.

As he drove north, he had all the windows down and the AM radio blasting the oldies station. He was happy, sweating, as the Buckinghams complained it was kind of a drag.

All of a sudden, he saw his father. Garrett was standing outside the package store on the side of the two-lane road with two of his buddies. He faced his friends with his eyes squinting in the bright afternoon sun, scanning the oncoming traffic with his arms crossed.

When he spotted Bobby's Rambler, he didn't move except to stick his right arm into the air and flick his fingers. As soon as Bobby saw it, he had to slam on his brakes. The pickup behind him honked as Bobby slowed then swerved off the road and into the parking lot that skirted the small building. White banners with red and blue letters announced the two-for-one six packs of cheap beer inside.

He pulled up next to his father. "Yessir?"

Garrett jerked his head with his two buddies watching. "Get out."

"But I was going—"

"Don't sass me. Get out. And bring your toolbox."

Bobby parked. He grabbed a small toolbox out of his cluttered trunk. "Mr. Tanner," he nodded respectfully as he walked up to them. "Mr. Hedeman." The two men nodded in return.

"I'm not getting any air," Garrett told him.

"But I just fixed that. It was working fine last week."

"Well then you did a crappy job. All I'm getting is hot." Garrett looked at Tanner. "I told him it was the compressor, but of course he said I was wrong."

"Dad, it's not the compressor."

"Oh? You can tell that from here?"

"I need to get out to the farm. I've got the new blades for the planter."

"I don't care what you've got. I want it cool."

Bobby took a breath as he turned toward his father's truck parked in the shade.

"The compressor's up front!" his father yelled to his back. "In case you forgot!"

"Bill, you gotta hear this," Bobby heard his father tell the other man. "This really happened. I was sitting there last night reading the newspaper. My youngest—you know, Tommy?—he comes running down the stairs as fast as he can. Just pounding his feet."

Bobby opened the hood and thrust in his head.

"He comes up to me and he says, 'Yessir?' Boy's just standing there, waiting. I look at him and I say, 'What're you doing?' And he says, 'You yelled for me to come down.'"

Bobby slammed the hood, then walked around to the driver's side as he stole a glance at his father. Garrett had begun to rock up and down on his feet. Back and forth he went, as he jangled the coins in his front pants pocket.

"He's real sure, like he heard me," Garrett said as Bobby climbed into the driver's seat. "I tell him he's full of shit. That I didn't yell. He stands there a minute, then goes back upstairs."

Bobby twisted himself upside down, so his shoulders were crammed on the floorboard and his legs were up in the air behind the wheel.

"An hour later, same thing happens. Tommy comes pounding down the stairs. He comes over to me and asks what I want. I tell him I didn't yell for him, and he says, 'Yes you did.' I say, 'No I didn't,' and he stands there. After a minute, he gets this funny look on his face and goes back upstairs. You know what it was?"

"He was scared to death," Bobby said under the dash.

"He comes back down with this tape recorder. You know, one of those new ones, with the cassettes? Tommy says, 'Listen to this,' and he turns it on. I hear him playing his guitar and singing some country song. And then there's me, after a few minutes, yelling at him to come down. Right there on the tape."

Garrett laughed. "It was me, from maybe a week ago. He was up in his room running this thing when I yelled. So every time he plays that song, he's got me yelling and he keeps running downstairs."

He laughed again, a short bark that carried. "I've got that kid so well trained he comes running."

Bobby listened for it, but the other men didn't laugh.

"Hey, Bobby!" his father yelled. "What are you doing?"

"Almost done!" Bobby turned himself back around.

"What d'you mean? It hasn't been five minutes."

Bobby sat upright, started the engine and stepped on the gas. He sat for a minute with the motor idling, then pulled on the hand brake and climbed out. He was smiling as he walked toward his father with his hand out.

"Here, Dad," he said. "I just saved you a hundred and fifty dollars."

"What's that?" Garrett held out his palm. Bobby dropped a glass bulb into it.

"It's a fuse," Tanner told him.

"Why'd you give me this?" Garrett said. "I told you it was the compressor."

"It was the fuse." Bobby grinned. "The air conditioner fuse was blown, so I just switched it."

"I told you to fix the compressor."

"There's nothing wrong with it, Dad. I told you. It just wasn't getting any juice. So I switched the fuse."

"Where'd you get it?"

"The lighter. On the fuse block."

"So the lighter won't work now? I don't have a lighter?"

"You smoking now, Squirrel?" Tanner said to Garrett. "I never heard of you smoking."

"I can put in another one when you get up to the farm," Bobby said. "I've got a five-pack. This fuse here only cost a dime."

Hedeman asked, "How'd you know it wasn't getting any juice?"

"I've got a screwdriver test light in my tool box."

"When that compressor blows," Garrett interrupted, "it's gonna cost me a hell of a lot more than a dime."

"What's wrong with you?" Tanner said. "Your boy's done you a big favor. You ought to be thanking him instead of getting mad."

Hedeman had turned to Tanner. "How'd he do that so fast?"

"He's always been like that," Tanner said. "His whole life. Isn't that right, Squirrel? One time, I came over to the house and he was sitting in the back yard. He'd taken the whole lawn mower apart. You remember that?"

Garrett wouldn't answer.

"He was supposed to mow the lawn, but the darn thing wouldn't start. So he just took it apart. Must've been in a thousand pieces. It only took you, what? A couple of hours to fix that thing? And put it all back? How old were you, ten?"

But Bobby was watching his father. "About that," he said quietly.

"Goddamn thing never did work right after that." Garrett threw the old fuse and it skipped like a stone over the gravel. "It better not happen to my compressor. Or to my planter. Hey, did I tell you boys what happened to that?" He scanned their eyes and began rocking again.

"Yeah, you told us," Tanner said as he turned again to Bobby. "You getting done with school this year?"

"Yessir," Bobby said.

"You heading out, or you gonna stick around?"

"I'm going to Nashville."

"For what?" Hedeman asked.

"Diesel mechanic school."

"What do you need that for? They ought to be paying you to teach them."

"Bobby," Garrett said. "I want those blades on right away. You don't have time to chew the fat. Get going."

15.

The next day, at the end of English, Miss Nunley passed slowly up and down the long rows of students, handing back tests the class had taken the week before. As she ambled, she had kind words for everyone who had done well. Bobby watched her spend a lot of time in the front. When she got to the back each time, then finally down the last row next to the window where he was, she didn't speak. She just slapped the graded papers down on the old desktops.

When she at last arrived at him, she leaned over and whispered that she had to see him after class. Then she handed Bobby his test with a bright red "F."

The loud bell rang a few minutes later and all the other kids poured out. Bobby waited until he was alone with her, then stood and began the long walk to the front. Miss Nunley sat at her desk. She closed her lesson plan and pointed to the closest desk facing her. He slid in. He had never been in such a seat before.

She leaned back and clasped her hands in her lap. He didn't say anything. "Bobby. We've got a problem."

He waited. She watched. Finally, he had to ask. "What's that?"

"That test there. The one you're holding. You only answered two. Two out of four. And what you did write I can't read, it's so messy."

She paused again, but he didn't speak.

"Bobby, what's going on with you?"

"I didn't have time to finish. That's all."

"You had the same time as everyone else. Four questions in an hour. Nobody else had any trouble with that timeframe."

He swallowed hard. "I guess I got stuck. You know, I spent too much time on the first two. I just didn't get to the rest."

"That's for sure. But even those I couldn't read. I've never seen handwriting like that. And the spelling."

"Miss Nunley, I did the best I could."

"That's the problem. I know you did. If you weren't trying so hard, I wouldn't have any trouble failing you. But you are. I see that. But you can't."

"Can't what?"

"I've thought a lot about this. I know what it means, what I'm about to say. But I can't pass you, Bobby, if you can't read."

"I can read!"

"No, you can't. Not well enough anyway. What I saw day before yesterday was someone who can't read."

"I did that assignment with the passage."

"I know this hurts, Bobby, but you can't. That's the truth. You can't go out in the world after high school and get a job reading at that level."

"What kind of job?"

"Any kind. Why?"

"You're wrong. I can be a mechanic."

"Is that what you want to be?"

"I'm going to school for it, after this."

"What school?"

"Diesel mechanic school. In Nashville."

"You got in? They accepted you?"

"Is that so hard to believe?"

She turned to look out the window. Young and pretty, this was her second year teaching. "What do you need to get in?"

"A diploma."

"That's it?"

"And the money. I've been saving up."

She thought about it, but finally said, "I'm sorry. But I just don't think I can pass you if you can't read. I should've figured it out by now, but all the other tests were multiple choice. Either that or take-home. You always passed those."

"I'm a good student, Miss Nunley."

"Yes, you are. And you've always done your work. You pay attention too. But if I passed you, what kind of English teacher would I be?"

She looked out the window again. He waited, hopping his foot below the desktop where she couldn't see it. Up front, the tick of the clock sounded like clanging metal.

"Bobby," she said. "This is a big decision, and it impacts you and your whole family. I know that. I want to talk to your mom and dad before I decide."

"You want to talk to my dad?"

"Yes, and your mom. I think they should both be here. And you too."

"You want to talk to my dad?"

"Is that a problem?"

He swallowed. "He's out in the field."

"He'll come. This is important."

"You're not from here, are you?"

She tilted her head. "What does that mean?"

"I don't mean any disrespect, ma'am, but he's a farmer. And farmers don't do anything in May but plant corn and drill beans. Day and night."

"On the weekends too?"

"Weekends too. He's out every night until ten."

"Oh. I see. Your mother then. You and your mother. That'll be fine." She looked down at her lesson book. "Can you do it to-morrow, after school? Three thirty?"

"Yes ma'am."

"If she can't you just let me know."

She nodded to dismiss him, and he slid out from under the small desk. He didn't leave, though. He stood and faced her. After a moment, she looked up at him when she realized he hadn't moved. "Yes?"

"Are you really gonna flunk me?"

"I don't know, Bobby. I don't know."

16.

He got home late that night from the farm and went downstairs to wash. When he came up again, his mother was in the den crocheting an afghan and watching TV with the volume low. She smiled as he walked through the dining room and gently patted the cushion next to her on the broad, rust-colored couch.

"Where's Dad?"

"He went to bed right after the game."

"Who won?"

"The Cards. Can you believe it? Chris Zachary shut out the Cubs."

Bobby stretched his long legs in front of him and crossed his arms over his chest.

"Ten nothing," she said, but he didn't comment. He put his tired eyes on the screen and, after a moment, his mother fell into her work again. The bright colors of the changing yarn danced in her hand as she stitched together apple green squares of wool with a single skein that went from yellow to orange to all the rest of the rainbow before turning yellow again. Her concave lap was piled with more squares she had cut out, and she was making holes in them with her crochet hook as she joined them together between seams of crochet. The half-finished afghan covered her thin legs and fell to her ankles.

The late news came on from St. Louis with a lead story about a farm worker, Juan Corona, who had been arrested in the fields of the great central valley of California. They were still digging up all the murdered bodies he had left.

Bobby didn't move and his mother didn't talk to him. It wasn't until the first commercial minutes later that he spoke. "Mom. Why did you marry Dad?"

The crochet hook stopped for an instant, but then started again. "I've told you that story. He asked me to the senior dance." She smiled at him through her thick lenses as bright blue yarn slid between her fingers.

"Not just a dance. Why did you marry him?"

"Did something happen today between you and your dad? Is that why you're asking? He did seem distracted when he came home."

"No. I was just wondering. You and your sisters, you must have had a lot of boys around."

"Not me. I only ever kissed one other boy before your dad, and I didn't kiss him until I was eighteen. My sister was the pretty one. I was this tall bookworm with these big glasses."

"But Mom, you're—"

"Shh. I know I'm not going to win any beauty contests. I didn't get my mother's good looks. I got the books, and she got the beautiful. That's what we always used to say. I'm sorry she died before you were born."

"You told me she never learned to read. Was she like me?"

"It was different back then. A lot of people never learned. I tried to teach her once, but she couldn't. There was something about the words themselves she couldn't get." Cora touched the rainbow yarn in her lap, then smiled over at him. "I think all my books got me married. Your father went out with a million girls before me, but he liked that I always had a book. He picked me. I couldn't believe it. This boy I liked had just left town, so I was sure I'd end up an old maid."

She lifted the hook again and the blue yarn started pouring.

"He told me he couldn't do numbers, but he could. He had me help him with this big math test, but he didn't need it. He told me later he got an A. He only did it to meet me, he said. And he was going to stay in town. A lot of boys left this old place and never came back, just like they do now. But your dad promised he'd never leave me, and he didn't."

She touched him then, wrapping her long fingers around his forearm. "I know he's not always easy on you, but he means well. He's a good man, and he's made a good life for us. You know he converted for me? He wasn't Catholic. That meant the world to my whole family."

"Is that why Granddad gave him that job at the dealership? Because he converted?"

"He didn't 'give' him anything." The yarn was purple now, having changed from the blue. "He earned it. He nearly died over there. Plus he was a great salesman, with all those stories he tells all the time. He was the best employee my father ever had."

"But I thought they didn't get along."

The yarn was vibrant red-purple now, a bright fuchsia. "No. It was my mom he didn't get along with. My dad hated to see him leave the dealership and go into farming. But your father became a big success, with more land than older farmers who've been at it a lot longer. Other men look up to him. He's always coming home telling me about some friend or other who's come to him for help."

"But do they come over, Mom? Has anyone ever been in this house?" Bobby blurted it, and his mother's eyes snapped over at him.

"They're busy! They're farmers." She began twisting the yarn between her fingers and the hook. "He has friends. You know how he goes to the grocery store for Mrs. Krause across the street. He even gets her cigarettes every week, even though he hates it. He doesn't have to, but he does it to be nice because she's old."

"She pays for it herself."

"Bobby!" The yarn was red now, whipping over the shiny silver. "He doesn't have to go at all, but he does. Your father has taken good care of us. It's been hard work since he got the farm, but he's done it, and he's never complained. Never once, about how many kids we have. I can't imagine the obligation he must feel. You've got to give him some credit."

They sat in silence for a minute.

"You resemble him, you know." Her voice had softened as the yarn had changed to popsicle orange. "You've got his chin, and the same freckles and blue eyes."

On the TV the weatherman began to talk, and they listened closely. When the man was done, Bobby asked, "What was Dad like before the war?"

"Oh, I don't know. Just the same."

"But Uncle Scotty told me once he changed. The war changed him. He said Dad was more tightly wound."

She thought about it. "Scotty's right. A lot of men saw things and they came back changed forever. Your dad never told me what he saw, but I know it was terrible. When he came back, he could never calm down, and he started to get mad a lot, for less reason."

"He didn't used to be like that?"

"No!" She was laughing but she caught herself. "But he's no worse than my dad. Once your granddad threw that Royal typewriter of his at me across the room. He nearly hit me, but I don't think he knew I was standing there. That's just the way he was. My job was to make sure I never got in the way. That and to come home with the right man, and I did that. Eventually."

Her yarn was yellowing as she played the hook. She had a rhythm with it, like it was an instrument.

"Why didn't Grandma like Dad?"

Her fingers paused. "What is this? Interrogate Mother night?" But she laughed. "My mother thought he had a mouth on him, and he did. You know that's why they held him back in high school? He said something to a teacher once. She flunked him, she got so mad. That's why it took him five years to graduate."

"Just like me."

"What? No, it isn't." She started crocheting again, the hook flashing. "Is something wrong?"

"I'm graduating with Debbie. A year late."

"That happened a long time ago. And you never mouthed off to anybody. You were always a good boy."

He keened his ears to listen to the sound of the house over top of the noisy television. All was quiet. He swallowed. "There's something I have to tell you."

"What?"

It all came out in a rush, gushing. "I might not graduate. I might not pass."

"What do you mean not pass? Which subject?"

"English. Mom, she knows I can't read."

"Of course you can read!"

"You know that page from the other night? She made me read another one in class. Right there, in front of everybody. I couldn't do it."

"You just need a little more time."

"I couldn't, Mom. I couldn't do it. She gave us an essay test last week. I only answered two questions, out of four. And she couldn't even read what I wrote!" Bobby's voice now was high and shrill.

"Shh!" Cora said, leaning close. "You'll wake him."

"She's right. You know she is. It's the same as before. I'm stupid. Everybody says so."

"I don't."

"Miss Nunley does, and Miss Denny. Lord knows Dad does."

"Bobby." She had dropped her hands to her lap. "You are not."

"Only stupid people can't read. That's what Dad says. You sit there and read a book like it's nothing. So does John. And Debbie. But I can't. I'm just like Grandma."

"So you don't like books. You don't need them. You're good with your hands. You want to fix engines. Go do that."

"But what kind of life am I gonna have, fixing trucks?"

"A fine life, that's what. A lot of good men do it every day. People know what you can do. Aren't you the one who just made the carousel for the prom all by yourself?"

"It was a class project."

"Sure, the rest of the class did what you told them. But didn't Mr. Engle ask you to do the drawings? And to figure out what you needed in order to build it?"

"But—"

"And didn't he make sure you were going to be around to do the work? Before he went to Mr. Harris and volunteered? He knows how smart you are."

"But what am I gonna do about school? I already paid half the money. If I don't pass—"

"You'll pass. You'll get to go."

"That's not what she says. Miss Nunley. Mom, she's serious."

Cora had forgotten her work. "She's really going to fail you?"

"She's thinking about it. But she wants to talk to you first. She wanted to talk to Dad too."

"She did?"

"I told her he didn't have time because he was out in the field."

"That's right. That was a good answer."

"So she said she has to see you. Tomorrow after school."

17.

"Mrs. McAllister."

"Miss Nunley."

"Come in. Please sit down. I know these desks are pretty tight. Bobby you can sit down here next to her."

They faced Miss Nunley side-by-side, his prim mother placing her pocketbook on the desktop and tucking her stem legs underneath her as she pulled herself up in the perfect posture of the straight-A student she used to be. Bobby slumped, planting his tense elbows on the thick wood table desk that jutted into his chest and crossed his forearms along the top of it, popping his shoulders. Miss Nunley had returned to her wooden throne, a huge battered square box of a desk four times as old as she was. She clasped her hands on the nicked glass that topped it, making a nest of her smooth fingers, the reflection doubled into a tangle of twigs.

She began. "Ma'am, I suppose Bobby has told you why I wanted to meet today."

Cora inclined her head but said nothing.

The two women regarded each other. Bobby heard four ticks of the clock. Miss Nunley squeezed her own hands and he watched the angles sharpen. "I'm sorry to have to say this, but your son's got a severe reading problem."

"No I don't!"

"Bobby," Cora said without moving.

"I should have figured it out by now," Miss Nunley said. "But I didn't. Bobby just can't read effectively."

"What does that mean?" Cora was calm.

"He's functionally illiterate."

"Functionally illiterate?"

"What I mean is, he can probably read some. Maybe he's even able to get by, right now. But he can't read well enough to function as an adult. And he can't spell or write so anybody can read it. I've never seen handwriting so bad."

Miss Nunley stopped, but Cora didn't answer. Bobby cut a look over to her and saw the same blank face she gave the grocery store cashier who pried into everyone's business.

"Mrs. McAllister, I can tell this doesn't come as a surprise to you. You knew about this, didn't you?"

"Of course I did. So has every teacher he's ever had, eventually."

"Then why didn't you do something?"

"I'm sorry?"

"Get him help, Mrs. McAllister. Teach him."

Cora leaned forward in her chair. "Miss Nunley, you're new here. You probably don't know Miss Denny. Eleanor Denny."

Bobby closed his eyes.

"She was his third grade teacher. The most wonderful woman. Probably half your class had her. When he was eight, she met with us, his father and I. And she told us she'd tried and tried, but she couldn't teach him how to read. His eyes jumped all over the page. Nothing she did worked."

"Did you try?"

"Miss Denny was the best teacher in the world. Every one of my children had her. She taught my two oldest, before she got Bobby."

"I don't follow."

"If anybody could teach him, she could. And if she couldn't, what was I supposed to do? What was anybody?"

"So you just gave up?"

"Gave up?" Cora's voice had an edge now, but he heard her round it. "Of course not. I encouraged his mind. Bobby has a wonderful mind. And his hands can do anything. I praised him every day when he left my house and went to school. I saw his face. I saw what that meant, to pack up his books and walk down that street. Every day for twelve years, Miss Nunley. And go to school. Do you have any idea how hard that is for a child who has trouble with books?"

Cora looked over at him. "And you're wrong, you know. He can read. He's worked and worked, all on his own. Now he reads just fine. It just takes him longer."

"Is that true, Bobby?"

Bobby nodded without looking up. He had found a new, wet scrawl of blue ink on the desktop that said "GO CARDS." Bobby had spit on his finger and he was rubbing for all his life.

"You just can't ask him to read something right off the bat," his mother said. "He's got to take it slow."

"Is that what happened the other day?" Miss Nunley asked him.

Bobby nodded again, his index finger working.

"And that's why you needed all that extra time?"

He nodded a third time, but just once. A bob of the head.

Miss Nunley thought about it, but then she said, "Mrs. McAllister, I appreciate what you're saying. But maybe someone here can help him if he stays another year."

"Someone. Would that 'someone' be you?"

"I'm not equipped—"

"That's my point. No one is. No one has any idea how to help him. That's why it doesn't make sense to hold him back again."

"Again?"

"Eleanor Denny told us to hold him back. So he'd have two years to learn how to read. But it didn't make any difference. Nothing made any difference. And don't you think that's hard too? It's a small town, Miss Nunley. You already see that. Everybody but you knows Bobby was held back. And if he's held back again, I don't think he'll ever live it down."

He had finished the stain and now his finger just hunted for specks. As it touched the wood grain, feeling it, his ankles started dancing, hopping up and down to bounce both his knees.

Miss Nunley said, "Bobby, I need to ask you something. Look at me."

He brought up his head. Her eyes were green. Green like the blades of spring grass he made whistles out of. You couldn't see that from his home in the back row.

"Those take-home tests. How'd you do them?"

Cora interrupted. "What are you asking?"

"It's all right, Mom," Bobby said, not breaking his teacher's gaze. "I wrote the answers. Then I checked the words. Once I got them right, I copied it all over again so it was neat."

"Did anybody help you, at any time?"

"You think he cheated?" Cora said.

"No," he answered over his mother. "No one helped me."

"My son doesn't cheat," Cora said. "And he doesn't lie. Everything he's done, he's done on his own."

"I believe you," Miss Nunley told her.

The clock ticked by, punching the silence as both women thought.

"What's his grade right now?" his mother asked.

Miss Nunley opened her black and white composition book on her desk and Bobby watched her find a page with writing down the left side, in a column. She found what she wanted and traced across the page following the top of her ruler, which she balanced over the open spine and used to press it down. "He's got about a D plus average now."

"Does that include this last test?"

"It's because of it, really. Before that, it was probably a C minus."

"So that's passing."

"It's not his grades. That's what I'm trying to tell you, his grades aren't the problem. At least they weren't up to now."

Cora cleared her throat. "What I'm trying to ask is this. If he can't read, then how can he have a C minus average?"

"He passed all the other tests."

"And he's done all his assignments."

"Yes."

"So how could he do that if he can't read?" Cora pointed at the book. "Your grades there prove he can. He may not read the same way you and I do, or as fast, but he can. Those marks prove it, and they're going to prove it to the principal of this school. And this is what I want to know. Why in the world would you want to punish this boy just because he's different?"

"But he just flunked a test."

"One test. That took down his grade, but he's still passing."

"Right now he is."

"There can't be any more tests between now and the end of the year. All he's got is the final next week."

She was right. Bobby smiled to himself. She had been paying attention.

"Yes," Miss Nunley conceded.

"So even if he fails the final, he'll pass."

"I don't know. He might not. I'd have to do the figuring, but it doesn't matter anyway. Senior English is a required course, and that means you have to pass the final. If Bobby doesn't, he can't graduate, no matter what his overall average is."

Bobby butted in. "Miss Nunley? You've already written the final, right?"

"Yes."

"So you already know if it's got an essay."

"Yes, but why?"

"I was wondering. If I don't do well on the essay part, can I still pass?"

She thought about it. "Yes, it's possible. But you'd have to do real well on the rest of it."

"How well?" Cora asked.

"He'd have to get a solid C or better."

"But if I got that," he hurried. "I'd pass?"

She looked down again at her composition book, pushing the ruler against the spine, then traced the pad of her finger along the ridge of it to recalculate his numbers. He saw the clear nail polish shine. She took a long breath before she answered. "Bobby. A solid C on that final is better than you have been doing. It's a jump up. So I don't know if you can do that."

"But if I can?"

She looked at him and he saw the bright, sharp green. "Bobby, if you can, if you really can, then I'll pass you."

"Woo-hoo!"

The teacher smiled. "You better do it. Nothing less. That's our deal. Not even a C minus, you get me?"

"We understand," Cora said.

At the door, his mother shook the teacher's hand, then held it as she said, "Miss Nunley, there's something I'd like to ask you. I'd like you to tell me you'll read that final with an open mind."

"Pardon me?"

"I don't mean any offense, but last night I read that essay test Bobby took. I asked him for it, and then I read that whole book again too. The Call of the Wild. It sure seemed to me like he answered those questions."

Miss Nunley took back her hand. "I don't agree with you."

"You don't have to. And I'm not asking you to change his grade. You're the teacher, and what you say goes. But I would like you to take that test back and read it over again. Maybe now that you know about Bobby, some of those words will make more sense to you." Cora smiled her eyes at her as Miss Nunley considered it.

"All right."

Cora dug in her purse for his test. He had had no idea that she had brought it. Miss Nunley promised to call as soon as she had finished marking his final. Yes, she assured Cora, she had their telephone number in the file. Yes, she would make sure to ask for Cora, no matter who answered.

"Thanks," Bobby said on the deserted stairs going down. Cora reached for his rough hand and brought it to her heart, hugging it close against her thin ribcage. Then she noticed his finger.

"Where did you get all this blue ink?" she asked as they stepped outside into the light.

18.

The next morning Bobby got up early. It was only six fifteen when he arrived at the farm, but Will was already outside working. He nodded when Bobby walked up next to the planter, then told the teenager to double-check the new disk assemblies while he mounted the last one in his hand.

When they had finished, Will said, "We need to talk. We don't have a lot of time. Your dad'll be here any minute. He's always here by seven, even on Saturdays."

Bobby was slapping his dusty hands against his pant legs. "What's wrong?"

"We're leaving. As soon as I get it all planted. I'm sorry."

"You mean for good? Where?"

"I don't know yet. I heard there's a job down in Red Bud."

"You're leaving and you don't have a job?"

The older man had closed his mouth and he was working it, chewing his own tongue. "There's no easy way to say this. I'm a Christian. Let me just say I'm not willing to work for your dad anymore."

"But you always have."

"I've only been here six years. You just don't remember because you weren't out here much before that. There were a lot of other men before me. I lasted the longest, that's all."

"But why now?"

"Because he cut me down to fifty percent. It was bad enough before, but now I can't even make a living. Not when I've got a wife that likes to go to the movies once in a while. And she wants her own house. At least to live somewhere that seems like it belongs to her. Not with some crazy man banging on the door every morning at the crack of dawn."

Will picked up a wrench and bent to put it in the large, red-painted toolbox that sat beside him on the riffling grass. "You know, all the time I've worked for your dad I don't think I've ever been right about anything. And I don't think I've ever once been allowed to finish a sentence. He's always right, no matter what. Even when he's wrong. And he's wasted a lot of money. His and mine. You know he tried to plant hybrid corn one time? The second year? Any idiot knows you don't plant the corn you harvest from hybrid seed. It'll come up but it won't yield. But your dad, this smart guy, he figures he can cheat Pioneer. He planted a whole field in it. It almost busted us."

Will shook his head, remembering. "Your dad's not stupid. He's smart. He's as smart as anybody I've ever known. But he's not a farmer like you. He doesn't give a shit about the land. He's just a card player, trying to make money and look good. That's all he cares about."

The day was hot. It was baking already and it was barely breakfast time. Bobby heard the clang of Anna's pots in the kitchen. Bobby nodded. "I know that's how he got the farm."

"What is?" Will's eyebrows had found each other.

"He won the money on the boat back after the war. He played poker with the other POWs the whole way. He was the best player, so he won all their money."

"It's not true. That's what he says, but that's not what happened."

"It's not?"

"You want to know the truth?" Bobby saw the weather in the older man's eyes. "Your dad was down at the dealership one weekend. It was back in fifty-nine. You know he used to work for your granddad, right? He owned it. Mr. Rowan. The old John Deere dealership, next to the gas station?"

"Yeah."

"Well your granddad wasn't there. Your dad was alone and Clyde Berrington walks in. You know him?"

Bobby nodded.

"Clyde tells your dad he needs six thousand dollars to pay off a gambling bet from the night before. He'd been playing poker, and I guess he put up the farm. See, the dealership was the only thing with a safe and any money on the weekends. So he comes in and gives the deed to your dad, and your dad takes six thousand dollars out of the safe and gives it to him. Puts the deed in the safe.

"Well, Clyde figured he'd get the deed back, once he got the money. But your dad, he goes to the bank on Monday morning and gets himself a loan. He puts that six thousand dollars back in the safe and he keeps the deed. When Clyde came back for it, your dad gives him the money and makes him sell him the farm."

"For six thousand dollars?"

"No. He paid a lot more for it. But the rest was all done with paper. Your dad's still paying it off. He put up the house as collateral."

"This house?"

"No. The one in town. The one you live in."

"You mean there's a mortgage on our house?"

"A big one. You didn't know that?"

"He got that house from my granddad. My dad grew up in that house."

"I know," Will said. "It was free and clear when he got it. But it's not now. Not by a long shot. See, overnight, your dad decided to become a farmer. Probably never would have done it, if that deed hadn't been sitting there in the safe. But that doesn't keep him from thinking he knows everything and telling us all what to do. The man doesn't know squat about farming, Bobby, but that never stopped ole Garrett. Oh no."

Will reached for a worn dishtowel on the grass. "Son, you're not like him. I mean that as a compliment. You turned out all right." He started to wipe his dirty hands. "It's none of my business, but if you ever want to be anything separate from him, you've got to get out of here. Go to that school. Even though you'd be a good farmer. A darn good one. You've got an eye for it, and a feel that your dad'll never have."

Will smiled, then it disappeared. "I just don't know what he's gonna do about getting somebody else. He's been through so many, everybody knows what he's like. People always ask me how I stand it. Heck, my wife asks me that every day. But maybe one of your brothers will want to be a farmer. Or one of your sisters will marry somebody who wants to do it. Until then, I guess he'll find somebody, somewhere. I just hope that whoever he gets knows more than he does."

Will threw the towel down again as Bobby asked, "When are you going?"

"Not until the planting's done. Your father and I worked something out that pays me. It's not much, but it'll be enough."

Will put out his hand, and Bobby took it. They shook much longer than they had to. "Watch yourself Bobby. That man's capable of anything."

19.

Bobby got up so early the next morning it was black outside. The only dim light came from the single bulb in the flat glass fixture that hugged the ceiling of the attic hallway. His father demanded that it be kept on all night, so he could check on them.

Little Tommy rustled as Bobby reached for his books and headed downstairs in his bare feet, taking care to lift himself by shifting his body weight to the dark banister whenever he neared one of the many steps that creaked. All the boys knew, as Garrett J. had when he had told Bobby, precisely which wooden treads woke the man sleeping with their mother in the master bedroom at the front of the house.

At the bottom, when he reached the dining room, Bobby turned to see whether gold light spilled from under the bathroom door to his left, across from his parents' room. Often his father woke in the middle of the night and Bobby heard him flushing the toilet downstairs after he had done one of his circuits. Bobby always wondered why the pounding never seemed to wake anybody else.

Every night before he went to bed, his father beat every outside door in the house. Starting in the basement, then traveling to the back door and finally the front door that opened to the overhung porch and the cement steps leading to the patchy grass that faced the main street, Garrett slammed each thick panel shut, vibrating the door frame, then tripped the dead bolt, then slapped the locked wood hard with his right hand. He did it again a second time and then once more for good measure, three times at each, with each set of movements faster than the last.

Slam ... turn ... SLAP! with his left palm as he gripped the door knob.

Slam, turn, SLAP!

SlamturnSLAP! This last one was executed in a single motion.

Sometimes he did it a fourth time, in the middle of the night, jerking Bobby awake and upright no matter how many times he heard it. He would sit blinking in the dark, then wait once he was lucid for long minutes before the toilet flushed with its high whirring sound and final hiccup, which was followed by the door to his parents' room being shoved closed against the tight door-frame. Bobby never put his head down again until his father was secured behind it.

Tonight, though, his father was in bed. All was dark and safe and quiet.

Bobby switched on the overhead carriage lamp that hung from the center of the kitchen and slid his books onto the table with two benches built into the wall, making an alcove next to the window where he had seen his father raging. Before he began, Bobby pushed aside the ruffled curtain and opened the closed and locked window, breathing deeply the moist, cool air that poured like water into the warm house.

Bobby listened, his books unopened on his mother's pink oil-cloth. The chorus of night bugs had stayed at the farm, along with the moaning owl and the wind that swept whistling up the steep hillside from the fields and through the clotheslines, flapping the sheets like truce flags in the moonlight. All he heard, despite all his trying, were the close-in, crouched sounds of town. A lone truck passed, bouncing hard over the tracks on the other side of Debbie's room. Bobby caught the bang of metal in the truck bed and the squeal of tires that needed inflating as the heavy chassis came down.

He began to study, and as he did a long train passed, moving quietly. At night, they were often a hundred cars long, filled with coal and corn and soybeans. Bobby hummed with the low rumble of the train as it rocked. Hundreds of small wheels pulsed the air with the rhythm of their love affair with the long steel ribbon.

The sky had begun to lighten by the time his mother came in fully dressed and asked him smiling if he wanted any breakfast.

"How long have you been up?" She tied on her apron with ruffles at the bottom.

"A long time," he said.

A few minutes later, his father strutted in humming, then crossed over to the stove to hug his wife. Garrett nuzzled her neck, which made her giggle. "Garrett!" Cora said. "Bobby's here."

Garrett didn't lose his smile. "I don't care. Don't you look fine today? Is that dress new?"

"You silly. You know I made it last year."

He turned to Bobby. "What are you working on?"

"English."

"When's the test?"

"Who said there was a test?" Bobby asked him nervously.

Garrett swung around to Cora, "See that? I was just making conversation."

Bobby shot a look at his mother, whose eyes were playing ping-pong from one man to the other. "This Friday," Bobby answered him.

"See?" Garrett was mollified. "I knew that. I pay attention."

His father sat at the head of the table, scraping the low wooden chair along the linoleum. "Close that window. You're letting the flies in." And then, like it was a new thought. "Hey, I've got an idea. This is Sunday. You ought to take the day off."

"I should?"

"And you know what? I was thinking. We don't get to spend any time together, you and me. You know, without having to work. We don't have any fun."

Bobby stared. Across the kitchen, Cora turned toward them from her post at the skillet. Below her look of utter astonishment, bacon frizzled, popping grease.

"So what do you say?" Garrett said, not taking his narrowed eyes off Bobby, who smelled the cloying fat. "Let's take the day off and take a ride."

"To where?"

His mother had opened her mouth but no words came out. Over Garrett's shoulder, Bobby saw her trying to think of something to say, to keep him there, so he could study, but she couldn't.

"Come on," Garrett prodded, his eyes not moving. "It'll be fun."

Bobby leaned sideways to ask her, "Mom. You want to come?"

"No!" Garrett snapped, then calmed himself. "There's no reason for her to go. This is just you and me. All boys."

Behind Garrett, Cora put both her palms up as she shrugged.

"Cora, what do you say?" Garrett asked like he had eyes in the back of his head.

She made big eyes at her son. "You won't be gone long? He has to study."

Garrett smiled his small teeth smile. "I'll bring him home as soon as I'm done with him."

After breakfast, Garrett told him to get in the truck. They barreled around the courthouse square, then sped on, blasting past the bank and the rich banker's old mansion next to it. The tall Victorian house was the county library now, its shiny oil portrait of the rich man now hanging in his great-grandson's bank-president office next door.

Outside town, the flat land became furrowed with shallow slopes, then turned into broad tabletops between wider and wider valleys where streams ran. Bobby couldn't see the rivulets, snaking deep, but he could follow the lush green of the trees that needed the extra water.

The tabletops fell away as the level spots became fewer. Eventually even the smallest fields disappeared. His father gunned it up and down the hillsides as they lurched on the topographic rollercoaster, with Bobby's stomach hitching as Garrett took the peaks.

Bobby couldn't smell anything but the musty inside of the pickup. His father had the windows rolled tightly and the air conditioner on. Bobby was frigid, but he didn't touch the lever.

Neither of them spoke, and neither turned on the radio.

After forty-five minutes, Garrett slowed to turn right, and they started bumping over the gullies in a dirt road. It was overgrown, with weeds even in the smooth parts where the tires ran. Trees hung over them with grasping branches that scraped the roof.

Bobby cocked his head to see out the windshield. "Where are we?"

"The next county. There's something I want you to see."

Garrett pulled up at an intersection. To their left, another dirt track climbed a steep hill. His father pointed, and Bobby saw the old graveyard at the top of it. Across the rutted dirt road sat a small white church that stood out against the gathering grey clouds.

Garrett turned and drove up, his tires skipping over the deep dry gouges. When he reached the top, he pulled over by the sign with the name on it: Rose Hill Presbyterian.

He climbed down and started walking, motioning without turning for Bobby to follow him as he marched ahead, past the rows and rows of old markers and crying angels with their heads bent. He trudged back to the last row edging the graveyard, far from the church. Bobby scuttled behind him as Garrett turned on his heel, making a sharp right turn, and strode to the last grave in the farthest back corner. From where he was on the church-side of it, Bobby couldn't see any writing.

His father stopped and waited, lifting his shoulders and holding his elbows as he stared at the stone. Bobby came up and Garrett pointed. Allen Newman and Elizabeth Sutton McAllister. Bobby's great-grandfather had died in 1918.

"You've never been here before, have you?" Garrett asked.

"No."

"I don't think I've been here in fifty years."

They stood facing it and past it toward the far-away church. The big stone marker had its back to God, its writing facing the wild, unkempt forest at their backs. Bobby felt the trees hovering close, bending low. The lawn around the stones had been mowed out a few feet but not an inch beyond his family's toes.

"I was right there when they buried him," Garrett said. "Over by those doors, watching them try to get that horse cart up that hill in the mud. You know that's what they used to have, funeral carriages. They used to put the coffins on those big carts. But the horses couldn't do it. The mud was too deep. So my dad and some of the other men took the coffin out and carried it by hand. They hauled it up the hill there, themselves. They were up to their knees in mud."

"How old were you?" Bobby asked.

"Six. It was a long time ago."

Bobby listened for birds while his father stared at the marker. When Bobby didn't hear them, he looked up. Across the sky, high platoons of them were hurtling like bullets. He turned to smell into where they had come.

"Son, there's something I want to say." His father looked up at him. "I want you to stay. This is your home. You don't need to go all the way to Nashville. This is where your life is. Us. We're the ones who are gonna take care of you. Not some stranger, somebody you don't know.

"I want you to stay, son. I want you to stay and work with me on the farm." Garrett paused, scanning Bobby's face, then smiled sheepishly. "Listen, I know what I am. I'm not easy. Some people call me a pain in the ass. But I can help you, Bobby. Help you become somebody. Somebody you're not ever gonna be away from here. And I can give you a life. As a farmer. You don't need to be a mechanic. Hell, I pay those guys to work for me.

"Why go to school to be something you already are? You can already fix every vehicle we have. I know that. You've been doing that since you were ten years old.

"And you're right about college. You sure can't do that. But what I'm trying to tell you is that you don't need to go to school anymore. You can make a living right now, on my farm. Working for me. With me. We can do it together."

On the spot where Garrett looked at him, boring into him, Bobby's face felt hot. It burned and his fair cheeks tingled.

"You know, you're gonna go to that school for two years. Two years of not making any money, and spending money you don't have, to learn something you already know. And then you're gonna come out and have to look for a job. You'll be what? Twenty? And you'll get your first full-time job, working in some shop somewhere. For somebody else. And what are you gonna make? It'll be okay, I suppose, but you're gonna have to pay for everything—your car, your house, everything. Out of that pay, whatever it is, and it's not gonna be much. You're not ever gonna build up anything or buy a house on what you get. Not for years. Nothing's gonna belong to you. You'll just be a guy with a toolbox trying to keep a job.

"And what are you gonna do when your boss wants you to read something? Or you have to fill out order forms? What are you gonna tell him, when you've got a wife and kids to support? That you can't read?"

Bobby looked down at his feet.

"Son, this is your home. Your mother and I look out for you. Who's gonna do that in Nashville, or wherever it is? We can take care of you and make sure you're all right.

"And I'll give you a good deal. I will. Fifty-fifty. That's what I'm willing to do. Fifty percent of the crop, and fifty percent of the cost. Even though you don't know shit about farming and you're only eighteen. Hell, I'll even throw in the house for free."

Garrett waited, but Bobby didn't answer. Instead, Bobby lifted his boot and jabbed the hard round toe into the grass. He began digging, kicking his foot in little cuts that gouged deeper and deeper into the earth.

Garrett kept on. "Someday maybe I'll give you more. Sixty-forty. But right now, you know and I know that you don't deserve it. If I gave you any more, it'd be a gift, and that's not what you want. You want to earn it."

His father waited. Bobby stopped digging because he had cut a worm in half with his boot toe. A piece of it wriggled and flipped without its head, twisting in the bright glare from the knitting clouds above them.

"Think about it, son. How many boys like you have their own house? And a job, right out of high school, that pays them fifty percent?"

The wriggling continued, slower now.

Garrett asked him, "So what do you think? Huh?"

"I've already paid half the tuition."

"That's no big deal. You'll earn that back the first year."

Bobby watched the worm finish dying.

"Shit," Garrett said. "You've been talking to Will."

Bobby didn't deny it.

"Crap."

Bobby was digging again, moving more earth with his toe. Only this time, he was trying to cover the body.

"I tell you what," Garrett said. "I'll do even better. I'll give you a deal I'd never give anybody else, because you're my son. If you stay five years and work for me, I'll change the title on some of my land. Let's say two hundred acres. I'll change the title so we own it together, you and me. Jointly."

Bobby looked up. "You will?"

"If you stay five years, I'll do it. I promise."

Bobby tamped down dirt on top of it. "I still don't know. I made plans, Dad."

"Think. You spend the next two years in Nashville, you've got nothing. You spend that time with me, and you've got money rat-holed. Plus two years from now, you'll only have three years to go before you can walk away and tell me to go to hell and still have that land."

"You'd still let me have it? Even if I left?"

"I give you my word. And in the meantime, you'd have that house to yourself, starting just as soon as they move out. I know you like that girlfriend of yours." He winked. "Even though her father's not worth much."

"Dad—"

"Aw, relax." His father tried to smile. The teeth were there, small and even like two rows of white corn, but the eyes didn't luster.

Bobby tried to sound like an adult. "I appreciate it, Dad, but I've got to think about it. This changes everything. My whole future."

"Well don't think too long. I want an answer. If you don't tell me by the end of the week, I'm gonna have to get somebody else. I need to have help for this fall, and I need to get somebody signed up."

"Yessir."

They headed back to the car leaving old death on the hill. As they walked, Bobby listened to the silent forest.

As Garrett pulled away, he said, "I don't want you telling your mother about this. There's no need to make her think you're gonna stay if you're not, even though that's what she wants more than anything. But you know that. And I don't want you talking to that girlfriend of yours. This is family business."

Garrett finally looked at the sky as they reached the paved road ten minutes later. "They say we're gonna have weather tonight. But I don't see it."

20.

"Bobby! Bobby wake up!"

Garrett's shout charged up the stairs. "Get down here! Now!"

Bobby's head jerked up. His eyes snapped open. It was pitch black dark and he couldn't see.

"And get your brothers! Move it!"

The hall light was off. It was never off. It had been glaring bright when he had gone to bed early, his brother John still up studying.

Bobby struggled out of his sleep and sat up. He turned his head to find John and Tommy. That was when he heard the noise, huge and deafening. A blasting roar. It rolled around him, tumbling on without breathing, deep as sound could go and still be heard. On top of it, drums were falling, banging down a staircase, and above it all, he could hear a thousand voices screaming, swirling above the house. It was the shriek of women, screaming for their children.

In the dark, Bobby shot a glance at the window. The sheet of rain that had been streaming down it was gone. The lightning flashed, but the rain had stopped.

There was nothing but this sound, and what the wind was doing to the house.

He swam out of bed and onto his feet. Bobby yelled, "Tommy! You okay?"

"I'm okay!" the little boy yelled back. Bobby could barely see him. Tommy was hopping, trying to pull on his slippers.

"Where's the light?" Bobby called out.

"The power's out!" John yelled from the hallway.

"Boys!" Garrett shouted. "Get down here! Now! Cora, have you got her?"

"Yes! We're coming!" Cora yelled.

The windows clattered and banged. The shutters slammed against the side of the house. On the edge of the roof, the tin gutters screeched and screeched, fighting to hold on. Dogs barked in the neighbor's yard.

Bobby found Tommy with his hands and pushed him forward. They felt their way down the stairs, counting the steps.

"Move!" Garrett yelled when they got to the bottom. He used a flashlight to point the way.

"We're going down!" Cora shouted from the kitchen. They moved toward her, following the beam.

"Mom!"

"I'm down here, John! Just follow us."

They all clamored down the wooden stairs. Garrett waited as he shooed them past, then stepped down and latched the door behind them. "Southwest corner! It's coming from there!"

They pounded down the stairs. The flashlight beam bounced on their backs, their hair, and then the concrete walls. At the bottom, they ran to the near corner, under the living room. Their mother was already there, with Debbie. She threw an arm around little Tommy.

They clustered together. With her free hand, Cora searched in the dark for each of them and touched them, patting and squeezing. The planks in the floor above them popped and creaked.

"Turn around!" Garrett warned. "Toward the wall!"

The portable radio was on, sitting on the washer in the dark, turned all the way up. A man's voice, high and tinny, was coming in and out, between the crashes of lightning and the waves of static that came though the box.

The roar got louder, like a train barreling toward them.

"Get down!" Garrett shouted.

Cora put her knees on the hard floor and brought Tommy in front of her, holding him tight, facing the "v" of the walls. The rest of them crammed up behind her, kneeling, with their arms around each other. Garrett stayed on the outside. He threw the flashlight on the floor and knelt down and spread his arms over his family.

"We've got reports … Mt. Olive," the radio chopped up.

Over their heads, the screaming came closer. Angry fists pounded and the basement window between them and the stairs rattled and shook. The storm door upstairs was thrown open, and it banged, banged, banged against the side of the house.

"My God," Bobby said. His chin was on Debbie's neck. He could feel his father's chest pounding against his back.

"Get your heads down!" Garrett yelled in his ear.

"Blessed art thou among women," Bobby heard his mother say.

The roar came toward them. It was outside, on the other side of the wooden boards. And then it was on them, covering them, and over them, deafening and thunderous, trying to get in. The rumble shook their feet with both hands.

They held their breaths and prayed to God.

They held onto each other.

And then, after what seemed like a year, they heard it move to the other side. The sound of screaming voices walked across the house, then out to the yard, then roared over the railroad tracks. The swirling, killing wind rolled away, tumbling and shrieking over the next house, and the next family.

The rumbling kept on, but they had been spared.

Long seconds later, the rain came back in a rush and hosed down the basement windows.

"This is WQMR, AM 930," the voice said under the crackling static. "We've got one right here. Ellen Decker just called. She's had one overhead. Never touched down, but it's gonna. You people in Ava, get yourselves under cover right now, if you're not already."

Garrett got to his feet. "We okay?" He bent over and picked up the flashlight, then swept it over them. They all straightened up, then stood up, moving a little away from each other so they could breathe.

"We're okay," Cora said, turning around.

"Dad," Bobby said, "Mrs. Decker's up on Carpenter. I used to do her lawn."

"Then she's right here," Cora said. "Right over there, on the other side."

Debbie said, "It was here. It was right here."

"But it never came down," John said.

"Stupid woman, calling in," Garrett told them. "Using a phone right now."

The radio repeated it. "Again, we've got a funnel cloud. Heading northeast out of Allensboro."

"Turn it off. I need to listen," Garrett said.

"Dad, it's gone," John told him. "It's raining again."

"I said turn it off!"

Bobby stepped over and snapped off the sound.

"Rain doesn't mean a thing," Garrett told them. "There could be another one coming. We've got to listen for it."

They stood in the darkness and heard only the rain. Through the basement windows they saw flashes of light and trees thrashing in the yard. But the rumbling sound was gone. It was nothing but a thunderstorm.

They watched and waited, all of them staring at the circle of yellow light at Garrett's feet.

Suddenly there was a crash in the far corner, then a tumble of clanging as metal hit the floor.

Garrett's head jerked back. "Jesus Christ! What was that?"

"I'm sorry, Dad. I'm sorry." It was Tommy, over next to the sound. "I knocked over your golf bag." They could still hear it chiming. "I'll pick it up."

"Don't you touch those clubs!" Garrett swung the beam into Tommy's face. "Leave them alone! You hear me?"

"Why?" the boy asked, confused.

"You want a lightning rod in your hand?"

"Garrett, honey," Cora said. "You don't really think lightning's going to come down here in this basement and run down a golf club."

"How do you know?"

"It's okay, Dad. I won't," Tommy said. "I just wanted to see what it looks like, out these windows."

"It's just rain now," Cora said. "Come back over here. Now why don't we all go upstairs and go to bed?"

"But how do we know it's safe?" Debbie asked. "It's still blowing."

"Because nothing heavy came down," their mother said. "We probably lost a couple of shutters, and the mailbox, I'm sure. But other than that, I think we're fine. Aren't we, Garrett?"

There was no answer. He had the yellow light pointed down at the floor again.

"Garrett?" Cora said.

The children turned toward him. The basement was all silence and yellow light.

"Dad?" Debbie said.

"Shh."

They all listened.

"You hear that?" Garrett said.

"What?" Cora asked him.

Garrett moved the light up over his head and stopped it on the floorboards above him. They could see his straining face in the glow. "You hear it now?"

A police siren had begun, loud and high over the top of the raining.

John said, "It's just a siren, Dad."

"Not that." Garrett shook his head. "That."

Then they could all hear it, a low rumble, steady, somewhere in the middle register. They heard just one at first, and then two, the same. Getting slowly louder and coming toward them.

Lightning flashed again, then thunder boomed. There was no time between the crash and the light, no time to count the miles in between.

They listened to the rumble. "It's airplanes, Dad," Bobby said. "Two of them."

"Get out!" Garrett yelled. "Now!"

"What's wrong?" It was Cora.

"Get outside! All of you! Right now!"

"In this?" she said. "Why? What is it?"

A police siren was coming close.

Garrett pushed over boxes as he moved toward the stairs. They tumbled. "Fast!"

"Dad!" John shouted, next to Bobby. "What're you doing?"

Garrett had found John. He was shoving him, shoving him toward the stairs and into Bobby. He was pushing them both. The flashlight bounced over everything.

Cora called out to him. "Garrett! What's wrong with you?"

"I want you all outside!"

In the jerking yellow beam, Bobby saw Garrett's face as it twisted. His father was scared, and Bobby had never seen it.

"Garrett!" Cora said. "What's happening?"

Bobby could tell that she was moving, coming over to them. He could still feel his father's pushing hand and he could still hear the two planes, droning, directly overhead.

"Garrett stop!" shouted Cora.

He did stop. He turned around with his eyes dancing over every surface, scanning. Afraid.

"Over here, Garrett. I'm right here. Look at me."

Tommy said, "Mom? I'm scared."

"Honey, it's airplanes," Cora told her husband. "It's just airplanes. Regular airplanes. Nothing more." She was behind Garrett's back now, looking over his shoulder to Bobby and John. "Flying toward the air force base after the storm. That's all."

Her voice was honey. She had changed it to soothe. "And the siren's gone. Listen. It's gone. You've heard it before. It was just a police car."

Garrett had his back to her. He couldn't see her face. He was still staring at Bobby and John.

She touched him from behind. She put her hand on his shoulder and began to stroke him, moving up and down his back. Stroking and lifting, stroking and lifting her hand. "We're all here," she said. "Right here. You're home. With us. We're all here."

Stroking and lifting. "And it's just a storm, and those are just planes. The same planes we hear all the time. We just never heard them in a storm before."

She started to nod at Bobby. She kept doing it, making a show. In front of her Garrett looked up. "See?" she said. "They're right here. John and Bobby. Your boys. We're home. You're not there. Look. Debbie's over there. And Tommy. Little Tommy. You see him? You're at home. Tell him, Bobby. I want you to tell him." She kept nodding as she spoke the words.

Bobby started to do the same. They nodded in unison. "That's right," Bobby said. "It's gone now. Everything's all right."

Facing them, Garrett closed his eyes. Bobby looked beyond him, to his mother behind.

His father dropped his arms and let them go.

"Bobby. John," she said. "I want you to take your sister and Tommy and go upstairs now. Bobby, I want you to get the other flashlight out of the drawer and bring it down. Then I want you to get everybody back in bed. You're the oldest. It's all over."

Bobby opened his mouth but she shook her head. "We'll be all right. And take the flashlight when you go up. We'll be fine. We'll be fine in the dark."

Bobby took the rest of them up without a word. In the kitchen they waited for him as he got the spare flashlight. He was about to go down the stairs again when he heard his father's voice from the dark basement.

"I'm all right," he was saying quietly to her.

"I know you are. You're fine," she said.

"It's just the goddamn planes. And all that thunder."

"I know. I know."

She raised her voice. "Bobby. We don't need that flashlight now. We're coming up. Just wait for us. Then we can all go to bed now and get back to sleep."

21.

All the next week, the sky shined a robin's egg blue. The storm had come through and scooped up all the clouds. It would be another week before the first puff appeared.

During that week, Bobby spent all his free time studying. His mother got his father to leave him alone. Every day, though, Garrett asked him what he was going to do, to which Bobby answered that he didn't know. Garrett said he needed to know by Sunday night at the latest. On Monday morning, he said, he was going to get someone else.

Bobby took his English final that Friday, on the last day of class. When he got home, Cora asked him how he had done and again he said he didn't know. He couldn't tell, with all the questions.

"Well," she said, "we'll just have to wait."

The next night, on Saturday, Bobby was going to take Sarah to a movie in another town. There were no theatres in Allensboro. Garrett said it would be all right, so long as Bobby didn't leave until after dark.

Sarah asked if she could spend part of the daylight hours with him too. She said she liked to be with him. Bobby then asked his father if she could come out to the farm. Garrett said she could, but only after six that night. He didn't want Bobby distracted until after they had finished the eighty acres by the far culvert, he said.

At six, though, Bobby was still out, working. He stood next to Will's pickup, waiting for his father to come around again on the tractor, so he could fill the bins with soybeans one last time.

He saw her car as she came down the long hill, a speck of blue trailing a cloud of yellow dust that tumbled and swirled as it rose high in the air above her. When she turned, it turned with her and followed her into the farmyard. He watched her car disappear behind the house and then he saw her, a minute later, walking in her short skirt toward the little ridge that ran parallel to the back door. She stopped in the sun and stood there shielding her eyes with both hands. She turned her head, looking for him, squinting out over his father's land.

Bobby stepped away from the pickup and took off his green John Deere hat, then waved it in huge arcs and yelled until finally she saw him. When she did, she waved back with both hands and started bouncing on her toes.

When Garrett stopped again on the tractor, Bobby told him she had come. His father looked up and asked what the hell she was doing here in the middle of the day. Bobby had to tell him it was six, like he'd required. His father denied having said it at first, but then relented. The beans they were pouring now were all he needed to finish the field. But Bobby would have to walk back up to the farm, Garrett told him. Garrett was going to leave the planter where it was, when he was done, and so he was going to be the one to take up the truck.

So Bobby began to walk, first along the edge of the field his father was planting, then over the short ditch to the next one, and the next, taking the thin dirt track that ran along each of them, whip-stitching the borders of the huge squares. When he finally reached the deep ditch and the cement bridge, he saw her again, standing next to the house. She was shaded under the narrow eaves in a yellow blouse, looking out over the green.

He stopped. He looked up at her, and he saw the house beyond her at the top of the hill. It wasn't anything. It was small and red, with an old covered porch on the road side, under a canopy of catalpa trees. The leafy trees fluttered in the breeze. He saw the silver gas tank on legs outside the bedroom window, glinting, and he saw the picnic table on the cement slab by the back door, a few steps from the Y-bent clothes poles with their drooping ropes that were empty now.

She finally saw him standing there, and she waved. She was all alone. Just Sarah and the redbrick and the white trim and the box hedge by the front steps, square like the house and Kelly green in the sun. And he saw the tall grass Will would never cut again against her legs, and her black hair blowing and the hand above her eyes, so she could see him.

The land came up to meet her, flowing over the hill and up to the house. He made a big gesture with his arm and pointed toward the bins in back. She turned her head and looked around, then nodded big so he could see it. She stepped back and disappeared as he kept walking. His father and his tractor buzzed behind him in his ear.

When he got to the top, he saw her standing next to Will, beside the auger. The huge corkscrew was turning, drawing the corn out of the bottom of the bin and up inside until it came out the top, spraying corn like a sprinkler into the wagon.

He walked up to her and he kissed her. Will smiled. Bobby put his arm around her and held it there. All around them, little brown corn hulls floated in the air.

Will said he needed something. He walked away, over to the back door and inside the house. All the while, the auger kept turning. It was loud and overworked and the belt was old.

A minute later, Will put his head out the door again. "Bobby! Your mother's on the phone."

Bobby yelled back at him, "Can you tell her I'll call her back?"

Will disappeared inside. He poked his head out again. "I told her you were out here with Sarah. She said you don't have to call her back. She just wanted to say that some teacher called from the high school. She said everything's all right. It's all set for graduation."

Bobby started to smile. "Thanks."

"What was that all about?" Sarah asked him.

"Oh. Nothing." His smile got wider.

"What?" She smiled back, watching him.

"I'll tell you later. It's nothing, really. I'm sure glad you got out here."

She lifted her eyes to the sky. Soft and soundless, it was snowing. Tiny curved lenses floated down. Shiny little boats of brown corn hulls bobbed in the current, rocking softly back and forth in the wind. Lighter than air, they rose up and fell again.

Bobby looked over at Sarah. They were all over her. She had been standing in them longer than he had. They were in her hair and covered her shoulders. Even more of them hung like a whisper next to her, about to light.

"What is this?" Sarah said. She held one of them in her palm. It was small as a beetle shell in the fold of it, shining golden in the sunlight. "I've never seen this before."

"It's corn hulls. Chaff, from around the kernel. You always get some when you shell corn. It comes off when the corn comes out of the auger. The corn goes into the wagon and the wind takes the hulls."

She looked up again. They danced in front of her. "Do you have a name for it?"

Bobby smiled. "We call it bee's wings."

"Bee's wings," she said. "What a beautiful name."

SARAH
Winter
1986

Fifteen Years Later

1.

"Boys, hurry up!" Sarah cried out. "You're gonna be late! The bus is coming."

Her seven year-old was down on his knees digging in his closet with wind-milling arms. High in the air, his backside made a "z" with the side of his legs, but the little boy was leaning so far in she couldn't see his head. "Kevin! What are you doing?"

A white ball of gym socks flew out of his hands to thump the wall behind him, then dropped to the growing pile of debris on the twin bed pushed up lengthwise along the wall in the tiny room. Paneled in wood from floor-to-ceiling, it looked like a knotty pine shoebox.

"Why aren't you dressed yet? You've got to go."

"I'm looking for my shirt!"

"I put it right there, on top of your bed."

"I don't want that one. I want my jersey."

"Mom!" a second boy called out.

"What?" she yelled through the wall. "Daniel, you need to get moving!"

"Did you sign my permission slip?"

"I found it!" Kevin waved a bright red shirt with a white number sixteen.

"You can't wear that!" she told him. "It's twenty degrees outside."

"I'll wear my flannel shirt over it."

"And where are you gonna find that?" She had her arms crossed as she stood between the kitchen sink and the dinette table, talking to Kevin over top of it and through his bedroom door. She could have pelted him with a melon ball, if she had had one, the distance was so short.

Daniel sped into the kitchen, swinging his eyes around. "I don't see it. Where?"

"There," she pointed. "On top of the microwave."

The miniscule rectangular farmhouse had been planted lengthwise to follow the ridge of the hill. The front room filled the first third with two windows at one end flanking a heavy door facing the gravel road. The kitchen filled most of the third in back. In between, two small bedrooms faced each other across a two-foot-wide linoleum corridor. Kevin's room was the third one, even smaller, sharing a hollow wall with Daniel's and opening directly into the kitchen.

The only bathroom was down the stairs that descended from the landing inside the back door. There were seven steps down and three steps up to the kitchen from the small flat square of carpeted floor.

Sarah felt a tug at her waist.

"Mom, will you help me?"

Kevin grinned up. He was small for his age and freckled, with startling turquoise eyes like his mother's. When he smiled big, as he was doing, his cheeks disappeared into skin pleats that rippled to big flaps of ears that stuck out like radar. He could wiggle them.

She took the jersey, then knelt to one knee to stretch the fabric over his head. She held out the flannel shirt, which was long-sleeved and bone white with a black plaid and thin red stripes running like blood through the weaving. As she buttoned it, she heard a key slip into the back door. "Daniel!" she said to her elder son. "I want you to go down and get your jacket."

The door opened. Sarah felt the blast of cold air but she didn't look up. "Kevin, do you have your lunch? Go get it."

"Where's Bobby?" Garrett called as he stomped his wet boots on the landing, pounding mud into her carpet. He hadn't closed the door.

She laid her hands on her two boys and turned them toward the same back door. "I don't know."

Two loud toots sounded outside. She hurriedly pushed them toward the landing where Garrett was, but he blocked them, getting his body in the way. "Sister," he said. "I'm talking here. I asked you a question."

"And I said I don't know. He didn't say. All he said was he had to go look at some pipe. Daniel, go!" The boy squeezed around Garrett and went down to the basement.

"Excuse me." She walked by him out the open back door, trailed a moment later by her clamoring puppies. "Daniel! Give him his jacket! He's going to catch his death."

She trudged behind them into the icy wind, pulling her acrylic cardigan around her as a blast gusted to slam the door on Garrett. She hugged herself and watched her boys charge across the brown yard. Daniel got to the bus first and stopped, then threw his arms out to block his brother.

"Sister!" he cried as he barricaded the doorway. "I'm talking here!"

Kevin plowed into him at full force. He couldn't stop himself, and the two of them banged hard against the side of the bus.

"Are you all right?" Sarah called, but they couldn't hear her. They had already climbed inside and were wrestling each other down the center aisle.

She danced in the frost, little shards of grass popping beneath her. She clenched her jaw to stop the clattering as she watched the bus pull away and get smaller as it hauled itself coughing up the long hill. At the top of it, all that was left was a tiny square of screaming yellow. It winked, then gave her back her world of solid brown.

As it disappeared, Sarah kissed her fingers and held up her hand.

When she got to the back door again, it flew open in her face as Garrett stormed out with his jacket flaps flying. She had to jump so he wouldn't knock her down.

"I can't believe you don't know where your husband is," he yelled over his shoulder. "As far as you're concerned, he might as well be dead in a ditch."

"Excuse me?"

"When he gets home I want you to tell him to stay where he is. Make sure he doesn't go anywhere."

"But I can't. I'm going into work," she yelled to his back.

"Then write him a note! Tell him to wait here and not move. I can let myself back in. I've got my key."

2.

She was alone as she drove, fidgeting. She kept the radio on and turned up the heater so it breathed on her feet with a gurgling wheeze. The smell of it was cooked rubber.

In the grey light at the bottom of the hill, she turned left onto the two-lane county road that ran straight like a knife's edge fifteen boring, empty miles south from the farm to the town square and the courthouse. Five minutes on her way, Sarah passed the package store, turning her head just long enough to skim the parking lot and the lip of concrete that skirted the building. Inside, the store looked dark but the glowing red neon promised "OPEN."

"We Are the World" chanted on the FM station as she passed the only cement plant within a hundred miles. Three old crusted barrel trucks waited silently next to each other at the foot of a tall, single smokestack that still slept in this early morning. Sarah listened, but she didn't sing along. The rhythm she beat on the steering wheel was her own, out of time with the loud chorus. She didn't even know she was tapping.

Once, she had to slam her brakes, pitching herself forward as she flung her arm out to keep her purse and her romance novel from flying off the passenger seat. A huge combine had been turning onto the paved road, but she hadn't seen it. The boxy machine was fifteen feet high and bright red, and it had been inching its way off a dirt track between two vast empty fields.

It wasn't Bobby at the wheel. The man was bareheaded. He honked hello as she passed, but she didn't glance up.

At the end of ten miles, she took a deep breath finally as she rose over the last hillock and saw the beaded string of little houses that marked the beginning of town. They were tiny places, just wooden cartons. Chain-link fences circled most of them waist-high. Inside the yards, sodden leaves banked against the wires.

Two large dogs leapt as she went by, barking sharply and jerking their ropes taut with their running to lift their whole front quarters off the ground. They scared her every time, as if she had never seen them.

She slowed to rumble over the railroad tracks, then glanced left. Garrett's pickup was gone. He was never home this time of the early morning. Cora was, though. Her brand-new silver four-door Chrysler LeBaron, which Garrett had bought her to celebrate her last birthday, glinted by the side door.

A block farther on, Sarah arrived at the square and continued straight along the western edge of it, past the courthouse on her left. The old, two-floor storefronts ringing the block had all been thriving when she was in high school. The county's population had spent its money in the shops under the overhang that jutted from the second stories all around the square and shielded the sidewalk below them even in the worst weather. But the stores were nearly all vacant now, along with their chipping front curbs. Behind the panes of plate glass that threw Sarah back at herself, cracked brown butcher paper hung long and curled, blocking her view of the emptiness inside.

3.

"Hey, Sarah."

"Hi Peggy."

"So did you tell Bobby yet?" The nurse leaned in holding a stack of thick files against her bosom. She had propped her elbow on the metal ledge and the forced curve of her breast had cocked her nametag.

Sarah sat below her, on the other side of the wall, looking up from her desk in the cramped room under the small sliding window that had been punched in the wall of the tiled hallway. "X-Ray Department" read the sign above Peggy's head.

"Not yet," Sarah said quietly. "I'm going to tell him on Kevin's birthday next week."

"Oh, he's gonna be so thrilled. I mean Hawaii. That's so romantic. I don't think I'll ever get there in my whole life."

Sarah nodded but she didn't smile back.

"You don't look very excited."

"I'm just thinking about next week. You know, that appointment."

"There's nothing to worry about. He's just a boy, that's all. Sometimes it takes them longer than it does the girls. He's fine."

4.

Sarah sat at home after dinner that same night with Kevin and Daniel, helping them with their homework at the dinette table. Kevin nestled next to her as close as he could squeeze his chair, while Daniel had spread out to occupy the other side, facing Kevin's door. He had taken Bobby's seat.

"Now I'm going to read these words," she said to Kevin. "Just like we always do, and you're going to write them down for me."

Daniel had his nose in his math book.

"'Still,'" she read from a piece of paper. Kevin stuck out his tongue and bent to write, smashing his thick pencil lead into the dotted lines of his tablet.

"No, honey," she said as she watched him. "Remember what's in the middle there. It's a short vowel. What is it?"

Kevin looked at her, his thick brown hair curling a question mark on his forehead. "I don't know."

"Sure you do. Say it for me."

"Stuh … stuh."

"No. Stih … stih. Like stick. Can you hear that?"

"e?"

"No. If it was an 'e,' it'd be steh … steh. It's stih … stih. Short i."

Kevin put his head down.

"The words don't change," she said as she watched him writing. "They're the same ones we had yesterday and the day before."

"Mom," Daniel said. "How many days in a leap year?"

"Uh, three hundred and sixty-six. Why?"

"I'm done," Kevin said.

"Good. Now let's go on to the next one. Listen to the sound, all right? 'Sh-ell.'"

"So when's the next one?" Daniel asked.

"What?"

"The next leap year."

"1988, I think. Why? What are you doing?"

"Calendars. So what happens if you're born on February twenty-ninth? Do you get a birthday when it's not a leap year?"

"Mom."

"I don't know."

"Mom!"

"What? Kevin, I'm right here." The boy was in her face, leaning close.

"What did Dad say? Did you talk to him?"

"About what?"

"My horse. I want a horse."

Sarah sighed. "Kevin, we've been all through this. You know we can't have a horse. We don't have any place to put him."

"There's the shed."

"How many times do we have to talk about this? It's not heated out there. A horse needs a proper home, just like people."

"But you said you'd talk to Dad."

"He'd say the same thing."

"You promised! My birthday's next week."

"Kevin, we need to do these words now. I want you to pay attention. The word was 'shell.' I want you to write it."

He didn't move. He just stared at her.

"Oh, all right," she said. "I'll talk to your dad, but he'll agree with me. Now write."

Kevin smiled. "I love you, Mom."

"I love you too, but that's not going to get you out of this. You've got a test tomorrow and you need to work. Pay attention."

5.

She couldn't sleep, so she was still up reading when she heard the back door. Bobby went downstairs to shower and change into the clean clothes she had put out for him, then quietly climbed the stairs to the kitchen. She heard the refrigerator open on the other side of the thin wall of their bedroom, then a plate chime on the counter before the clunk of the microwave door. It beeped as she reached for her robe.

He had pulled out the same chair Daniel had occupied earlier that evening as he sat with a full plate of the meatloaf she had made for dinner. The smells of Irish Spring and ground beef filled the air. His hair was wet and combed and his face was scrubbed raw along with his nails, which were bitten.

Bobby faced Kevin's closed door with a glass of milk and his green John Deere hat close to him on the oblong table. Sarah eyed the hat, which was grimy and stained with sweat and dirty fingers.

"So how'd it go?"

"Real good," Bobby said. "They're gonna let us have it. The only thing we have to do is get it out and get it up here. We'll have to get a flatbed truck, but that's no problem. We can find one of those. It's getting it out of the ground that's gonna be hard."

"Why?"

"There's gas in it still." He took a bite. "Residual gas. Left over from when they were using it. It's gas pipe. You've got to cut it up in order to move it. And to do that, you've got to use a torch."

"But how do you do that without blowing up?"

He smiled at her. "That's the whole trick. You've got to hit it with the torch until it pops through, and then you have to stand back and hope the explosion doesn't kill you."

"You're kidding."

"I don't know anybody who's actually died. At least not recently. But that's not the hard part. You've got to get it all done in one day, because if you don't, the gas will settle in the bottom again. That's when fellows really get hurt. They forget about the gas that second day and they light that torch into that hole they've already got."

"You're out of your mind! Why are you doing this?"

"It's good culvert." He was tan even in winter, with freckles that never went away. "Once I put it down, it's gonna last a hundred years. Plus it's free. It doesn't cost us anything. Texaco said all we have to do is come get it out. I've got to have better drainage down there. That old pipe isn't worth a damn."

"You're serious." The yellow stag with its antlers leapt at her from the hat next to her husband. She sat across from it and him, on the other side.

"Where else would we get the money?"

She heard Kevin's door open and twisted around. She smiled at her little boy and held out her arms. "Did we wake you?"

He blinked in the blinding light. "Daddy?"

"Yes, son?"

Half asleep, Kevin stumbled around the table to get to his father. "Did you talk to Mom? Can I have it?"

Bobby glanced at her as Sarah shrugged. He pulled Kevin onto his lap, putting his lips close to the curly mop of hair. "You know there's no room."

"There's the shed."

"We keep equipment in there. You know that. We've got trucks and rollers and planters. It's full."

The little boy had burrowed into his chest, rubbing himself against the softness of Bobby's shirt. "We could move them."

"He'd be cold."

"We could get a heater. I know you've got them in the shop."

"But we'd have to brush him, and feed him. And what about the pond, in the ice? We'd have to break it up every morning." Bobby wrapped his arms around him.

"I'd do that."

Bobby sighed. "But he'd get lonely. He'd be out there all by himself. What's he gonna do while you're in school? That's not a life for a horse. Is it?"

Bobby laid his cheek on Kevin's head. "Now I want you to think about something else you want, and tell me tomorrow. Okay?"

Kevin finally nodded.

"Good. Now can I put you to bed?" Bobby cradled him in both arms as he stood. Kevin was mumbling, but Sarah couldn't hear what he said. Bobby lifted the boy high to maneuver him around the table, then dipped him down so Sarah could kiss him goodnight. She closed her eyes as she touched her mouth to his peach forehead.

"I love you," she said to her murmuring son. "Always have and always will."

Bobby took him into his room, lifting the blanket to tuck it snugly under his chin. Bobby bent to whisper something that Sarah couldn't hear, then backed out silently on stocking feet. Sarah watched it all from where she was sitting.

"You must be tired," Bobby said. "How were the boys tonight?"

"The same. Always the same. I wish you were here. You think he's all right?"

"What do you mean?"

"You know, St. Louis."

"Oh. Yeah. I think he's fine."

"I'm really worried." Her fingers started the same absent tapping. She touched the fake wood of the table with the pads of her right hand, repeating over and over the same tight rhythm.

"Why? Did something happen tonight?" he asked.

"No. We did his spelling words, but I still don't think he's got them right. I'm gonna have to make Daniel drill him again on the bus."

6.

The next morning was the same, only Bobby was with her. They stood outside in the frigid cold and waved as the bus chugged out.

She pulled her cardigan close around her. "You want some more coffee?" she asked, her breath making curlicues. "I can make a new pot."

"Yeah, thanks."

She took his mug and went inside.

Garrett's truck was there when she came out again, dressed in her hospital scrubs and her soft, silent, thick white shoes. She couldn't see Garrett but she could hear his voice as she started across the gravel farmyard with Bobby's steaming coffee.

"I want you out of here! You go work for somebody else! I'm not gonna put up with your crap anymore!" Garrett was yelling and he wasn't taking a breath.

"Dad, I'm telling you. I wasn't in the truck. I swear. I was out looking at pipe."

Sarah stopped short, then realized she was freezing.

"Don't give me that shit! I must've called you a hundred times."

They were in the back of the machine shop, in the shadows. Sarah tiptoed toward the huge open door.

"It must have been turned off or something," Bobby told him.

"So you're turning off the two-way now? You don't want to talk to me?"

One of their big grain trucks was parked in front of her on the concrete lip, nose first inside the shop. Bobby had been working on it with the hood up. He and his father were on the other side of it, at the far back of the building. She couldn't see them.

She bent to put the mug on the gravel, then knelt so both her knees hit the sharp stones. She leaned forward, wincing as she put her palms down, then squinted to see under the low chassis of the truck.

Garrett had cornered him. "You better call me whenever you leave! And I want you to call me every night, you hear? So I know where you've been."

She saw Garrett's legs take a step toward Bobby. Then she watched as her husband's boots backed up.

"Goddamn son of a bitch. Making me sit there, waiting for you to call. Like some woman. And look at this truck!" Garrett said as he took another step. "Running around down there in Cobden when you've got this to do. New pipe. Stupidest goddamn thing I ever heard."

"But we got it for free." Bobby was trapped in the far corner with nowhere to go.

"I don't give a shit if they paid you! We don't need it, and I don't want it."

"But it's under water out there!"

"You don't tell me what to do. I tell you!"

Bobby was crammed up against an old lathe. The two sets of boots touched toes.

The gravel cut into her knees and the soft heels of her hands.

"I don't care who you are," Garrett said. "I'll throw you out so fast. I'm talking to you, you dumb shit. Do you hear me?"

She tried not to breathe.

"Huh?" It was a grunt. Sarah heard it. It wasn't language.

"Huh?" Garrett grunted again, his toes shoved right up against Bobby's.

"Fight him," she mouthed as she strained to see.

"Answer me!" Garrett raged at him.

Then Bobby said it.

"I hear you, Dad."

"Don't," Sarah told the gravel. "Please don't. Tell him to go to hell."

"Say it's mine," Garrett told his son. "Say I own it."

She waited, praying with her head down, but then Bobby answered.

"Of course it's yours. I know it's yours. You're the boss, Dad."

7.

"Hey, Sarah."

"Hey, Bill."

The handsome young paramedic leaned in through her tiny window. "You okay? You don't look very good."

"No. I'm all right."

"You want to get some lunch? It's twelve. The cafeteria's open."

"No, I'm sorry. I'm going out."

"You mean to the Dairy Queen?"

She finally smiled. "You know, you're right. That's about all there is. It's either that or eat here. I bet you miss Indianapolis."

"Not really. I mean, how much sushi can a man eat?"

She made a laugh.

"That's it? That's my best material," he said, his blond hair flipping surfer-style over his forehead. "But seriously, where are you going?"

"A fish fry. Our friend Lester's throwing it."

He raised his eyebrows. "I've never been to one of those."

"You haven't?" It was Peggy, who had just come down the hall. She had a cup of coffee in one hand and her pack of cigarettes in the other. She smelled like smoke and outside.

"You're still coming, aren't you?" Sarah asked her.

"Oh shoot. I forgot. But if I don't get those trays in the autoclave, I'm not gonna have anything I can use."

"You're not going to make me go by myself again."

Peggy looked at Bill as they clustered at the window and tilted her head. "Take him. He'll be new meat for the Dead Peckers."

"The who?" Bill said.

"Oh, they won't be there," Sarah told her. "It's raining."

"Excuse me," Bill said.

"You want to bet?" Peggy answered. "Every single one of them is gonna be sitting on his two-way, trying to find out where the free lunch is. Everybody knows there's a fish fry someplace when it rains."

"Hey!"

"What?" Peggy finally turned to him.

"What's a Dead Pecker?"

Peggy gurgle-laughed. "Sarah, you have got to take him."

"It's a bunch of old guys," Sarah told him. "My father-in-law's one of them. That's what they call themselves."

"The Dead Peckers? That's a real name?"

"They've got this farmhouse down on 153," Peggy said. "It's empty except for the card table in the middle of the living room. I've been there. You don't want to see that bathroom."

"What do they do?" he asked.

"They hang out and play cards. Drink beer. Somebody's always got a pot of chili going. The fire department gets called a couple times a year."

8.

Fifteen minutes later, Sarah pulled off the road and into a thick covey of farm buildings. She parked all the way in back by a chain-link fence.

"Now what am I supposed to do here?" Bill asked as they got out.

"Just be your usual charming self."

Bill smiled. "You think I'm charming?"

They walked toward a metal building with huge sliding doors. They were open and the space they left was wide and tall above the building's cement slab. Inside, two long folding tables had been put together, with two rows of empty folding chairs on either side. Men were standing at the front, near the doors, holding cans of soda and watching the drizzle that dripped off the overhang. As Sarah and Bill came toward them in the mist, the loitering men all turned to watch.

"Is my slip showing or something?" Bill whispered.

"Welcome to a small town."

As they stepped out of the rain, most of the men said hello to her, but only one or two of them knew Bill. When they came up to him, he shook their hands eagerly. In a minute, he had met everybody and was already the center of a circle of laughing men.

Sarah found Lester and kissed him. He told her Bobby was in the back.

When her husband came out a minute later, he kissed her and shook hands with Bill, then stood off to the side with a can of soda pop. He smiled when he was supposed to, but she saw that he didn't have anything to say.

A few feet away from them, square vats boiled oil. Huge thermometers hung down into them over the sides, and two big wire ladles were propped up against the legs, dripping grease on-to the cement.

Two enormous men were cooking catfish and French fries. One of them wore army fatigues and sucked a butt as he ladled the batches in and out of the grease. His black hair stuck out of the cap that was pulled low on his head. The other man wore a big apron that flapped below his knees. It was covered in dirt and grease spots.

Next to one of the vats, a giant jar of Zatarain's sat on the floor. Every few minutes, one of the men picked it up and poured some out onto a plate, then dredged more catfish or French fries in it and started a new batch. When it was done, he picked one of the ladles off the floor and lifted the food out, then turned and dumped it on the table behind him, onto one of the mounds growing on top of a layer of paper towels. He banged the ladle hard against the metal vat and sent oily bits flying. The floor within ten feet was littered with shiny balls of catfish and French fry and breading. The crowd knew enough to stay far out of his way.

A small hillock of white onions, sliced into half-moons, sat next to the growing piles of catfish and French fries. Next to that was a haystack of lemon wedges with the seeds still in, piled next to paper plates and plastic forks. At the far end stood three rolls of paper towels.

"What's with the dog?" someone asked Lester. A skinny black mutt stood between two of the cars outside, staring across the rain at them, sniffing the air.

"She's a stray," Lester said. "Been out there a couple of days. She won't let me near her. Looks like she's been treated pretty bad. Anybody want her? She'll come around if you treat her right."

The men cooking gave Lester the high sign and he waved his arm. The crowd began to line up at the paper-towel end of the food table. The men motioned to Sarah and another older woman, who was Lester's mother, and the two of them stepped up first. Once they were out of the way, the men smiled and fought and elbowed each other as they built huge pyramids of catfish and French fries on their extra-reinforced paper plates.

"Hey, Slim!" somebody called out and the fat man in army fatigues turned around. "Where's that hot sauce of yours? I can't live without that stuff."

Slim lumbered to a corner and fished around in a cardboard box that sat on a pile of bags of seed corn.

"Uh-oh," another man said. "Dead Peckers at six o'clock."

Sarah looked through the wide open doors and saw Garrett coming toward them under the spitting drizzle with two other white-haired men. One of them wore overalls. The other had on a pink-striped shirt. Short Garrett was walking fast, to stay in front.

"What're you doing here?" someone called to him.

"Same as you," Garrett said. "Hey, Lester."

"Garrett," Lester said.

From her seat, Sarah scanned for Bobby. He was at the back end of the food line. He had swung his shoulders so Garrett couldn't see him.

She watched her father-in-law stride up to Bill, who put out his hand and smiled. "Bill Davis. Nice to meet you."

"Who are you?" Garrett said without introducing himself.

"I'm a paramedic. I work out of the firehouse."

"You the new ambulance driver?"

"Paramedic. Yeah."

"We're gonna need this guy pretty soon," Garrett said to his buddies.

"Garrett, how'd you hear about this?" someone asked.

"Same as you. On the two-way. Hell, the whole county knows. Lester, you want to keep it a secret, you need to tell people to park out back."

"That's okay," Lester said. "There's food for everyone. And if we run out, Slim here will cook you some more."

"Oh yeah?" Slim said as Lester laughed.

The men all sat down. Garrett took one far end, next to Bill and across from his friends. Sarah kept her seat in the middle. Once he got his food, Bobby sat as far away from his dad as he could, at the other end, talking with Lester and a stranger. Sarah leaned back and looked down the table often, but Bobby never looked up. When he was done, he pushed his chair back and leaned forward and listened, staring silently at Lester and the new man, whom Sarah didn't recognize.

More and more men arrived, mostly alone and in pairs. At one point, a truck from the gas company pulled up and a crew of four jumped out. The long table quickly filled with men in jeans and overalls and uniforms, all of them in billed caps and heavy work boots.

After they had served everybody, the two cooks sat down, their backsides spilling over small folding chairs that creaked as they protested. The men tipped them back against the wall and lit up. Their stubby fingers shined with grease.

"So you met everybody in town yet?" Sarah heard Garrett ask Bill.

"No. Not nearly," Bill answered.

"You meet Jim Lawler? Over at the funeral home?"

Bill shook his head, so Garrett leaned in. "When you do, he's gonna ask you how you are. And you better tell him you're fine. Because if you tell him you feel poorly, he's gonna follow you around all day."

Bill laughed. Garrett put his fork down and wiped his hands. "You know how he shakes hands?" Garrett put out his hand and Bill took it. As he shook, Garrett put his index finger out straight on the underside of Bill's wrist. "You know what he's doing?"

"No."

"Checking for a pulse."

Bill laughed again, a loud hee-haw that surprised everyone.

Garrett pointed at his buddies across the table. "You need to watch out for these two. This one for instance." He pointed to the man in overalls. "Percy. He took out an ad in the paper about a month ago. Telling women they could have an all-expense-paid trip to Florida for two weeks, and to call this number."

A couple of the other men began to laugh.

"You know whose number it was?" Garrett asked Bill.

"No."

"Shorty here." Garrett pointed at the other man, in pink.

"You?" Bill said.

Shorty nodded. "I got about a hundred calls."

"Anybody you wanted?" Bill asked him.

"Just his wife," Shorty said, pointing to Percy. Bill laughed again.

Shorty asked Bill, "Have you been stopped by the police yet?"

"No."

"Well let me tell you."

"Don't tell that one!" someone called out. "There's ladies present."

Shorty lifted his head and located Sarah and Lester's mother, staring. "Let me just apologize in advance, then. Anyway, I'm sure you've heard this one before."

Sarah shook her head no, but Shorty kept going. "Well," he said to Bill. "I'm coming back from Ramsey one night and I get pulled over by this cop. He's just a kid, about twelve. Anyway, I was moving. Probably going eighty."

Shorty pushed his chair back and stood up, then stepped back from the table. "So he pulls me over and I jump right out of the car, holding the seat of my pants back here."

Shorty grabbed the seat of his overalls in his fist and pulled them away from him. He started making little short hops back and forth. "'I gotta go. I gotta go,' I tell this kid. He asks me why I'm speeding, and just keep telling him 'I gotta go, I gotta go.' Then I run off into the bushes. You know that kid was still there when I came out? He follows me up to the next gas station, and I figure I better pull in. You know, like I got to go clean myself. He didn't drive off until I hit the men's room."

"These guys are a scream!" Bill told her as Sarah laughed along with the men.

"Did you ever get to Florida?" he asked Percy when the laughter died down. "You know, on that all-expense-paid vacation?"

"Sure did," the old man said. "I went by myself. Stayed with my daughter. Now that's a story."

"Oh no," someone said down the table. "Here we go."

"You want to hear it or not?" Percy called to the man.

"Got to see a man about a horse," Garrett said. Sarah watched him get up and start toward the back of the building. He was looking down the length of the long table as he went. He stopped when he saw Bobby at the far end.

She watched Garrett turn on his heel and come back across the cement, then lean over and whisper in Bobby's ear. A few words. Maybe a sentence. When he was done, Garrett straightened and headed toward the toilet, his shoulders rolling. Sarah also saw the new bounce in his step.

She watched her husband flip his wrist and check his watch on the underside of his forearm. He said a few words to Lester as he got up, then pushed in his chair politely, shaking hands with the new man across the table. Bobby approached her. "I'll see you at home," he said, laying his palm on her shoulder. "I've got to finish that truck."

She watched him cross the floor, his boots quiet as sneakers, then step out in the rain and turn right and disappear.

"One night when I was down in Florida," Percy was saying, "I was out late. I don't remember what I was doing. Playing cards or something. Anyway, my daughter lives in one of these developments, you know. Where all the houses are all lined up? So I come home late and I come in and all the furniture's gone. There's nothing in the house anymore but this one white recliner, sitting in the middle of the living room. I figure she's moved out without telling me. And I hope they're gonna come back in the morning and get me. So I sit down in this recliner and I go to sleep."

"Uh-huh," Bill said, egging him on.

"Well the next morning, when nobody comes to pick me up, I go outside and I check the number. Turns out I was in the duplex right next door to my daughter's place. I get her on the phone and she tells me she's just called the cops and she wants to know where I am. I tell her to look out the window, because I'm standing in the kitchen next door, looking at her."

Sarah suddenly saw her father. Drenched with rain, he was followed by two much younger men, teenage tough guys who looked like they worked at the rail yard with him. She didn't know either one.

A few of the men on her side of the long table saw them too and began watching. Others began to turn, seeing the vigilance, and the huge hanger of a building grew still. Lester twisted in his seat as he sensed the change in the weather, then stood. The two young men stopped walking and eyed him as he got up, but Sarah's father kept coming, shuffling toward Lester, his dirty jeans pouching at the knees and drooping in the back over his scuffed black dress shoes.

It was so quiet Sarah heard the brush of her father's denim and the thumping of Lester's boots on the concrete floor as they walked toward each other. Lester smiled and thrust out his hand. Chuck Winston wiped his palm on his pant leg before he took it and pumped hard, his smile growing. With his other hand, Winston smoothed his hair, which was white-grey and too long, with one thin lock that curled like Kevin's over his forehead.

Winston introduced Lester to his two companions, who ducked their heads once each but didn't speak. Lester waved them all over to the food table, gesturing wide as he offered them what was left of the catfish.

Sarah shot a look at Slim, but neither of the chefs had gotten up. They had leaned back even farther in their folding chairs, tilting them and spreading the great hams of their legs over the sides. Like the rest of the crowd, both men were wary. Slim had forgotten the cigarette spit-pasted to his lower lip.

Winston and the young men crowded the food, shoveling as much as they could on their plates as fast as possible. When they finished scooping the fish, they started on the fries, making great thatches stacked high above the white Styrofoam. Her father was done first and turned to find a spot for them to eat alone together all while Sarah smiled as she waited for him to see her.

But then he froze. He had spotted Garrett. She watched her father's face close tight before he turned away, swinging on his heel and walking toward the big open doorway that led out into the rain. Lester called to him, waving his arm to come back in, he was welcome, but Winston just thanked him kindly and kept going. Surprised, the two young men trailed him clutching their food. Sarah got up as her father stepped outside and turned right like Bobby had around the side of the huge open doors.

Her shoes padded across the wide floor as she felt everyone watching her. She lifted her head for them as if it was no big deal, as if the day were clear and the rain had stopped as she stepped out to follow him, only it hadn't. The wet plopped on her face as her white shoes sunk in mud.

"Dad, where's your coat?" she asked as she approached him. He was alone, stuffing his meal, leaning against the corrugated metal and under the high lip of the roof that cut some of the worsening rain but not enough of it. "You're going to catch your death. Come inside."

"I'll be all right." He shoveled another bite with his head down.

She dipped to peer into his face. "Why are you wearing your dress shoes?"

He smelled of body odor and dirt. "Can I take you home?" she asked.

"No," he said, taking a big mouthful. But he wasn't focusing. "My sunnygirl. You always take care of me."

"You know how worried I get until you come home. Did Mom say something? Did you two have another fight?"

"I got this new job over in Carmi. It pays good."

"Are you all right? There was plenty of room inside, at the table."

He looked at her and blinked. One, two, and then he was with her and angry. He spat it. "You know what that son of a bitch did?"

"Who?"

"It's time somebody did something about him. Goddamn asshole. I was at the package store this morning. You know, Mastin's?"

"Dad—"

"Garrett the Goddamn Squirrel was in there yesterday. Mastin said he was mad as hell. Looking for Bobby. Mastin told me he just went off about you. About how you were costing Bobby a fortune. Just spending him blind. He said Bobby never should have married you."

"He did?"

"He said you're the reason Bobby comes up with all these ideas all the time. About the farm. And what they ought to be doing. He told Mastin Bobby's so squeezed he'll do anything. 'She's got his oysters in her hand' is what he said. 'And she keeps squeezing.'"

"He didn't really say that."

"He said Bobby's a fool. Letting you run him. That he's willing to do anything just to get you some money."

"That's not true! I work full-time. I have ever since Kevin started school. We save every penny! How could he say that?"

"Because he's an asshole."

"But it's not true!"

The stray black dog inched out from under a car.

"What does that have to do with it?" her father said. "He says what he wants. Whatever works. I'm not talking to that son of a bitch. Not ever again. I don't care who he is. I don't understand why Bobby didn't take that offer last year and get you out of here."

"What offer?"

"You know, from Mack Swartz. To stake him."

The rain had collected on her cheeks and dripped down her chin. "What are you talking about?"

Her father stopped. Wet too, he scanned her face. "You didn't know? Shit. I shouldn't have said anything."

"I want to know."

He wiped the end of his nose and sniffed. "Mack Swartz offered to stake him. Last year. On some ground down near Indian Mound. Real good black dirt. But Bobby wouldn't do it."

"Stake him. What does that mean?"

"He said he'd cover the down payment. It was five hundred acres. Mack told Bobby he could just pay him back when he got the money."

Sarah thought. "What kind of terms did he want?"

"That's the whole thing," he said. "It was free money. He just wanted to help get Bobby out."

"When was this?"

The dog was closer, smelling the grease on Winston's hands even through the rain. She moved closer, her fur wet and clumping as she wagged her bony tail.

"Last year," he said. "When Bobby had that record harvest and he had to build those new bins. Mack saw the whole thing. He told Bobby he could tell that him and Garrett weren't getting along. So he offered to stake him. Bobby wouldn't do it."

"Why not?"

"He really didn't tell you? I don't know. It doesn't make any sense to me."

"Sarah?" It was Bill, leaning out the open doorway, calling over to her.

"Who told you?" she asked her father.

"Mack did. He told me himself. He couldn't figure it out either."

"Sarah?"

She turned toward Bill. Her hair shone with raindrops that glistened, too, like freckles across her face.

"I don't mean to interrupt," he called out again. "But I was wondering when you were heading back."

"Uh ... Soon. Let me just say goodbye to my dad."

Sarah felt a thump on her right leg and looked down. The dog nuzzled her, beating its tail.

9.

Bobby kept to himself all that same evening. At dinner he didn't say a word, and he disappeared downstairs as soon as it was over. It was Sarah's job to get the boys ready for bed and to read to them until it was time to turn out the lights.

When she was done, she went down to find Bobby playing pool in the small, wood-paneled back room behind the washer-dryer. He didn't speak as she parked herself on the arm of the old, rump-sprung couch that pressed against the foundation under their bedroom.

He lined up a shot. He stroked and sent the white cue ball skidding. It banged into the seven and sank it, then rolled backward in a straight line to stop magically behind the black eight. He sank the eight, and the nine, and bent over to get the rack off a hook by his knees. He put it flat on the felt and started taking the colored balls out of the bin. She watched him arrange them carefully in a diamond inside the wooden triangle.

"That's not how you usually do it," she said.

He didn't look over. "I'm playing nine ball."

When he broke, he pumped so hard the cue ball crashed into the diamond and sent one of the balls flying off the table towards her. She jerked her arms up to protect herself as the ball slammed into the concrete by her head, then smashed into the old end table next to her.

"Sorry." He bent to retrieve it.

He made a new diamond and broke again, then lined up his first shot. The cue ball hit the one, which rolled down the table and smacked the nine. The nine clunked in the pocket. He picked up the rack.

"I don't understand what you're doing," she told him.

He still didn't glance at her. "You're supposed to sink the nine. If you sink it on the break, you win. If you don't, you have to sink every other ball in order, until you get to it. You have to sink the nine last."

"But that's not what you just did."

"No. I used the one to sink the nine. If you hit the nine with another ball, you can win that way too."

She crossed her arms. "Who makes up these rules?"

He looked up then. "You gonna let me play, or not?" He wasn't smiling.

Silently, she watched him for a long time. No game lasted more than five minutes, and some were over on the break, when Bobby sank the nine. Once, he sank the cue ball and cussed himself, but otherwise he didn't talk.

Sarah looked away after a while and up at her troll dolls on two long ledges that made a single shelf filling the top of the opposite long wall, creating a cornice of small plastic creatures with bug eyes. She had forty of them in all sizes but all with the same straight extended arms and splayed fingers, fat bellies, and colored wisps of hair.

She smiled for the first time since coming downstairs.

The only other furniture in the room, apart from the pool table, was the couch and the two end tables on either side. On the short right-hand wall, under the front door upstairs, another set of two ledges was piled neatly with the boys' old toys and board games. A rusted metal globe sat at one end, at the crux where the two walls and the two sets of ledges came together.

She stared up at that corner, and then she saw it. The toys had been moved to one side, shoved down the ledge toward the right,

away from the corner. A tall stack of oversized paperback book-
lets had been crammed in beside them, arranged in a tidy pile
two feet high topped by the upstairs floor. They were so high it
would take a ladder to reach them.

"Bobby?"

"Yeah?"

"Why are those down here?"

Holding the cue stick, Bobby lifted his head to follow her finger. "I just wanted to get them out of the way."

"But those are your house-plan books."

He hit the eight ball so hard it rattled into the pocket. He
strode around the table to the other side.

"I don't think I've ever seen those off the living room table,"
she said. "You've been drawing house plans since we got married. Every night, just about, after the boys go to bed."

He hit the nine ball off a rail but it ricocheted, hitting two
more side rails before it stopped rolling.

"Why are they down here?"

"It's no big deal, Sarah. I just got them out of the way."

"But you don't do it anymore. You don't work on them."

"Sure I do."

"Not in a long time. Months, maybe. I never thought about it
before. Does that mean you don't think we're moving anymore?"

"I just moved them. What are you getting so worked up
about?"

"Those were important to you!"

"Not anymore."

"What did your dad say to you today? To make you run out
of there."

"I don't want to talk about my dad tonight." Bobby was angry.

"But he's terrible. He says things that aren't true. He's mean!"

He jammed his pool cue into the floor, clunking the fatter end of it onto the cement so it pointed straight up next to him like a javelin. She saw him take a deep breath to calm himself, like she was a child he had to explain to. "He's not gonna change, Sarah. He's seventy-four years old."

"Don't give me that."

"How many times are we gonna talk about this? Ignore him."

"Is that what you do? Ignore him?"

"I try, but you won't let me. You're always bringing this up. You're not gonna change him."

"But he's worse. It's getting worse." She had closed her eyes. "You know what he told Mastin Banks? He told Mastin you never should have married me."

"How do you know that?"

"Dad told me at the fish fry, after you left. Mastin said Garrett claims I'm spending you blind. That you'll do anything to get me money."

"Jesus."

She put her hands over her face. "I'm the reason. It's always me."

"Shit. Not again."

She bent her head, losing control of the wave. After a moment, Bobby laid his stick on the table and came over, putting one arm around her bucking shoulders. She tried to push him away, but he wouldn't let her. Bobby held on. It took a minute, but eventually the sobbing let up enough so she could speak again.

"Why do you put up with it?" she asked. "He's affected our whole life. He keeps you away from here. This is your home! Our home, only you run away whenever he comes, and he's here all the time. I want you home!"

"My father's an asshole, Sarah, and you've always known that. He's never changed, and he's not going to, but you've never changed either. I've been hearing this for twenty years."

"But he said it so that everybody could hear him. Dad told me he said it right in the middle of the store. Why?" She had started crying again.

"He rages. That's what he does."

"But why?"

"My sister thought it was the war. He was a prisoner for over a year. He was in one of those pick-up platoons. He killed a lot of Germans before they got him. I think when they found him he was the only one left. He'd been hiding in some building, and it came down on him when it was bombed."

Bobby was rubbing her shoulders now.

"Jeanne met this guy once who had gone to school with him. I don't remember his name. He was from someplace around here. He was over there and he saw Dad in the hospital, after the Allies freed the camp. He said he didn't recognize him. Dad was down to a hundred pounds. They didn't think he was gonna live."

"So it was the war? Is that why you put up with it?"

The rubbing stopped. "At least until he's dead and we don't have to have these conversations. I love you, but I'm tired of them. I've had a long day."

She started shaking her head. "I'm tired of them too, Bobby. Real tired." She swung her leg off the top of the couch and stood. "I'm going to bed."

10.

Two days later Sarah dressed her boys up for Sunday supper. She spit and polished them until they shone.

In town, her mother-in-law greeted them all warmly at the back door. Cora threw her arms around Kevin, hugging him tightly to her thin bosom as he rolled his eyes under the white bow of her polyester blouse. She tugged at Daniel too, but he was larger and evaded her, offering only his cheek before the two boys ran through her bubble-gum pink kitchen toward the blaring television in the den.

"Shotgun!" Kevin yelled as Bobby followed them.

"It's my turn!" Daniel shouted back.

"Hey!" Garrett called out so loudly Sarah could hear him. "You two be quiet. I'm trying to watch."

The smell of frying chicken filled the room. Next to the stove, hot pieces sat on a paper lunch bag dotted with blossoming grease spots. Steam covered the windows over the sink from the green beans and the potatoes that were boiling. On the counter, two layers of chocolate cake cooled on a rack.

Sarah asked Cora what she could do to help. At first, Cora told her to sit down and relax, but Sarah tried again, and then a third time. Cora finally pointed to the refrigerator, where homemade icing hardened on the top shelf. Sarah took it out as Cora lifted the pot of potatoes and poured them into a colander in the sink, the wet steam rising to cover her square glasses and mist her white hair.

"Whew, this is hot," Cora said as she poured them. "Have you told Bobby yet about the trip?"

"I'm going to tell him next Saturday, on Kevin's birthday."

"Oh, what a nice idea. When are you going?"

"February thirteenth, next year."

"So you'll be there for Valentine's Day." Cora spooned the potatoes into a big ceramic bowl. "I've never been to Hawaii. The farthest I ever got was California, during the war."

"Really?" Sarah said as she angled the long spreader blade upward around the cake. "Why were you out there?"

"I worked in a factory, calibrating gyroscopes." Cora opened the refrigerator. "I took Garrett J. and moved out to San Diego to live with my sister while Garrett was gone. I got a job repairing airplane instruments. Tanks too." Cora smiled to herself.

"What did Garrett say about that?"

Potato steam traced curls that turned in the air between them. "I didn't tell him until I was gone. He nearly killed me when he found out, but he was already in Belgium. I timed it just right, but of course I didn't know what was going to happen to him."

Cora had taken out the hand-mixer.

"This trip will be good for Bobby," Cora said as the machine whirred. "He needs a break. This recession and everything. It's making everybody crazy."

"I guess it is. Maybe that's what's going on." Sarah nodded to herself.

"I just can't believe you paid for it all yourself, without him finding out. How did you do it?"

Sarah smiled. "We've been eating spaghetti and tuna casserole pretty much non-stop, and I've been saving every penny for the last three years."

"Thank goodness for your job at the hospital. What with beans so far down. They're under five dollars. And this is the second year it's been like this."

"I know. Bobby talks about it all the time."

"It hasn't been this bad since we started farming. Thank Heaven the yield's up, thanks to the good weather."

Sarah turned to her, the blade in the air. "You think it's the weather? You don't think it's—"

"That's what my husband says—"

"—Bobby?"

"— and he's always right. He's been doing it a long time. Thank goodness Bobby built those new bins last year. We'd never have enough room if he hadn't done that."

"No. We wouldn't," Sarah said pointedly, but Cora wasn't listening.

Cora added butter to the bowl. "Good weather helps everybody. Remember seventy-seven? That was the best year we ever had, up to then. I remember that summer. It was beautiful the whole time. All my husband ever talked about was retiring and playing golf. That was the first year Bobby took over the farm. Garrett said he wasn't doing it anymore. Boy, he sure changed his mind."

"He sure did," Sarah said, behind her, but Cora couldn't see her face.

Bobby walked in. "Mom, you've got about a minute before the half."

"I'll go see what the boys want to drink." Sarah walked into the dining room, past where the wooden table was already set for only five. She changed her mind, though, on the other side of it and turned instead toward the bathroom on her left. When she came out, she asked her sons and Garrett what they wanted to drink. He ordered ice tea and wiggled his TV tray up closer. She turned back to the dining room.

She was next to the table again when she heard Bobby's voice, low and urgent. "Did Dad say something to you about that pipe?"

Sarah stopped. She couldn't see him yet.

"Mom?" Bobby said. "Why do you look like that? What did he say?"

"Ah Jesus!" Garrett yelled behind her in the den. "Stop him! What are you doing? Fifteen yards!"

"It's that Mayes," her son Daniel said. "He's a rookie."

"Why can't we have somebody like that?" Garrett demanded.

Bobby said to his mother, in the kitchen. "Tell me what's going on."

"Nothing" Cora said, nearly in a whisper. Sarah stretched on her toes but still could barely hear. "It wasn't that bad."

"Field goal!" Garrett yelled. "Can you believe it? Ten nothing, with nine seconds left."

"I don't know why he doesn't just yell at me," Bobby said angrily. "Why does he have to yell at you too?"

"Shh! He'll hear you."

Sarah heard dishes coming out of a cabinet.

"There's the gun!" Garrett called out. "Boys, go tell your grandmother."

"Let it go," Cora told Bobby. "The pipe. It's not going to happen."

Sarah turned her head to look behind her. Kevin and Daniel had stood up, and they were coming.

"But we need it," Bobby told his mother. "It's under water out there."

"He doesn't think so. You can't argue with him so much."

"Hey, Mom!" Kevin shouted. "Did you see that? Some of the people in the stands had paper bags over their heads!"

Cora said, "And Bobby? Tell your father where you go from now on."

11.

It took an hour and a half to get to St. Louis and the two of them were quiet most of the way. As they drove west, Sarah asked Bobby what he had told his father in order to get the day off.

"I told him you had to have some tests done at Barnes Hospital."

"What kind of tests?"

"Female stuff." Bobby smiled as he drove the truck. "It shut him up."

The flat fields slowly turned to asphalt, then the asphalt turned to chain link and debris. They drove by more and more old bombed-out, run-down buildings as they came into East St. Louis, the back alley of the white city across the bridge. A thousand dirty, smoking cars and trucks clogged the filthy tangle of roads that converged at the wide ramp on the Illinois side, beneath the Arch.

Sarah dropped her eyes as they started over the narrow, muddy water. She missed the thicket of steel girders as she began shredding the tight, dry wad of tissues in her hands. It started to snow on her navy blue trousers.

They passed the Budweiser eagle flapping his wings in neon lights on a giant billboard and the round Ralston Purina plant with its black and white checkers in a wide band. At last, Bobby took the off ramp at Kingshighway and curved around to the smaller side streets near the hospitals clustered in that part of town. He finally found the number they sought on a low-slung two-story brick building and pulled over to the curb, where meters doled out quarter hours. Bobby was fishing in his sport coat pocket already as he opened his door.

But Sarah didn't move.

With one foot on the curb, he hesitated, watching her fingers fight with each other, tearing at the tissues.

"Are you all right?"

"No," she said, littering her lap.

12.

"Well," Dr. Weiss said as he sat and flipped open the manila folder. "Where should we start in our discussion about your son?"

Unusually tall, the gray-haired psychologist had greeted them personally in the reception area, telling Sarah how good it was to see her again.

"Call me Alan, please," he told Bobby as they shook hands.

His office was large and, except for his brown wooden desk, furnished entirely in the chrome and black of 1980s modern. In a far corner, where two floor-to-ceiling panes of glass came together, two uncomfortable box-frame director chairs faced an expensive Italian leather sofa that was cut in a rectangle with little buttons on the leather squares. Outside, through the wall of glass, Sarah could see the twiggy back of a hedge with brittle, twisted, naked branches.

She sat on the couch but didn't lean back. She perched, tucking her toes under the silver frame, crossing her ankles. Bobby parked himself next to her and tried to get comfortable. He attempted to put his arm up on the back of the armless sofa but gave up.

"I'm sorry," the doctor said from the director chair he had taken across from them. "This was all my predecessor's. It's not my style, but I haven't had time to change anything."

"No, it's fine. I'm fine," Bobby lied.

Dr. Weiss looked at his file. "The school says Kevin's having difficulties with written language. His reading is substantially below grade level, and his writing is poor. Not just his handwriting but his ability to spell and write comprehensible sentences. He's also having trouble with phonics and word constituents."

"What are those?" Bobby asked.

"He can't seem to break words down into their phonetic parts, which of course means it's nearly impossible for him to read. And he can't write for the same reason. He also switches letters and numbers, like 'b' for 'd' and '6' for '9.' And he skips words when he reads aloud. His eyes jump all over the page. The teachers say he doesn't see punctuation. But that's very common."

Bobby cleared his throat, punching the air like a backfiring engine. Sarah looked at him, but he didn't speak.

The doctor waited, watching him, but then continued. "I found the same things when I tested him myself. I think his primary problem is that he can't seem to distinguish the different sounds that letters make. He hears fine. You had him examined by your pediatrician at home, so it's not his hearing, or his vision. It's something in his mental processing.

"Like for example, if you tell him to spell 'cat,' he'll get the 'c' and the 't' right, but the middle's a mystery. He puts in random letters. He's also not able to distinguish letter blends, like 'ch' and 'tr.' By second grade, most children can decode words with double blends, like 'trunk' and 'clunk.' Kevin can't." The doctor looked down at his file. "The school says he sings the alphabet whenever he's trying to spell. That's unusual for an eight year-old. They've usually outgrown that by then."

Bobby leaned forward and put his forearms on his knees. He clasped his hands and started bouncing them.

Dr. Weiss waited once more. "Bobby," he said. "Are you all right?"

Bobby shrugged and didn't answer, but his clenched hands kept bouncing.

"Fortunately, he's not disruptive at all. There's no indication of any hyperactivity. But he's clumsy, though. That's pretty typical. Does he fall off things?"

Startled, Sarah said, "All the time. I'm always worried he's going to get himself killed."

Dr. Weiss nodded. "And he's distractible. Several times, he veered off into some idea of his own."

He smiled towards Bobby. "Before I forget, Kevin asked me to tell you he wants a horse for his birthday."

Bobby didn't smile back.

"Now, based on this, as well as my long talk with Sarah, we selected a battery of tests. They included things like the Bender Gestalt and the Weschler IQ. I chose those because—"

Sarah interrupted. "Doctor, what's his IQ?"

"For that, there are two parts. One's a verbal score, and the other's performance. Spatial performance. Things like puzzles I give him, and pictures with details he needs to see. There's a separate score for the verbal and the performance, and then there's a number which is sort of an average of the two.

"Kevin's verbal performance score was 100, which puts him in the fiftieth percentile. He had some trouble with some of the questions, like how many nickels are in a quarter, but his performance section was really quite extraordinary. There, he got a 130."

"130?" Sarah looked at Bobby, who had turned his head.

"Yes. He's very, very good with his eyes and hands."

"Isn't that gifted?" she asked.

"It depends on the school district. But yes, most of them consider a child to be gifted if he scores 130 on either part of the test."

"Kevin's gifted? Our son's gifted?"

"One-thirty puts him in the top two percent. Ninety-eighth percentile. He's incredible, really, spatially. Let me show you something." Dr. Weiss stood and went to his desk, where he picked up a small green box. In it were red and white plastic pieces that fit together snugly and made a pattern, like a star pattern on a quilt. "In one of the tests, I showed Kevin different designs with this, and I asked him to recreate them for me. Kevin not only did every one, but he did them all faster than any other eight year-old I've ever seen. Your son's quite a builder, too."

"So there's nothing wrong with him?" Sarah said. "He's not retarded?"

Bobby turned to her. "Retarded? What made you think that?"

"No," the doctor said patiently. "He's quite normal. He's just dyslexic."

"He's what?" Bobby said.

"Dyslexic."

"What's that?"

Bobby was leaning so far forward now he nearly fell off the sofa. The doctor put the file on the small table in front of them and looked Bobby in the eye. "Dyslexics have trouble making the connection between spoken language and written words. Some very smart people have real trouble sounding out words and spelling them. We know it's not a function of intelligence. Retarded children can be taught to spell, so it's not about brain power. It's about how the brain is organized."

"Kevin's brain is different?" Sarah asked.

Dr. Weiss nodded. "Schools teach to the majority, and most of us think in words. Sarah, do you talk to yourself inside your head?"

"Sure. All the time."

"So do I. And when you need to buy milk, what do you say to yourself?"

"That I have to go to the store to buy milk."

"Me too. But many dyslexics think in pictures more than words. One man I know was first in his class at law school. He told me that when he has to go to the store, he puts a picture of the front of the store in his head, and then he puts in pictures of what he has to buy. Actual pictures. He doesn't think in words at all."

"I do that," Bobby blurted.

"I know," Dr. Weiss said quietly.

"You do?" Bobby said.

"I saw your reaction when we started to talk."

"You're dyslexic?" she asked Bobby. "You've got the same thing?"

But Bobby spoke to the man. "Is this hereditary? My grandmother never learned to read. My mother's mother. Nobody ever knew why."

"Yes," the doctor said. "It can skip generations."

"I used to sing the alphabet too."

"You never told me!" Sarah said.

But the two men were talking as if she weren't there. "For people like you, Bobby, and for Kevin, the normal way that schools teach children to read and write just doesn't work. For people who think in words, like I do and Sarah does, it's relatively easy to go from saying 'cat' inside our heads to writing 'cat' on a piece of paper. But for someone like you, it's much more difficult because the word 'cat' isn't living inside your head. What you've got is a picture of a cat, and not the word."

"That's exactly right," Bobby said, speaking quickly now. "You know, it got so bad I nearly flunked out my senior year. I almost didn't graduate."

"You did?" Sarah said.

"My English teacher found out I couldn't read about a month before graduation. She told me and my mother she had to flunk me."

"Who did?" Sarah said, but Bobby wasn't listening to her.

"My mother had to go with me to beg her. She even accused me of copying homework. I sat there not being able to say anything while my mother had to convince her to let me graduate. Can you imagine being so stupid your mother has to beg?"

13.

Bobby didn't say a word once they left the building, as they walked down the sidewalk to their truck, or after they climbed in. He didn't speak as they pulled out, found the interstate again and began the long, slow, rush-hour trip east toward downtown and the clogged mile-wide bridge over the Mississippi. He didn't turn to Sarah to ask if she wanted to eat. He never switched on the radio. His eyes rested without blinking on the whizzing asphalt in front of them. He crossed one of his thin wrists over the other, then forgot them both on the hard top curve of the steering wheel.

On the passenger side, Sarah hugged herself and rooted her gaze out her own window. Like Bobby, she didn't really see any of the billboards that stuttered by or the downtown buildings above the highway. She had propped her right ankle on her left knee and she jerked her foot without stopping until Bobby got them on the other side of the river.

"You weren't ever going to tell me, were you?" She said without turning.

He came to. "What?"

"You never were, but you've got the same thing. You know how much it would have helped me if I'd known that? I could have him helped better, and I could have helped you."

"But I had no idea I was dyslexic. I never heard that before today."

"But you knew you did the same things when you were a kid. Why didn't you tell him? Don't you realize how lonely he is?"

They had reached the flaking husk of East St. Louis, the torn up, decaying city on the other side.

"And why didn't you tell me?" she said. "You went in there today and you told a perfect stranger things you've never told me."

She looked over her turned shoulder at him. "You knew whenever you asked me to write anything. How many checks have I written in the last twelve years? How many Christmas cards?"

The land had finally opened on the far side of the new strip malls as the wide, flat fields once again began quilting the ground. They started to pass planted rows and metal silos whose cone caps caught the sun.

"Why didn't you ever tell me about school? It was Joan Nunley, right? I know Joan. I must see her twice a week in the grocery store. All these years, she knew but I didn't."

Bobby's voice took on the same edge. "What did you want me to tell you? That I nearly flunked out of high school?"

"That's crap!"

"I'm a farmer! I stayed in my hometown."

"But you wanted to go to Nashville."

"But I didn't! I work the land. I don't have to read."

Sarah heard a honk behind them.

"Go around!" Bobby barked at the rear-view mirror. "Damn Mercedes."

"Alan just told us never to give up or let Kevin give up, but that's what you did," she said. "That's what you're doing every day when you work Garrett's farm. I want our son to have more. I want him to have—"

"What?"

"—what I wanted! A marriage, with my husband. I want a man who puts me above his father! Isn't that what you promised me?"

"I never—"

"Forsaking all others, Bobby. You said it. We stood there and you promised. Only you never did it, did you?"

"What's so wrong with our life?"

"It's not ours! It's yours! And that means it's your dad's. He controls you. And if we're not careful Kevin's gonna have the same life."

"What's wrong with my life?"

The black Mercedes sedan honked again as the teenagers sped by them. One of the kids gave Bobby the finger.

Sarah shifted so she faced him. "We're supposed to be a team, but we're not. Not while there are secrets. I've told you everything about me since I was seventeen years old. But you haven't."

"I refuse to—"

"Why didn't you tell me about Mack Swartz? He offered to stake you."

"Who told you that?"

"Why didn't you do it?"

"Because you can't support a family on five hundred acres, that's why."

"But you had the land up here, too. Garrett lied to you and it took him ten years to do it, but it's yours now. Yours and his. That two hundred acres is in both your names. Isn't that enough, along with your percentage as a tenant farmer?"

"The minute he found out I was making my own money off my own land, Dad would have thrown us right off. And then where would we be?"

14.

There were three empty plates on the table when Sarah got home from the hospital the following afternoon. Next to each of them was an empty glass.

As she was rinsing, she noticed a crumpled ball of paper next to Kevin's backpack, which he had dumped on the table. She picked it up. She was about to throw it away when she saw handwriting on it she didn't recognize. She laid it out on the table and flattened it with her fist.

Mrs. McAllister. Kevin was involved in a fight today with another boy at lunch. One of the male teachers had to physically separate them. Needless to say, this behavior is unacceptable and will not be tolerated from any student at this school.

Please call my office at your earliest convenience to set up a time to meet. Your husband should attend as well. Rest assured that I'm also meeting with the other boy's parents.

It was signed by the principal, Robert Jacobson.

From the window above the sink, Sarah caught a glimpse of Bobby and Daniel far below, walking together in the field closest to her at the base of the slope. She didn't see Kevin.

She put on her winter coat and went outside again into the bitter cold.

"Mom!" she heard Kevin yell as she closed the back door. He was running up the gravel road. "I saw you drive up! Come on! I want to show you! You're not gonna believe this."

"Kevin! Button your coat and come over here. I need to talk to you."

"Mom, I want to show you!"

"We can do that in a minute." Once he was next to her, she said to him, "Now tell me. What happened in school today?"

He cast his eyes down, dipping his head. "It's no big deal. Dwight and Smitty made fun of me again, in front of everybody, that's all. Come on." He tugged at her coat.

She wouldn't budge. "What did they say?"

Kevin let out a sigh. "It's the same thing they always do, Mom. They make fun of me. Call me a baby."

"Why'd they call you a baby?"

"Because I can't read fast. They said I couldn't even get Hop On Pop."

"When did this happen?"

"At lunch. I was sitting with Ryan. They said I had to go back to first grade with all the other babies."

"So what did you do?"

"I hit him. Dwight. He's the one who said it." He smiled then. He smiled up at her. "I banged him up pretty good."

"Kevin! Hitting somebody is nothing to be proud of. What did Ms. Wilkins say?"

"Nothing."

"You told her?"

He shook his head.

"Why didn't you tell her what they called you?"

He rolled his eyes at her, then tugged on her again. "We're witching."

"You're what?"

"Witching. Me and Daniel and Dad. That's why I came to get you. Come on!"

She relented, letting him pull her. After a minute, they reached the bottom of the long hill, then started across the cement bridge that spanned the wide drainage ditch. There weren't any railings on the sides to keep them from falling, and even some of the edge itself had cracked away. She grabbed his hand tighter as they walked across it. The straight drop was more than twenty feet, and deep standing water filled the bottom.

"Kevin," she said as they were walking. "You can't let those other boys bother you."

"That's what Dad said too."

"So you and he talked about this?"

"Uh-huh. Dad says I'm just like him. We're the same. Him and me."

She looked down at him. He was smiling. "Daniel doesn't have it," Kevin said. "You don't either. It's just him and me and Grandma Rowan. We're dysleptic."

"Dyslexic."

"He said I'm just as smart as everybody else, but I'm different. That's all. I just can't read very well. But I can do other stuff the other kids can't. Like build things. The only thing they do better than me is read, and write. And that's not gonna be for long."

"No?"

"Heck no. Dad told me. He said I was gonna learn to read and write just fine. He said you were gonna teach me. And maybe I'd get a tutor."

Kevin swung her arm as they walked.

"I'm glad you talked to your dad," she said.

"Me too."

They started across the field where Bobby and Daniel huddled in the middle together, looking down at something.

"And did he tell you not to get so mad at Dwight?"

"Yeah. He says I got to let it just roll off my back, when somebody says something. And never, ever start a fight."

"That's good."

"But if one gets started, don't stop until you destroy the guy."

She stopped. "What?"

"There's two ways to fight. Either you don't fight, or you fight to win. And if you've got to fight, you don't back down until the other guy stops. No mamby-pamby."

"He said that?"

Bobby was fifty feet away, staring down and walking with Daniel. "What else did your father say?"

"That if someone's making fun of me, I should make fun back. That if I hit him when all he's doing is talking, I lose. I look like an idiot. But if he starts it. You know, hits me or rushes me, I've got to give it back as good as I get. It doesn't matter that I'm smaller. He's gonna teach me how to fight."

"He is?"

"Isn't that great? Just me and him. In the shed. Oh-oh. I wasn't supposed to tell you that."

She called out to Bobby. "You told him you're going to teach him how to fight?"

Bobby looked over.

"Sorry, Dad!" Kevin called out.

"He's got to know how," Bobby said as they approached. "This isn't gonna stop, Sarah. He's gonna get it his whole life."

"He should just walk away then."

"He walks away, nobody's ever gonna leave him alone. We can't be there every minute. He's got to learn how to handle this. On his own. He might as well learn now."

She looked at him for a long moment.

"I guess you're right," she finally said. "It's just too bad he has to. But Kevin, I don't care what your father says. If we get another note like that from Mr. Jacobson, you're gonna be grounded for a month. You hear me? Neither one of you boys is ever gonna start a fight. I don't care what names they call you."

"Why is this now about me?" Daniel asked, his palms out.

"There's starting one," Bobby told her. "And then there's finishing one."

"I understand that. But Kevin, I'm telling you. I don't want to ever hear about you starting a fistfight with anyone. And Daniel, that goes for you too. I'm serious. No fights. And you," she said to Bobby.

"And me, what?"

Sarah smiled and shook her head, then Bobby smiled back at her, the grin coming in like a slow tide over the deep ridges in his tanned face.

"Now," Bobby said to their boys. "Let's show her what we've been doing."

"Back up." Daniel waved at her. "Watch." He had two L-shaped pieces of coat-hanger wire in his hands. Daniel held them out like pistols, with the long ends of the wires over top of his fists, pointing straight ahead, with the short ends sticking out of the bottoms of his hands. They were parallel when he started walking, but after a few steps they began to creep in. Two steps later, they swung together and crossed in an "x" in front of him, but he hadn't moved his hands.

"That's the old tile, down there," Daniel told her.

"Tile?" Sarah said.

"Not tile like floor tile, but tile that's little pipe that comes off a big drain."

"You did that," she told Daniel. "You made those metal things come together."

"No, I didn't. They do it by themselves."

"Neat, huh?" Bobby was still grinning.

"The wires cross when you walk over the old tile," Kevin said.

"You really want me to believe that these two coat hangers magically know where the old tile is?"

"It's some kind of electromagnetic field," Bobby said. "I remembered it this morning, when I was thinking about how to find it buried down there. You try it."

He took the wires from Daniel's hands and passed them over. "Don't hold them too tight. Don't grab. Just let them sit on top." He arranged them so the wires pointed straight out in front of her, over the tops of her fists. When she moved her arms, they swung a little.

"Keep your arms stationery," Bobby said. "Now walk over that way."

Her three men stayed close. After she had taken a few steps, the wires began to move. She kept going, maneuvering around a crawdad pile that stuck up like a giant sombrero in the middle of the field. As she did, the wires swung together and finally crossed. She looked at Bobby. "What is this?"

"The wires are crossing over the tile. Every time you go over tile or culvert or any water, it does that. Utility lines too. I found the line to the house this morning, under the road."

She looked down at her shoes. "There's tile right here?"

"It's happening every ten feet. Coming off the main in the middle of the field over there."

"So how did you find the main? The same way?"

"No. They're always down in the low spot. Every field's got a low spot. I saw it this past summer. The beans were a different color along the top of it, and I could see it from the house. This morning I just started back there, where it was, with these coat hangers. The tile's coming off it in a herringbone."

"How did you know to do this?"

"I saw Gus Riordan do it once. My mom's uncle? I was a little kid."

"It works over tile," Kevin said. "And water too. And power lines. They crossed when I was under the power line up by the house before you got home."

"I think I can find all the old tile this way," Bobby said. "Without having to dig up the whole field and be wrong. You know how much time this is gonna save us?"

"Grandma Winston!" Daniel yelled.

Sarah turned to look up the hill and saw her mother driving down the dirt road toward the house, a swirling ball of dirt trailing behind her old car. She glanced at Bobby, who was smiling again. "Do you know why my mother's here?"

"I thought maybe you'd let me take you out for dinner," Bobby said. "I called her and she said she'd be happy to watch the boys."

15.

They made love when they got home from the Mexican restaurant in Ramsey. Afterwards, she lay with one ear on his chest. It was late, and the house was quiet.

She asked him softly as he stroked her hair, "So you were in a lot of fights when you were a kid?"

"Not just when I was a kid."

"What are we going to say to the principal? He wants us both there."

"We're gonna tell him what Dwight and Smitty said to Kevin. And I'm gonna tell him he better take care of it or he's gonna hear from me."

Sarah smiled to herself in the dim light. "I love you," she said.

He lifted thick locks of her hair and dug in with his fingers. She could feel the pull on her scalp. It felt good, as if he were taking possession. Bobby whispered as he combed her, "I love you too."

She pressed her cheek against the sinews of his freckled chest. He was strong and wiry.

"We ought to do that last part more often," he said.

She raised herself up. Her breasts swung beneath the white undershirt of his that she wore. It was short-sleeved and v-necked and thin. "I want to show you something."

"You mean there's more?" He laughed.

She laughed too as she reached across him, rubbing against him as she opened the drawer in her nightstand, then pulled out a thick envelope. She handed it to him as she sat up to watch.

"What's this?" he asked as he sat up too.

"I was going to save it for Kevin's birthday but I want you to have it now."

He lifted the flap and pulled out the papers, then unfolded them and slowly began to read out loud. "February 13. Depart Lambert Field. TWA non-stop to LAX. LAX to Honolulu. Four nights Sheraton Waikiki."

"Keep reading."

"Honolulu to Kauai February 17. Two nights Kauai Beach Resort. Kauai to Maui February 19. Three nights Maui Beachcomber. Depart Honolulu February 22, LAX."

He looked at her. "You did this?"

She nodded.

"You paid for this?"

She nodded some more.

"It's all paid for?"

She couldn't stop.

"How'd you do that? Hawaii. This is great! You're great. I can't wait!"

16.

When Sarah crossed the driveway the next morning, she saw a pair of boots sticking out from underneath the chassis of the huge old grain truck. With the tall door of the machine shop open, it was cold inside. Bobby had the space heaters blasting from the rafters. The coils on both glowed red.

Stepping inside and leaning over to speak to the boots, she said, "Honey, I've got to go to Mt. Vernon before we leave. I have to get some things. Those old shorts of mine just aren't going to make it. Not in Hawaii. And I'm gonna need a couple of dresses too. You know, for dinners. And there's that luau show the last night."

The boots didn't reply.

She laughed. "You're gonna need some new things too. Maybe a couple of those wild shirts with the parrots. Of course you could get those over there, I guess. That plane ride, though. It's going to be long. You're gonna need something comfortable. We both are. You think that's all gonna be in the stores? After Christmas? You know, bathing suits and all that? I've seen that resort wear but I don't think it comes out until later."

She waited but he still didn't speak. "Well, I guess we can deal with that later, after Kevin's birthday. Well, I'm going. Anything you need at the store? I'm gonna stop after work."

"No, thanks." She barely heard it through the underside of the truck.

"I'll see you later." She strutted out happily into the morning sun. She was at the door of her car when he called to her.

"Sarah?" He had come from the shadows, wiping his hands on an old towel.

"Yeah?" She had her hand on the door. He kept walking toward her across the gravel. "What?"

He stopped, facing her at the car. "I'm sorry. I can't go. I can't. We can't. I've just got too much to do here."

"Are you talking about Hawaii?"

"I've just got too much. I'm sorry. I know how much this means to you."

"What is it you have to do?"

"I've got to rebuild that tractor. One more time. And the combine. I've got to figure out what to do with that."

"But you do that every year."

"It's a lot of work. You know. And with this recession, we can't afford any new equipment. I've got to get us through another year."

"But you can do that when we get back." She had put her hands on her hips.

"It's a long time to be away."

"It's a week!"

"Eleven days, actually. And then another couple, getting over the jet lag."

"But that's why I planned it then. It's February. That's three months from now, so you can get everything done."

"Can you get the money back? Is it refundable?"

She sputtered. "I guess so."

"That's good, at least."

"What are you saying? That we're not going? After all that? Everything I did?"

"I'm sorry." He had stopped wiping his hands.

"But it's all set. My mom is gonna watch the boys."

"So let's go down to Kentucky Lake for a couple of days."

"In February?"

"I don't know. I'm just trying to help."

"Trying to help! You can help by going to Hawaii!"

"Sarah, it's not like you asked me. You could've talked to me before you did this. It's not my fault I can't go."

"Now you're blaming me?"

She jerked the door open and smacked it into Bobby's knees.

"You're overreacting," he said as he hopped back. "It's just a trip. Be reasonable."

"So now I'm unreasonable too." She climbed in and slammed the door, then twisted the key in the ignition. She floored it in reverse, not looking where he was as she backed up so fast the wheels spun on the gravel.

"Sarah!" he yelled after her.

She heard him but she didn't slow.

17.

Sarah went to her parents' house that night for dinner. When they were done, her father cleared the plates as her mother walked down the hall to the bathroom. At the kitchen sink, her father turned as soon as they heard the door shut.

"I'm sorry about the other day," he said quietly. "Did you talk to Bobby about that land?"

"Yeah."

"What did he say?"

"He said you can't support a family on five hundred acres."

He thought about it, then shook his head. "If Mack was gonna stake him, he wouldn't have had to pay that money back for a long time."

Her mother walked in again, and her father said, "I'm gonna go lie down. You don't need me for this one." He patted Sarah as he walked by.

Esther Winston replaced him at the sink. Her hair had grayed since awards night in the school gymnasium, and her large bosom had lowered to her waist. "He always forgets something," she said. "Your dad thinks he's done, but he's not." She ripped off a paper towel to wipe the countertop.

Sarah stood to take the salt and pepper shakers off the table. "I saved up for that trip for more than three years."

"You can get a refund, right?"

"That's what he said! But I don't care about that. I wanted to get away together. Go someplace different. Just us." She took the Morton's salt from a cabinet and slammed the container on the counter. Her mother was scrubbing the range top with her paper towel and her whole upper body shook.

"He's not too busy, Mom. That's ridiculous. And there he is, standing there, telling me like I'm gonna believe it." She screwed off the top of the salt shaker and began pouring.

"Don't take this the wrong way, but didn't you think about all this before you made those plans? All those reservations?"

"Think about what?"

"That Bobby might not go?"

"Are you defending him?"

Her mother turned. "No. I'm just asking."

Sarah screwed the top on and reached for the pepper. "It never occurred to me that he wouldn't go."

"But he's doing what he always does. He's worrying about his father and his reaction. Bobby's not going to do anything, he's so afraid of him."

Sarah stopped and stood facing the shakers on the counter.

Her mother's voice softened, watching her back. "You and I both know Bobby's afraid. He's not ever going to do anything to buck his father. That shouldn't be a surprise to you. You tell me all these stories, all the time, about something that Garrett's done, and Bobby won't stand up to him. What was it the other day? That pipe."

Sarah turned to her, surprise on her face. "He always does this?"

"Garrett?"

"Bobby. He does?"

"Of course. Don't you see that? He's always been like this, ever since you've known him."

"He has?"

"You mean you didn't realize?" Her mother paused, suspended, with the paper towel in her hand. "It's the same thing with your dad."

"I don't want to talk about Dad."

Her mother put the towel in the trash under the sink, then moved to the table. "Come. Sit next to me." Once they sat, she began. "You still believe what you do about your father."

"Mom—"

She put up her hand. "Listen to me, please. You've believed this one thing all your life. That he's going to come home to you, and everything will be okay. No matter what the actual truth is, you believe it. Nobody can change your mind. It's stuck."

"Mom."

"You've got this idea in your head and the facts don't matter. You've been doing the same thing with Bobby. You don't like the facts. But it's time you saw the truth."

"There's nothing wrong with Dad!"

"But there is, and Bobby's no different either, than the way he's always been. You just don't want to see it. I love Bobby like I love your father, but I know the way it is. I just never understood before why you didn't. You are always so surprised by both of them, each time they do it. But I guess we can tell ourselves powerful lies, especially about the people we love. Maybe that's why you were always so mad at me. But with Bobby, you act like this is the first time every time this happens, and you're actually surprised. And then you get mad at him like he's supposed to be different. But it's not going to change until Garrett dies."

Sarah played with the grain of the table wood with her right thumb.

"I'm not perfect," her mother told her. "But I'm not the big problem in this house, except that I'm still here. That makes me as much to blame as he is."

Her mother touched her hand. "I made my choice," she said. "I'm not sure I made the right one, but at least I made one. It was conscious." She leaned toward her daughter. "You have to make a choice too, one way or the other. Either way, you need some peace. Either you stay with him the way he is, or you go."

"No!" Sarah tugged her arm out from under her mother. "I didn't marry that. Not the way he is now. Weak. Submissive. He was different back then."

"But you're wrong. You did know. Remember, we talked about this. We talked about how Garrett mistreats him. You hated it."

"But I didn't know that—"

"Bobby doesn't stand up to him? Is that it? Sarah, look at me. Deep down, you knew. Did you ever see him stand up to him? Did you ever see him defend you? I know what Garrett says about you. I hear it. Chuck told me about Mastin too, the minute he walked in the door here. Does Bobby ever tell his father to go to hell?"

Sarah bent her head.

"This is what you've got," her mother told her softly but firmly. "This is what you signed up for. I know how much you loved him. He's just got this one flaw. This big one. Just like your father."

"But I don't want to be married to that!"

"But you are. Like I am. And you've got children. You make your choice, and then you live with it. Either way, it's yours. No one can help you. Not even your dad. And Sarah? It seems you've already made your choice. You're waiting with Bobby until Garrett's gone. Until he dies, and then you think you'll be free of him. Only thing is, you won't be. By then, Bobby will be the way he is forever."

Sarah whispered. "I don't want that."

"Maybe it's not so bad. You just might love him a little less."

"But I don't want to love him less!"

"What's wrong with that?"

"That's how you feel about Dad."

"Shh. Then are you prepared to leave him?"

"No. I want him to change."

"But how, when he's never done it?"

Esther Winston lowered her voice so the sound couldn't leave the kitchen. "You're going to need to figure out how to turn him into somebody you can love again. If you can't, you owe it to both of you to leave him. Because if you don't, your children will come to hate you."

"Mom!"

"Sarah, I know how that feels."

18.

As she pulled in, her headlights caught him. Bobby stood bundled on the ridge ten steps from the back door. Their house was dark inside. It was nearly midnight.

Sarah got out and walked to him. He faced away from her, staring down the steep hill and across the low, flat valley. Miles off, tiny lights flickered on the other side.

Their breaths froze in a night cold and sharp as a knife. She put her gloved hands inside her coat pockets and hunched her shoulders. He didn't move away from her but he didn't speak.

After a moment, she asked, "Is that Hank's place over there?" She pointed with her gloved hand across the valley.

"No." Bobby raised his own to show her. "He's that one, with the yellow light."

"How do you know that? He's five miles away."

He shrugged.

She breathed her breath into the cold night.

"I need to know something," she said eventually. "How can you tell Kevin to fight back like you did, when you won't defend yourself or this family?"

He jerked back. She had never spoken to him like that.

"I'm sorry," she said evenly. "But I can't do this anymore. I can't stand by and let it happen, and then have you tell me it's not going to change. It takes too much out of me, Bobby."

"So what are you saying?"

She turned toward him. "You deserve his love. Not his hate. But you don't ever get mad enough to change things. I've been driving around for hours, trying to figure that out. Why do you need him so much? Is it because you think you can't read?"

He didn't answer. When he finally spoke, his voice was dull and resigned. "I don't get to have what other people have, Sarah. Don't you know that by now? I don't get to have a dad who's proud of me. I'm stupid, and he knows it. He's seen my report cards. You know he used to get so mad at me he wouldn't sign them?" Bobby laughed to himself. "It sure was different with my brother. We used to ride around in that truck with Garrett J's report cards in the glove compartment. Dad would haul them out all the time and show them to anybody he could. They used to fall out on me when the damn thing opened up."

Bobby took a deep breath. His air froze as it twirled in the void between them. "Nothing can change until he's gone."

She rushed in. "Can you still take Mack's offer? I did the math at my mom's tonight. Even if he found out and kicked us off, five hundred acres, if it's yours outright, is about the same as your fifty percent. You get half now, don't you, on all this twelve hundred?"

He shook his head. "We'd have a mortgage."

"But it wouldn't be that much. We'd only need a little house."

"It's not the house. It's the land. We'd be paying for the land. You know how much the debt service would be on that five hundred?"

"Mack said he would stake you."

"For a while. We'd still have to buy it eventually. And we couldn't do that. Not without the income from here. We'd need that, in order to support ourselves."

Her voice fell. "No matter what I say, you have an answer."

"That's because I've thought about this for years. Every day."

"That's not what I mean. What I mean is you'll always have some reason why you can't change this. That's why you moved those house-plan books."

She stared off into the night, a few inches but a world apart from her husband, until she crossed her arms finally and cleared her throat to say, "Bobby." Her voice had become strong, and it carried in the still night. "I don't believe in ultimatums. We each get to decide. That's what I've been doing since I left my mother's. I only want to tell you the truth, so you can make your own decisions. I'm just about to ask you to move out."

GARRETT
Fall
1991

Five Years Later

1.

Garrett put his key in the back door and opened it. He came in, stomping his muddy boots on the square of linoleum that now covered the landing. Kevin and Daniel, both teenagers, were up the short flight of stairs, hunkered down behind two piles of their schoolbooks at the same old dinette table.

"Hey, Granddad," Kevin said absently as he came up.

"Hey boys." Garrett passed them and continued down the hall. "Where's your mother?"

He found her in the next bedroom, folding laundry. He knew she heard him, but she didn't look up. "Where's Bobby?"

Sarah shrugged.

"When did he leave?"

She picked up an undershirt and spread it on the bed. "I don't know. He was already gone when I got home."

"He was supposed to stay here for DB Grain. Have they been here?"

She shrugged again, and he leaned out the doorway. "Hey boys! Has DB Grain been here?"

"No, Granddad," Daniel said.

Garrett walked back toward the messy kitchen. "Jesus Christ!" he yelled at her through the wall. "Don't you ever clean up?"

He went around the boys to the sink, then looked out the window and stopped dead. "What the hell. Did your father plant winter wheat down there? When he got done harvesting those beans this morning, did he plant wheat? I see the planter."

"I think so," Daniel said.

177

"I didn't tell him to do that."

Garrett heard the back door open. He spoke without turning around. "What the hell do you think you're doing? You planted winter wheat down there. I didn't tell you to do that. Now we can't plant corn. It'll be too late next spring once we harvest it. That field's not gonna be good for anything but beans."

The boots stopped at the top of the stairs. "I know that," Bobby said, his voice calm. "I don't think we ought to plant much corn next year. We ought to be planting beans. Not just us, but everybody."

"Oh, you do, do you?" Garrett stood by the sink with Bobby on the other side of the table, near the back door. The two boys sat round-eyed between them, watching the tennis match.

"You know how many acres we've got right now, planted in corn, in this county?" Bobby said. "Sixty thousand. It was forty last year."

"It rained, remember?"

"That's my whole point. We've got so much corn planted right now the price ought to be zero. The only reason it's not is the drought. It knocked back the yield. If we plant all that corn next year and the weather's good, we're all gonna be screwed. Every one of us."

Garrett snorted. "Where'd you get that piece of information?"

"I ran the numbers last night."

"Don't kid me. You got it at Pam's."

"The sandwich place?"

"Standing around with all your buddies." Garrett threw both his hands in the air. "Oooh," he squealed, shaking them. "Let's all stay away from corn now! The bottom's gonna fall out. Ha! You're all a bunch of women. You know what I'm gonna do? I'm gonna plant corn. Every field I've got, except for that one you see out there, because you've already planted it with winter wheat. Goddamn you, Bobby."

Bobby spoke again, still as calm. "Why are you gonna plant corn? You're gonna lose money."

"Because all of you idiots are planting beans! You're too stupid and scared to think for yourselves. This whole county's gonna be swimming in beans. I'm gonna make a killing. But don't plant any more wheat!"

Bobby sighed. "I can hear you, Dad. You don't have to yell."

Garrett hovered over the table, just above Daniel's head. "Then let me be real clear. No. More. Wheat. Now what's the story with DB Grain? Did you call them?"

"We're gonna lose money if we sell the crop now. We've got the bin space. We might as well wait. Why not sell it after the first of the year?"

"This is the best price it's been in three years."

"Yeah, but the price now, in October, is always the worst. It's only gonna go up. And we've still got plenty of cash. I asked at the bank. Mickey says we're fine."

"You talked to Mickey Shaw?"

"Yeah. Why?"

"That's my account. You don't talk to him about my business unless I'm there."

"My name's on that account too."

"It's my money. I don't care what the account says. I want you to call DB Grain."

"We could be at two forty by April. I read it. You know how much of a difference that is, versus what the price is right now? That's eight percent. That's twenty-five thousand."

Garrett laughed. "You read it. That's a laugh. Daniel," he said to the head below him. "You're a smart boy. I bet you keep up with the stock market. How's it doing?"

"Uh … good, I guess."

"Do you know how good? The S&P's up eighteen percent. Kevin."

"Yessir?" The boy stared up at him from the across the table.

"Answer me this. If I can get eighteen percent putting my money in the stock market, then why would I take eight percent to keep it out? You just heard your father. He wants me to hold onto my money and let it sit there, and then sell it in six months for eight percent. You boys think that's a good idea?"

Kevin blinked.

"Of course not. Bobby, these boys already are smarter than you are." Garrett lifted his head. "Hey, Sister!"

There was no answer from the other room.

"Sister! I want you to come and hear this."

Sarah finally answered through the hollow wall. "Garrett, I can hear you just fine."

2.

The next day, Garrett came out of his eye doctor's office in one of the old wooden two-story buildings that ringed the courthouse square. He walked slowly toward his truck under the warping tin overhang, watching his feet on the cracked pavement of the crumbling sidewalk. He curved his back to stare at the ground and avoid tripping.

"Hello! Mr. McAllister!"

Garrett turned to see a man wearing a business suit behind him hurrying to catch up. He was waving. "Mr. McAllister, that is you! I wasn't sure. It's good to see you again." He put out his hand.

When Garrett didn't answer, the man said, "I'm Kenny Dermott. Dottie's son. I'm Lester's brother. I was a year behind Bobby in school."

Garrett took the hand. "Oh, yes. Where are you now? You went off someplace."

"Chicago. I came down yesterday because my mother had a stroke."

"I'm sorry."

They started walking west together toward the bank. "I was just in the Dairy Queen," Dermott said as they passed empty storefronts. "There's nothing left. It's the only thing open. Even Cotter's is closed. That's where my mom used to get all her furniture."

"So what do you do in Chicago?" Garrett tried not to watch his feet.

"Public relations," Dermott said.

"For who?"

"For myself. I just bought the company."

Garrett glanced way up to the taller man's face. "How many people you got?"

"Twenty-three, as of Friday. It was payday." The man laughed.

"You got a lot of business?"

"We do all right. Hey, I want to see Bobby while I'm here. Is he still up at your place?"

Garrett stopped.

"What is it?" the man asked. "Is Bobby okay?"

Garrett's smile had gone. "Of course he's there. Where else would he be?"

"I'm sorry?"

"Bobby's a fool. He doesn't do a damn thing. All he does is come up with these hare-brained ideas all the time. It's all I can do just to get him to harvest my crop. I'm seventy-nine years old. Why do you think I'm still working all the time?"

Dermott stared down at him, dumbstruck.

"You know what he did to me last week? He built me a corn stove out in the machine shop. It burns corn, instead of butane. He told me it was gonna save me money. Stupidest damn thing I ever heard, burning your own corn."

"But is it going to save you money?"

"You don't burn your own corn! You sell it."

"But is it chea—"

"He was just messing around! He's a loser. Always has been."

"But my brother says he's doing well."

"That's me. He works for me. Why does everyone keep making that mistake? I'm the one who's got fourteen hundred acres now."

"But Lester says—"

"He doesn't even own his own house! You know that little box up there? He wouldn't even have that if it weren't for me. I don't charge him rent. They've been there for twenty years and he's never paid me a dime. What kind of a man does that? He's pushing forty. Where's his self-respect?"

Dermott didn't answer.

"You know what I mean?" Garrett looked up expectantly.

Dermott put his hand out. "It's been nice talking to you, sir."

"I mean seriously. Is that someone you'd want working for you?"

"I have to go."

"Why can't I have a son like you?"

3.

The next day, the Cardinals played the Vikings at noon in Minnesota. The football game screamed from the new color television in the old house. Garrett's same old armchair faced it, but it was empty. There was no one in the kitchen, either. It was Sunday, and Cora had gone to church.

The toilet flushed in the bathroom on the far side of the dining room.

The back door in the kitchen opened and heavy boots hit the floor. A moment later, Bobby walked through the doorway into the dining room. He was filthy, and his coarse brown hair was wet and stringy under his green John Deere cap.

"Tupa was a punter back at Ohio State," the television announcer said. "He only played quarterback one year."

Bobby walked into the den, toward his father's chair. Garrett shuffled out of the bathroom behind him, clutching his newspaper. "What do you want?"

Bobby turned. "God that's loud. Is Mom here?"

"No. What are you doing here?"

Bobby picked up the remote and switched off the TV.

"Hey! I was watching that."

Bobby reached into his pocket and pulled out a piece of paper. "I'm gonna start paying you rent. Today." He held it out.

Garrett didn't move. "What's that?"

"A check. For a hundred and twenty-five bucks. I figure that's right. If it's not, just tell me. I'll pay whatever it is."

Garrett took the check and looked at it.

"I'm paying you that every month."

"Why?"

"Isn't that what you want?"

Garrett raised his eyes. "Don't you talk to me like that."

"Aren't you happy? It's another hundred and twenty-five dollars a month."

"What's wrong with you?"

"Isn't that what you want?"

"I want you to get out of here and get back to work!"

But Bobby didn't move. "Before I go, we need to get one more thing straight. I was supposed to get that house for free, remember? You said that way back when we started. That's how come I only got fifty percent. So if I'm gonna be paying you rent now, we need to up it to sixty, starting immediately. That's what it should have been, anyway, the last ten years."

"You're out of your mind."

"I'm nothing but a tenant, right? The tenant gets sixty."

"You're nothing but a hired hand! I gave you that house. It's charity! I should be paying you by the hour. You don't even deserve fifty percent."

They faced each other, the taller man staring down the older one without flinching. "I can get ten of you down at the square. They line up. You ought to be working for minimum wage."

"You don't mean that." Bobby was all icy stare, daring him.

"It's a gift! You're not worth crap. All you do is dig up fields and run around. You're unemployable. And now you come in here and demand sixty percent. Who do you think you are, telling me what I have to pay you? I've been supporting you the last forty years!"

"You don't support me!"

"I support your whole family. You wouldn't even have that house if it weren't for me!" Garrett tapped his own chest with two of his fingers. "I'm the reason you can afford that wife of yours and those kids. Me! I'm the provider. I make the decisions."

"No you don't!" Bobby took a step toward him. "You just think you do because I let you." Bobby tapped his own chest. "Open your eyes, Dad. Who do you think put in those new bins?"

"We didn't need them!"

"I did! And who got the yield up, so we needed them? Me! And who did all the tile? Huh? And who put down all that new culvert?"

"It was a waste!"

Bobby took another step and leaned forward. The two men stood toe-to-toe. "We're getting a hundred and forty bushels an acre now! Did you ever get that? You used to be glad to get eighty, remember? You'd never even dreamed about a number like that. I spent five years doing that. Five years!"

Bobby towered over him. "Every winter. I dug up every inch of that ground. Myself, with my two hands. And I had to pay for it too. You didn't pay any of it. And it wasn't even my land! But you sure got the benefit of it, didn't you? And you still do. Those checks just keep rolling in."

Bobby waved his hand in the air. "Lookee here, Cora! Here's another check from DB Grain!" He looked down at his father. "So let's go back over this. I didn't hear you right. That part about being the provider. Who did you say it was? Me?"

"You don't provide for me!"

"Who's watching the goddamn TV?"

Garrett's right hand came up fast and slapped him hard. Bobby's head jerked back but he didn't grab his jaw.

"You don't do shit, Dad. You never have."

Garrett's hand swung up again and slapped him hard once more.

Bobby didn't move. He didn't touch his own face. "Is that the best you've got?"

Garrett's whole fist came up then, but Bobby caught it. His reflexes were so fast he caught the wrist in mid-air. Garrett struggled but Bobby held on like a father clutching a squirming toddler. "Don't you ever do that to me again. And don't screw with me, old man. I'll bury you."

"Get out! Get out of my house and don't come back!"

Bobby let go. "I'm going. I don't need this any more."

"You get out of here! All of you! As soon as you get done with the harvest. I want you out of that house!" But Garrett saw nothing but Bobby's back, walking away from him through the dining room. "I want you gone! I'll get somebody else!"

Bobby's boots came down on the kitchen floor.

"Next month! You hear me? I'll get somebody good!"

The back door opened.

"You can starve for all I care! You and your whole family."

The door slammed shut.

4.

The next morning, Garrett drove to a vast field he had south of town.

One of his huge combines was already running, tearing dry stalks of corn that fell like timber between the long, sharp, shiny metal cones on the front. They looked like the claw of a giant hawk, stretching, swooping down to snatch a mouse.

One of his big grain trucks was parked at the edge of the field and there was an enormous cart in the center, but no one was in either one. The only human being in the field was driving the churning combine.

Garrett honked. The man nodded and pulled hard on the brake. He put both hands on the brake stalk sticking up next to him in the glass cab and jerked it up fast.

The grinding couldn't stop. It only slowed. The man kept pulling, straining hard. It took another ten seconds for the huge machine to thump to a squealing halt.

"Harold!" Garrett yelled through the open window of his truck.

The man opened the door of the cab and stepped out onto the metal platform high above the wheels. "Yessir?" he shouted, standing ten feet off the cornfield.

"Where's Bobby?" Garrett called up.

"I don't know, Mr. McAllister. He never showed up."

"Did you call him at home?"

"Yeah, but there was no one there. So I've been trying to do this all by myself. It's pretty tough with only me, though. Are you gonna stick around?"

"Where's Larry and Vern?"

"Up at the farm."

Garrett started to pull his head back inside his pickup.

Harold lifted one arm. "Wait! What do you want me to do? This grain. That cart's about full. Where do you want me to put the rest of it?"

"Take it up to the bin. Where else are you gonna put it?"

"But all the bins are full."

"We only just got started. They won't be full for another month."

"But they are. This is the most corn we've ever had. And Bobby's says it's gonna rain. You don't want it all to get wet because we have to leave it out here, do you?"

5.

Garrett barreled down the steep hill toward the tiny farm-house. Two of his other men were working a field at the bottom, another minute past the cement bridge that spanned the wide drainage ditch. When Garrett spotted them, they were far-off specks.

He turned hard and careened into the gravel farmyard as he always did, but this time his vehicle was the only one. Through the yellow dust, Garrett could see the place was deserted. Bobby's truck was missing, and so was Sarah's car.

As he climbed out, he saw that the huge sliding door of the machine shop had been pulled closed, and padlocked. Across the patchy grass, the barn door was locked too. All the farm equipment that was always parked outside in the open was gone. There were tracks showing that it had been hauled inside.

Garrett went to the barn and peeked in through the door crack. Everything had been parked in the shade. Even his power-boat was there, in the corner, resting safely on its trailer.

He turned toward the house. The dog's pen was empty. He looked around. The black bitch was gone.

He unlocked the back door and went up to the kitchen. The counters had been scrubbed clean. Washed dinner dishes rested neatly in the drain board. He opened it, but the old Frigidaire was bare.

Garrett went down the short hall. On every bed, clean sheets had been folded and stacked. There were no clothes in the closets that yawned open, and there was nothing anywhere in the rooms. All that was left was his old furniture, and even that had been wiped clean.

In the small front room, the old black and white television had been put back in its place. The color set and the new corner cabinet had been moved out.

He went down the stairs. In the basement, there was only one light on, in the game room behind the washer dryer, whose metal lids gaped open. The insides of both machines were empty and clean.

Garrett followed the light back behind the machines and through the doorway. It was the fluorescent light above the pool table, and it flickered. Under the winking, something glinted on the old green felt.

He looked at them, and then he started counting. Forty-one keys stretched the length of the table. Over the green, they made one long, straight row. Big keys and little ones, and some on rings but each alone. They had been separated and laid out singly, every one of them the same, a precise one inch apart. He was seeing a perfect marching five-foot parade.

All of them turned the same way—flat sides toward the wall and the jagged edges facing like teeth toward his neck. They were arranged in logical order too, starting with the house keys, nearest him. Garrett opened his palm and looked at his own copy of the same one. The outbuilding keys followed them, including the one to the padlock on the shop, and then the twenty-three keys to all the vehicles. Bobby had left him every one.

Garrett looked up, to the ledges that lined the upper walls near the ceiling. The woman's stupid, childish dolls were gone.

6.

That same afternoon, Garrett sat down in the wingchair facing the old, ornate, carved wood desk from the 1860s. Beyond it, through the tall wide antique window, he could see across the street to the courthouse.

"Thanks for meeting with me on such short notice." He bent to place his papers next to him on the floor. As he did, a much younger man pulled out the leather desk chair and tugged gently on the crease of his navy blue trousers. Once he sat, the man stretched his white dress shirtsleeves on the bare desktop.

"Of course. What can I do for you, Mr. McAllister?"

Above Garrett's small white head three oil portraits of Mickey Shaw's ancestors judged them both. All three had been presidents of the bank that ruled the county.

Garrett lifted his chin. "Mickey, I'm glad you were here, because I wanted to tell you this myself, in person." He hesitated, saying the words with a slight reluctance. "I thought you deserved that. There's no easy way for me to say this."

Thirty-two year old Shaw clasped his own hands. He was paying close attention. Garrett saw this and went on, his old man's voice beginning to quaver. "I've been with your bank now for what? Fifty years? Even before I had the farm, I had all the dealership accounts with you, or with your grandfather, I should say. Your family's always had every one of my accounts. The operating account, the capital account, everything. I've got all my loans with you too. For all the land, and the equipment."

He faked a laugh. "Hell, if I went under, you'd get everything." He looked at Shaw, seeing the tension. "So, what would you say? I move about four hundred thousand through here every year. Isn't that right?"

Shaw cleared his throat. "That's right, I guess. I don't have your account in front of me."

"And I pay what? About fifty thousand in interest to you every year?"

The man nodded.

"And what kind of assets do you get if I go under? About four million altogether, right?" Garrett shook his head. He seemed sad about it. "That's what makes all this so damn hard. I'm sorry to have to say this, but I'm gonna have to move it. All. Right away. I don't think I have a choice."

Garrett waited, but Shaw didn't speak.

"That's why I wanted to come in. I needed to tell you in person, out of respect. I'm gonna have to move it all to Union Mercantile. It's nothing personal. I just don't see any other way."

Shaw was at a loss. "If there's anything we can do. You know, to make you change your mind. I don't mean to pry, but if there's something we're not doing …"

"Oh no. You've always been very solicitous."

"Are they giving you a better rate?"

"No."

"Does somebody in your family work there now?"

Garrett shook his head.

Shaw stared. "Then I don't get it."

Garrett turned to check that the door was closed, then leaned forward in the high wingchair. "Union Mercantile's in Ramsey," he stage-whispered.

Shaw waited. "And?"

"That's fifteen miles away."

"I'm sorry. I still don't get it."

"I need to get my money out of town. And I'm gonna have to put it all in my name." Garrett sat back, watching Shaw process.

"You mean, without Bobby? Is Bobby all right? Is there something wrong?"

Garrett took a loud deep breath and sighed as he let it out. "Bobby's my son, and I love him. He's my own flesh and blood. You know I wouldn't ever say anything against him. Not to you, not to anybody else."

Shaw leaned toward Garrett across his desk. His shoulders crawled up next to his ears.

"But there's something going on," Garrett said quietly. "I don't know. But it's something. We used to talk about everything. And I used to know where every cent was. But not now. We're not talking, and he's spending money on I don't know what."

Shaw cast a glance at his office door himself. "What do you mean specifically?"

"There's money going out of the operating account. I don't know where it is."

Shaw considered it. "Have you bought any new equipment lately? Or any new land?"

"No, that's just it. There's nothing I know of. The money's just gone."

"How much?"

"I don't know, exactly. That's part of the problem. I'm sure there's a good reason."

"Have you talked to Bobby?"

"Yeah, but I'm not getting a straight answer."

"What does he say?"

"He won't talk. He walked out on me yesterday. I brought it up and he stormed out."

Shaw's eyes strayed to the portraits above Garrett's head, then he checked the fat Windsor knot bulked under his chin. "Does he owe anybody any money?"

"I don't think so," Garrett said, watching him think.

"He doesn't gamble. I've never heard that. He doesn't play cards. No drug problem?"

"No, hell no." Garrett paused. "The only thing I know of is the fighting between him and his wife."

"Sarah? What are they fighting about?"

"I don't know. They stop whenever I get there, but I can hear it when I come in." Garrett monitored Shaw's young face.

"You know," the banker said finally.

"What?"

"Well. If they're fighting, like you say." Shaw hesitated. "I hate to say this."

"Tell me. I can take it."

"Do you think there might be some other woman?"

"What?" Garrett reared back. "Bobby would never do that!"

"I'm sorry. I didn't mean anything."

"How can you say that?"

"I'm sorry." Mickey held both hands out to calm Garrett. "But you know what my dad used to say? That when a man started spending money for no good reason, there's usually some gal. Somebody that maybe Sarah's found out about. Like maybe he's paying for her, or buying her stuff."

"That's ridiculous!" Garrett bellowed. "My Bobby loves that girl. They've been together since they were kids. Hell, I don't think he's ever even been with anyone else. Twenty years."

He stopped, then swung his small white head to look past Shaw out the tall window.

After a moment, Garrett slumped his shoulders and sank back in his chair with a breathy sign. "I know he loves her, but

I'm with you, now that you say it. I'm trying, but I can't think of anything else."

"I'm so sorry," Shaw told him.

"Damn. It all fits. I just have to hope it blows over. But I've still got to get my money out of here, so he can't get it. At least not until he comes back down to earth."

"You mean it's all joint?"

"Yeah, I've got it in both of our names. Everything. All the accounts."

"So he can take it out whenever he wants," Shaw said. "All of it, any time. And spend it on anything he wants. Wow. Then I have to say you're right. I'd do the same thing if I were you. It's just too risky." Shaw glanced up again at the portraits on the wall.

"It jeopardizes the whole family," Garrett said as he watched him. "Course, Mickey, if you looked at the bank statements, you'd think they were fine. He's being real careful. It's something only I could see. Nobody at the bank would ever see it."

"I appreciate your telling me this. I know it's not easy," Shaw said, already having moved on. "But this affects us too, here at the bank. So I'd like to work with you on it. I mean, I hope we're both wrong. I really do. But no matter what it is, it's a good idea to close those accounts. At least right now, until we know more about what's going on."

Garrett sighed again, audibly. "That's why I'm here."

Shaw shot his cuffs as he thought, fidgeting. "But why do you have to go all the way to Ramsey? Why don't you just keep them here and change the names? Open up new accounts? That way we could keep the money. I mean we could keep it close by."

"Wouldn't Bobby find out?"

"Who's going to tell him? I trust you, Mr. McAllister. I know you're doing this for his own good. Plus it helps me. We can't be giving money to people who aren't using it wisely. And his name's on all your loans. If the money's in your name, the loans aren't in jeopardy."

"You wouldn't tell him where the money was?"

Shaw shook his head heartily. "He'll end up thanking us both later on. You're going to be taking good care of the farm, right? You'll keep spending the money as you always have, to improve the asset."

"I sure will."

"Then really, you're just taking care of it until he comes around."

Garrett brightened. "Okay. So how do we handle this?"

"You simply close the accounts. Since they're in both your names, you have the right to close them whenever you want to. So you do that. Then you open up as many new accounts in your own name as you want."

"But what about the credit line and the notes and all that?"

"Let's start with the line. What's the balance?"

"Zero, right now."

"Then that's easy. The line expires when you close the account."

"So what if Bobby tries to borrow money?"

"He won't be able to."

"You mean he can't get any more money from you?"

"No." Shaw continued. "But the notes on the loans are more complicated. I would have to get my Board's approval to take Bobby's name off. It's our policy. We like to see both generations on the debt. So you're both responsible for paying it back. Bobby's net worth—"

"He's not worth anything."

"Huh. I didn't think that was true. But anyway, he backs up the notes just like you do. So I may not be able to get his name removed. But now that I think about it, that's not bad, from your perspective. Or the bank's. Having Bobby's assets securing the loans on your farm."

"I feel bad doing that." Garrett made a face. "The debt's over a million dollars."

"You shouldn't feel bad. You're not the one with the girl-friend. And it's not like the collateral's any different. It's still the same land."

Garrett suddenly took in his breath.

"What?" Shaw asked him.

"The land," Garrett said. "I didn't think about that. Don't I have to change the title too? Until this blows over? We own some of that land together. Two hundred acres."

"How is it titled?"

"Joint tenancy. It all goes to him if I die, right?"

Shaw nodded.

"And it's worth a lot," Garrett said. "At least fifteen hundred an acre. If I died, he'd get land worth more than three hundred thousand. There wouldn't be anything to stop him from giving it straight to her. This woman. Or he could sell it. And it's right in the middle of my land. We changed the title to two hundred prime acres."

Shaw was thinking.

"Mickey," Garrett said. "Don't you need to approve a change of title? The land's collateral for the loans, so you need to ap-prove it, right?"

The banker nodded. "But the land's the same land, whether it's in your name or both of yours. It doesn't change what it's worth to the bank, since you're still going to be on the debt."

"So I can do it?"

"Yeah," Shaw said. "The bank's okay. Consider this your au-thorization. But how are you going to do it? You need both of you, to sign the papers. Either that or you have to have his written consent."

"I've got that. I've got his Power of Attorney right here." Garrett pointed down to the papers next to him on the floor. "I just got it out of the safety deposit box."

"Will that work?"

"It ought to. It gives me the right to do anything I want. You know, to protect his interests. And isn't that what I'm doing?" Garrett raised his eyebrows.

"I guess so," Shaw said.

"So I'm okay. All I have to do is get a lawyer to do the paperwork."

Shaw nodded. "I guess that's right."

Garrett asked Mickey Shaw one last question as he stood and shook the younger man's hand. "What happens if Bobby tries to cash a check?"

"He won't be able to. If he comes in, I'll tell him you closed all the accounts. Don't worry. I won't tell him why. I'll just tell him he's got to talk to you."

7.

Garrett drove back to the farm. Larry and Vern were working now in a field closer to the cement bridge, but Garrett didn't join them.

Garrett walked into the house and dialed the wall phone. "Harvey Biggerstaff," he said, then waited. "Harvey. Garrett McAllister. I'm fine. Yeah. Listen, did my son call you? He did? So you're coming today? Good. Listen, we've been so busy out here I haven't been able to go over the sums. Can you tell me what the deal is on this?

"Is that your base? And what'd he say about the bushels? How much have we got? Sixty-five thousand. You sure? Damn, that's good. How much is that altogether? Before dockage and your trucking expense. What's that trucking gonna be? Ten cents? You're killing me! It never used to be that much. Yeah I know I'm an old guy. So what's the bottom line on the corn? Two thirty-two a bushel. I'll take it. Yeah, scale grade's fine.

"Now what about the beans? How much you gonna pick up? Twenty thousand. That much? And what's the price on that? Five forty-eight. That's good. Listen Harvey, I want you to do something for me. I want you to go ahead and make those two checks out to me. Yeah. Just my name. Leave Bobby off.

"Why? Because I'm gonna have to sign them over for some new equipment and Bobby's out of town for a little while. Yeah, and the dealership's gonna want those checks. You can? Great. Oh, and Harvey? Can you send them to my house? Not here to the farm. I need to get them deposited right away.

"Can you tell me what those totals are again?" Garrett closed his eyes to memorize. "One hundred fifty thousand eight hundred dollars on the corn. Yeah, I got that. And one hundred nine thousand six hundred on the beans."

He hung up the phone, whistling, and started opening drawers. When he found a telephone book, he pulled it out and plopped it on the counter, then flipped to the yellow pages in the rear. He didn't slow down until he got to the listings for "Attorneys" and began reading the big, bold-print ads that covered every page.

8.

Garrett walked by the old yellow brick building twice before he saw the street number high on the glass transom, under the awning. Through the small glass hole that was eye-level in the door, he saw a steep staircase to the second floor. The grayish carpet was worn and black shoe marks scuffed the walls. He looked up and down Main Street, then stepped up to push the button on the intercom. A moment later it buzzed back.

He had only gotten to the third step when a loud voice asked if he needed help. "No. I'm just old and forgetful," Garrett said as he climbed, puffing his cheeks in and out. "You're Neil Spencer, I take it?"

"That's right." The man smiled widely at him from above. "And you don't have to be old to be forgetful. I do it all the time."

They shook hands and Garrett let Spencer guide him into a small, cramped, open room ringed with file cabinets and doorways to tiny offices he could partially see. On top of the cabinets, books and files were stacked two feet high, along with staplers and computer disks and boxes of paper. Some of the stacks were tipping, and some of the papers lay on the floor. In the middle of it all, a young woman was typing. She had a telephone headset hooked to her ear. Over the drumming sound of her fingers, a man was shouting at somebody in one of the tiny back rooms.

Spencer led the way to a miniscule office with a single window facing a redbrick wall. An old metal desk and its scratched chair were pushed up against one side. One other small chair sat in a corner across the five feet of open middle space.

He apologized for the mess and invited Garrett to have a seat.

"Thank you for seeing me on such short notice," Garrett told him.

"Now, what can I do for you? Something about changing title to land?"

"You can do that, right?"

"Oh sure. Where is it? Here in Greene County?"

"No. I'm over in Jefferson County, next door."

"I've done it there too. Now why don't you tell me what you need."

Garrett had squeezed himself into the tight side chair. "It's hard to know where to begin. All I can think about is how pissed off my son is, at me. I don't blame him either. I'd be mad too, if I was him."

He tugged on his clean jacket. "See, I'm a farmer. I've got more than fourteen hundred acres, pretty much all over. You don't know me, do you?" He paused.

"No."

"And you don't know my son? Bobby McAllister?"

"No. I don't think so."

"I only ask because you look like you're about the same age. Anyway. About ten years ago, I was real sick. I had pneumonia. They put me in the hospital. The doctors didn't think I was gonna live. I didn't think I was either, for a while. I got worried about what Bobby was gonna do if I didn't make it. You know, he's on the farm with me. So he would have had to make all those payments on our loans. I remember we had a couple of big ones, and the annual payments were due pretty soon. I didn't want him to have to wait for probate. Those payments have to be made on time, you know. So I decided that I was gonna change title to some of my land. So Bobby could get to it, and sell it or do whatever he wanted. Right away, if I died. Not have to wait until probate closed."

"So you put it in his name?"

"No. I made it joint. In both our names. From mine to both of us."

"Did you change all of it?"

"No. Just two hundred acres. I wanted him to have enough to get by."

"And you never changed it back. Is that it?"

"No, I never did. I got better and I just forgot about it. And now my other kids are screaming."

"Why?"

"Well my will. It says that everything gets divided equally. You know, after my wife dies. But with Bobby having this property, that means he gets more. His whole share, plus that two hundred."

The lawyer was writing furiously, taking notes at his beat-up desk. "How did all this come up? I mean, why now?"

"About a month ago, my daughter asked me. We were talking about buying some property, and she remembered it, and she asked. Course, I couldn't lie. I had to tell the truth. That I'd forgotten it. Naturally, all hell broke loose. Now I get a call from at least one of them every day. And they're calling him too. Bobby. And every time they call him, he calls me, to get this thing fixed. So that's why I'm here. I should've done this a long time ago, but I didn't. And you know the other thing?"

"What's that?"

"What happens if I get hit by a truck or something, before this goes back? Bobby'd never hear the end of it. I'm getting so I'm afraid to walk down the street." Garrett smiled at him but the lawyer kept writing.

"I understand," Spencer said without turning.

"I need to get this done right away. Can you do it? Change it back?"

Spencer was thinking as he wrote. "Where's your son in all this?"

"He wants to get it done. He only did it in the first place because I asked him."

"So he doesn't want the extra land?"

"Oh no." Garrett shook his head. "He just wants what he's supposed to get. Same as the rest of them."

"But where is he, though? I mean physically. He's not here. You came by yourself."

"Oh. That. He and his wife are out of town. One of those surprise things, for an anniversary. He wouldn't tell us where they were going."

"He's not here?"

"I've got his Power of Attorney. That ought to do it. That's what he said."

"He told you to use his Power of Attorney?"

"Yeah, it was either that or cancel his trip, and he wasn't gonna do that. Not with that wife of his. I even forgot we had it. He had to remind me. You want to see it?"

"When's he coming back?"

"This weekend. At least, that's what he said. I know I'm really pushing it." Garrett smiled sheepishly. "I've only had it this way for ten years. But if it's not done by the time he gets back, he's gonna kill me."

"Bobby knew you were coming to see me?"

"Well, he knows I was gonna see a lawyer."

"So he wanted the two of you to use the same one?"

"Huh?"

"I'm only asking because of the ethics here. See, your interests aren't the same. You and your son's. Because you're gaining property from him, and he's losing it. You're really adverse, if you think about it. So if he were here, I'd have to suggest that maybe he ought to have his own lawyer, to represent him."

"Oh no. That's the last thing we want to do. We don't need two lawyers. No. Bobby wants me to get this thing done. And he for sure isn't gonna want to pay for another lawyer, all on his own. I told him I'd pay for it. It's the least I can do. I got him into this."

"So he consents to this?"

"I told you that."

Spencer had turned to face him. "Please don't get irritated. I'm just trying to understand. You're sure he's out of town?"

Garrett looked full on at the lawyer. "I swear to God I have no idea where he is."

Spencer nodded. "You know, I completely believe you."

He took the document Garrett handed him. "Why don't you give me a minute to read this. Hmm. Okay ... General Power of Attorney. Collect money. Commence actions ... vote ... buy land. Here. Here it is." Spencer raised his voice and read out loud. "'Execute and cause to be recorded any and all deeds or other documents that may be necessary with respect to any transactions involving any property.'" He turned to the next page. "And here. 'Make, sign, acknowledge, and deliver any contract, deed, or other document relating to real estate or personal property.' Yeah. This will cover it."

"So we can do it?"

"I think so. Let me finish." Spencer flipped to the last page. "Did you see this? You have the general power to perform any other acts of any nature whatsoever that ought to be done or in the opinion of my attorney ... "

He looked up. "That's you. Not me. You're acting as your son's attorney-in-fact here." He read on. "'... in the opinion of

206

my attorney ought to be done, in any circumstances as fully and effectively as I could do if acting personally.' Hmm. And it's durable. That's good."

"What's 'durable'?"

"It means this power doesn't terminate if your son becomes disabled for any reason. It says so right here, at the bottom. It has to be durable, in order to work in this state." He held the last page up to the florescent light. "This is the original."

"Yeah. I was there when he signed it. We did both at the same time."

"You have one too, that names him?"

"Yeah. You want to see mine?" Garrett handed him the other one.

Spencer read for a moment. "They're identical."

"Yeah. Sam Ross said they should be."

"Sam Ross? He did these?"

"That's his signature right there."

"I know Sam. He's a good lawyer. Why aren't you using him for this? Isn't he a lot closer to you over in Jefferson County?"

"He's too expensive. Plus he makes a mountain out of everything. I figured it'd be cheaper to have you do it."

"So how'd you find me?"

"The phone book."

Spencer nodded then tapped all the pages on his desk to straighten the corners. "May I keep these?"

"Sure. And I brought a copy of my will if you want, so you can see that equal distribution business."

"Thanks." Spencer took it from him. "I'll give them all back to you next time we meet. Now, let's talk about my fee to change the title."

9.

"Well, I did it," Spencer said the next day.

"Can I have it?"

"I think we need to talk a little first." The lawyer picked up some typed pages off his desk. Garrett could see the words "Warranty Deed" in bold print on the top of the first one.

"I had some follow-up questions for you." Spencer said as he held the papers. "I have to tell you. I'm having some trouble with this." The lawyer shifted in his chair.

"What trouble?"

Spencer took a deep breath. "After you left, I started thinking, and I realized I had quite a few problems with it, in fact."

"Like what? You said it was simple."

"Let's step back and look at it from the point of view of someone who's paranoid. You know, someone who thinks there's a bogeyman around every corner, like I do." Spencer smiled. "And let me apologize in advance. I simply want you to understand how this might look to someone who didn't know you. Someone who's looking at it from the outside.

"Let's say there's this elderly man, and he seeks out the services of a lawyer he's never met before. He got his name out of the phone book. And he comes in and he asks this lawyer to change the title to some land, over in another county. And it's not land he's got in his own name, but something he's got with his son. It's joint. And what this man wants to do is change title in a way that's detrimental to the son. Take the land away from him. And the son's not here to participate. Or give his consent."

208

"He consented."

Spencer spread out his hands. "On top of that, this man tells the lawyer he's got to get it done right away. Chop chop. Before the son gets home from wherever he's gone. Only the man says he doesn't know where that is. Now I'm sure, Mr. McAllister, that you can appreciate how all this might look to the objective observer. And that's totally apart from the Power of Attorney. Which is a whole other problem."

"What?"

"Oh, the document lets you do it. It's legal. But the whole thing looks funny to me. That Power of Attorney's not specific to this transaction. It's a general Power of Attorney that applies to everything. And it's not just that. It was drawn up a couple of years ago, so it obviously wasn't done for the purpose of this transaction."

"So what are you saying? That you won't do it?"

"I'm just telling you how it might look to someone who didn't know you."

They stared at each other.

"So I got to thinking about our conversation yesterday, and I realized that I probably should have gone over something with you that I didn't."

"What's that?"

"Fiduciary duty. See, by virtue of that Power of Attorney, which names you as his attorney-in-fact, your son has made you his fiduciary. That means you have a duty to act in his best interest when you use it. Whenever you do anything in his name. You can't be acting for yourself, or taking advantage of him. Everything you do has to be for his own good."

"Is there a reason for this speech?"

"I just want to tell you that somebody might say you weren't acting in your son's best interest here, given the circumstances, particularly since he's not here to tell us precisely what he wants."

"So what's your point?"

"I'm obviously not doing this very well. What I'm saying is that I need for you to explain to me better what's going on."

Garrett sat back at last, exhaling. "I told you all that yesterday."

"Well, that's the problem." Spencer shook his head. "I'm sorry, Mr. McAllister, but it doesn't make any sense. I do a lot of real estate work, so I know what that land's worth. It's got to be worth more than a quarter million. I'm having trouble understanding how losing half of that is in your son's best interest, particularly when he's not getting any consideration. You're not paying him, are you? I didn't think so. What do I say when somebody tells me that I helped take a hundred and twenty-five thousand dollars away from your son, when he's supposed to be my client too? That's why I need your help here."

He stopped. There was a pause that filled the room, but Garrett didn't answer. Spencer said, leaning forward, "That's why I need for you to tell me the truth."

He paused again, but Garrett didn't open his mouth. "I've got another problem. What you said doesn't make logical sense. No offense. You told me you changed the title in the first place so Bobby could sell the land if he needed to, if you died while you were in the hospital. But you didn't have to change the title to do that. You could have just transferred some money, or made the payments. You weren't unconscious, and either one of those things would have been free. As it is, you had to pay all kinds of taxes and fees in order to get it recorded as joint. You even had to pay Sam Ross.

"I've got another problem. You seem like a smart guy to me. Real smart. It's just not plausible that you're gonna forget this for ten years. I don't care how sick you were, at the beginning there." Spencer was shaking his head. "I've got to tell you, this whole thing doesn't add up. With all due respect, sir, the truth is ... I don't believe it."

The two men eyed each other.

Spencer said, "I'm not here to play any games with you, sir. So I'm just going to tell you what I think. I'll just say it, and we'll see where we go from there. I think you and your son own that land together. Really own it. Not just as a favor to you, but because it's his too. And I think you want to put it in your name. I don't think he knows about it. I don't think he knows anything at all.

"Now I could tell you that I won't do this. Shake your hand and show you the door. But I realized yesterday that I didn't know why. I don't know why you're doing this. And there could be a perfectly good explanation. I just don't know what it is. So that's why I did the Deed for you. I wanted to have it here, so we could talk about it. Maybe you'd tell me the truth."

Spencer waited. Garrett didn't answer.

"I know it's difficult," the lawyer said. "There's got to be a good reason why you don't want me to know. Family business, or something secret. But I just can't give you this. So you're not doing yourself any favors by sitting there."

Garrett looked at him for a long moment, then dropped his eyes. He began to shake his head, then sighed deeply. "He's got a woman."

"A woman."

"He's screwing somebody and it's not his wife. And if anything happens to me, he's gonna get that land. And if she's who I think, she'll make sure she gets it right away. And my grandsons and their mother will all get screwed. That land's been mine for thirty-two years. I bought it when I started farming. It belongs to those boys. My boys. I love them. Not to some cheap round-heel who blows him better than anybody else."

Spencer thought about it. "But what does changing the title do? It just gives it to you. It doesn't get it to the boys."

"I'm gonna leave it to them directly."

"You're going to change your will?"

"Yeah. I have to."

Spencer nodded. "So that's why you're not using Sam."

"What am I gonna say to him? Bobby's screwing some woman in town? I can't do that. You know how long they've known each other?" Garrett shrugged and tried to smile. "I'm sorry, Neil. I didn't mean to lie to you. I just didn't want to tell you."

Garrett watched him. Spencer was staring, his face impassive. They looked at each other across the narrow room.

Then the lawyer smiled. "You know, you're really good at this," the man said. "You may even be better than me."

"What are you talking about?"

"But you need to be more consistent. You gave me your will, remember? Yesterday. Bobby's got a full share. Just like you said. You haven't cut him out of anything."

"I haven't done it yet."

Spencer shook his head. "Why would you be so anxious to change the title and not ask me to change your will at the same time? You've got fourteen hundred acres. A fifth of that is …" He looked up at the light. "Two hundred and eighty acres. That's more than he's got now. So if you're going to change the title, why aren't you changing the will? No. You're not stupid. Like I said, you're real smart. You wouldn't do that."

"So what are you saying?"

Spencer said it fast and hard. "What I'm saying is I don't believe you. I think this is all crap. Just like the other story you told me. I think you made the whole thing up."

Garrett stood as his chair clattered. "I won't sit here for this."

"Oh yes you will."

Garrett took a step toward the door.

"I wouldn't do that if I were you. Aren't you forgetting something?"

"What?"

"The Power of Attorney. The original. Who's got it?" Spencer smiled.

Garrett looked over at the man's desk.

"Oh, don't worry," Spencer said. "It's not here."

"You can't keep that!"

"Keep your voice down."

"That's my property!"

"No, actually, I don't think so. It belongs to Bobby. He signed it. And it seems to me that I ought to give it back to him. I'm his lawyer too, right? Isn't that what you said?"

"You can't do that!"

"Sure I can."

"I'll turn you in!"

"To the bar? And say what? That I wasn't really his lawyer? Because you were trying to screw him? Commit fraud? And I caught you? Is that what you're going to say? Think about it, Mr. McAllister. You sue me, or you file charges. Whatever it is. What are you going to say about why you came here?" Spencer still smiled, looking up. "No. I think you've got yourself a much bigger problem now than you did when you came in here."

"Screw you!"

"That's not nice. And it's sure not going to get your Power of Attorney back. So what's it going to be? Do you really want to walk out of here? Because if you do, feel free. I'll just return it to Bobby personally."

"What do you want?"

"Really, Mr. McAllister. I think you ought to sit down so we can discuss this as two rational men."

Garrett didn't move. "Tell me."

"Well, I think the first thing I want to do is call Bobby. You know. Like I said. I need to make sure this is all something he knows about."

"Bobby's not here."

"You know, I actually believe that part. That's the only thing I do believe. So, maybe I just leave him a message, telling him who I am and why I'm calling. And I wait for him to call me back."

"Cut the shit. What do you want?"

Spencer leaned back in his chair and crossed one leg casually over the other, ankle on knee. "You know, I thought about that last night. I think what you need is to put me on retainer. A man like you probably gets into trouble all the time. And I do everything. Criminal. Civil. I can even look at that will."

Garrett still stood. "How much?"

"Speaking as your attorney, I think you could use a three-year retainer agreement. We'll make it open-ended. One payment up-front buys all the time you need. That'll also preclude me from representing anybody else against you. If that ever comes up."

"How much?"

"Fifty thousand. Payable immediately. I know it's a big slug right now, but you'll get the last two years for free. Isn't it worth it? For all my expertise?"

Neither of them spoke.

Garrett finally said, "Twenty."

"Fifty."

"Twenty."

"Fifty. And I'll tell you why. When Bobby gets done talking to me, he's going to go to your bank. And what's going to happen there? I mean, which one of those stories did you tell Mickey? I know him too. You can't do business around here without knowing the Shaws. So did you tell him the will story, like you told me yesterday? Or was it the girl? You had to tell him something, to get him to agree to this. Everything you've got is pledged as collateral against those loans you were telling me about. You're a smart guy. So I know you got his approval to do this. You had to. You're not going to risk a default."

"Go to hell."

The lawyer laughed. "It was the woman. I'd pick that one too. It's a real good story. Something another man would like. I know I did."

"Thirty."

"Fifty. I'm going to have to get ready to be sued. By your son. For participating in this thing. Because if he's got any sense, he's going to sue me too, as well as you. For fraud, misrepresentation. And he'll try to get punitive damages, from both of us. Fifty thousand's really a lot less than it ought to be, given what my exposure is. It ought to be a hundred."

"Thirty-five."

"I'm getting tired of this. I called people over in Jefferson County to ask about you. And you know what they said? They told me you really do have all that land. And a lot of kids. Including that one other boy of yours who couldn't stand you. But nobody remembered you being in the hospital ten years ago. They sure didn't remember you almost died." He shrugged. "They told me you're a real son of a bitch, Mr. McAllister. But your son's a different story. People like him. And they have a lot of respect for him, and what he's done. He's got a name in your town. So here's my point. If he sues you, he's going to sue you in Allensboro, of course. And he's going to ask for a jury, because he's got a right to one. And I'm willing to bet you that most of those people will already have an opinion about you. And about him. Not enough to get them excused, but enough to make this easy for Bobby. And when he gets that judgment against you, he's going to get a judgment against me too. And I'm going to be the lawyer. The one all the way over here in Ramsey. The one who did the dirty deed."

He smiled. "Pardon the expression. But that's what's going to happen. I'm going down with you."

"I don't have fifty thousand."

"Sure you do. You've got it right there in your operating account. Or you're about to. It's October. You've been harvesting all month. You should be nearly done by now. Don't try to snow me, Mr. McAllister. I'm a farm boy myself. You can get a check for the whole amount right now. Oh, and I forgot. It's got to be certified too."

10.

"You ought to read this before you sign it."

They were in Spencer's office again, with Garrett once more jammed in the one tight chair in the corner. "Just give me the pen. I want to get out of here." With the papers on his lap, Garrett scrawled his name. "Now give me the Deed."

"You give me the check first."

Garrett took it out of his inside coat pocket and handed it over. Spencer scrutinized it carefully before he locked it away in his desk drawer. "There's one other thing I need you to sign. I realized last night that I don't have anything that documents what you told me, about why you want to change the title. I also didn't have anything that tells me your son specifically consents to do this. So I wrote this letter to myself, from you, for your signature."

He picked up two typewritten sheets off his desk. "I dated it last Monday. All I did was repeat what you told me the first time. About how you want to change title in order to give all your children an equal share. And I included a statement about how Bobby wants you to do this, as soon as possible, and he wants you both to use me. I also put in what you told me, about how he's out of town, but he wants you to use his Power of Attorney."

"Just give it to me," Garrett told him.

After Garrett signed, the lawyer locked it up too, then finally passed over the new Deed.

"Let me explain this," Spencer said, putting on a teaching voice. "What you've got here is a Warranty Deed. It names you and your son as grantors. You in your own name, and your son by virtue of his durable Power of Attorney, which names you as his attorney-in-fact. After that comes the description of the land you're changing the title to. And the last thing is the Power of Attorney itself. It's attached to the back. So what you have to do is take this all to the Recorder of Deeds at the courthouse in your county. Myrna Roberts. You know her?"

"Of course."

"You give her this, plus a check for fifteen dollars. It's fifteen dollars per grantee."

"But there's two of us," Garrett said. "That's thirty."

"There are two grantors. You and your son are the ones giving the land, so the two of you are the grantors. You're the only one getting the land, so you're the only grantee. Just you, so it's fifteen dollars. You give all this to Myrna."

"The Power of Attorney too?"

He nodded. "You'll get it back when the Deed's recorded. You know how that works? The two separate books? There's a grantor book and a grantee book, and they're both alphabetical once you get the right year."

"So if Bobby goes in and looks for it, he's gonna see it? Those books are public record, right? Anybody can go in and look through them."

"But Mr. McAllister, think about it. How's he going to know to look? It's not like they send him a letter. And he's got no reason to look in the grantor book at all unless he sells something else and needs to check that it's been recorded right. Has he got any land of his own?"

"Hell no."

"Well then, it may be years before he does. By then, Myrna will have started a new book. She does that every few years when the old ones fill up. But even if she's still using the current one, this transfer's going to be way back. Pages back. There'll probably be a hundred transactions between this one and the new one he's going to check. He's never going to see this unless he starts flipping back pages for fun."

"But his name's gonna be in that other book too."

"No it's not. Remember, the only grantee is you."

"So for him to find out, someone would basically have to tell him."

"Uh-huh. Otherwise, he'll never know."

11.

The next afternoon, Garrett yanked open the double doors, then quick-marched down the deserted hallway with his work boots clip-clopping on the marble floor. When he got to where the two main corridors crossed in an X, he swerved right, hugging the wall, and skirted behind two of the four wooden benches that faced each other to make a diamond in the intersection. At the far end of the second hall, he sailed in through an open doorway, above which hung an old-fashioned, white-lettered sign:

Myrna L. Roberts
Clerk and Recorder of Deeds

Two other men stood at the long counter that cut the room from side-to-side and created a large, bullpen work area behind it for the employees. On the far wall opposite the doorway, an office door was closed, although the light was on behind the pane of frosted glass. A pert young blonde stood at the counter helping one of the men while the other man waited. At a desk, an older woman wearing reading glasses wrote carefully in longhand in a thick, leather-bound book.

The pretty blonde cleared her throat, and then did it again, only louder, and kept doing it. The older woman finally looked up, saw Garrett above her half-lenses, then stood and went over to the closed office door. She knocked and stuck her head in.

Myrna Roberts came out immediately and closed her door, then motioned to Garrett as she walked to the wooden counter, a full six feet down the wide counter from the others.

"Garrett," she said as he moved over.

"Myrna."

"I assume you came back for your Warranty Deed. The one you dropped off yesterday." She pulled a big wire basket from under the counter, then put it down in front of her on the old wood and started rummaging. "Is this it?"

"Did you record it right?"

"Excuse me?"

"I want to come through, behind there, and have you show it to me."

"You want to come back here in the stacks?"

"The books are public record, right?"

She had an elbow on the counter. "You really want to check my work."

Garrett leaned across. "The last time I looked, Myrna, you were a public servant."

She turned and walked away, her heels clicking. Garrett opened the gate in the counter and followed her as she disappeared through an archway in the back wall that led to another room filled with tall bookcases and fat volumes on shelves to the ceiling.

He lost her for an instant but found her again at the far end of a long, cramped row. Next to her, a tall window looked out over the browning square. The sun caught the bright red roof of the Dairy Queen outside on the kitty-corner.

She rose on the balls of her feet and reached for a book. "1980 - " and "MNO" were written on the thick spine.

"Is that the grantee book?" Garrett said.

"Of course it is." She banged the book down on a small table and opened it, then put her finger on the little round tab that marked the "M's." She flipped it, then turned many thin pages of handwriting until she got to the last one, the most recent one, where the "M" entries stopped. Myrna pointed, stabbing the last entry. "There. You happy now?"

He looked, then nodded. "It shows I'm the grantee for the land."

"Gee thanks," she said. "I didn't know that."

She went to close it again, but he stopped her. He put his hand on her arm. "What's that?" he said, looking down.

"What?"

"That."

He put his own finger on the page. "That looks like Bobby."

"It is. Why?"

"Robert R. McAllister. It says right there."

"Garrett, I can read."

"What's he doing there?"

"That's his new parcel."

"His what?"

"His new ground. You know about that."

"What new ground?"

"Over by the old coal mine. The one he just bought."

Garrett looked at her.

"You know about that, don't you?" she asked, her bright eyes peering.

"He's the purchaser? He bought it?"

"They bought it together. Him and Sarah. A couple of months ago." She sighed, then pointed. "Read it. It's right there. Robert R. and Sarah W. McAllister. Tenants by the entireties."

Garrett didn't say a word.

"You didn't know about this?"

"How much is it?" he asked her. "How much land?"

"Hard to say. It's all in metes and bounds. But I'd say … maybe two hundred acres. That one."

"That one?" His little eyes got round. "You said 'that one.'"

"He's got more. He's got a whole farm out there. You mean you don't know?"

"Show me. It's all in here, right?"

"I'd have to find them. It might take me a while." She ran her finger up the page. She scanned each entry quickly, then moved to the next one, then flipped back a page, and did it again. She turned another. "There."

He pushed her finger out of the way. "Robert R. McAllister," Garrett read out loud. "Where is it?"

"Same place. It's all contiguous. The old Van Mueller farm. You remember. Out by the old coal mine. They split it up when Mr. Warren died."

"1989," he read. "How much land is it?"

She thought. "Another three twenty, maybe."

Garrett put his own finger on the page, then began to slide it slowly up, going backwards. He flipped back another page, and then two more.

Myrna stopped him. "There."

"1987," he read out loud.

"I remember that one," she said. "That was the first one. They came in together, acting like newlyweds. Giggling the whole time and holding onto each other like there wasn't anybody else in the world. We all laughed about it. They looked so happy."

"All this in four years."

"They acted like that this last time too. Sarah was thrilled. She said they were done. That was where they were gonna build their house. She told me they were gonna put in a lake at the bottom of this hill, and put the house on the rise above it, with a deck."

"When did the two of them come in?"

"Two months ago. Maybe three."

"How much has he got? Altogether."

Myrna shrugged. "Seven fifty maybe. You mean apart from the two hundred he had with you?"

"Who'd he buy it from? The sale didn't make any noise."

She peered down. "Ellen Kline. She's some relative. She doesn't live here. I think she's on the West Coast."

"Who did the paperwork?"

"Sam, I guess. Doesn't he do all your legal work?"

12.

Garrett drove along the hard road back toward Ramsey. Past the turnoff to the coal mine, he slowed and looked right, up a gentle hill. In the distance, near the top of it, there was a combine with dust swirling around it like bees.

He turned right and curved south, then went west on a dirt track. He got closer to the roaring machine but he didn't slow down.

He leaned forward to peer through the windshield.

He couldn't make out the man's face. It was too small and far away, but Garrett could see the green John Deere cap he was wearing. He was sitting high on the seat too, with his wrists crossed casually over the wheel.

It was a big field, and Bobby was almost done with it.

13.

The woman at the reception desk told him to wait, but he wouldn't. He blew by her and charged down the hall.

"You son of a bitch!" he said as he rushed into Sam Ross's office.

Ross was at his desk on the phone. "Yeah, I'll tell him," he said, then hung up. Ross stood.

"You set me up! You helped him buy it!"

"You're raving, you know that?" Ross was calm.

"Did you two have a good laugh? The old man, he'll never find out. We won't tell him. You're my goddamn lawyer! You can't help him screw me!"

"He didn't."

"He bought the land! I'm gonna sue you."

"For what?"

"For conspiracy."

"You didn't even bid on it."

"It's a conflict of interest, your helping him."

"No it's not."

"He's my son!"

"He's a grown man! He's none of your business. You didn't want that land. You and I talked about it at the time. And you just saved me a phone call. I'm not your lawyer anymore. If anybody asks you, I want you to tell them I had nothing to do with what you just did to Bobby. You don't think I know? Myrna called me the minute you left. She wanted to know why the hell I did this to Bobby. I couldn't believe it. Using that Power of Attorney."

"It's legal."

"It's crap!"

"It says I can do whatever I want."

"You can't use it for yourself, to take his land. And Bobby says he didn't know a thing. That was him on the phone. Do you have any idea how much he could sue you for? He could take you for everything you've got. And he ought to!" Ross put both his hands on the desk and leaned into them. "That's what I just told him. And I told him I'd be a witness at the trial against you."

"You can't be!"

"Sure I can. I can be a fact witness. And even if I can't, I can make sure everybody knows I had nothing to do with this. Bobby wants to see you. He says you already came by today, so you know where he is. It's all up to him, but if I were him, I'd sue you for fraud, conversion, and everything else. Do you have any idea how much the punitive damages could be? Bobby wants me to tell you that you've got exactly one hour to get out there."

"Or what?" Garrett smiled at him. "What's he gonna do to me?"

Sam Ross smiled back. "You want to know?"

Ross made him wait for it.

"At four o'clock he calls your wife."

14.

He sat down hard on the driver's seat and put the key in the ignition.

He stopped as he realized, then looked next to him on the empty seat.

He thought about it, then glanced at the floor of the passenger seat and at the floor where his own feet were. He leaned all the way over, pressing his right shoulder into the cushion on the passenger side, then picked up the mat there, and then the one under his boots, lifting his old legs. He grunted as he sat up again.

Garrett pulled down the visor, then shoved his right hand into the crack at the base of his seat, running it behind him and under his own rear end.

He stared at the wheel, then stared out the windshield and across the street, eyeing the front of Ross's office. He opened his palm and looked at it, then looked back at the front door, then down again at his hand.

He opened his truck door and climbed out, then checked the grass on his side of the chassis. He knelt, grimacing as he did and holding his knees, putting both hands on the curb and doubling over to peer under the axles. He struggled up, then stepped back to search the bed of the truck. He walked around to the passenger side and checked the asphalt under the door.

There was nothing, anywhere. He scanned up and down the street.

Garrett's papers weren't there. The new Deed and Bobby's Power of Attorney were gone. He'd left them at the courthouse.

15.

He swerved into traffic, flooring it heading back to the square. It took him ten precious minutes before he pulled over at the curb.

When he did, he only had forty-five minutes left to get to Bobby.

Garrett winced as he marched up the walkway toward the main doors of the courthouse. At the top of the cement steps, he threw the doors open and started sprinting down the hallway. His work boots clicked hard and echoed on the polished floor.

When he got to the middle, he rounded the same corner where the benches were. He could already see Myrna's sign at the end of the hall. He was moving so fast he didn't see anyone or anything. He passed the benches and kept his eyes focused on the far door.

"Garrett!" a voice called out.

He kept going.

"Garrett! I'm back here."

He turned. It was Cora, in a pink dress. She sat on one of the benches he had passed in the middle. "I'll be right back!" he yelled back at her. "I have to get something. It's some taxes I need to pay. And then I have to meet somebody." He gave her the back of his hand above his shoulder.

"Is it this?" she called out.

He stopped and turned. She had her hand up. From twenty feet away, he saw the papers as she waved them. "Is this what you came for, because I don't see anything in here about taxes, and I've read every word."

"Don't you speak to me like that," he said as he marched back toward her.

"You're stealing his land!"

He stopped in front of her. Towering over her, he thrust out his hand. "Give me those."

"I will not!"

He made a grab for them. She snatched them away, shoving them under her backside and sat down again on top of them. "Now you tell me what's going on."

"You're being ridiculous, Cora."

"She said you stole his land. Myrna says she talked to Sam. He told her it's not legal. That Bobby didn't know."

"He only got that two hundred acres in the first place because you made me. You wouldn't shut up."

"He had to wait ten years. You promised him five. Sam said you had to go outside the county to find someone to do this."

"He threatened me. You weren't there. He tried to hold me up."

"No he didn't!"

"He tried to slug me! And he demanded sixty percent. He was gonna bury me! That's what he said. Bobby even left us in the middle of the night, just like Garrett J. did."

"Garrett J. didn't walk out on you. You stopped paying him. Is that what you did to Bobby?"

Garrett pointed at her pink lap. "Do you know where that land is? Right in the middle of my ground. At the bottom of that hill. Two hundred acres. You know what happens if he tries to sell it? If it's joint, he can do whatever he wants. Hell, he could give it away! We'd be screwed, Cora! He could bring in the damn circus. I was trying to protect us."

"From what?"

"Huh?"

"He's no threat to you. He's got his own land now."

Garrett leaned in, looming over her. His voice got quiet. Deadly. "You knew."

"Knew what?"

"About his land. That he bought the old Van Mueller farm piece by piece."

Cora took in her breath.

"You kept this from me," he said.

"He said you'd do something to them if you found out. All of them, and not just him but Sarah too, and the boys. He said you'd throw them off. I told him he was wrong."

"Give me the papers."

"He said I didn't know you. And it's true. I got all dolled up to come down here, when Myrna called me, because I figured I'd see you when you came back. I didn't know what it was you'd left."

"How did he do it?" Garrett demanded, but she didn't hear him. She was talking to herself.

"He didn't threaten you, and he didn't hit you. That's not like him. You must have hit him. I bet you did it when you found out about his land. And then you threw him off with his whole family. Our family. And you went to some lawyer to get this done."

She had gone inside, figuring this out, her eyes darting behind her thick glasses. "But wait," she said. "You didn't know. Myrna says you had no idea. She had to show you. So you did this before you knew. Before you found out he had someplace to go. You just threw him out, and Sarah and the boys."

"Cora!"

But she wasn't listening. "You threw him off for sixty percent. And then you did everything you could to make sure he didn't have a home."

"Excuse me." A stranger hurried past, scurrying to avoid them.

"You've been cutting him out since he left, too. Haven't you? So he doesn't have a choice but to come back to you. He's not Garrett J. Garrett J. could leave you. He got an education. Bobby didn't have a choice. That's what you thought, before you knew about the land. So you were taking advantage. What else did you do?"

Garrett gripped her wrist. She struggled but he held on, boring down on her. "How. Did. He. Do. It?"

In her fear, she talked quickly. "He bought land from a woman who doesn't live here, and he bought it at the other end of the county, so you wouldn't find out."

"Where did he get the money?"

"Ow! He leveraged it. And they've been saving for years. "Sarah's salary from the hospital. Plus they worked the new land right away."

He held on, pressing tight. "Who co-signed the loan? Somebody had to."

"Esther did, but only the first parcel. She's off it now, and—"

"Did you sign it too?"

"No!" she cried. "I don't own anything on my own. You know that. I don't have any collateral. The bank wasn't interested in me."

"You talked to Mickey Shaw?"

"No. We went out of town. Bobby told me you'd find out if we went through Mickey."

He dropped her wrist and turned. "Come on. I need to be somewhere." He began to walk.

"I'm not going anywhere with you!"

He turned around again to see a birdlike skeleton in a ruffly pink dress. "What are you gonna do? Not feed me for week? Refuse to do my laundry?"

"I'll leave you," she said as she rubbed her wrist with her left hand. "And I'll tell Bobby. I'll make sure he knows everything, and he'll come after you."

"You're gonna tell him to sue me? Good, because you know what I'll do? I'll make him read. These papers under your butt, in that courtroom down that hall right there. I'll give him those, and I'll make him read. Every goddamn word, out loud."

"You wouldn't!"

"The whole damn town loves Bobby, but he's been lying to them. He can't read and they don't know it! I'll humiliate the son of a bitch and show him up to everyone in this county. I'm gonna do whatever it takes to protect this family, just like always."

16.

When Garrett made the turn, he could see Bobby's combine still thundering over the ground.

Garrett bounced off the road and headed straight toward it, through the soy beans. The brittle short plants snapped. The gray twigs flew up and hit the grill at the front of the truck, then traveled. They snaked their way up the glass of the windshield, then over the top, filling his sight, making it impossible for him to see.

Garrett charged forward through the forest in front of him. He could hear the branches scrape the roof. He didn't slow down. He just estimated. He kept going toward the combine with his foot pushing the pedal down.

There was nothing but sky at first, between the mat of beans, but then he saw the top of the combine, and then the cab, and finally Bobby in it. He was glaring at Garrett, looking right at him in a straight line, but Bobby hadn't pulled on the handbrake. The combine kept coming at him at full throttle.

The sickle flashed. The slashing metal teeth caught the sun as they ripped back and forth just a few feet off the ground. The big cartwheel below them was rolling in front of the combine, felling the plants and bringing them towards it, where the fatal sickle was meeting them, cutting off their life. They were shark's teeth in a shark's mouth, only the teeth didn't bite down. They ripped from left to right like scissors in two belts covering the length of the combine, champing with the power to take off a man's head.

Bobby sat above it, right above it, in the driver's seat. Two feet below his shoes, the killing metal bit the plants.

From inside the truck, Garrett saw Bobby, and then the sickle. He looked up out his windshield and waved his hand telling Bobby to stop.

Bobby didn't move. Garrett watched him. Bobby set his jaw and continued to stare.

Garrett honked. Bobby leaned forward.

Garrett put his foot on the brake and stopped his truck. Bobby was sixty feet in front of him and still charging.

Garrett pounded on the horn, but the machine kept coming. Garrett hit the sound hard, over and over, but Bobby didn't move. He came barreling towards him, with his hands on the wheel.

"Shit!" Garrett got out and left the door open. He stood in the field and raised his fist.

"You stop this thing!" Garrett yelled at him. Bobby was fifty feet away.

"You stop it!" Garrett shook his fist.

He was knee-deep in soybeans, standing fast in front of the chomping machine. It kept thundering, coming toward him. It was twenty feet away.

The combine was close enough now for Garrett to see the smile. He looked up into the cab far above him and he finally caught it. Bobby was grinning as he came to cut him down.

The sickle was ten feet away from him. It was going to kill him. The wheel and the metal were going to shred him.

Garrett leapt back in the truck, throwing himself prone across the seat.

The left end of the sickle struck the truck's door, slamming it hard against the chassis. The door hit the frame but couldn't close. Garrett's boots stuck out enough to stop it from slamming.

But the sickle had enough clearance now to move past him. Just a few inches, but it was enough.

He could feel the wind from the cartwheel. He heard the roar of the blade. His feet were saved though, along with the rest of him. The screaming machine rumbled past.

He waited, then pulled himself out again, standing in the field as the combine squealed to a stop.

Bobby opened the door of the cab and stepped out.

"You nearly killed me!"

"Get out of here!"

"You tried to kill me!"

"You stole my land! And where's my money? Mickey Shaw won't talk to me, and it's all gone. And I want my check. Harvey says you called him."

"I don't owe you shit. Jesus, you hurt me!" Garrett threw out his arm, waving it around him. "Look at this! You didn't have the balls to tell me about this land. How old are you? Ten?"

"I don't have to tell you! And that land's mine. You can't change the title."

"You wanted it to be in the middle. Right in the middle of my land, so you could screw me."

"I picked the land you didn't steal. I picked the parcel you bought from Mrs. Wilcox, where you paid her full price. Not anything from Mr. Barrington. Will told me when I was a kid that you got it for half price. Mr. Barrington was stuck for money. I went to the courthouse, and I counted the transfer stamps. I figured out what you paid for it, and he was right. I wasn't gonna have anything to do with that ground."

Bobby looked down at the earth far below him. "This is mine. Mine and Sarah's. I want you to leave and never come back."

"I'll take you down!"

"You're not doing anything to me. That's why you came barreling out here, tearing up my crop. If you had any leverage, you wouldn't have come out on time. But don't worry. I'm not gonna sue you. But you better make damn sure I get everything that's coming to me from this year's crop. And I want my money. Whatever you said to Mickey Shaw about me, and I know you told him something, you're gonna tell him you were wrong. You got that?"

He pointed toward the road. "Now go on. Get out of here." He turned to get back into the combine.

"You're not gonna sue me?" Garrett yelled up. "What's the angle?"

Bobby stopped. "There's no angle. I'm thinking about Mom. She loves you, and the truth would destroy her if she found out. So this is gonna stop. It's over. But don't make any mistake about how much that land means to me. Not just the two hundred, but all of it. I took care of it like it was mine even though it wasn't and it was never gonna be."

He shook his head. "I'm the one who did all the work. I got the cows out of the levee after it rained, remember? All those carcasses? Blown up like that?

"You never burned stalks in the spring. Watched the fire burn out, at the edge of the field, where it hits the green. Do you know why it stops? You don't. Remember that time you got so mad at me, when that fire started under the truck and I dragged it all over the field? You'd think you'd be worried about me, maybe blowing myself up with that fire coming out of the exhaust pipe, but no, all you cared about was the seed. I told you it wasn't gonna hurt it, even though I had scorched the whole field, but you didn't believe me. You know what I had to do? I had to lie to you. I told you I'd replanted it, but I hadn't. I knew it was gonna come up, and it did. It was alive under there. No matter what you do to it, Dad, it's still alive.

"You know what else? I planted wild grass on the other side of the stream. I've got a band over there, about a hundred feet wide.

Only I'll never see it again. It's filled with birds and snakes. Wild birds. You've never been out there. I've been over it a thousand times.

"You've never gotten out of your truck. I don't think I've ever seen you do it, except to get up on the tractor when you felt like it. You had to be the big man. You know how many clutches you've blown out, driving so slow? You run up and down the road like a maniac, and then you creep in the field. You're scared of it. Like it's gonna bite you." Bobby laughed.

"In all these years, I've never seen you get out and walk. Actually walk your own farm. You've never done that. Have you ever picked up your own soil? Do you know what it smells like after a rain? There's not an inch of that farm I haven't picked up in my hands. You never get dirty, Dad. And I never get clean."

"How'd you do it?"

"Is that all you care about? I farmed your land when I knew you'd be out there. But when you weren't, I coordinated with Larry and Vern and everybody else you hired. They didn't know where I was. They just knew to use the two-way and that I'd be back in an hour. I sure thank God for your TV."

"Screw you!"

"You were planted there! With that damn newspaper. You know how much I planted here, on this land, every April when I knew you were watching the Masters' Tournament? And March Madness. Then there's baseball, then football, until it was all harvested. Didn't you ever wonder why I started missing every game? Think about it. Sarah started bringing the boys over. I haven't been to your house for Sunday supper in five years."

Bobby jerked his thumb. "Get out of here."

He bent to step back into the combine, but then turned around. He pointed back behind Garrett, at the crushed line in the field where he had driven the truck. "I saw the way you came in here, mowing down everything in sight. I want you to go back out the same way. Just follow your tracks, straight out. I don't want you to trample any more of what's mine."

He stepped in and closed the door.

Garrett climbed into his truck as Bobby's combine started up and moved away.

In the shadow of the driver's seat, shielded from the sun, Garrett looked over at the Deed on the seat next to him and smiled.

DANIEL
Summer
1994

Three Years Later

1.

"I can't talk to her. I don't know what to say." Kevin twisted to look behind himself at the girl. "She's beautiful," he said to Daniel. "Why would anybody like that want to go out with me?"

"Because you're smart, that's why. And you're funny."

"I'm dumb, plus I look like an elf with these stupid ears."

The two brothers huddled in the back corner of the Dairy Queen parking lot behind the busy drive-through at the end of an alleyway that ran to the curb along the nicked brick wall of an old empty storefront. Daniel was leaning against that brick wall as they talked. Over Kevin's much shorter head, he saw twenty yards out to the street and the crowd of girls who stood in a big circle on the bright, hot sidewalk, showing off their pale legs in their new summer shorts. There were at least fifteen of them, with a few more out of sight around the front of the building. A few minutes before, Daniel had seen them line up to buy their ice cream at the take-out window that faced the square.

They were licking their cones now, as they stood baking. Even from where he stood, Daniel could see their heads bob as they flicked their little cat tongues. One of them had fiery red hair, and it glistened. Her mass of corkscrews tumbled copper in the light and floated up shining whenever the humid breeze blew across from the courthouse, lifting her ringlets and sending them sideways into her mouth. All the other girls had put their hair up, but not this one. She had left hers free despite the heat.

Daniel knew her. Her name was Lisa and she was a freshman like Kevin. Daniel watched her as the smell of hamburger grease hung like the moisture in the air. They were all cooking already, and it wasn't even noon yet.

Daniel poked his brother gently in the chest. "Don't you ever call yourself dumb. You're not, and there's nothing wrong with the way you look."

"But she's so smart," Kevin said. "She gets all A's!"

She stood a step back from the throng. She wasn't talking, and none of the other girls were trying to bring her in. They were all too busy trading insults with the three teenage boys who taunted them from eight feet away, under the deep shade of the red roof overhang. The boys stood shoulder-to-shoulder facing out, each with his right foot propped up against the wall of the Dairy Queen and both hands plunged deep into his jeans pockets.

They weren't the only hungry boys, these three pimply flamingoes. They were just the bravest of the hovering bunch. Much of the rest of the male population of Allensboro High School was either gawking farther back in the packed parking lot or yelling to the girls as they circled the square, honking and leaning out of their parents' cars and trucks. Antlike in their tight formation, the driving teenaged boys inched up the long hill from the cemetery into the county square, then waited to turn left at the northeast corner, in front of the Dairy Queen, after which they immediately began playing bumper cars for the right to pull in.

But nobody was leaving, so there was a pile-up. The boys with no chance gunned it and went around the square again. In the last few minutes alone, Daniel had seen the same dented gray Econoline van make four separate laps, with the same two sophomores dangling out the passenger-side window as they pounded on the metal and shouted at the girls.

"Come on." Daniel started walking toward the front.

"No! Wait! What are you gonna do?" Kevin had trouble keeping up.

Daniel was much taller, and his legs were long. "I don't know yet. But I'll think of something."

"Don't embarrass me."

"Hey Jim!" Daniel shouted as Kevin pattered alongside. "What are you doing?"

One of the flamingoes yelled back. "You want to help me?"

The boy had an odd haircut, with brown bangs so short they sliced across the very top of his high forehead. If they had been any shorter, they would have stood straight up. It looked like a barber mistake, but it wasn't because the squatter, fatter boy next to him had the same cut.

"Help you what?" Daniel called out as they approached him.

"Trying to get these girls to pay some attention!"

One of the girls shouted back. She was the blonde ringleader. "Well that won't happen, Jim Stoddart, and you know it!"

Daniel shot a glance at the redhead. She was looking at Kevin, but then she turned her eyes to him. It was only an instant, but Daniel saw them in the bright late-morning June light. They were blue, dazzling blue.

As they stopped, Jim said to Daniel, "You ready to get out of here?"

Toronto Blue Jay blue. Miami Dolphins.

Jim said, "Hey! I'm talking to you about this trip."

Daniel came to. "Yeah. How about you?"

Kevin piped up. "At least you get to go. She won't let me." He raised his young voice as he imitated his mother. "You're too young. You're not old enough," he said through his nose.

"You're fifteen," the fat boy next to Jim said. "You're the same age as me and I'm going."

"That doesn't matter. I'm not mature. You never know what I might do. I could hurt myself, like I did last year. I could fall off the boat again." Kevin had put his hand on his waist and stuck his hip out.

"But there're no boats in Washington."

"She won't even let me stay here alone. You know they're going to Hawaii next week? She's not gonna let me stay at the house. You know, this weekend, while Daniel's gone. And even when he gets back, we're gonna have to be at my grandma's. We're gonna stay there until they get back."

Daniel asked him, "When did she say that?"

"This morning," Kevin said.

"But I'm sixteen!" Daniel said, and his three friends nodded. "I'm gonna stay by myself!"

Jim lifted his head. "Hey Amy!" he yelled to the same blonde girl. "You want to have a party at Daniel's next week when we all get back here? His parents are gonna be away."

Every single girl swiveled her head then. They were all looking now, and Jim was suddenly smiling. "Tell them Daniel."

Even redheaded Lisa was looking over with her glorious eyes. "Uh, yeah!" Daniel called out. "I'm gonna have one."

"You can't—" Kevin said.

But Daniel didn't hear him. "I'm gonna have the house to myself, me and my brother here." Daniel threw his arm around Kevin. "Hey Lisa!" He put Kevin's neck in a hammerlock.

"Let me go!" Kevin fought to get free, but Daniel shoved Kevin's nose under his armpit. "Lisa!" Daniel shouted again. "You want to come? You know Kevin, right?"

Kevin was struggling, pounding Daniel's chest.

Daniel yelled at the redhead again. "Are you gonna be around?"

"Let me go! I look stupid!"

A man's voice called out. "Daniel! Over here!"

Clutching his brother, Daniel turned toward the street. Crammed in under his arm, Kevin had to stutter his feet.

His grandfather had pulled in, cutting the wheel so hard at the last second that his right front tire had hopped the curb. Nose in but slanted way out, the huge pickup blocked two lanes of traffic. Behind the shiny chrome grill, Garrett had stuck his small white head and his left arm out his driver's side window. They were only separated by three feet of sidewalk.

The honking started. Every driving boy wanted old Garrett dead.

His grandfather flicked his fingers as Kevin punched Daniel in the ribs trying to get free. "Can't it wait?" Daniel called out as he held on tightly.

"Let go of your brother," Garrett said. "I only want to talk to you."

2.

"I need to get back soon," Daniel said as his grandfather gunned it, turning right at the corner. Daniel had to grip the inside handle of the door.

"I need to pick up Kevin and get him back home to do his homework before Mom gets off work."

But Garrett didn't answer. He left the square, driving north. They passed the cement plant and the package store, but Garrett didn't slow.

"Are we going to your farm?" Daniel asked. "Because I—"

"No." On the other side of a short bridge, Garrett braked hard and turned left onto a dirt track that stretched due west. The sun shifted as he turned so it gleamed off the red lacquer of the front hood into Daniel's eyes.

It was icy cold in the truck, but Daniel stood it. He didn't dare move the vent so it stopped blasting in his face.

They bumped over deep dry ruts that sent the new pickup flying, then bounced past field after planted field, turning right finally at the end of a lush parcel of sprouting soybeans. Green fuzz napped the ground.

They humped onto the asphalt of another paved road skirted by little ranch-style houses. Garrett finally stopped across from one with the word "Pimper" peeling off a big rusted mailbox on a wooden stake in the front yard. He raised his arm and shot it across the seats, so it nearly struck Daniel in the nose, then jutted his finger to point out Daniel's window. "That's my field there," he said. "It hasn't been planted yet."

The boy looked. The ground on the other side of the closed window was barren and dry, with clumps of earth that had been hurled up by a disker, then left as litter in chunks on the parching field. Up to the far tree line that Daniel could see on a little rise that marked his horizon, more than a hundred acres sat fallow and unused. The sun beat down, cooking it.

The air-conditioning condensed the air, making fog that had begun to cloud the front windshield. "You want to know why?" Garrett said. "My hired man quit. He called two nights ago and told me his wife couldn't stand me. It's my house. And she wanted to paint it. So here I sit now, without any help to get it planted. And I've got another one besides this Pimper ground."

"What about your other men? You've got others, don't you?"

"Larry and Vern quit last year. They took a job over by Carmi. I have my suspicions about who got them that job, but I'm not gonna tell you. Let's just say that someone doesn't want me to leave this to you. He wants me to have to sell it, so he can say he was right. That I'm not as good as he is. But I'm sure as hell not gonna give him the satisfaction. This is yours, Daniel. Yours and your brother's."

Daniel turned his head. "Mine?"

His grandfather was watching him. "Didn't you know that? Everything I've got is coming to you. You're gonna split it with the rest of my children, but you're the one who'll farm it. It'll be yours, Daniel. You're gonna be the one I hand it to."

"Why me?"

"Your two uncles aren't gonna do it. They're city boys. They're not gonna come back here."

"But what about Dad?"

Garrett snorted. "Not with that big house of his, and his own farm. He's already got enough. He doesn't need me. And he sure won't help me out. No, son. It's you. This is gonna be yours someday. And I want you to learn how to farm it, starting right now. There's not a lot of time left, for me to teach you."

Daniel frowned.

"Oh, don't worry," Garrett said quickly, catching the boy's concern. "I'm all right. But I'm eighty-two."

Daniel turned to look out at the vacant ground. "But what about Kevin?"

"He can't drive yet. I did the math last night. You can drive now, right? You're sixteen."

Daniel nodded. "But he'll be old enough next year."

Garrett held up a hand. "I'm sorry to say it. I know you're close, but I'm not sure he's got the mental horsepower. Don't get upset. I'm talking about you here, not your brother. I want you to start right away. Tomorrow. Tomorrow's Sunday. I want you to get up early and come out—"

"I can't. I'm sorry, Granddad, but I've got finals, and they start on Monday and they go all week. Mom would kill me if I came out here to help you. She won't even let me help Dad. Not until after I get back. And even then, I've got stuff to do for him."

"Where are you going?"

"Washington, D.C. Nearly the whole school's leaving Friday, and we're not coming back until Monday night. And then Mom and Dad are gonna be gone the whole rest of next week."

"Where?"

"Hawaii."

"Huh. That must be costing him a fortune." The muscles of his jaw worked under his papery skin. After a pause, Garrett said, "So it's money, just like him. How much?"

"I'm sorry?"

"All right, all right. I'll pay you the same as my hired man. Only we'll break it down, so it comes to some kind of hourly.

Plus that way we can tell your dad you've got a job. I hired you, to work for me full-time all through the summer. Okay?"

Daniel shook his head. "But Granddad, I didn't—"

"Don't worry. I'll make you earn every cent. And once you graduate and start working for me full-time, we'll make it a flat rate. Some kind of salary."

"You will?"

"Of course I will. You're my grandson. My heir. Later, we'll talk about a percentage. After you've worked for me a couple years."

"What's a percentage?"

Daniel saw a small smile.

"You don't know?" Garrett said. "It's a percentage of the crop. You'd get it every year. Of course, it wouldn't be much to start off with, and you'd have to share expenses. But I could throw in that house up there."

"You mean our old house? The one up at the farm?"

"It's my house. Not yours. But yeah. What do you say? Wouldn't you like to live there? Are you gonna shake on it?" Garrett put out his wrinkled hand with its straight fingers pointed at Daniel's heart.

The boy looked at it but didn't take it. "What about Dad? And Mom. They're gonna have to say it's okay."

"Leave that to me. I'll talk to him. In the meantime, don't say anything. You know how he is. If he thinks we've been organizing this without him knowing, he'll get mad as a wet hen. So let's act like this is a new idea, okay? When are they coming back?"

"A week from Sunday. The nineteenth."

"When you get back from Washington, we'll talk some more. But shake my hand here, so I know you're on board with this. And you're okay with helping me next week, until your father gets back. I've got over two hundred acres to plant."

Daniel hesitated with icy air blasting his face. "I guess so. I mean, as long as I can do whatever Dad wants too. But you're gonna tell him, right?"

"Just as soon as he gets back. But you don't say anything to him until I can. Now let's shake on it."

"But what about Kevin? If you're paying me, you should be paying him too, to work for you. He's good. He just can't drive yet. But he can help me. And he can do it too, next week."

"All right, dammit. I'll use him too, if I can get you. Now give me your hand. There. Good."

3.

When Daniel climbed out of the pick-up again at the Dairy Queen, he couldn't find his brother. The crowd was gone and the place was deserted. The only car left was their mother's, which they had brought with them. The furnace inside, caused by hours with windows closed, hit Daniel as he opened the car door. No Kevin, though. And no note.

Sweating, he went into the fast food place and checked the men's room, then stopped at the counter to ask one of the girls, who told him the kids had all left about twenty minutes before to catch the two o'clock in Benton of The Flintstones. No, she said, she didn't think Kevin had tagged along. Yes, she knew him, and she knew what he looked like. No, he didn't go.

"Aren't you the one who was grabbing him?" she said as he turned away. "We were laughing in here, through the window. He looked pretty stupid, the way he was. He kept struggling, but he was too weak."

Daniel got in the car and drove straight at the same corner where Garrett had turned right, passing a Christmas tree of road signs as he drove west out of the square and into the strong afternoon light. He went for a mile, never topping thirty as he moved his head from side-to-side. He didn't see Kevin. He even slowed to peer in through the plate glass window of the hardware store, then searched the broad front lawn of the library, but his little brother wasn't anywhere.

He rounded a curve that brought him alongside the high school's cracked and crumbling tennis courts. Farther on, where a high chain-link fence began, he squinted through the wire at the oval track and the grassy football field inside it. He was about to turn around and try a different set of streets when he spotted Kevin storming with his head hung and his arms pumping pistons along the dirt path that edged the outside of the chain-link fence. Daniel would have clipped him with his mother's car if it had been nighttime. Kevin was charging without thinking that close to the road.

Daniel rolled down the window as he pulled up behind him. The wet heat hit Daniel in the face. "Kevin! I'll drive you home."

Kevin didn't turn.

"It's not safe! Come on! I'll take you."

Daniel slowed to match Kevin's pace. "Did you hear me?"

Kevin flung his arm out, for Daniel to stay away from him.

"What's wrong?" Daniel yelled as he leaned out.

Kevin whirled around, his face dripping. "You made me look like an idiot!"

"I was trying to help you!"

Tears mixed with Kevin's sweat. "Help me what? Look like a moron? You think she's gonna go out with me now? Even Granddad saw it."

"I didn't—"

"They all laughed!" He started walking again. "I don't need you! I don't need anything you've got."

Daniel trailed him, crawling in the car. "I'm sorry, okay? I didn't mean it."

His brother stopped and twirled around again. Daniel had to slam the brakes on. "You think I'm an idiot because I can't read. And you have to take care of me. But you don't! Mom thinks so too, but I'm only a year younger than you, and you get to do stuff. What about me?"

"Kevin, I've fixed it. It's Granddad. He's got a job for us, all summer, and he's gonna pay us. Full-time. We're gonna get what Steve gets. Remember him? Well he's gone, and Granddad wants us to replace him. You're gonna make money, so you can take her out."

Kevin thought about it. "He's gonna pay us?"

"A lot! Now get in the car so we can get home. And if you want, I'll talk to Dad. I'll tell him you're no baby. Neither am I. We want to stay at home when they're away. Who wants to stay at Grandma's?"

"You will?"

4.

Daniel found his father upstairs that night in their new house, sorting the mail as he ate a late dinner of fried chicken wings and cole slaw. Bobby said he had been in the field all day, listening to the corn grow as he sprayed liquid fertilizer.

"You don't really hear it," Daniel said as he pulled out a chair at their solid oak table.

"You think I don't?"

"Where's Mom?"

Bobby chewed, then took a sip of sweet iced tea. "Gone to bed. She has to get up early to work a double shift. Peggy's out again with her chemotherapy."

Daniel looked out to see the bright floodlight that illuminated the wooden back deck, which stood on tall pilings at the level of the kitchen. When Bobby had built the house, he had sunk twenty four-by-fours deep into the cement of a walk-out he had poured downstairs, outside the rec room. The high deck extended the whole length of the house in the back and looked out over the water.

Daniel could see past the deck down the hill to the lake, which his father had created even before the house had been finished. Two acres wide, it filled the bowl of a little valley. Bobby had put an island in it, for something to swim to, and he had bought Kevin a rowboat, which was now tethered to a stake. The boat's white hull reflected the bright spotlight, but from the distance of the house, the glow was ghostly, like it was bathed in moonlight.

Daniel leaned toward his father, feeling the cool of the tabletop on his forearms. "Dad, there's something we need to talk about."

Bobby tossed an envelope onto the table. "Shoot."

"It's about Kevin and me staying here, while you two are gone. I'm sixteen years old. Why can't we stay by ourselves? I'll be back on Monday. He doesn't have to go to Grandma Winston's, and neither do I. She treats us like babies."

"Your grandmother?"

"No. Mom." Daniel lowered his voice. "And why can't Kevin stay alone while I'm in Washington? Aunt Gina's down the road. She can come over any time she wants. Or call. He's old enough. I know I am."

Bobby thought about it, but then said, "What would he do here all day by himself? You're not gonna be back until Monday."

"Have Gina pick him up, or call Smitty's mom. They can pick him up and take him someplace, then bring him back here. All he wants to do is sleep here, to say he did it. Come on."

Bobby looked at the doorway. Beyond it was the living room, then the hallway on the first floor leading to three of their five bedrooms. Daniel's mother slept in his parents' room at the end of the long, carpeted hall. "I don't know," his father said.

"It's only three days, and I'll be back. I can take care of him after that until you get home. Haven't I always done that?" Daniel put a smile on. "And I won't charge you. It's free."

A slow grin warmed Bobby's face. "You're good, you know that?"

"Dad, she's old! And her house smells, and she's got all those little ceramic things."

"You mean the mice?"

"Yeah, what is that? Is that where Mom gets it, with all those weird troll dolls?"

They were laughing now as Bobby made a beaver dam with the chicken bones on his plate. "I'm serious," Daniel said. "You know how he's gonna look when his friends find out he's staying at Grandma's? He's stuck here while we all go to Washington. Do you know how many other sophomores are coming? But not him. He's fifteen, but you don't act it."

"Daniel—"

"He can't read very well. So what? Why does everybody have to treat him like a baby? He's not stupid, and no one should treat him like he is."

The smile was gone. "I don't."

"Yes you do, with all this protection. You're telling him he's not smart. That he can't do it. You guys treat him like he's different, but he's not. A lot of people can't read well. Who cares?"

"He does."

Daniel was fluttering his hands, talking with them. "But I don't! Nobody does. And you shouldn't. But you guys—you and Mom—you act like it's this big deal. Even Granddad …" Daniel stopped himself.

His father stared. "Grandad what?"

"Uh … never mind." Daniel put his hands in his lap.

"Did he say something?"

"No."

"Then why did you mention him?"

"I've just heard him. You know, at Christmas, or when we go over there. He treats Kevin different, that's all. Younger. But you and Mom, you do the same thing. He's gonna be out of here in a few years, just like me, and he's got to start being responsible. It would be good for him to stay by himself. And it would be good for me too, for us to be together. Please?"

Bobby didn't answer.

"Pleeeeese?"

5.

To get to the airport on time the next Friday morning, they had to leave the house by 6 a.m. By 5:45, everybody except Kevin had eaten, and Bobby had gone out to the garage. When Daniel went to check on him a few minutes later, Bobby was laughing to himself with the trunk of the SUV wide open.

"What's she got in here?" Bobby gestured to the four huge suitcases and three carry-ons piled on the cement foundation. "It's only nine days, for cripes sake. Once we get there, she can buy whatever she wants. It's not like we're going to some desert island. I can't get it all in here. Where's Kevin?"

"Still in bed."

"Where's your stuff?" his father said, looking down. "Can you bring it out? I need to know what I'm working with. Better get it before she brings something else out."

Daniel went inside and downstairs to retrieve his overnight case, walking through the rec room where the new pool table was near the huge color TV. On his way to his room at the end of the hall, he passed by their bathroom and Kevin's room to his right. Daniel saw his brother standing, staring out his ground-level window toward the lake with his arms tight across his chest. He was naked except for the worn-out pair of red Cardinals pants he used as pajamas.

Daniel went in. "Listen, Kevin. I need to talk to you. Dad's upstairs and so's Mom. We don't have much time before we have to leave."

Kevin pointed. "You see the ducks?"

"Pay attention. This is important."

"Look."

The new day's sun glimmered on the rippling lake, with little sparkles that kissed the wavelets.

"Don't screw up, okay, while I'm in Washington? Don't do anything funny or we'll both be at Grandma's. And don't have anybody over. Not even Smitty, all right?"

Kevin nodded once, but he still didn't look at him. "There's only three."

Five ducks padded across, two adults and three babies. Daniel saw the feathered male in front.

"You see?" Kevin said. "There're only three left. Dad says the turtles got the other one, probably last night. That's two. They've already gotten two ducklings. Two out of the five they started with."

"Kevin—"

"The mother and father there, why don't they just fly away and take their babies to somewhere safe?"

The three little ones bunched tightly in a short line behind their mother. Daniel watched the male as he reached the far shore and stepped out, wagging his tail to shake off the water.

"They keep swimming like they don't care," Kevin said. "They just lost a baby. Don't they know that? It's terrible. I told Dad we ought to get rid of them. The turtles. Why do they have to do that? Pull them down like that? They've got plenty of other things to eat. But he says we can't find them all, even if we tried. But I bet we could. I bet we could get them all out of that lake."

Kevin turned to Daniel. "Don't you think? You and me and Dad, we could find them."

6.

When Daniel came up from the basement, his mother was slapping a piece of paper on the refrigerator door, anchoring it with little round black magnets on all four corners. She had drawn two perpendicular lines that intersected in the center, then filled the four boxes with her handwriting.

When he asked her what it was, she said, "It's a calendar of every day this weekend. It goes through Monday night, when you get home. I've got every minute planned, except when he's sleeping. I've even got your cousin Bryce sleeping over one night. Gina says she can keep him late tonight too, after dinner, and not bring him home until he's comatose."

"Mom."

But there was no stopping her. "This is a big thing, him staying alone. But I guess you're right. It seems every man in this house is against me on this. You keep telling me I can't treat him like a child anymore."

"He's gonna be all right. She's just down the road, and there's Grandma Winston. She doesn't have anything to do at night. And if you want, I can call him from Washington."

"No, I'll call him. Probably a couple times a day. I don't care how much it costs." She stopped to think. "I've locked up everything."

His mother had on a new sundress that was short and baby blue with bright green toucans all over it. "I think he's got what he needs. I washed all his clothes."

Daniel rolled his bag outside and gave it to Bobby, who asked as he wedged it in, grunting, "Where's Kevin?"

"Downstairs still, looking at those ducks."

Bobby put all his weight into closing the door. "He's not happy unless they're fine. He doesn't seem to understand that things don't always work out that way. Where's your mother? Don't tell me she's got something else."

Daniel smiled. "You know she's got this big schedule for him on the refrigerator? Poor guy, he's booked every minute."

"I had to go along with it so he could stay by himself. That reminds me. I need to tell him to bring that canoe in, and take down that lasso. I don't want him falling off that boat again."

Daniel cocked his head. "What did he do with the lasso?"

"He's got it up around the deck, around a piling, and he's been swinging on it from out on the walkout. He thinks he's Tarzan swinging on a vine, only it's got a loop in it so he can stand up."

The house door opened and Sarah finally stepped down two steps into the huge three-car garage.

"Woo-wee!" Bobby said as he eyed her. "Don't you look nice?" She held her new sundress in both hands and spun around for him. "Where'd you get that? Victoria's Secret? You think maybe I could help you get out of that later?"

"Dad! That's gross!"

But Sarah had stopped, and she was frowning. "Why aren't you wearing it?"

Bobby put on a big pout. "You're not gonna make me wear that."

"Oh yes I am."

"I couldn't find it," Bobby said. "I guess it got lost somewhere."

"No it didn't." Sarah turned to go inside again. "You're always hiding things, Mr. McAllister, but I always know where they are."

"What's she getting?" Daniel asked when she was gone.

"A shirt with the most god-awful hula girls. She says I've got to wear it. It's payback."

"Payback for what?"

"For not taking her before. Listen, I need to tell you. I almost forgot. I need for you to drill the beans on the one-sixty up by the railroad. I didn't get the chance to do it before we got rained out. It's probably gonna take you a couple of days."

"Uh …"

"I'll call you if there's anything else. But you need to do that field so I'm not behind when I get back."

The house door opened again. "Here it is!" Sarah trilled, waving the bright yellow fabric. "I found it! I told you."

Daniel said to him in a hurry, "Dad, I need to tell you. It's Granddad. He wants me to work for him. Starting this summer, pretty much full-time. He's gonna pay me, and he wants Kevin too."

"What?"

"Put it on!" Sarah began to sashay across the long garage.

Daniel ducked his head to whisper. "He wants me to start as soon as I get back. So I may not have time."

Sarah flapped the garish rayon. "Bobby!"

But Bobby said, "He wants you to do what?"

"He wants us to learn how to work the farm, so we can do it after he dies. He's old, Dad. He's eighty-two, and he doesn't have anybody to farm it after he's gone."

Thunder appeared on his father's face, so Daniel talked fast. "He wants to pay us full price. The same as he was paying Steve. We're gonna make a lot of money. And when I graduate, Granddad said I can live at the house, and he'd give me a percentage."

"A what?" Sarah said. She had come up.

Bobby said it too. "A what?"

"A percentage of the crop. Why? What's wrong?"

"Oh my God," she said. The shirt was forgotten.

Bobby said to her, "Now he's starting with them."

7.

"You're not working for him," Bobby said, his hands balled into fists. "Not ever. You're going to college. Get in the truck."

"But Dad!"

His face had closed and he clenched his teeth so hard his jaw had corded. "Get in the truck. We're going."

"But what if I want to?"

Sarah told him, "You don't understand."

Daniel skyrocketed. "You're busy telling me, but nobody's asked!"

She said, "There are things you don't—"

"Do I ever come into this? Do I get a vote?"

"No!" Bobby said. "You don't."

"And what about Kevin?"

"Don't you yell at me!" Bobby's voice was as loud as Daniel's. "No more discussion."

"Oh now I'm the baby? You're treating me like Kevin. Like I'm stupid!"

"Your brother's not stupid!" Sarah said. "How can you say that?"

"I don't believe this," Bobby said.

Kevin opened the house door. He was still in his pajama bottoms and no shirt, holding himself as he stepped down from the kitchen, clutching both his elbows with his hands. "What's going on? I can hear you guys yelling all the way downstairs."

"Kevin," Bobby shot back. "Did you know about this?"

"About what?" Kevin stepped down to the garage in his bare feet.

"I told him last week," Daniel said. "As soon as it happened. So what?"

Bobby turned on him. "Last week and you didn't tell me?"

Daniel paused, but then he said it. "He made me promise not to tell you."

"And you agreed?"

"We can't go," Sarah said. "I'm not gonna leave them. We're gonna have to—"

"No!" Bobby barked. "We're not gonna delay this trip again. I'm gonna call him, right now, and I'm gonna tell him to keep his hands off our boys."

"No!" Daniel said. "You can't do that!"

Kevin said it too. "That's not fair! I need the money."

"Kevin," his mother told him in a soothing voice. "You're too young—"

Kevin's voice rose. "Why do you keep saying that?"

Bobby had turned and was heading for the kitchen. "This is gonna stop right now," he said over his shoulder. "Kevin! I want you to get that boat in. Get it out of the water. No more back talk. Turn it over on the bank. And I don't want you out there while we're gone. And Daniel! Get that lasso down. Kevin help him. Now quick march, both of you. NOW!"

8.

Sarah followed Bobby inside and closed the door to the kitchen.

"What's his problem?" Kevin padded angrily in his bare feet toward the open automatic door.

"Fuck him!" Daniel turned toward the kitchen. "I'll be right out."

Daniel heard his father's shouting before he saw him. Bobby gripped the handset as Sarah stood glued to him while the words spit out like bullets.

"I don't give a shit what time it is!" Bobby told Garrett. "Wake up and listen to me! No, I will not lower my voice. I can't believe you did this. Going behind my back to get my boys. Yeah. He told me everything."

Bobby shot Daniel a look. "Just now. Right as we were getting ready to leave. Hawaii. What do you think he said? Of course I believe him. He's not gonna work for you, and neither is Kevin. What do I care? Sell the farm! It makes no difference to me. You want to see them again? Yeah, that's my leverage. You better keep your goddamn hands off!"

9.

"Now let's go," Bobby said. "We're late. We need to get to the airport. You." He pointed at Daniel. "You go out there and help your brother with that boat."

"Dad!"

"You heard me! I can't believe you went behind my back. Keeping secrets from me. You two thought you could manipulate me. Get me all soft and willing to do what you wanted after I'd been in Hawaii for ten days."

"That's not it!"

"Don't you think I know how he works?"

"Mom!"

His mother squared her shoulders as she stood tall next to her husband. "I agree with your dad one hundred percent."

"This is totally unfair! Both of you! You won't even listen."

"We don't have to," Bobby said. "You live in our house, and you live by our rules. You don't manipulate me. I'm ashamed of you. Now go!"

10.

Daniel found his brother below the deck, on the walkout. He was tugging on the rope, snapping it back and forth as he tried to get the lasso down without going up to untie it from the top, where it was looped around a corner piling.

"I can't believe him!" Daniel said.

"I can't get it," Kevin said to the rope.

"Fuck him!"

Kevin kept jerking it.

"Just leave it." Daniel told him. "Fuck them both. Don't take it down. We'll get it when I get back. Or better yet, let's leave it up for when we have that party."

Daniel put his hand inside the rope loop four feet off the ground. "How do you get up into it?"

"You have to hop. But Dad said—"

"I don't care!" Daniel heard how loud he was, so he checked over his shoulder. Quieter, he said, "We'll take it down before they get back. He'll never know. But we don't have to tell him, and we sure don't have to do everything he says."

"We're gonna have that party?"

"Sure as hell. Next week. And they're gonna want to swing in this."

Kevin looked at the thick coil in his hand, then up at the top of the piling. "But Dad will see it when he pulls out. It's on the corner here, on the edge of the deck."

"I'll distract him so he doesn't."

11.

"— call you tonight," she was saying to Kevin. "As soon as we get to the hotel. You know there's a big time change. You ought to be back here by then. You're having dinner with Gina."

"I know, Mom," Kevin said as he trailed her. "You told me a hundred times."

Bobby held his hand out, and Sarah grasped it. The SUV was so high she had to climb on the running board to get in. "I want you to put that shirt on," she said to Bobby. "As soon as we get on the plane. I'm not going to let that man ruin our trip."

Bobby closed her door, but then she opened it. "Kevin, you're going with Lester this morning. He's going to pick you up at seven, so you need to get dressed."

"Mom—"

"You need to be ready."

"— it's only six fifteen."

Bobby flicked the fingers of his right hand. "Come on," he said without looking at Daniel. "We're late. Get in."

Sarah kept talking through her open door. "He's going to drop you off at four, and I want you to take a shower before your Aunt Gina comes to get you. I don't want you sitting on her new upholstery in dirty clothes."

"Sarah," Bobby told her. "Close the door."

At last, they pulled out of the garage. Kevin walked with them across the cement.

"I love you!" Sarah called to him through her open window.

"Dad," Daniel said from the backseat. "When you come around the front, there's something I want to show you."

"Have fun!" Kevin yelled back at her.

Once they had backed into the driveway and started forward around the front of the house, Daniel pointed out the passenger-side window next to his mother. "Look Dad. It's over here."

Bobby turned his head to look right, where Daniel pointed.

"When I'm done doing the lawn next week," his son said as his father drove away, "do you want me to cut that part over there? Can you see that little section over by those far trees?"

12.

The next afternoon, the Park Ranger in her brown-striped uniform finished her spiel from the stage about the assassination. She pointed with a flourish to the spiral staircase at the rear of Ford's Theatre, which circled to the balcony and the box where Lincoln was shot.

Once Daniel had gone up to see it, he and his friend Jim came down again, then took the larger staircase to the basement, to the museum. A large, square room painted gray, it was filled with tall display cases arrayed between two rings of thick columns. In the center, the biggest box of all was flooded by a spotlight mounted in the ceiling.

"Hey, look at that," Jim said as they drew near. Behind the glass in the square case, a life-sized white mannequin wore Lincoln's actual evening clothes. The dead president's charcoal overcoat lay stretched across the wide bottom.

"Man, he was huge," Daniel said.

"I bet that would fit you."

"Nah. I'm only six-three. He was taller than that."

Jim peered. "Is that the gun?" A tiny pistol had its own small glass box adhered to the outside of the case with a printed sign. "Damn. It's a Derringer."

As Jim bent to read the small type, Daniel swung his head to scan the darkened room, then glanced at the restrooms on a landing at the top of a short flight of steps. Girls were there, but Daniel's eyes kept sweeping over the crowd and then down again, into the shadows on the other side of the stocky gray pillars.

"I need to pee," Jim said. "Need to go?"

"No." Daniel stood casually where he was until Jim entered the restroom, then turned quickly to search the farthest corner of the museum, where twenty busts of Lincoln rose in the semi-dark into a pyramid that stopped just below the ceiling. In front of them, a long flat case ran diagonally from corner to corner.

He saw her there. Redheaded Lisa had her back to him, staring down into the top of the glass. She was alone. Every one of the friends she had been spending the day with had left her.

Daniel spun, tangling his legs and nearly falling before he located five of her friends moving away from her across the large room in a flying wedge, giggling as they made a noisy, glamorous beeline for the bookstore. The door of it had been cut into the long wall opposite the bathrooms, and there were two big plate glass windows of merchandise. He could see two of the girls already pointing at what they saw.

Daniel turned again. She was still bent, her red curls tumbling into her sight. He took a deep breath and then his first step into the shadows.

When he had walked halfway toward her, though, he stopped himself. He shot a glance at the bathroom again, then ducked behind a seven-foot-high case jammed between two pillars in the outer ring. Inside the narrow case, a broad signboard hung, taking up nearly all the width. In his secret hiding place, shielded by the placard, Daniel was hidden from behind too. Jim wouldn't be able to see him in front of the tall video machine in a black box that was playing non-stop behind Daniel.

Daniel spread his legs and positioned himself so he could see through one of the two slivers of space on either side of the signboard. It was an inch wide, but he could see her.

In the loud room, sound fell away. He forgot about Lincoln, and death.

As he watched her and what her dancer's body was doing to the case, Daniel's mind went home again, back to their new house, and this girl was doing the same thing to him, only he wasn't him. He wasn't a person. He was the hard, yearning surface of the lake as he had seen it that last morning. Her fingers were on him, and he was rippling with her touch.

Lisa rubbed the smooth top of the case with her soft hand, caressing it, moving her palm along the cool hard of him, her fingers outstretched to feel the glass. With the other, she held her cascading hair back. She had tried to tuck it behind her ear, but it escaped and kept falling, so she had to hold it, hugging her ringlets beneath her chin.

She rubbed her lithe body along the side of it, stroking the glass with her right hip and the curved top of her thigh. She was stroking him too. Against his own case, he could feel her against him.

She caught each pinpoint spotlight as she swept along, shining the bright light back out like a beacon turning from a lighthouse. Rising, Daniel watched the glow of her suffused with red. A warning.

But he was lost.

13.

At nine o'clock that same night, Daniel sat with Jim at a beat-up old square-topped table at the back of the windowless, cavernous party room of their budget hotel off Pennsylvania Avenue. The bare overhead light bulbs had been dimmed. The base line of the rock music thumped so loud Daniel felt the driving beat in his elbows, coming up into his bones from the battered table. Across the room, a handsome DJ held court in a corner behind the empty, fold-up dance floor that had been put over the stained carpet. Nearly all the girls, including Kevin's Lisa, had pressed themselves as close to the flirting, knowing young man as they could. They bobbed to the base as they each tried to grab his attention.

The boys ate pizza and pretended not to care. Most of them lined the walls holding cans of soda, although some had perched on metal seats with ratty cushions around a few of the tables. Other than Daniel and Jim, none of them sat with any girls. The two of them, however, were graced by the blonde ringleader's presence.

"Is there any more, over by you?" Jim shouted at Daniel over the din.

"Are you kidding?" Daniel yelled back. "You're not still hungry. You ate that last one all by yourself."

"I want to dance," the blonde said to Jim.

"Go dance then." Jim reached for the last piece of pizza.

"But I want to dance with you!"

"Janet," Daniel said to her. "Have you seen his dancing?"

Daniel felt a hand on his shoulder and turned. One of the chaperones was leaning to talk in his ear. "Daniel," the middle-aged teacher blasted. "You need to come with me."

She wasn't smiling. "Did I do something wrong?" Daniel yelled at her. But she had stepped back so he could scoot his chair and follow. "Just come," she said.

Daniel shot a look at Jim, who shrugged.

The shorthaired, stout woman walked ahead of Daniel and quickly out the door of the dark party room, then took a left into the hallway. The bright lights struck him, making him blink. Even through the wall after she closed the door, Daniel could hear the music and feel the constant pounding like a heartbeat in his chest.

She led him down the narrow corridor lined with guestrooms. "Mrs. Lindan," he asked as he marched. "Am I in trouble?"

The woman shook her head but didn't look at him. She wasn't mad, but Daniel couldn't figure out what she was. She stopped at a door.

"Is this your room?"

She nodded as she slipped her key into the lock, then held the door open as she motioned him inside. "You go in now." He stepped into the room and she closed the door, leaving him alone.

The room was a rectangle, with the door on one of the short sides, then a long wall to his right studded with beds. There were three of them, all queens, and they were all made up and tidy. The place was spotless and organized, not like his room, which he shared with two other boys on another floor with another chaperone.

The long boxy room was dark, as dark as the party room. There was only one light—a black lamp shaped like an lantern with orange crackle glass suspended from a thick chain that swagged over the lone table at the faraway end. There were two black plastic chairs there too, just like in his room, crammed into the tiny space between the last bed and the brick wall. One of them was still pushed in under the small round table. The other had been pulled out.

Daniel squinted. Someone was there, sitting under the hanging lamp.

It was his father.

"Dad?"

Bobby sat under the one light.

Daniel said, "Are you all right? Is something wrong? You're supposed to be in Hawaii."

Bobby stood up. He smoothed his pant legs. "Come here, son, and sit."

"How did you get here? What's wrong?" As he came closer, Daniel saw his father's gray face and then the red in his eyes.

"Sit down, son." Bobby pointed at the bed next to him.

"Is it Mom? Is she all right?"

"She's fine." His father spoke softly now.

"Then it's Kevin," Daniel said. "Is he all right?"

Bobby sat in one of the plastic chairs as he waited for Daniel to sit on the edge of the queen bed. When he did, Bobby leaned forward, putting his forearms on his knees. "Son—"

"What is it?"

Bobby clasped his hands and Daniel saw they were shaking. "There's something—"

"Is he all right?"

"—I need to say. I need for you to listen, and be quiet now." Bobby took a deep breath. "There's been an accident."

"An accident? What kind?"

"Daniel. Your brother's been killed."

"What?"

"He's been killed. Kevin's been killed in a terrible accident."

"What accident?"

"Kevin's dead."

"He's dead? Where?"

"Back at the house."

"Today?"

"Yesterday."

"Right after we left?"

"No," his father said. "Last night, before your Aunt Gina got there."

"Was he in the boat?"

"No, but they don't know yet."

"Who doesn't?"

"The doctors."

"There were doctors there?"

"No. He was alone. He was in the rope. That's where he was when she got there. She said he got caught in it."

"The rope? You mean that lasso?"

"She was gonna pick him up, remember? Your mom had it all planned. But when Gina got there, he was on that swing. He was in it. Caught up in it somehow. That's all I know." His father spoke without emotion. He was just delivering words.

"He was alone? No Smitty or Dwight?"

Bobby shook his head.

"Did he fall?"

"They don't know. That's why they have to do an autopsy. Dr. Frederick this morning, he said it was the law. They have to, because he was alone, and underage, and because of how he died. Mysterious circumstances. They have to do a complete autopsy."

Bobby had no emotion. It was like he was reading words off a page. He flicked his wrist to look at his watch. "They're doing it right now. Right this minute. Dr. Frederick has to be somewhere tomorrow, so he wanted to get it done tonight. He wants to get the lab results before the inquest." His father's voice stopped, but he didn't look up. He had gone somewhere that looking at his watch had taken him.

"What's an inquest?"

Still the eyes on the watch. "It's after the funeral. They think they can have it done before everybody goes home, so we can all know. Your aunts and uncles and all your cousins."

"Funeral. Jesus. So we can all know what?"

"How he died." Bobby was hunched, looking at his watch. "What time is it here?"

"Uh…" Daniel looked at his own watch. "Nine twenty. Why?"

"It's an hour later here, right? So it's eight twenty, and they started at seven. It's been an hour and twenty minutes. So they're about halfway done." His father spoke robotically. "Dr. Frederick said it was gonna take three hours, with all they have to do. It's Tuesday. The funeral's Tuesday. I wonder—"

"Dad."

"—if they'll be done by the time we get to the airport. They're doing it right now. Can you believe that? As we sit here in this room."

Daniel grabbed his father's hands. He lurched forward as he took them. "Dad, look at me."

As he spoke, Bobby looked at Daniel's fingers gripping his knuckles. "It's the only way they can know for sure. It's because he was all by himself and no one saw. So there's nobody to tell them what happened. They said they can't even guess."

Bobby started blinking. "He was alone. I left him alone, so I could take my little trip for my second honeymoon. I made her leave him there alone. She didn't want to. There was no one. He died alone. He died alone."

Bobby's shoulders started bucking as the sobs broke through. "It's all my fault."

"No!"

"Gina's not strong. If I'd been there, I could have helped him. I could have gotten him down. Or I could have made sure he never got up on that swing in the first place. Daniel, why didn't he take it down? I told him to take it down. Why didn't he mind?"

Daniel came off the bed and dropped to his knees in front of his father.

Bobby grasped him, folding in half to hold his son tightly against him. "Kevin's gone because I went to Hawaii. I should have taken down that swing."

14.

Their plane for home took off an hour later. Mrs. Lindan had already called them a cab. It was idling at the curb, waiting, when she had put her hand on Daniel's shoulder in the darkened party room.

On the plane, Bobby told him about Gina's call. She had left a message at the Honolulu hotel, that they needed to call her as soon as they arrived. When Sarah called back, she answered on the first ring, but then she wouldn't talk until Bobby too had picked up another phone. He bark-laughed as he told it. He had heard about his son in the bathroom, sitting on the closed lid of the commode.

Gina was crying so hard she could barely tell them. She was so sorry, she said, but he was already gone. When she had found him, there was nothing she could do but get him down. She laid him on the cement of the walkout, but he wouldn't breathe.

Bobby and Sarah had taken the very next flight to St. Louis, leaving Hawaii at 6:30 that same night. The plane landed hard on the tarmac of Lambert Field very early the next morning, and when they straggled off, the two of them still had on the same clothes they had left in.

"You mean that shirt with all the hula girls?" Daniel asked as the car sped to the airport.

Bobby tried to smile.

At the hospital, Dr. Frederick had been waiting. He took Bobby aside and whispered to him as he explained what he had to do.

After that, Bobby and Sarah both prayed with Father Parham from their parish. The young priest had been there all night, keeping a vigil next to their boy.

Bobby had gone in then with Father Parham, to see Kevin. Sarah couldn't bring herself to walk down the hall. Bobby told Daniel his brother looked like he was asleep, only he was transparent. Through his skin, you could see his veins and the small purple bruise like a thumbprint at the base of his neck.

They had finally pulled up at home exactly thirty hours after they had left it. Kevin was gone, but two Lawler's men lingered on the hot front porch, sweating in the black suits they wore despite the mid-day temperature. Bobby said he had called the funeral home on one of his five trips to the airport pay phone in Honolulu.

Once the Lawler's crows had gone, Bobby at last took a shower and changed. He had eaten finally, then said goodbye to his wife.

She had told him she didn't trust them. The airline could do anything with her only surviving son. They could crash the plane, or decide to cancel it. They might even route him somewhere, anywhere, by mistake.

"Go get him," she had said to Bobby. "Go get him and bring him home. I don't want him to be alone, when he hears this. Go keep him safe."

15.

She was already flying when the headlights hit her. She had come out the front door, hopping the stairs to the grass and running with her arms out as she was screaming. "Daniel! Daniel, you're home!"

"Stop!" Daniel said to his father. "Stop the truck."

Daniel threw open the door and leapt out, then started racing toward his mother. "Mom! Mom, I'm here. I'm home! I came home!"

They collided. She threw her arms around him.

"I'm okay." He lifted her up.

"Oh God. Thank God, Daniel. You're home."

16.

By Sunday supper the next day, they had all come. Every single one of his aunts and uncles and all of his cousins were squeezed like sardines in his kitchen and in his living room and out on the screened-in back porch. Daniel tried to inch by all the relatives and half the townspeople. "Excuse me. Excuse me." As he moved he could barely breathe.

Their eyes were bloodshot when they came in, and they all started crying again as soon as they caught sight of him. Even the men, who dragged shaking fists under their noses as they sniffed.

They all had to clutch at him too, like he was their blanket. Everywhere Daniel went in the house, some adult on some couch reached up to pull him down. They stared at him and they held him as they looked deep into his eyes. They demanded to know how he was, really. Really truly. And then they waited, blinking up, as if he was actually going to say.

He told them he was fine, really. But you look terrible, they said. Grief-stricken, just like your parents. They wouldn't release their grip until he smiled and reassured them that yes, he would survive this.

They were whispering too, leaning in close to watch each other's lips. Most of them stopped when they saw him coming, and shut up, but some of them kept on. They hunched ever closer and started hissing, their soft sibilants sounding like air escaping from a hose.

His mother's two sisters spent the day on the back porch with his Grandma Winston. His mother's third sister, his Aunt Diane, had flown in from Florida with her husband Stan.

Bobby's sister Jeanne had arrived from Knoxville late the night before, but she had already gone by the time Daniel and his father had pulled into the driveway. She was staying with his grandparents in the old house that still faced the railroad tracks. Jeanne would be coming back, Bobby told him, later that afternoon.

His Aunt Debbie and her family had arrived very early that morning. She and his Uncle Dave had loaded up their five kids and driven straight through the night, as soon as they heard. The baby was still warm and sleeping when they had tumbled in the kitchen door at breakfast.

His Uncle John had pulled up then, with his wife and his three boys. They hadn't stopped once on the race from De Kalb.

Tommy, the youngest, walked in by himself with his duffel bag a few minutes before noon. He had gunned it, he said, all the way up from Houston. It had only taken him eleven and a half hours, a new record.

"But that's nearly 800 miles!" Debbie said as she hugged him.

In the kitchen, platters of cold cuts and rolls filled the counter space, along with cut vegetables and warm casseroles and chips and dip. The oak table was groaning too, under the weight of all the pies and homemade cookies. Even the new woman manager of the bank had brought a mountain of fresh fruit, cut into little balls and spilling out of a watermelon.

Daniel's mother came out from her room once in a while to greet the changing multitude. After a few minutes, though, Sarah always headed back down the hall. She shuffled slowly, touching the walls for balance and watching her feet. Sarah talked all right, but her words were choppy, and she didn't cry enough. And she didn't respond when somebody hugged her. Even his father couldn't get her to focus for more than a few seconds at a time.

Daniel saw his father having to play host to everyone. As they walked through the door, they were already searching for him. They wouldn't talk to anyone else until they had cornered him in the kitchen or out on the porch. Very often, they had to wait their turn. Then, the men stood awkwardly while the women clung. His father had to hold them and let them cry it out. After a while, the left shoulder of his knit golf shirt was wet. Daniel could see the growing, messy circle of dark green.

The men stepped up, and they hugged and slapped him, pounding Bobby hard on the back. He was flinching by noon, but he let them do it. His father took it all, from every one. Daniel saw them hand him their pain, and Bobby take it. He hugged them and told them all the same thing. Yes, it was awful. Yes. But they would get through it. They would, as a family. Yes, yes I know, she looks terrible too.

Bobby never broke down. He never cried in public. He took too long a few times when he went down the hall to check on Sarah, but whatever he did with the door closed, he did with her.

Twice, his father pulled him aside and whispered. He wanted to know if Daniel was all right.

"Yeah, I'm fine. Don't worry about me. How's Mom?"

"Not good. I don't know how we're gonna get through this. Father Parham's gonna be here in a little while, to talk about the funeral, but I don't think she's gonna be up for that. We'll have to do it ourselves. Daniel, can you to talk to him with me?"

"Is it the sedatives?"

"Yeah. Maybe they gave her too much. She doesn't know what she's saying half the time. I don't know how she's gonna get through the funeral in two days. She's supposed to be off of them by then, but I don't know."

An hour later, three of his little boy cousins came up to him and asked if they could see the lasso.

"I don't know where it is." Daniel told them the truth. "It was already gone when we got home. Somebody must've taken it down, but I don't know who."

The boys trooped down to the rec room anyway. They all did, sooner or later. Even the grown-ups went to stand and stare out, peering through the sliding glass door at the concrete walkout and then up, at the wooden beams of the deck off the kitchen upstairs.

Daniel went to his room, but they wouldn't let him stay there. Some aunt or uncle always knocked and asked too loudly in a high, bright voice how he was, and whether they could get him anything.

Across the hall, the light was on in Kevin's room. Everything inside was the same as his brother had left it, except the bed had been made and there were now clothes laid out carefully across the coverlet. Blue dress slacks were there, next to a newly ironed white button-down shirt. Kevin's sport coat hung on the back of his chair, unbuttoned. Across the navy blue lay a red-striped tie his mother had draped around the collar.

Sarah had been in there much earlier that morning, after Lawler's had called to say that Kevin needed clothes. When he had first gotten up, Daniel had found her ironing the white shirt crisp while she cried.

17.

"Father, we don't understand how this tragedy could have happened to this family."

More than fifty people were gathered in the living room to hear Father Parham. Next to Daniel, Bobby held onto Sarah, but she didn't look like she was there. As he stood with his eyes closed, thinking of Kevin, Daniel tried to breathe, but then it hit him, the heavy, sweet perfume of the fifteen flower arrangements in screaming summer colors all around him. It was all he could do not to bolt.

"Kevin was such a good boy. I believe with all my heart that he's with you. We want to celebrate that he's with you, but that's hard for many of us. We can't make sense of what's happened to this wonderful young boy, and to this good family. Please God in Heaven. Please give them some peace. We know he's with you. We know it in our minds, because that's what your Son taught us. But please help us know it in our hearts.

"We ask you to help them, and to comfort his poor aunt, who found him. His Aunt Gina. Help her Lord, to find some peace after what she's seen. And this father here …"

Daniel swung his eyes over to Bobby, who was looking down.

"I don't know what to say. But you do. You know what it's like, to lose a son. Your precious Son. Please help this father know there's a reason for this. And give this woman strength. This poor mother who has just lost her son. She loved him Lord. I saw how she looked at him every Sunday in church.

"A mother brings her child into this world, trusting that he's going to live. They're supposed to outlive us. It doesn't seem right for him to have to leave her first. I can't imagine what she's going through. Giving a child back to You must be the hardest thing any mother could ever do. Help her. Please help her Lord to see that you'll take care of him. Help her to feel what he feels, right now. He feels the warmth of Heaven's breath.

"Help these parents understand they're not to blame for what happened. And for not being here. Sometimes, You just have to come and take Your children home. Even the young ones. And the strong, healthy teenagers. It doesn't matter if their parents are here or not. Sometimes we don't get to say goodbye. Not in words. Not directly. But help them understand that he's up there. He's waving down to them right now. He's fine, and he's happy. He can see them even if they can't see him.

"And finally this boy. This young man here."

Daniel felt his father's hand. It gripped his fingers. "Help him with his crushing grief. He's just lost his only sibling. They were so close. I watched the two of them playing every week. Daniel, I know how much Kevin meant to you. I just pray to God that He will get you through this. Everyone in this room, in this whole town, knows he was your best friend."

18.

"Daniel, it's time," his father said. "We need to meet with Father Parham but I don't have a Bible. Can you go down and see if my mother's is still there? I think I saw it in Kevin's room. She was praying before."

In Kevin's room, in the single drawer of his brother's nightstand, distraught Daniel found her Book. On top of it, as she had slid it in, his grandmother had laid a small photograph of Kevin taken at school that year, along with a new green sprig of baby's breath. The tiny white buds had been plucked from one of the bouquets littering the house upstairs.

Daniel lifted the Bible and felt its weight. It was wrapped in a homemade dust jacket of pink oilcloth that was thick in his hands and shined like the old covering on her kitchen table. The stitching had been done with gold thread on a thick needle that created two flaps for the hard covers to slip into. In the light, he spotted fingerprints on the stiff, smooth front.

He began walking toward the rec room, but as he went he opened the Book, paging through it carefully so as not to tear the paper-thin, gold-rimmed leaves. He was trying to locate a particular passage about a son who falls prostrate in front of his father.

The Bible pouched a little inside the back flap of the homemade cover. He opened it all the way, but it didn't lie right. There was something tucked inside. In the hallway, he stopped walking, then looked up to check the rec room to see if anyone was there.

In that one moment, it happened to be empty. Daniel turned away from the inside stairs, anyway, and brought the Book in close to his chest. He curved his shoulders and ran his fingers inside the back flap. He felt the edge of a fat square of thick paper that had been folded many times and shoved deep inside the bottom right corner. He struggled to get his man's fingers in far enough to pull it out.

19.

Bobby stared down silently at the single typed sheet. Father Parham had handed it to him as they came in, when Daniel and his father had sat on the twin bed in Daniel's room. After he closed the door, the young priest squeezed himself awkwardly into Daniel's little desk chair, then turned to face them. Daniel noticed the man's odd, thick-soled black tennis shoes as the boy stared at the floor.

"There sure is a lot to plan," Bobby said to the priest from the bed. "Look at all the blanks on here."

"It can be pretty daunting, I know."

Sitting next to him, Daniel craned his neck to look at the sheet in his father's hands. The page was a list with blanks going down the left side and fine print across from each entry. "So it's not just the people we've got to find," Daniel said. "It's all the rest of it too. What they'll read."

Father Parham said, "I can help you with that. I brought this book. It's got most of the readings in it. You just have to go through it and decide what you want."

Bobby asked, "Is there an order?"

"It's what you see there. It starts at the beginning of the celebration, with the placing of the pall, and then the first reading. See those spaces? And then the psalm follows, and the second reading, and the gospel and so on."

"I need people for each of these?" Bobby asked, surprised.

"Yes. Everything with a blank."

"'Eulogy'," Daniel read out loud. "What's that? There's no blank for it."

"It's discretionary," the priest said. "You don't have to do it, though most people choose to. It's usually a family member who talks about the deceased."

Daniel thought. "What about Tommy, Dad? He'd do it and he'd be good. Kevin really likes him. Liked." Daniel heard himself and stopped.

"I can ask him," Bobby said. "That's good. What else?"

"The readings are the biggest part. You have to choose them, and the readers have to read them in plenty of time, so they're familiar with them before the celebration begins. We've only got another day, and the early part of Tuesday."

Bobby nodded as he thought. "There's Gina of course. And my brother John. He'd do it. That makes two."

"Dad, can I read?" Daniel asked.

"No," Bobby said. "It's not your job. Plus you're in no condition to—"

"I'm fine! I want to do it."

"I don't think—"

"But Dad! I really do. Please."

"Daniel," Father Parham interrupted. "I know how much it means to you, to be a part of this. I see how upset you are. But I was in there just now, with your mother, and I have to tell you she's not doing very well. She's barely hanging on, and she may not be any better by the time of the celebration. So I'm worried that if she sees you up there, it might be more than she can bear. You know, if you're up in front, reading. Healthy and strong and standing there, next to him, in that … " The man paused.

"Oh," Daniel said. "I see."

The priest thought. "But you know. You could be the one to place the pall. The cloth. You know, that goes on top. And we could do that in front, after the procession. That way, you could still do something that was meaningful to you, but you wouldn't be up there for too long. And you'd be moving the whole time. She might not notice, because it's a lot of action."

"Yeah," Daniel said, nodding. "That's all right."

"Bobby, is that okay with you?"

After Bobby said it was, and Father Parham had written it down, they started again to go down the list, filling in the blanks with the pen the priest had given them. It took some time, but eventually there was only one left, next to a reading of a psalm. Bobby tapped on the paper and said to Daniel, "Should I ask Lester to do this one?"

"But he's not family," Daniel said. "What about Granddad Winston?"

Both the priest and Bobby looked up, then at each other. "No," Bobby said. "I don't think so."

"I have to agree with your dad," Father Parham said.

A moment passed, then Daniel shifted on the bed. "There's no one left," he said to Bobby. "It's got to be you."

"Me?

"One of us has to read, and if it's not gonna be me, it's got to be you."

"Actually," the priest said. "The immediate family isn't expected to."

"But Dad," Daniel pleaded. "We're all he's got. Everybody else lives out of town. I love them, but it can't be all of them without at least one of us. If I can't, then you have to. It's not gonna be Mom."

"Daniel, I can't. I'm sorry, but I can't."

"Because you're too upset? It's just words, right?" Daniel turned to the priest. "All he has to do is read?"

"Son." Father Parham said, reaching out to touch Daniel's shoulder.

"Dad! We can't leave him up there with strangers."

"They're not strangers." It was the priest.

"They see him twice a year!" Daniel said to his father. "If you won't do it, then I will. I'm not gonna leave him up there alone!"

Bobby closed his eyes.

"Oh God! Alone! I can't believe I said that. Dad, I'm so sorry."

Bobby wiped one eye with his thumb, then blinked. "It's all right. Really." He turned to his son. "I know exactly what you mean. And I feel the same way. And so does your mother. So if it's that important to you, I'll read."

20.

Daniel shouldered by all the people wolfing sandwiches in his kitchen. He didn't say a word as he pulled open the back door and stepped down to the cool hardness of the garage's concrete, then marched straight out to the white glare of the blinding sun. He squinted as his feet crunched on the pebbly gravel of the driveway, but he didn't slow as he passed behind the twenty cars and trucks jammed in like his hungry relatives, squeezed cheek-to-jowl and facing down the long hill toward the lake.

The grass was short when he got to it, and it smelled like the summers he used to have. His father had been out cutting it on the riding mower before dawn, in the ghostly morning. Daniel had lain awake in his bed listening to the moan.

Daniel had his back to the house, but he could still hear them. They sounded like geese honking on his back porch. "Wa wa wa" was what he heard, even when he turned away and made himself not see them.

He headed out in a beeline, not stopping until he got to the edge, to one of the two stark lines where the velvet nap of the lawn met the wilderness. Bobby had never cleared the valley all the way around. On the far side of the lake, opposite the house, it was chaos, with tall, waving rushes and wild pampas grass that matted thickly on the steep hill. The thatch was so dense that all the many sharp rocks were hidden, as were the sinkholes and soft spots and dark clumps of crowded, waxy shrubs. Only the four-wheelers could get around out there, and even they slid on the mushy slope as often as they got to the top of it, losing power as teenage boys stood on them and skidded back, out of control.

Daniel stopped short on his side of the line and took a deep breath on the shorn lawn, and then another. After he cleared his lungs, he turned finally, and looked down.

It was blazing hot, and August humid. The drum of cicadas thumped in the air, circling slow and deep in a bass rhythm that revved under the high squawk of all the mourners. Even where he was, the honking still came out to him from the house.

On the lake, four ducks glided in formation on the glassy water. Daniel spotted the bright male first, way out in front. He was so far ahead of his mate and their two babies paddling furiously that he had nearly reached the shallows on the other shore. The female sliced through the water quickly, trying to catch him, while far behind her two ducklings struggled to keep up. They were all in a line, but there were at least ten feet between her and the first of her two children.

Daniel counted, and then he lifted a finger to touch each of them in the air, counting again.

They kept moving silently. They didn't see him. Back from each of their tails, two lines of ripples made an arrow in the water. There were four of them, one for each of the ducks, and together they made a herringbone embossing the shine. Daniel glanced behind them, then turned his head to peer back at where they had all started. It was in the wild part down on the shore to his left. He tried, but he couldn't see into the muddy flats there past the bangs of rushes. The tall reeds bent so low they furred the edge.

He jumped his eyes over the male and out in front of him. Nothing swam ahead, or foraged at the roots of the young green plants along the far shoreline.

Daniel narrowed his eyes and scanned the oval rim all the way around. Nothing else was paddling anywhere that he could see, or shaking its tail. The third duckling Kevin had seen two days before was gone.

Daniel plunged across the line and started running. He flung his whole body into the wild, into the prickly, saw-toothed grass that grabbed him and tore at his pants. He hurtled down the hill, heading for the water, seeing nothing but the lake, but then his running feet caught in a hole and he went down. He tumbled, rolling once, but then he saved himself. He struggled up, clutching onto a bush, but then the branch broke and he started skating. The boy was surfing, fighting to keep his balance by flailing his arms.

He crashed down onto his rump and started skidding. His muddy feet went first, and then his spine. He hit the rocks with a yelp, and his arms swung out in a cross from his body. The palms of his hands felt the hard Braille of the slope.

The male duck reached the shore, and he shook himself. Everything flapped until it was only his tail.

Daniel burst out of the jungle muddy and clamored down to the rocks that lay hidden under the water, where they had started.

On the other side of the lake, the mother duck got out and followed the male. Behind her, as they got to the shore, her two babies struggled to stand up, but they couldn't find a spot that was shallow enough to put their feet down. They started flapping their wings, quacking to her to come back. They both called to her, but she didn't help them. They were stuck out there on their own.

Daniel looked down at his feet, but he didn't see it. His eyes saw only submerged plants and fish. There were minnows and flies, but nothing else.

He doubled over, and then he knelt, first on one knee and then on both. He put his shins and then both his elbows into the mud. He dove both his hands into the warmth that was drenching his clothes and seeping into his tennis shoes. Daniel searched frantically under the rocks, grasping, feeling with the spongy tips of his tender fingers. He smashed them as he poked and jammed them under the stones.

He staggered up, making two big sucking sounds as he pulled his legs out and tried to move them. His plastered pants must have weighed a hundred pounds. He couldn't straighten his legs anymore, so he walked like Frankenstein.

He collapsed again, and started to grope along the shore. He got up, went down, and then up again, each time a few feet farther away. The rocks under the surface cut him, and they made his arms bleed.

He finally stopped, and sat back and looked down at the desperate ripples he was churning in the water. The circles jumped so much they didn't reflect back his face. He was crying but he didn't know it. All he saw was a broken boy breaking apart in the lake.

21.

"Hey." Tommy smiled as Daniel walked up. "You know, you've got about a hundred people up there having heart attacks. They're all lined up. Can't you see them, up along the kitchen window? And look there. You've got another crowd out on the porch."

Daniel looked up to the house where his uncle pointed.

"Every single one of them thinks you've lost your mind. So you better wave to them if you don't want them coming out here. If you don't, we're gonna have to take the old ladies to the hospital, because they're gonna come out here and trip on this hill."

He raised his arm and starting swinging. "Come on!" he said, and Daniel did the same thing. They pumped their arms like they were parking airplanes, and in an instant thirty white hands fluttered back at them from the house. They looked like moths slapping their wings against the porch screen and the kitchen window.

Tommy turned to sit down, but he tripped. "Jesus," he said as he regained his balance. "What did I just step in? A gopher hole?"

Daniel laughed. "A snake hole." He patted the hill. "But it's okay. They're probably gone by now, I was making so much noise. I've made it all nice and smooth for you."

"I can see that." Tommy lowered himself. "I can also see your hands and what you did to your backside. Jeez, what were you looking for? I didn't see all of it. They had to come get me. But what's over there? What's under the water?"

"It's gonna sound pretty dumb," Daniel said, turning his eyes away from his uncle. "I was looking for turtles. They keep getting at the ducks. The little ones. I thought maybe I could find one, but I couldn't. But I know they're out here."

Tommy looked at the lake. "You mean them? They look okay to me."

"No. There used to be three ducklings. Now there's only two. It happened while I was gone, because there were three of them two days ago. The turtles, they don't go for the adults. They're too big. They want the babies they can grab."

In the thick air, the cicadas kept humming. "Boy," his uncle said. "They sure make a lot of noise."

"The bugs?"

"No. All those people. I bet if you listen you can hear every word. No wonder you came out here. But it doesn't help. They must be driving you nuts. Are you okay?"

"Yeah."

"Well, if there's anything I can do."

"I should just ask."

"Jesus, that's what they're all saying to you, isn't it? I'm sorry. I sure hope I do a better job with this eulogy."

As they sat, the hot sun did its baking work, drying Daniel out and replacing the lake water with salty sweat that began pooling under his arms and skimming a fast track down between his shoulder blades.

Daniel heard tires crunch and looked over. They both watched his Aunt Jeanne get out, then walk to the passenger side and open the heavy door for her mother. Old and frail, Cora unfolded herself, then leaned on her daughter as they headed toward the open garage that led to the back door of the kitchen.

Tommy said, "Huh. He didn't come. I haven't seen him. Did he come and leave before I got here?"

302

"You mean Granddad? No, I haven't seen him."

"You mean he hasn't been here at all? I know he's mad at your dad but this isn't the time for that."

Daniel turned. "He's mad at Dad? Why?"

"Oh I don't know. With him you never know, but I do know your dad pissed him off royal last year." Tommy was smiling. "I mean, look at this." Tommy swept his arm in front of himself. Muscled and thirty-four, he was the youngest and coolest of his father's siblings. "Look at this house, and the lake and the boats and your dad's truck. And that farm of his that he did without my dad knowing. He has to be jealous."

"Jealous?"

"Isn't it obvious? But then there's always been something else too. Something special about your dad that sets him off. I don't know what it is. I never have known. But this last thing, this past year, sure got his goat."

Tommy was still smiling. "My dad tried to get him back, but your dad wouldn't do it. He told him no, and it pissed him off."

"He wanted us to move back to the farm?"

"No, he just wanted your dad to help out. Work for him, like he did before, before you moved out and your dad built this house here. You know why? He can't get anyone to stay. He keeps chasing them off. They walk out on him. Bobby was the only one who never left. Not until it got so bad that he didn't have a choice about it. Last fall, my dad sent one of his buddies to negotiate as his proxy." Tommy laughed. "Oh, he was vague about it, but your dad knew exactly what he was after. Your dad turned him down flat."

"Who was it?"

"You mean his buddy? Some old guy. Is Shorty still alive? But I tell you what, it would have been hell no if he had asked me. I don't know how Bobby stood it all those years. But I'm glad he did, for my sake, because otherwise it was gonna have to be me. Or John. One of us. But damn." Tommy looked across the lake, at the house. "I didn't know it was this bad. He's got to be really pissed not to show up."

Tommy shook his head to himself. "Damn. He could do the same thing he did to Garrett J."

The cicadas droned in the heavy air, cycling around without stopping.

Daniel wiped the sweat on his cheek. "What did he do?"

"He cut him out of his will, and he cut out his daughter. Hope. You know, your cousin. As it stands now, it's divided into fifths. She doesn't get anything. It ought to be in six parts, with Hope getting her father's share, but he got mad, and he cut out Garrett J. when he left town, and he's never changed it. So his own granddaughter gets screwed."

"Jeez," Daniel said. "Does Grandma know?"

"Yeah, she's been working on him for years, but it doesn't matter. It doesn't make any difference. And now he's not here. I bet he's gonna cut out your dad now, too, if he hasn't already."

Daniel brought his hand up to his forehead, putting his palm against his skull.

"What is it?" Tommy said, leaning toward him on the slope.

"Shit." Daniel whispered it.

"What?"

"He told me last week, but I didn't realize it. You know what he said? He said, 'Everything I've got is gonna come to you.'" Last week, before I left on my trip. He said I was gonna split it, with the rest of his children. He said it was mine, mine and Kevin's. He wants us to farm it for him."

"What did he say about your dad?"

Daniel tried to remember. "That he already had enough, what with his own farm and this big house. Enough. That's what he said."

"Ah nuts, so then he did do it. He's cut him out. Does your dad know?"

Daniel shook his head. "No."

"You didn't tell him? Crap. My dad's old. He could go any time."

"I know," Daniel said. "He told me that too."

Tommy started hopping the wooden heels of his boots, making holes in the grass as he bounced them. "What an asshole. Daniel, I don't want you to tell your father. I'm gonna try to fix this without telling him. This is the last thing he needs to know right now."

"But—"

"Maybe after the funeral I can take my sisters and brothers over to the house and talk some sense into him." Tommy was thinking out loud, his words slow as he put them together. "I just thank God they're all here now. Can you imagine what it would be like if it was just Bobby and me? I don't know what I'd do if Dad got mad at Bobby one day and decided to leave it all to me."

He glanced at Daniel suddenly then, shooting a look over to him that Daniel noticed. Tommy screwed up his face. "I can't believe I said that."

"What?" Daniel said.

"God I've got a mouth." Tommy broke off a fat blade of grass.

"Why? What did you say?"

Tommy started to turn it between his fingers. He spread it flat, then ran it over the top of one knuckle and smoothed it with his thumb. "It's just the same as you and your brother. Only nobody got pissed."

"What's the same?"

"Well," Tommy said slowly, measuring his words. "You get it now. Everything they've got. Your parents. It all comes to you."

Daniel swung his eyes away from his uncle.

"Are you okay?"

"I get it all," Daniel said quietly. "Kevin doesn't get it now."

He turned on Tommy. "But I don't want it! Granddad gave it to me, but I don't want it. It's not fair to him, and it's not mine!"

"Not fair to who? This place is yours—"

"Not this place!"

Tommy put his hand out. "Calm down. You're not making sense."

"I don't deserve it! And now I get it all, the whole share."

"What are you talking about?"

But Daniel wasn't listening. He had swung his sweating head to scan the driveway and the graveled space at the end of it where all the cars and trucks were parked.

"Tommy," he said in a rush as he eyed the vehicles facing them. "My dad's truck's blocked in. Yours isn't. Can I borrow your keys?"

22.

Daniel banged through the screen door and into the kitchen. Garrett sat at one of the old wooden benches at the table in the alcove, eating a late supper Cora had made. "You've got to change it, Granddad! You've got to change your will and give it back to him."

The old man sat alone with a magnifying glass next to the weekly town newspaper. "How dare you barge in here after what you pulled the other day. I don't have anybody now, and it's the middle of June."

"I don't want it!"

"And why aren't you home, playing court?"

"What?"

"With all those friends of his, and my whole family. All my children are there, and I'm sitting here by myself." Garrett pushed his plate.

"I don't want Kevin's share. I don't want Dad's either."

"Why are you wet? You're covered in mud."

"I didn't know you'd cut Dad out."

"Sure you did. Your eyes lit up like a damn Christmas tree. And his dying doesn't change anything. Your brother. I'm torn up like everyone else, but I have to say it. You're the one I wanted. And now it all comes to you, your father's whole share. That's the right answer anyway. There was always something wrong with Kevin."

"No there wasn't! I'm not gonna take it!"

Garrett's fist pounded the table. "You're gonna run this farm just like your daddy. And you're gonna run it after I'm gone. All those kids of mine, over at your house right now, jaw-boning? They're gonna need you 'cause they can't run it themselves. And you know what?"

"What?"

"Nobody's called me. And it's been three days. My own son hasn't had the decency."

"So how did you find out?" Daniel was confused.

"That Gina, or whatever her name is. She called my wife, not me. And that was Friday night. It's Sunday. What does your father think? That I'm off in Tahiti or wherever the hell they went to?"

"I'm sure he didn't—"

"He's making me look bad! Everybody in town's over there except me."

"I can drive you. I've got Tommy's—"

"I'm the head of this family. Not him."

"I'll take you right now."

"Not without an invitation. And you come in here and tell me to change my will? So I put him back in?"

23.

Daniel rounded the corner in a run, then found his father at last on the far side of the house by the first-floor bedrooms. His father was plunging two enormous goose-necked watering cans one-by-one into an open, filled rain barrel at the bottom of a downspout. "Dad! There you are."

His father held them aloft. Water rivulets snaked down his father's arms. "Are you all right? Where did you go? Tommy said you borrowed his car."

It was seven already, but the sun still beat down on them from a full hand's-breath above the trees that lined the tops of the slopes that made up the rim of Bobby's valley. His father had built their new house in a soft bowl of land traversed by a streambed at the bottom he'd dammed into the lake. Above where they stood, from every angle, pine trees poked the sky.

He trudged down the hill toward the four massive terra cotta flowerpots Grandma Winston had bought and installed that day at the edge of the walkout. Tagging along behind him, Daniel said, "I went to Granddad's. Yeah I did, and you know what? He's sitting there all alone. Nobody's called him."

Bobby kept going, hauling the heavy cans and sloshing water. "Gina called him. I asked her to do it when I talked to her the first time from the airport."

"But you haven't called."

Bobby stopped, the cans clanking. "Why doesn't he call me? The phone works two ways, you know."

"But he's family," Daniel said. "We need to go get him."

Bobby started to walk again, down the hill. "Screw him. He knows how to get here. Why's he making Jeanne drive my mom?"

"Dad!"

Bobby turned to him. "Now he wants to be the victim? All of a sudden he's had a stroke and can't drive?" Bobby went over to the first huge flowerpot at the edge of the walkout, where purple and white petunias twirled their candy-striped petticoats. He nearly upended the can, he drowned them so fast. Water careened off the blossoms and onto the hot, bleached concrete.

"But Dad."

"Listen, Daniel. He's always like this." The drops were fading already on the scorching pavement. "He's got to be the center of attention. If he can't be, he'd rather stay home."

The drops were gone. "But he's your dad," Daniel said. "And no matter what, he's still alive. You've still got time to fix this."

Bobby moved to the next flowerpot and upended the other can. "I don't want to fix it." He clipped his words. "I'm fine with the way it is."

"You've got to fix it before it's too late!" Daniel's voice caught. "I want him to read, Dad. I want Granddad McAllister to read at the funeral. I want you to call him up right now, and ask him. He'll do it. Just put him in the place of Mr. Dermott. He's your friend, but he's not family like Granddad."

Bobby had twisted around as Daniel spoke. His eyes had become tiny and black, like shiny beetles squinting in the light. "No. Your granddad would just make a scene like always. He'd think of something to make everybody look at him."

"No he won't. I—"

"Why is this so important to you all of a sudden? You didn't mention any of this to Father Parham."

"But if he does something, you can stop him."

"Did he say something to you at the house? Is that why you're crying? Is it those ducks? Tommy said—"

"How are you gonna feel when he dies?" Daniel jerked his arms. "He could be gone any day now. How are you gonna feel when you realize you could have fixed this? But you didn't?"

"Daniel—"

"People die! They die all of a sudden, and they don't come back!"

Bobby let go of the cans that clattered banging and rolling on the grass. "Is that what this is about? You think you're responsible somehow for Kevin? You're not!" He threw his arms wide as he stepped toward his son. Daniel lunged into them and hugged his father and didn't let go.

"It was me!" Bobby said into Daniel's neck. "I should have taken that thing down. I wasn't mad at you two. I was mad at my father, but I took it out on you. Daniel, I'm so sorry."

Crying, Daniel held on, bending his head down so he could feel his father's shoulders.

"Hush," Bobby said as he stroked the back of Daniel's head as if he were a baby again, his rough hand soothing and stroking away the nightmare that Daniel slept with. "You didn't do a thing. Don't blame yourself. When people die, we always think about what we could have done. It's natural."

Daniel wept, snuffling hard as he tried not to. His father went on, stroking his son's wet, sweaty hair up and down, up and down, trying to soothe him. "If you want me to ask your granddad to read, I will," Bobby said. "If that's what you want, it's no big deal. I'll do it. We'll do it together, your granddad and I. Would you like that? Shh. It's all right."

24.

Bobby gently closed the door to their bedroom, then locked it. Sarah had already gone down the hall on one of her slow, meandering circuits of the house that took her through the living room and the kitchen, then downstairs like a spirit floating to Kevin's far room.

Daniel waited as Bobby dialed the phone.

"Dad," Bobby said.

The yelling started. Daniel heard the shrieking through the line. "I'm sorry, Dad. Okay? I should have called you."

But the shouting kept on. Bobby listened, then pulled the phone away from his ear. Daniel put his two hands together in a pointed steeple. "Please," he mouthed. "Please."

Daniel strained to hear but couldn't make out the words. The voice on the other end of the line, though, was lower now, in a calmer, deeper register. "Yes," Bobby said. "I remember Garrett J.'s funeral. No. I didn't know that you drove over that day to pick up your dad. Yes I heard you. You had to wait for him to finish his breakfast. Yes, I should have done that. I should have come and gotten you and brought you to the house."

He sighed. The voice went on. Finally he interrupted. "Listen, Dad. There's something I need to ask. Are you listening? Okay. We want you to be part of the service on Tuesday."

Daniel let out his breath.

"Yeah," Bobby said. "The service. Yes I'm serious. Big?" Bobby raised his eyebrows. "You want something big to do, as the head of the family?"

"Please," Daniel whispered. "Don't let him get to you."

Bobby took a breath and started in again. "This will fit right in. We want you to read. Read. Read a passage during the service, up in the front of the church. I don't know. They say a thousand. It was ... whose idea?" He glanced at Daniel, who jabbed his own finger at his father's chest. "Mine. It was my idea," Bobby said. "A passage from the Bible. We've already picked it. No, it's not maudlin. You've been to funerals. Family members. John's doing one, and so is Jeanne. Tommy's doing the eulogy. I'm doing one. Daniel asked me. Why are you surprised? A psalm. I'm reading a psalm."

Bobby's voice took on an edge. "Something about being a father. No, I haven't read it. Daniel picked it out. Because Daniel asked me. Daniel. Yes. It's important to him. Yes, I can."

Daniel mouthed, "What's wrong?"

Bobby saw him and turned his back. "No. I'm not gonna say no to him. What's it matter to you?" He was mad. "No, he doesn't know."

He was shaking his head fast. Daniel could see the back of it. "No, I'm not gonna put Mom on. She's downstairs. No, I'm not gonna come talk to you." His voice was raised now.

"Well then I guess I'm gonna embarrass you. You're gonna have to deal with it, same as always. I'm nothing but a great big embarrassment."

"Dad!" Daniel waved his hands behind Bobby's back, trying to get his attention.

But Bobby went on. "It's important to him! Simple as that. Then stay home! I don't give a damn. You want to miss Kevin's funeral?"

He shouted. "Fine!"

He slammed down the phone. "What an asshole!"

Daniel put both his hands over his face.

25.

Tuesday morning came gorgeous, bright and blue, with a shining light that waxed the fields and fired the walls of the old church where his funeral would be. It was high up, like a castle, crowning the lush top of a steep hill no one could plant.

The blazing white of it shone out over the valley. The old plaster walls sent the warm sun back to the land.

At the door of the church, there was a stone landing. At the far end of that, a ribbon of steps tumbled halfway down the hill and stopped at a small rose garden by the front parking lot. The Virgin Mary prayed there with her arms outstretched next to the asphalt. She was surrounded by a circle of pink roses that fluttered and smelled like heaven as they embraced her. The creamy soft color set off the robin's egg blue of her dress.

On the other side of the parking lot, a little gray road began and fell down the rest of the slope to the valley. Narrow to begin with, it ran in a straight line that seemed to get thinner and thinner until it finally disappeared into the green.

The day was cooler, almost like September, and the soaring birds sang high and light. Down in the fields, down on the flats of the broad valley, a sweet breeze had come up that kissed the land. The growing corn stalks were dancing in it. They whispered together, rustling, and tossed their long leaves like a woman's hair.

The bell of the church tolled, calling them. Bong … bong … bong, it echoed deep and low, out over the thrusting plants and into the tired ears of the farmers working. The men straightened up when they heard it and rubbed their backs. They turned their heads and listened as their eyes found the gleaming walls.

Up on the hill, a mile above them, the mourning bell was calling them home.

They were all on their way. City people were coming, and mine workers, and farmers. They were driving already up from town and from far off, on the interstate that took them to Indiana and beyond. Every single one of them—the wives, too, and the children—had scrubbed and brushed and donned their Sunday clothes.

The first of them had already arrived and were waiting. Bill Davis and his young wife watched their toddler hop along the paving stones that led up to the Virgin Mary. The blowsy flowers waved along with the pink ruffles on her dress.

Teenage boys stood in a loose circle away from their parents. Jim was there with his hands in his pockets, leaning under the shade against the brick wall of the church.

Close by, a younger group of boys imitated the older ones and pretended they weren't. Dwight watched every move as Smitty slouched and spit.

Lester pulled up then, with his wife and two teenage daughters, followed immediately by Miss Nunley, who parked her old Cutlass under a tree.

The whole town began coming in a slow caravan that stretched all the way down the long hill and into the cornfields. It was everyone Sarah knew from the hospital, including Dr. Frederick and nearly all of the nursing staff. It was every farmer who had ever met Bobby in three counties, as well as every high school child and everyone in the middle school, including every teacher and every parent that Kevin ever met. It was every clerk in every store, and every postman. Every child who had ever worked at the Dairy Queen, or been there, or heard about it. It was every single person they ever knew.

They all waited patiently in their vehicles, and then came forward. They turned in forever one-by-one to their left, filling the church parking lot and then the alley behind it, and then the back, and then the back of the church hall, and then the grass. They started to drive into the graveyard, and left their trucks on the dirt tracks. When those got full, someone signaled and they had to begin parking outside, on the road.

The line went on forever. When they were done, the row of vehicles stretched down the hill more than a half-mile.

26.

His mother was crying in the limousine as they rode. Bobby held her as Daniel sat across in the big wide bench seat that faced them, and looked out the tinted back window at the sky.

As they got closer and the limousine slowed, his father pulled a wet lock of hair from his mother's face. Her cheeks were streaming. Bobby said to her, "Just remember, all you have to do is get through today."

She pulled back then, and looked up at him. The sudden strength in her voice surprised Daniel and made him look inside the car again and away from the dark birds following them.

"No Bobby," Sarah said as she shook her head. "It isn't just today, or one day. It's the first. I'm going to have to get through this same day every day for the rest of my life."

27.

Sarah gasped as they made the left turn into the church parking lot.

Kevin's hearse was parked in front with its swinging back door open. A Lawler's man was bent at the waist as he began to pull him.

"Hey look," Bobby said, pointing suddenly out the opposite window. "Isn't that nice? Peggy came. And Carl. And they brought Lisa. What do you think, honey? Is that a new dress Peggy has on?"

Daniel had turned his head too, to see the family through the smoky glass.

She stood next to her parents. Redheaded Lisa saw him and put her hand up in a little, awkward wave. She couldn't see him but he could see her, and he stared at the spiraling curls as the soft breeze took them.

"Oh God," he said under his breath.

28.

Garrett burst through the door into the small, private sitting room. "Are we supposed to wait here? Nobody told me. I've been standing in front of the church for an hour."

"No you haven't." Cora said as she trailed him in. "I'm sorry. I couldn't stop him."

Daniel had turned to look from his post in a corner of the room on the high second floor, far above the filling sanctuary. He had been staring out the one window, thirty-eight feet straight down to the jammed parking lot.

The lady who had brought them there had told them to wait for the next half hour. She would keep well-wishers away from them until it was time to go down and begin the celebration.

"Come in," Bobby said to his father. "You can sit down."

Garrett stopped in front of him. "Get up. I want to talk to you." He jerked his chin. "Out in the hall."

"No."

"What?"

Bobby stayed on the couch next to Sarah. "Whatever you have to say, you can say in front of everybody."

Cora had taken one of two small wooden chairs in a corner. "Why don't you come sit down?" She pat the chair next to her.

In response, Garrett spread his legs at parade rest. "I'm not gonna let you make a fool out of yourself." He glared down at Bobby. "You're not going out there. I'm not gonna let you embarrass me and this family."

Sarah slowly said, "Not let him do what?" She slightly slurred her words with the sedatives she was still taking.

"Aw, Jesus," Garrett said to Bobby. "She doesn't know either."

"Sure I do," she said. "He tells me everything."

"Sister," Garrett said to her. "You stay out of this."

"What did you call me?" She leaned forward. "That's not my name! My name's Sarah!" They could have heard her in the hall.

Cora said to her in a soothing voice. "I know you're not yourself today. They're coming for us soon, and we're—"

"He needs to call me by my proper name," Sarah said. "It's been twenty-three years."

Garrett loomed over her. "What's wrong with you?" He slowly said every word, parsing them like he was talking to a foreigner. "If Bobby goes out there, he's gonna embarrass this whole family. Including you."

Sarah thrust out her chin. "He could never—"

"Bobby can't read!" It was a thunderclap.

"Of course he can!" It was Daniel. They all turned to where he stood. "It's Kevin who can't read. Couldn't."

"Aw, shit," Garrett said. "Kevin too? Cora, did you know about this?"

"No," Bobby said to himself.

"Yes," Cora said. "I did."

Surprised, Bobby turned to his mother, but she was looking at Sarah. "You were always working with him with those notebooks."

"You knew," Garrett said. "And you didn't tell me?"

Cora shrugged. "It was from my side of the family. Plus it was none of your business." She smiled at Sarah.

Sarah smiled back as Garrett boomed, "Daniel, have you got this too?"

"No!" Daniel said.

Garrett turned to Bobby. "You kept this a secret. Yet another secret from me. You and that wife of yours. Yeah! You there! But now I see it. You coddled him, just like she did!" He pointed at Cora. "Her little Bobby."

"Garrett!" Cora said.

"You and that woman here. Miss Say—rah. You're the reason he's dead!"

Sarah gasped.

"You be quiet!" Daniel shouted.

"Stop right there!" Cora told him.

"You and I both know," Garrett said to Bobby. "You never bothered to take down that swing. That goddamn swing! He died up there because you couldn't discipline him. He wasn't afraid of you. Why do you think you're alive today? You're afraid of me!"

"Shut up!" Daniel shouted.

"That's why he's dead!" Garrett said. "And what about you?" he said to Daniel. "You were supposed to watch him!"

Bobby leapt off the couch. Sarah struggled up too. "This isn't his fault!" she said. "It's mine. If I hadn't let him stay alone. If I had listened to my instincts, he'd be alive. And you know what?" she said to Garrett. "If I hadn't wanted that big house in the first place. That big house away from you! We wouldn't have that deck, and he wouldn't have been swinging on it. My son's dead because I wanted to get free!"

She slapped him. She hauled off and hit his face as hard as she could with the flat palm of her hand.

He reeled back. She had hurt him. "I hated you!" she cried out. "For taking my life, and my house, and most of all my husband. You kept him away from me so he didn't come home."

Cora had gotten up too, now. She put up both her hands and implored them. "Please. All of you. Remember why we're here today. They can hear us out into the hallway."

Garrett glared at Sarah. "I'm right about what I think of you. You're Winston's daughter, and he's worthless. The whole town knows it."

"That's not true!" Daniel said. "You'll say anything, won't you? Like you did last week, when you wanted me to work for you. I didn't know what you had done to Dad. You never told me you cut him out. I had to figure that out with Tommy when he got here."

"What?" Bobby said.

Daniel told him. "He cut you out. I didn't know until I talked to Tommy."

"What?" Sarah said, struggling to catch up.

"That's all right," Bobby said to Daniel. "You didn't do anything wrong except trust him, like I did. I've known for years about the land."

Sarah spoke finally. "What did you know?" she asked Bobby. "What about the land?"

Cora interrupted, astonished. "Bobby? You knew all the time?"

"Sure," Bobby nodded at his mother. "But, did you?"

A heartbeat of pause. "Yes," Cora said. "I knew."

"But when?" Bobby asked her. "When did you find out?"

"The day it happened. At the courthouse. When was that? Ninety-two?"

Bobby said, "Ninety-one."

"No." Daniel interrupted them. "It wasn't then. It was last year. That's when he did it. That's when Granddad changed his will."

29.

Cora twitched her head around. "His what?"

"His will. Granddad changed his will, and left it to me. Me and Kevin. We were supposed to split it. Dad isn't gonna get his share. Only I don't want it. That's why I went over there, Dad. I wanted him to change it back, but I couldn't tell you."

"Wait a minute." Sarah threw up her hands. "Wait!" Daniel's mother had straightened, and she blinked to clear her eyes. She regarded them all with a new, fully grounded self-possession, and when she spoke again, she took her time. "Let me get this. I'm behind a couple of steps." She looked at Garrett. "You. You cut your own son out of your will. Did I hear that correctly? And you."

She turned to Daniel. "You promised not to tell that he wanted you to work for him, maybe the whole rest of your life. Not go to college. And you."

She turned to Bobby. "What were you talking about, you and Cora just then? What happened in ninety-one?"

Bobby hesitated. He didn't answer. Cora didn't say a word. "Honey," Bobby said. "It was a long time ago. It's not important anymore."

"But it is." Sarah gazed at him with unwavering eyes. "I'm apparently the only one who doesn't know what's going on." And then she waited, her face like stone. Nobody moved.

Bobby spoke. "He changed the title to the two hundred acres up at his farm. He put it all back in his own name."

323

"You mean our land?" She spun around. "How could you do that?" she said to Garrett. "He worked for it."

"He never told me he had his own land!"

"That was me!" Sarah said. "I told Bobby not to tell you. It was the only way we could get our own parcel. So if you want to blame somebody, blame me."

She shifted her eyes to Cora, standing next to Garrett. "And you," she said. "You knew all about this."

Cora shook her head. "I didn't know about the will."

"But you had to," Daniel said to his grandmother. "I'm sorry, Grandma, but Tommy told me about Garrett J. He told me Granddad did the same thing to him. He cut him out when he left town. It's been years since then. And you know how angry he's been at my dad."

Cora didn't answer.

"What's wrong with you people?" Sarah said. "You're cowards, all of you. Even you," she told Bobby. "And you. My own son. What are you all afraid of? I don't get it. Him? Look at him! What does he do to control you like this?"

"He doesn't control me," Bobby said.

"He sure does!"

"I'm my own man!"

"You think so?" She stared back at him. "There's nothing I've wanted more. But he controls you because you still care what he thinks of you."

Garrett spoke up then. He was smiling, and they all saw it. "You know, for once Sister, you're right." His voice was lethal. "You're afraid of me. That's why you hate me so much."

"Go to hell, Dad."

"If you weren't afraid, you would have told me about your farm."

Bobby moved then. He put both his hands on Garrett's shoulders and turned the old man against his will, shoving him toward the door. "Hey!" Garrett said as he fought back.

"Get out!" Bobby forced him with straight arms across the floor.

"Bobby!" Cora had stepped to block them with her thin body. "You've got people in the hall, and this is a funeral."

Sarah said to her, "Why can't you see? He's lied. He's stolen Bobby's land, and now he's cut him out of his will. All you do is defend him."

"Sarah!" Cora said.

"You know what your children call you? They call you a saint! But is that what you've been to them? Your son here. You know what he thinks of himself? He thinks he's stupid, and there's nothing I can do to fix it!"

Cora reared her head back. "Bobby, is that true? Do you still think you're stupid?"

30.

The small room grew still. It was almost imperceptible at first, starting as the slightest tilt of his head, but as Daniel watched it became a tipping, and then a rocking as Bobby began nodding without speaking, his head up and down, up and down.

Finally, he spoke. "Mom, he was all you had. I knew you were afraid. You didn't want to be alone with six kids and no income. But I've thought about this a lot. We were the price you paid. Not you, but us. We were the ones who never had a choice."

"Jesus Christ." Garrett walked over to the window.

"I was never once afraid of losing him," Bobby said. "I was afraid of being without you. I'd do anything to make you approve of me. I wanted you to tell me I was all right. I believed everything you said, and what you didn't say, so I wouldn't have to be alone. Mom, I was alone in that house, with all those people. He'd rage at me, and I'd be the only one. I made myself believe every word he said, because you did. Sarah asked me once where you were when he was raging. You were standing right there, but you didn't do a thing. Never. You didn't stand up to him. It was like you agreed with him and what he did to us.

"I know you loved me, Mom. I know you do. But you loved him more, and you made your choice. No matter what the cost was, only the cost was mostly me." He turned to his father and spoke to his back. "Dad, you were the one who could never do any wrong. It wasn't me. I wasn't precious Bobby, like you say. You were perfect. Whatever you did to me, it was okay with her."

Cora gasped.

"Mom," he said. "Why didn't you tell me about the land? You've known for years about the title, and what he did."

She didn't answer.

"Was it Dad? Did he say something to make you keep it a secret?"

It was tiny at first, but finally she was nodding like Bobby had been.

"What did he say?"

She spoke in a whisper meant only for him, but Daniel heard it. "He said he was going to make you read. If I told you and you tried to get it back, he said he'd make you read in public, at the courthouse, in front of the whole town. He said he'd embarrass you. I didn't want you to get hurt."

"You bastard!" Sarah cried out.

"Sarah, be quiet," Bobby said. "But Mom, that was my decision, not yours. By doing that, you decided for me, without ever giving me a choice. You treated me like a child. Dad was right. You coddled me. And you made me feel stupid because I couldn't read."

Garrett turned around. Daniel saw the dark eyes glistening with satisfaction.

"And Daniel," Bobby said. "You were right. That day, when you said Kevin was smart but we were treating him like he was dumb. We were making excuses for him." Bobby said to Cora, "That's what I did to my own son."

"Damn straight," Garrett muttered.

Bobby looked at Sarah. "But he wasn't." Bobby smiled at his wife, remembering. "Kevin was smart. He was so smart, and he could do things. Somewhere in there," he said to Sarah, "my little boy must have gotten a piece of you, along with all the crap he got from me."

Sarah said to him, "No."

"Dad," Daniel interrupted. "You don't get it."

"Get what?"

"You two are the same. You can't read very well. Isn't that where we started this? You can't, can you? Only you never told me."

"No," Bobby admitted to his son. "Not very well. I still can't. I skip words, and they jump all over the page. I have to hold them down with my fingers. Sometimes I have to do it with my whole hand."

"Why didn't you tell me?" Daniel asked. "Were you ashamed?"

There was the slightest incline of Bobby's head.

"You weren't ashamed of Kevin."

"Lord no," Bobby said. "Of course not."

"Then why would you be ashamed of yourself?"

"This is bullshit!" Garrett said. "People can read. It's that simple. Every kid learns how to in first grade. If you can't read, you're stupid."

Daniel ignored him. "Kevin was smart, Dad. Just like you. I always thought you were the smartest person I ever knew. That's my whole point. If Kevin was smart, then so are you."

Sarah said to Bobby, "I can't build things. I've never made a house."

"They're right," Cora said at Bobby's elbow.

Sarah said to Bobby, "Kevin was your son. I loved him, but he was your son."

Bobby looked from one to the other. The muscles of his face had gone slack. It took a lifetime for Bobby to say it. "You think I'm smart. Because Kevin is."

"Yes," Daniel told him.

"Yes," Sarah said too.

"No." Cora said. "You've got it wrong. You've got it all back-wards."

There was a soft rap on the door. Esther Winston ducked her head in as she held it open. "Sarah, Bobby, I'm sorry to disturb you, but we've got to get down there. I've greeted the last one and we don't have any more seats. They're standing in the aisles. We need to start this. I've got to go light that candle in the front."

Once Mrs. Winston had closed the door again, Bobby raised his voice above their new, hurried movement. "Dad," he said. "I'm gonna read this. I'm gonna go out there, and I'm gonna read the whole thing. That's another thing I learned from my son here. This one. Not Kevin. Nobody cares. They don't care how I do it. I'm not doing this for them. I'm doing it for Kevin, and Daniel too, because he asked me.

"You've got a choice," Bobby said to his father. "You can either go out there with us or you can stay here. I really don't care anymore where you go, or what you say to yourself. The only thing you get to decide today is what you're gonna do."

Bobby clasped Sarah's hand, then turned to his son. "Daniel?" The boy took his father's other hand. They stood as three and turned toward the door.

"Bobby," Garrett said. "You're a fool. I'm not going out there."

Bobby answered, "Suit yourself. Mom?"

"You stay right here!" Garrett told his wife.

But Cora had turned to face him. "Garrett McAllister," she said. "This isn't yours to decide. Not anymore. You've done it my whole life. I get to make my own decisions now."

She turned to Sarah and in a small voice said, "I'm sorry I've hurt you."

"Cora," Sarah responded warmly. "I can't do this without you. You lost a son, but somehow you got through it. I need you. Come with me. Take my hand."

Sarah offered it. Cora clasped it and took her first step. Now it was four of them.

"You're not going out there!" Garrett said. "That's final!"

Cora turned to him once more. "You listen to me. I'm going, and then I'm leaving you. When this is over, I'm moving out. And you can stay here, if you want, but I tell you what. You say you don't want people to talk? Well just don't come down with us. Have you thought about that? Not walking into this church? On this day? With this family? You think about that. You just sit here by yourself and you think about that."

31.

Cora closed the door behind them and they began to walk, their fine leather shoes clomping on the hardwood in a staccato that reverberated off the long walls around them. Four sets of feet drummed down the sunless hall. When they got to the end of it, and to the landing, Cora touched Daniel's arm. She held him back as she said softly to his father, "Bobby, you're going to have to go down first. The men from Lawler's are there, and they're going to want you and Sarah to be at the front of the line."

"I'm all right," Daniel said. "Go."

They stepped down in pairs then, into the boxy staircase of the church's tall bell tower. It descended the height of three stories, in six flights, each one separated by a left-hand wall that made it impossible to see beyond the end of the stairs at the next landing. Overhead, bluish fluorescent lights slanted from the tilted ceiling.

The bronze bells had been quieted now, many floors above them.

Daniel couldn't see far ahead as he went down, but he could smell. The strong scent of the incense hit him in a dense fog halfway to the vestibule. Spiced and heavy, it lurked on the stairs, then smothered his nose and stung his eyes as he descended, making him cough at the same moment his parents made the final turn within the spiral of the staircase. They rounded the last landing and headed down to the tiled vestibule inside the double front doors of the old Catholic church.

"Please wait," someone said, and they all stopped. The four of them bobbled, then stood in their assigned pairs with Cora and Daniel holding hands still three steps above his parents on the last tread.

Daniel didn't recognize the voice that had spoken. He leaned forward to get a better look, but he couldn't see anything in the small gap between his parents' shoulders except the gray slate of the lobby floor.

"Erskine!" the same man said in a stage whisper. "You need to move him."

It was then that Daniel heard the rolling of wheels and the organ start way off to his right in the bowels of the sanctuary. Its brass pipes were mammoth round stalks that corrugated the whole front wall behind the altar.

A woman began to sing Ave Maria. Bobby had chosen it, and the alto's rich voice filled the vast space all the way to the rafters. As he waited, hearing it, Daniel imagined the gates of heaven opening.

"You can come on now," the Lawler's man said, and they all descended. Daniel's parents stepped down finally onto the tile. Cora pressed Daniel's hand.

He saw Kevin. His brother waited lying inside the new closed casket on the cart. Sarah cried out, and Bobby grabbed her.

Daniel couldn't take his eyes off it. The coffin gleamed. Its shiny polish poured like honey over the yellow pine. There were brass handrails, and they twinkled from the candles that dotted the vestibule.

Mrs. Winston rushed over. "Sarah, are you all right?"

Father Parham swept up then, dressed in his long white cassock. "Sarah," he said. "I know it's hard. But remember, all you have to do is get down that aisle. You don't have to do anything. All you have to do is sit there, and it'll be done.

"We're going to be there with you," he told her. "And I'm going to keep an eye on you from wherever I am in the church. If you need anything, let me know. Wave or something. I don't care. I'll come over. And Bobby, that goes for you too. Now where's Daniel? There you are. And Mrs. McAllister. Where's your husband?"

Somehow Mrs. Winston had known, for she piped up then, telling Cora, "If it's all right, I'll walk with you, so you don't have to be alone. The two of us. Daniel, you can walk with your mom, and help her if she needs you?"

Sarah slowly lifted her head and squared her shoulders. She pulled away from Bobby at last, standing alone on her own two feet. "Come," she said to Daniel. Her face was running, and one of her flooding cheeks had red lines from where it had been crushed against Bobby.

In the boy's hand, his mother's fingers felt like paper. Even through his sweat, he could feel the skin and the bones that one good squeeze could shatter.

Father Parham moved to the front of the cart, then called to two altar boys to bring over the cross and the incense. He told the one with the crucifix to heft it high, then turn it, so that Jesus faced the rows and rows of pews crammed to overflowing.

Daniel blinked as he looked out over the curved lid of Kevin's box. In front of him, every seat was filled, and both of the side aisles, and every inch of the short brown carpeting at the back. His whole town was there, and most of the county. It was a sea of people in a dark, swollen tide of heads and backs and hats that swept two hundred feet to the marble altar and out again, to the plaster walls and up, to the old wooden balcony and the crowd there too, that stared down at him. When Daniel glanced up, they were watching him, scrutinizing every move.

It was dark, this ocean, like it was midnight. Despite the bright morning, no happy colors flowed. All he saw in this teaming dock of a thousand waiting souls were dull, muted grays and navy blues, sooty charcoals and somber blacks. As he stood he heard murmuring over the sweet voice of the woman singing. Then he heard a baby squall. Daniel looked for the child, but he couldn't find it. There was no newborn grasping his mother in the rear pews.

Daniel looked beyond them all, all the way up to the altar. At the foot of the marble, a tall white candle burned. The tiny flame flickered.

The organ stopped. At the front of procession, at the lip of the church aisle that stretched far in front of them, Father Parham, like Jesus, put out both his arms.

"Don't you start yet!" a voice called out. "Don't move until I get there!"

Daniel turned.

"Where do I stand?" Garrett charged across the tile. "Here?" He shoved himself in next to Cora, in the middle between the two old women. Mrs. Winston allowed it, and so did Cora. Both their faces they had made blank, but their eyes were flashing.

"Let's go," Garrett said to the priest. "What are you waiting for?"

The priest turned again to face the assembly. Daniel heard a loud click and looked up to eight large stereo speakers that tilted from the rafters. "The grace of our Lord and the love of God be with you all," Father Parham's voice boomed straight down from Heaven.

A thousand throats answered from every corner. "And also with you."

Four Lawler's men stepped up and grabbed Kevin's handrails. "Please rise, and face the back of the church." The tide rose, as a single body, and turned toward them.

Sarah broke.

The organ started.

The hired men pushed Kevin on out.

Daniel clutched his mother as she collapsed into his dad. They almost had to lift her, and drag her, in order to get her useless feet to move forward.

They started singing, everyone they ever knew, in every row. They wanted Sarah to hear them. A thousand hearts were trying to hold her up.

"And ... he will raise you up ... on eagle's wings."

Daniel and his parents shuffled slowly behind the cart. "Bear you on ... the breath of dawn."

The coffin glistened. "Make ... you ... to shine like the sun! ... "

Daniel was walking while his brother rode. "... And ... hold you ... in the palm ... "

They were there. " ... of his hand." They had gotten to the end, to the front pew.

Kevin went on. The Lawler's men rolled him to the candle and then swung him around, so that his head lay under the altar. They bowed, all four of them in unison, then turned in their shiny black suits and scuttled like crabs up the side aisles to disappear.

Daniel slid into the bench after his mother. Bobby waited as he stood, so he could sit on the center aisle. Garrett did the same in the pew behind them, taking his seat on the aisle after Mrs. Winston and Cora slid past.

Moving quickly, Father Parham had already taken his position. He held a cloth as he nodded at Daniel. The boy bobbed up and made his way to him. It seemed to Daniel like a hundred miles.

He took the white shroud and began to unfold it, then spread it and smoothed it over the wood. He stroked the box with the palm of his hand.

"How often in life did we clothe Kevin," the priest said. "Now his brother covers him once more with the pall."

After a prayer, Daniel went back to his seat. The boy kept his head down the whole way and his eyes riveted on the dark veins that coursed through the white marble.

"The first reading will be given by Kevin's uncle, John McAllister," Father Parham said from a throne-chair in a corner after a moment. Daniel's Uncle John buttoned his suit coat as he strode with a white sheet of paper. The tall crane of a man crossed to a lectern that had been set up on a high platform fed by three steps on the other side of Kevin, opposite the priest who had taken his place in the background.

John climbed the steps, then smoothed his paper. "Please respond," he said, then snapped back. He had been too close to the microphone that curved into his face on the top of the lectern.

John backed up a step and then said again, "Please respond with 'The Lord God will destroy death forever.' This is a reading from the book of the prophet Isaiah."

They hurried. They hastened to all answer as one. "The Lord God will destroy death forever," said a thousand voices in unison.

"On this mountain the Lord of hosts will provide for all peoples a feast of rich food. On this mountain he will destroy the veil that veils all peoples, the web that is woven over all nations. He will destroy death forever." John sighed. Daniel heard the rush of air through the high speakers. "The Lord God will wipe away the tears from all faces. This is the Word of the Lord."

John stepped down and walked to Kevin. There wasn't a sound as he clasped his hands in front of himself and bowed deeply.

"Our next reading will be given by Kevin's aunt, Gina Carlyle."

She was in tears already as she rushed to the front, nearly running into John as he took his seat. "This is a poem," she said once she too had unfolded her sheet of paper. "It's called 'There She Goes.'" She straightened herself, then took a deep breath that Daniel heard over the loudspeaker. "I am standing upon the seashore. A ship at my side spreads her white sails to the morning breeze and starts for the blue ocean. I stand and watch her go. Until ... at last ... at last ..."

She stopped. "Until ... at length she hangs like a speck of white cloud just where the sea and sky come together, to mingle with each other. Then, someone at my side says, 'She's going! Watch! Watch her go!'" Gina gasped, then let it out. Against the far wall, Father Parham leaned forward to watch her. "There," she said in a ragged voice. "She's gone! She's truly gone! But gone where? Gone from my sight—that is all. She is just as large in mast and hull and spar as she was when she left my side, and just as able to bear her load of living freight to port. Her diminished size is in me, and not in her. And just at that moment when someone at my side says, 'There, she's gone!'—there are other eyes watching her coming, on the other side of the water, and other voices shouting out the glad tiding, 'Here she comes! I can see her now! Here she comes! I am glad you have become one of us!'"

Gina choked as she caught her breath. Father Parham got halfway out of his seat, but she signaled to him that she was all right. "Life is eternal. And love is immortal, and death is only a horizon. And a horizon is nothing save the limit of our sight."

She was done but she didn't step down yet. "I love you, Kevin," she said to the box. It was a whisper, meant to be heard only by the dead boy, but they all heard it.

Sarah started to sob. Daniel reached for his mother next to him in the pew.

"Our next reading will be given by Kevin's father, Robert McAllister."

Daniel heard murmuring as Bobby stood up. To get a better look, people were shifting and stretching their necks.

"This is stupid," Garrett said behind them.

"Shh!" Cora said.

They all heard the stomp as his hard toes struck the risers. Bobby climbed the three steps, fumbling for his own piece of white paper. He got to the lectern and stood behind it, then looked out at the huge crowd. He opened the sheet and spread it flat on the wood like the others had, pressing it with the heel of his left hand to take out the sharp wrinkles. Bobby took his time, then kept his eyes down as he stared at the words for a long, long moment. It seemed to Daniel that he had never seen them before.

Bobby lifted his whole right hand and put it down on top of the paper. Daniel had visions of it blowing away, but there was no wind inside the church. The candle flame didn't struggle.

Bobby cleared his throat. "Please respond." But he bolted up as John had done, and looked at the microphone. He moved his body back and said again, without distortion and clearly, so they all heard every word. "Please respond. 'The Lord ... is kind ... and merce ... merciful.'"

He began.

"Merciful and gray ... gracious ... is the Lord. Slow to anger ... and abow ... abounding in kindness ... Not accor ... ding to our sins ... does he deal with us, nor does he ... require ... no, requite us ... according to our crimes."

Bobby paused. A thousand throats answered him. They were loud, too loud, and it came at them in a loving wave. "The Lord is kind and merciful!"

Daniel turned to his mother, who was smiling.

"As a father … " But Bobby stopped. He read it to himself again, moving his finger. "As a father … has compassion … on his children, so the Lord … has compassion on those who fear him, for he knows … how we are formed. He remembers … that we are dust … "

Bobby stopped again and closed his eyes. "Dust. We are dust."

The crowd jumped in. They couldn't do it fast enough. "The Lord is kind and merciful," they announced as one. They willed him to go on, but he couldn't. He just stood, holding the sides of the lectern with both trembling hands and squeezing his eyes shut.

"Man's days," Bobby choked out. " … are like those … those of grass. Like a flower … " Daniel heard the crying start that couldn't be stopped. It came up out of his father, out of the depths of him, and every gulp and gasp was a hurricane that was destroying him. There was nothing but tearing inside this man.

"Aw shit!" Garrett said behind them.

Bobby's shoulders shook with the pumping.

Father Parham stood.

Bobby turned his head to look at his dead son, who slept next to him, never to awaken under the white cloth that Daniel had given him. "My flower," Bobby said in gasps to Kevin. "My flower … of the field … He blooms. The wind. The wind sweeps over him, and he is gone. Oh God. He's gone."

Garrett moved. So did Father Parham, who started flying across the church. "And his place," Bobby got out. " … his place knows him no more."

Bobby fell back. He banged the lectern, but Garrett was there already. He had rushed up the aisle, billowing air into Daniel. Garrett grabbed his son and held onto him like a baby. "I'm here," Garrett said. "It's all right. I'm here."

"Bobby," the priest said as he arrived next to him.

"Hold on," Garrett said. "I'm gonna take you home. This has been too much for you." He didn't realize it, but the packed church heard every word.

Father Parham said, "Are you all right?"

"Of course he's not!" Garrett spat at him. "What were you thinking, having him read?"

"But Dad!" Bobby said. "I need to finish this."

"You're not finishing anything," Garrett said. "You're coming home with me so I can watch over you."

Bobby struggled to get free. "It's important to Daniel."

Thirty feet away, Daniel whispered. "No it's not."

"It's important," Bobby was saying again to Garrett. "Can you do it? Daniel wanted you to read anyway. So can you finish it?"

Daniel made to get up and read it himself, but Sarah grabbed him. Her sudden grip was tight on his arm.

At the front of the church, Bobby had stepped out of Garrett's embrace and was facing him. "Please, Dad. Can you do it for Kevin? And Daniel?"

The priest nodded at Garrett. "It's almost finished, sir. He was nearly done. Come on Bobby, let's get out of his way. Mr. McAllister, we'll be standing right over here."

They shuffled off and left Garrett alone at the lectern. There was complete silence in the church as everyone in every pew and standing in the aisles on both sides waited. Garrett looked down then, to study the sheet that lay in front of him. After a long pause, he looked up and out, to the two thousand eyes that were staring, eager for him to start again so they could join him in loving Bobby and Kevin.

Garrett blinked, and blinked again, then reached into his front coat pocket for his glasses. He put them on and stared down, blinking fast at the page. He cleared his throat, then started.

"As a fa," he read. "No."

He stopped. "Days are like. No, that's not it."

He looked up again and out at the crowd, but nobody came forward to help him. He glanced down and picked up his right hand. He put it down flat on top of the paper. "Please ... respond. Oh. We did that."

They answered anyway. It surprised him and he popped his head up as the church bellowed, "The Lord is kind and merciful."

He waited but they were done, and he had to look down again. "Merce ... merce ... merci ... ful ... and gray ... gray ..."

He was taking forever.

"... gray ... gracious ... Yeah, that's it."

Sarah's mouth fell open.

"... is the Lord ... Slow ... slow to ... anger ... and ... ab ... abow ... abow." Garrett stopped. Over the loudspeaker, Daniel heard him take another breath.

"My God," Sarah said to herself.

"And ... abow ... abow ... "

"I didn't know." Cora said from behind them in a whisper. "I never knew. He never told me."

In front, far away from them, Garrett started to shift a little on his feet. Then he started over at the very beginning. He jumped to the top of the page. "Merce ... merci ... ful and gray ..."

"But he reads the newspaper," Sarah said to herself.

Then he hopped ahead without any reason. "Slow to … anger and … abow … abow … "

"All the time," Sarah said.

Daniel shot a glance at his father, who was standing against a front wall with Father Parham. His face was frozen like he wasn't there.

"Not accor … accor …" Garrett stopped. The assembly was confused by the sudden silence, so they said it in unison. "The Lord is kind and merciful."

Garrett lifted his arms and grabbed the lectern. He gazed out, unseeing now, and he blinked, then dropped his eyes again to the paper. Clutching the wood, his blue-veined hands were white and Daniel could see them shaking. "Nor does," he tried to read. "Nor. Father."

He made no sense. Garrett was skipping words now. He looked up once again. He had started swaying. It got worse, and he began to circle. His body rolled like a marble in a jar. He wasn't reading anymore, or even trying to.

Daniel glanced at Bobby, who was staring at the floor.

"Is he okay?" someone said somewhere behind them. That was when Daniel finally heard the whispering that breathed throughout the church. They were talking. They were all shushing about Garrett and asking what was wrong with the elderly man. "Do you think he's sick?"

Garrett must have heard them too, for he began to frown but he couldn't focus. He was looking up now, his eyes swimming over the top of the crowd.

Daniel glanced over. Bobby was shaking his head as he stared at the slate floor. Daniel saw Bobby look up then and across the wide church front toward Sarah. His mother and father made eye contact. Bobby nodded. No one else could have seen it, the movement was so small.

It took a moment, but Sarah answered him. She began to nod back at him. And then she smiled. A tiny one, meant for Bobby alone, but Daniel saw it.

His father started to walk. He left the priest, taking strong, pounding steps toward Garrett, who was still swaying as he held the lectern. Bobby touched him. He put his calming hand on Garrett's arm. "Dad," he said. "You know you can't see that."

"What?" Garrett said. "Sure I can!"

Bobby looked up and out over the entire assembly. He said clearly into the microphone, carefully forming every word, "You forgot your glasses."

"I did not."

But Bobby smiled wide out to the congregation. "Those are your old ones you've got on. You can't read a thing. I'm sorry. I shouldn't have asked you to read that with those old things."

The throng smiled back at him, relieved.

Daniel turned to his mother. Sarah had on a grin Daniel hadn't seen in days, not since the hula girls and the laughter as they were leaving.

"Father," Bobby said to the priest. "Is it all right if we just recite the Lord's Prayer?"

"Of course," Father Parham said. "You can do anything you want."

"Dad," Bobby said. "Could you help me?"

He had clamped his arm around his teetering father, who wasn't swaying anymore because of the strong embrace. The old man's voice filled the church and he didn't mangle a word as he and his son said it together.

"Our Father, who art in Heaven. Hallowed be thy name ..."

32.

As they filed out, Daniel dug deep in his pocket.

He found her alone, standing next to the second limousine from Lawler's as the men loaded Kevin's coffin into the hearse. "Grandma McAllister," Daniel said softly as he held out the small, stiff piece of folded paper. "I'm sorry. I took it."

She looked down at the creamy square in her pleated hand. "You read it?"

The boy nodded. Overhead, birds sang, their song high and light over the growing rumble of gunning motors as people started their engines for the long drive to the cemetery south of town.

"That's all right, Daniel. It's time we all knew. No more secrets, huh?" She smiled at him through her thick glasses.

"It's not my business to tell. You tell it, when you want to."

"Thank you. I think there's maybe been enough for one day." She opened the pink Bible in her hands and tucked the fat square away again.

"Grandma?"

She looked up. "For what it's worth, I think he's right," Daniel said. "In that letter. He knew you were strong."

Her smile left her. "Not strong enough," she said. "And blind. I was blind."

33.

At four o'clock the next afternoon, Daniel sat mutely in the courtroom next to his ashen father. The place was jam-packed, but the crowd of spectators had left the two of them and Lester alone as the sole occupants of the first long bench at the front of the public gallery. Against Daniel's shaking knees ran the short, wooden half-wall that divided the chamber in two and kept the lawyers from the people. On the other side of the gate, a balding judge presided over the formal inquest into Kevin's death.

"Now Dr. Frederick," the young state's attorney was saying. "As the coroner for Jefferson County, did you have occasion to conduct a medical examination of the deceased?"

"I did," said the white-haired man in the witness chair. His voice was deep and rumbled like an earthquake. "I performed a complete autopsy. But before I did that, I went out to the house to try to understand what had happened. Everything I saw there confirmed to me what I already thought I knew. Kevin—and I've known this child his whole life—Kevin died in the most freakish accident I've ever encountered. And I've been the Medical Examiner for the last twenty-three years."

The lawyer nodded, then glanced down at his pad. "When did you go out there, exactly?"

"That very night. It was in the evening, after I pronounced him dead."

Bobby sighed. Daniel glanced at him, but Bobby stared straight ahead.

"It was Friday the tenth," the doctor was saying. "I asked his aunt to come with me and let me in. Ms. Gina Carlyle. She assured me that she hadn't touched anything. Neither had the paramedics. I talked to Bill Davis and his partner myself."

The lawyer flipped a page and ran his finger down the pad. "Doctor, based on the autopsy you performed and your examination of the scene, have you reached a conclusion with a reasonable degree of medical certainty as to the cause of death?"

"I have, but son, I think you're going a little too fast."

A ripple of laughter swept the room. It was only for an instant, but it lifted the weight. "But if you want that part now, I can give it to you," Dr. Frederick said. He cleared his throat and read in a loud voice from his notes. "His death was caused by tracheal crushing and subsequent asphyxiation."

"Can you explain—"

"Sure." The doctor shifted in his seat so that he faced the four men and the two women in the jury box on Daniel's left. "His windpipe was crushed, and when that happened, he couldn't get any oxygen to his brain, so he passed out. And then he died. He died real quickly."

The lawyer looked up from his pad. "How quickly? Do you have an opinion?"

"Oh, death was nearly instantaneous."

"Thank God," Daniel heard his father say.

"Doctor," the young lawyer went on. "Have you also reached a conclusion as to the mechanism of the boy's death?"

"I have, but let me tell you first about what I saw at the house when I went out there. That'll help in explaining all this. When I got there, the rope was still hanging down from the deck. Now the house is a single story, but the land falls away behind it, and there's a small lake in the back, down this hill. So the back of the house is really two stories, and there's a den downstairs, and a

346

couple of bedrooms, and a bathroom. And there's a wall of windows on the lake side and a walkout cement slab that's under the wooden deck upstairs. The deck comes off the kitchen. Can you visualize all that?"

The lawyer nodded. "Go on."

"There was a rope attached to the deck. Tied tight to one of the supporting columns, above the planks. So it hung down. And at the bottom, there was a big loop, and a knot in the loop about chest high. It's hard to visualize, I know. Think of it as a tire swing, without the tire. Just a big loop in the rope and a knot."

"How big was the loop?"

"About two and a half feet, I'd guess. It was certainly big enough to go around my chest. Now, there wasn't any blood on the cement, or any evidence of a struggle. The rope was just hanging there when I saw it. Still attached to the deck."

Dr. Frederick glanced up, as if he were going to see it. The whole courtroom lifted their chins into the air. "And I talked to the aunt. Ms. Gina Carlyle. She's the one who got him down. He was up in the rope when she arrived there, she told me. She said that when she found him, the rope was across his chest, under his armpits, and that big knot was against his neck. It was anterior, not posterior."

"It was what?"

"Anterior," the doctor said. "In the front of the neck. Not posterior. Not behind. It was on his Adam's apple. And she told me the boy's toes were dragging on the cement. He could have stood up. There wasn't a mark of any kind on his legs. That's how I knew that he had stepped up into it, to swing on it. He hadn't come down on it from above. Because if he had, there would've been abrasions on his lower legs, where he hit the cement. The only bruising Kevin had was on his neck."

"So what happened?" the attorney asked.

"Well, I also talked to some of his friends, and they told me that boys around here these days are twirling lassos. They're doing all kinds of things with them too, including tying them up and using them as swings. If the rope's long enough, they can get pretty high. And they can stand up with both their feet inside that big loop."

"Was it dangerous, what he did?"

"No, it shouldn't have been. I don't think the bottom was more than four or four and a half feet off the ground."

"So he fell?"

"No, I don't think he did. I think Kevin was swinging, standing up inside that loop. And I think he was holding on to the rope somewhere above that big knot. You know, they have to have a big knot, in order to get the weight just right so they can swing it in a circle above their heads. And when he got high enough on the upswing one time, he just clumsily lost his footing. I think he fell through. His whole body just shot through that loop."

Daniel took in his breath.

Bobby turned. "Are you all right?"

"I think the rope came up," the doctor said. "It shot up over his back, and then it got caught up under his shoulder blades. Maybe he was leaning back when he went through. I don't know. Anyway, in all probability when it caught under his arms, the force of it, the sheer momentum snapped the front of that rope taut up against his throat. And what hit him was the knot. It slammed into his trachea with tremendous force. His own body weight created the momentum as he came down."

Daniel couldn't answer. He was hardly breathing.

"Now doctor, now let me ask you this. If someone had been there, with him, could he have survived this?"

The balding doctor leaned all the way forward in his seat. "No," he said, looking straight at Bobby. "No. Absolutely not. And nobody should ever think that he could. You can't survive a crushed trachea, no matter what you do. And in this case, there were no signs of struggle. There was no attempt to extract himself. Mrs. Carlyle didn't find the boy with his hand up by his throat, or in between the rope and his neck. You know, trying to pull it off. That's completely consistent with what I'm saying. He never had a chance. He was gone too fast."

There was complete silence, as if there wasn't a soul in the courtroom.

Dr. Frederick took a long moment before he went on. "This was just a freak accident. That's all. An incomprehensible, terrible accident. He just fell through that rope when he was playing on it. He was alive one moment, probably laughing, and then he was dead."

His voice softened now, and filled with comfort. He spoke to Bobby directly, as if they were sitting alone together in the living room. "I've known your family for a long time," he said. "And I've known Sarah since before the boys were born. Your son Kevin was a fine boy. And a fine young man too. Just like his brother, who's there next to you. I'd be proud to have either one of them as my sons. Nothing in this world can make any of this comprehensible."

Bobby took a ragged breath.

"All I can say to you, Bobby. And Sarah too. I know she's not here today. She's still far too distraught. Is that there're countless ways to leave this world. And of all the ways there are, to exit this world, this isn't the worst way. I've seen so many children die, over the years. It's the worst part of my job. The children. And all I can tell you, the only meager comfort I can presume to offer you, is that it wasn't agonizing, or prolonged. After that rope hit him, he didn't feel a thing, and he was gone in the twinkling of an eye.

"I can't begin to comprehend what you're going through. No one can. It's the worst nightmare any parent, any loving parent, could ever have. But for you, and Sarah, and Daniel there, it's real. It really happened. And all I can say is this. Of all the ways there are, to leave this life, the way your boy left you wasn't the worst."

34.

They all waited in the courtroom so they could be there for the final verdict. No one approached them for the quarter-hour it took.

"Accidental suffocation" was what the jury foreman wrote. Daniel saw the paper before it was swept away to be filed formally down the hall in the courthouse. It was a public document, he knew, that anyone could see any time.

Daniel and Bobby said goodbye to Lester, then let the crowd disperse before they got up from their seats in the empty room and headed slowly down the air-conditioned hallway. They left together, letting the glass front door swing shut hard behind them.

The heat and humidity hit them as soon as they stepped out.

As they descended the three stairs to the walkway that crossed the square, Daniel counted cars and trucks in every parking spot. He saw men and women from the crowd at the inquest entering the few shops that were still open for business. He spotted others heading across the hay-green grass toward the Dairy Queen, where a line of vehicles already waited for food at the drive-through.

A few of them waved respectfully at Daniel and Bobby as they walked.

They strode silently toward Bobby's truck, which was parked along the curb next to an alleyway around the corner from the front doors of the courthouse. His father didn't speak, and Daniel was in no condition to.

As they approached the vehicle, Daniel's grandfather stepped in front of them from the alleyway. Daniel hadn't seen him until he appeared in view. He had been watching them, Daniel realized, as Daniel noticed the alley and the jutting side of the storefront that had shielded the man.

Mr. Winston staggered. Bobby reached for him, but he moved away.

"Are you okay?" Bobby asked him.

"I'm fine." He was reeling and stumbling on the sidewalk as he struggled to keep his balance.

"Do you need me to drive you home?"

"No." He reached a shaking hand toward the truck. The man's eyes were pink and the rims oozed stuff that had caked in the inside corners. But he was crying too, with water coursing white streaks in his dirty face. The man put both hands on the truck hood to keep from falling. "I should have been there." He slurred his words, and Daniel had trouble understanding. "We shouldn't have left him alone."

"You were away," Bobby told him gently. "I know that."

"All my life, I've been away."

Daniel could smell him. It was stale kegs of beer and body odor and acrid pee. "I'm sorry," the old man said. "This is all my fault."

"No!" Daniel said. "Granddad, it isn't. It's—"

"Shh!" Bobby said. "Let me get you home. Where are you living?" He tried to embrace the man so he could steer him.

"I don't deserve a home!" He pushed Bobby away. "But I have something to give her. That's why I waited for you. I couldn't go in there, with all those people. Tell her I love her. Tell her I'll be back soon. I don't know where I'm going, but I always come back to my sunnygirl."

He thrust his filthy hand out toward his grandson.

"Give her this," he said to Daniel. "Give this to your mom." He held a troll doll in his palm, whose shaking he couldn't stop. The white plastic was absolutely clean, smiling at Daniel with its loopy grin and splayed fingers wanting to hug him. Even the spun plastic cotton-candy hair was white, sticking up. Somehow, his grandfather had been able to keep it pristine.

35.

All his out-of-town family gathered at the house for one last dinner, then they packed up their suitcases and their dusty, tired kids and strapped everything anywhere on their cars that they could find a spot. His many aunts and uncles made sure the seat belts were tight, and they kissed their children, and then they kissed them again.

"Well, I guess we're done." John stood next to the station wagon that would take them back to De Kalb. "It's funny. Without this, we never would have known about any of it, but most of all about Dad."

"You think it changes things?" Tommy asked his older brother as they stood in the driveway.

"No, but it makes more sense. He's more human now. What if we'd never found out? It was only by chance that he had to read."

Tommy looked off. Somewhere distant, they could hear coyotes. The keening sound of their yearning was punctuated by the insistent slam of car doors.

Tommy answered. "Think of all the people who never find out. They live their whole lives thinking it's them rather than their dad, or their mother. Until yesterday, we were just like them."

36.

"We'll see you soon!" his Aunt Debbie yelled as she waved out her window.

"Don't forget!" Tommy shouted from his sports car. "We'll be back for Christmas and it's here at your house this year. Daniel! I'll call you."

The long, slow caravan began to bump away, bouncing as it left the gravel of the driveway and hit the ruts of the dirt track that curved and rolled over the gentle hills that Bobby had left fallow between his house and the county road.

"Sarah!" his Aunt Jeanne yelled out. "You call if you need me! I'm only in Knoxville." She was the last one, the Volvo caboose of the train. When she turned into the last curve they could see from the house, her taillights glowed red behind some tall bushes for a moment, but then were gone.

Daniel heard the engines for another minute as they snailed along the half-mile, but then they were gone too, petering out. All was quiet again, except for the crickets that had started in the darkness.

"Well," Bobby said as they stood on the front porch. "I guess that's it."

He smiled then as he turned to Sarah, but it was only his lips. His eyes were watching her.

She turned. "Excuse me," she said as she reached for the screen door. "I need to go make up your mother's bed. She must be tired."

She went in. The piston wheezed as the door closed.

Daniel asked his dad eagerly, "So what happened? I asked Aunt Debbie, but she said to ask you, and then we all had dinner, and I couldn't talk to you. So did he change it, and give it all back? Who went over there? I know it was Tommy—"

"No." But Bobby was looking through the screen. "It was all of them."

Daniel waited, but Bobby didn't turn his head. "Yeah? And then what? What did they do to him?"

"I don't know. I wasn't there. I guess they all sat on him, and got him to agree."

"Agree to what? Tell me. I want the whole story."

Bobby turned. "My mother told them, while you and I were at the inquest yesterday, and then she and Tommy drove them over there. One of the guys called me after we got the verdict. He said he was in the men's room at the courthouse on the first floor when he saw them speed by like bats out of hell. He recognized your grandma's LeBaron, but not the others. He said she was way out in front.

"When they got to the house, they had a little talk with him. You know John even turned around his chair? They've never done that. It's never been turned away from the TV. John said it was about time he joined the family."

"That's great!" Daniel said.

"And after that, they picked him up pretty much bodily and threw him in the car. You know who sat with him? They put him in the middle, so he couldn't get out. You know who sat by the door?"

"Who?"

"Jeanne. She was so mad at him she couldn't talk. They told me. That's what she did for me. And you know who did the driving? My mom. I don't think she's ever done that. He doesn't let her drive it when they have to go anywhere."

Daniel laughed. "They went over to Sam's," Bobby continued. "You know, Sam Ross's? Mom called ahead to make sure he had time. And you know what Sam told her, when she told him. He said, 'I wouldn't even think about charging you for this.' But he had to talk to Dad anyway, once they got there. I bet Sam didn't like that. But he had to make sure that he was all right with doing it. So he met with Dad alone for a while. When they came out, Sam told them Dad had signed everything. Sam had the papers in his hand, and he said he'd record them."

"So when is that?" Daniel asked. "Do they do that tomorrow?"

"Nope. Debbie made them all walk over to the courthouse right then. You know what my dad did? They made him walk in there himself and talk to Myrna. You know her. Myrna Roberts, the Recorder of Deeds? They made him stand there, until she did it. Debbie told me what Myrna said. She said she'd waive the fee and pay for it herself, but they said no. They wanted Dad to pay it. And he did."

"That's great. So you got it back? I'm not on it?"

"Yeah, but not just me. Your cousin too. Hope gets her full share, just like me. She gets the same share that would've gone to her father, only now it's hers. And I got the two hundred acres too, on top of that."

"You did?"

"It's not even joint anymore. It's all mine. And it's amazing. That land's in the middle of his farm."

"So it's back the way it should be." Daniel smiled. "But what was that about the newspaper? Mom was saying that at the funeral. Talking to herself. I heard her."

"He reads the newspaper all the time."

"Yeah. I see that."

"But it's not the stories. Your grandmother asked him, right after the funeral, and he admitted to her that he only reads the crop prices. It's all numbers, and he could always do math. It's words that escape him, just like they escape me."

"So it's all fixed now. We've got all the answers."

Bobby turned again to look through the screen and into the living room. Beyond it, Daniel could see his mother at the dining room table, unfolding a new cloth and smoothing it with her hands over the wood.

"No, it's not," Bobby said, his eyes on Sarah. "It's not fixed. Not the important stuff."

"You think she's gonna stay?" Daniel asked him. "Grandma McAllister. Do you think she's gonna leave him like she said?"

Bobby shrugged. "I don't know," he said, still peering in. "But she can stay as long as she wants, as far as I'm concerned. And I know your mother feels the same way. Daniel, I need to go in now. You do too. It's time to—"

"Dad, there's something I don't understand."

Bobby waited but his thoughts were already inside the house.

"Why did he do it? He never did the right thing before. Is it because they finally stood up to him, like you did?"

"No." Bobby shook his head. "It wasn't them, or me. It was her. For the first time it was her too, along with us. It was her, and all of her children against Dad, and that's why he made things right. Because of Mom."

37.

He couldn't sleep. Daniel was alone for the first time in their huge basement.

For two days, four of his boy cousins had been camped out on the sectional and sprawled in sleeping bags on the rug in front of the wide-screen TV, but they had gone now, and abandoned him. The first-floor underground was empty and cold from the air-conditioning.

Daniel padded to the bathroom in his faded blue gym shorts, and then seeing the bright light spilling down the stairs, he made his way slowly up to the kitchen. No one was there, but he saw two dirty plates on the counter next to the sink. A new pot of coffee was brewing and nearly done. The last of the water spluttered through the filter.

The TV was on, but it was mute. Daniel smelled the aroma of the beans as he glanced up at the clock at the bottom of the high, small TV his father kept in a cabinet above the oven. 3:04 a.m., CNN said.

"Dad?" But there was no answer. Daniel stuck his head into the living room. A square box of Kleenex lay on its side on the floor by the couch, next to one of his mother's romance novels. The book faced down with its spine cracked on the carpet.

"Mom?" he said. "Are you guys out here?"

It seemed every light was on in the house. He squinted as he rubbed his eyes. "Dad? Mom?" he whispered into their room at the end of the hall, but no one answered. Other than his grandmother, who was asleep in the guestroom on the same hall, there was no one but him alive in the house.

In the kitchen again, he switched on the back floodlight, which fired up the deck and grayed the short grass on the slope. Daniel leaned forward to peer into the darkness, then cupped his hand so he could see better through the window glass.

Bugs flew. They started coming. There were a million of them, spinning circles in the cloudy beam, but other than them nothing moved. His parents weren't standing by the lake, or sitting on the back deck.

Daniel opened the door to the garage and peeked out. His father's truck and his mother's Taurus were there, but one of the two automatic doors was up. He stepped down, out of the house, and touched the concrete. Bare-footed, he felt the gritty coolness with his toes as he walked across the floor and leaned out, holding the doorframe where it met the driveway.

Daniel listened, straining to hear.

He picked up a voice, talking softly. He listened harder. It was his father, talking in a monotone that made it sound like a bee buzzing. Daniel stepped onto the bristly grass. He crossed his arms above the gathered top of his gym shorts over his bare chest and hugged his elbows as he walked.

"Dad?" he said as a coyote started howling. Far off, it was joined by another one closer in. They took turns singing, mourning the loss of the moon, which hung as a big round white plate above the trees.

"Sarah, I'm sorry," he heard his father say as he padded closer. "I never should have done it. I should have told you. All these years, I've been keeping secrets. First about my reading, and then about the title to the land. And Mack Swartz, and my Dad. And how I felt about it. How angry I was, and ashamed of it. I couldn't support you, and I couldn't let go. He owned me, Sarah, and I never knew it. Even after we moved out and I had my own farm, I thought I was free of him, but I wasn't. You were right. It was like you said."

Her voice interrupted, "Bobby—"

"I'm the reason he's dead. I got mad at him. Him and Daniel, then I yelled at them to take down the swing. I only did that because my dad had been screaming. I had gotten him on the phone, and he yelled at me, and I was furious. And I took it out on them, instead of him. Kevin wasn't gonna take down that swing. He was mad at me because of what I said to him. Daniel too. They were as mad at me as I was at my own dad. I would have done the same thing if I was him."

Daniel kept coming across the dewy grass. He felt the wetness between his toes.

"No wonder he's dead, Sarah, and I'm the one who did it. There's nothing anybody can ever say or do to make me change my mind. I didn't grow up. I stayed a child for too long, and I let him run my life. And your life, even though you didn't want it, and the kids. Since the church, I've seen it all. All the fear I had, all the secrets. I've gotten to see what I've done to my life, and to yours. God, I'm sorry."

Daniel was close now but couldn't actually see them. Through the clear night, though, he could hear the tremor in his father's low voice. Daniel kept coming but then he stopped when his mother spoke with a tone he had never heard before. Even at the church.

He could hear the anger in it and the resentment. "Bobby, I want you to listen to me. This is important, and I need to say it. Do you realize how much you've hurt us, and hurt our marriage, because you've never let us be a team? It's supposed to be you and me, only it wasn't and it never has been. All these years, it was just you. You kept me on the outside. You kept us strangers, and you did it deliberately because there were things you didn't want me to know. You hurt me and you hurt our children."

She wasn't crying.

"Sarah," Bobby said. "I know what I've done. I've treated you like you were the enemy, and I've kept all my secrets to myself. I don't know why I did it, but—"

"You need to."

"What?"

"You need to. You need to find out because I deserve to know." Her voice was firm, and now Daniel could see them. They stood silhouetted against the glitter of stars, marking a dark void that was a single blanket wrapped around both of them. He could see now that they were spoons, with his father holding her from the back.

His mother turned. She left Bobby and took a step away from him, leaving the blanket. She faced his father head-on. Daniel could see her in the moonlight. The milky light cast a shadow that sharpened her features.

Daniel saw her set jaw and her resolve.

"I deserve an answer," his mother said to Bobby. "I want you to think about it, but I need to know. I need to know why you put him above me and both your children. I need to know why you lied, because not telling is the same as lying. And I need to say this. It's going to make the difference to me, about whether I go on."

"But Sarah!" his father said. "You know I love you!"

Daniel cried out. "Dad!"

He raised his voice then, right then, so they would hear him. "Mom!"

He ran forward into the light.

They turned. He saw the surprise in their faces.

"Dad, I'm here! Mom! I need to talk to you. It's about Kevin, and about what happened. I need to tell you what I've done."

CORA
Summer
1994

That Same Night,
At the Same Moment

1.

Cora McAllister was still up, even at that hour. She had turned her nightstand light off in the guestroom when she had heard Daniel calling out, looking for his parents. She had waited to turn it on again until she heard him open the back door and then it shut as he went into the garage.

She had heard her son and Sarah leaving a few minutes earlier. She hadn't heard the sound of any motors, though, so she knew they were nearby, probably walking.

Since Kevin's death, she had had trouble sleeping herself.

Daniel would find them and they would stand together, Cora thought as she propped herself up on two pillows against the small headboard. She balanced a large coffee-table book on her old knees to make a writing surface, and she reached for the lined school paper she had found in Kevin's room earlier that evening.

Quietly, reverently, she had touched his things. She had held his schoolbooks and caressed the top of his wooden boy's desk. All along the top of it, little ceramic horses ran. She picked each of them up and stroked its muzzle against her cheek.

She looked at a cantilevered house perched over a waterfall on the front of the book on her lap. Heavy and colorful, it was about the work of Frank Lloyd Wright, which she had given to Bobby when he was twenty-four. He was a new father then, and a proud one, and he had told her he liked to draw house plans.

It was fifty dollars. Like Sarah, Cora had saved for it secretly.

She began to write with a pen she had borrowed from the kitchen.

June 1994

Bobby, I am keeping this letter in my Bible for when I'm gone and you read this passage at my funeral. You and I already talked about this today. You told me I was never going to die, but I know better.

Please wait until you've buried me to read this. That's my last wish. Once you've read it, please give it to Daniel.

She took a deep breath.

Kevin's death was my fault. You think it's yours, or your father's, but it wasn't.

I was young and frightened of being alone when your father asked me to marry him. I never thought I deserved anyone else, but you did, Bobby. You and your brothers and sisters also deserved a much better mother.

If I had taught you to stand up for yourself earlier, this wouldn't have happened. If I had done it myself, it wouldn't have begun. I'm sorry. I taught you to be afraid of him because I was, because standing up meant losing him, and I could never do that. He was all I had, or so I thought.

I kept telling myself he was a good man every time he had an excuse that I clung to. I kept telling you—and me—there were reasons. I defended him even to you.

I know I defended him in my own home, in your home, where you were supposed to be safe. You weren't. I thought danger was on the outside, but it wasn't. Your father was there. I wasn't protecting you. I was protecting me.

I told you to be nice to him. I kept trying to tell you to be better. I told you it wasn't his fault, it was yours. The lie I was telling myself was more important than you were. I see that now. But of course you believed me in your tender heart because I was your mother. You took what I was feeding you from my own hands.

You can't forgive me. This time I will carry this because you won't read this until after. It won't be possible for you to look at me with those eyes of yours and forgive me again. I don't deserve it.

Promise me it stops here. It stops with me. No more secrets. No more lies.

I love you. Mom.

She folded the lined sheet of paper into thirds and slipped it into her Bible at the page she had discussed with him. She laid the pink Book next to her on the soft bed, then took off her glasses.

Hidden safely once again within the pink oilcloth back cover was another sheet of paper folded many more times over. It was old and frayed now, with its edges softer still than they had been when Daniel read the callous words in his locked bedroom.

On the top of the folded square, she had now written too.

Cora reached up then and with her old, thin arm turned out the light.

This is why.

Acknowledgements

This book would not have been possible without Jesse Kornbluth, who believed in it and in me, the neophyte novelist, from the beginning.

Standing with him are David Baldacci and Robert Bausch, both of whom for some reason felt the same about Farmer's Son. I am also grateful to Peter Matson, who treated me without kid gloves, as though I belonged. For the most salient question, "Why did both of these women stay?" I am deeply grateful to Walt Bode at Harcourt. I also thank Larry Kirshbaum, Aaron Priest, Suzanne Gluck, and Nicole Aragi for reading it, too. Speaking from the vast unwashed village of unpublished novelists, I thank them all for spending their precious time on a debut book from an unknown about a topic that's never before been novelistic, for an audience that—I was told by others—"doesn't read. Dyslexics don't walk into Barnes & Noble."

Now, with the advent of ebook devices that can blow up the font as large as anyone needs, and with the coming of audio capability for book reading out loud, the technology has finally arrived. At last, these devices can help my eyesight-challenged daughter and others read.

I am also deeply grateful for the phone call one day from a slush pile reader at an agency, who introduced herself as she wept, then told me she would do everything she could to get Farmer's Son in front of her boss. The reader's brother, she said, "was Bobby," and no book had ever been written about him or their family. Similarly, I thank a very accomplished man I've known for decades, who read my manuscript many times, then wrote me one day out of the blue to say, "I am Bobby." He had been too ashamed before to reveal his dyslexia but Bobby's story, he said, had given him courage. Those reactions, and others, got this novel into your hands.

I am by no means an expert on dyslexia. All substantive mistakes are entirely my own. What little I know comes from small research and the golden help of Dr. William R. Stixrud, a specialist in Silver Spring, MD, who taught me some basics and encouraged me to write a cinematic book with short, visually vivid sentences.

I am deeply grateful to my family and to my writers' group for their charity and dogged reviews, over many years, repeatedly, of every page. A rough idea became a real novel with the help of these Gentle Readers. To Ellen Dyke, I owe years of gratitude for her edits and patience.

I thank my two daughters for their love and encouragement, and for helping to format Farmer's Son in a way that's most accessible visually on the page. I also thank them for the cover design, whose font is Century Schoolbook, the same type used in the old Dick and Jane primers that Bobby McAllister would have seen as a boy.

Finally, and of course, I thank Bobby. Wherever you are.